P9-DFL-317

Also by Patrick Robinson:

One Hundred Days
(With Admiral Sir John "Sandy" Woodward)
True Blue

PATRICK
ROBINSON

HarperCollins*Publishers*

Nimitz Class is a work of fiction set in the near future. The premise of the novel and descriptions of naval operations and protocol are grounded in fact. However, certain liberties have been taken in the interest of creating a compelling narrative.

FIRST EDITION

Designed by Ruth Lee
Illustrations by ML Design

Library of Congress Cataloging-in-Publication Data

Robinson, Patrick, 1940–
    Nimitz class / by Patrick Robinson.
        p.   cm.
    ISBN 0-06-018755-7
    I. Title.
PR6068.01959N5   1997
823'.914—dc21   96-46872

97 98 99 00 01 ❖/RRD 10 9 8 7 6 5 4 3 2 1

Nimitz Class is respectfully dedicated to the officers and men of the United States Navy and the Royal Navy . . . to all of those who go down to the sea in warships, and who sometimes face great peril, in great waters.

FLIGHT DECK LAYOUT OF A NIMITZ-CLASS AIRCRAFT CARRIER

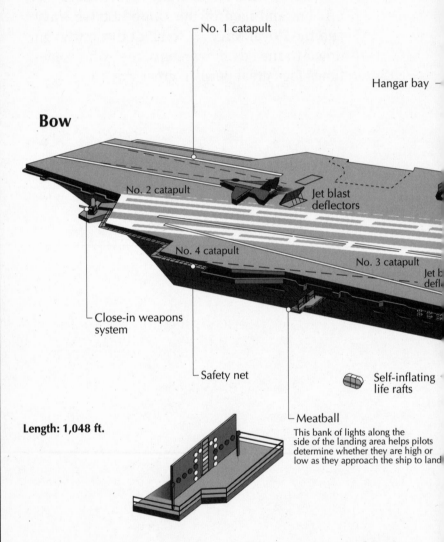

No. 1 catapult

Hangar bay

Bow

No. 2 catapult

Jet blast
deflectors

No. 4 catapult

No. 3 catapult

Jet b
defl

Close-in weapons
system

Safety net

Self-inflating
life rafts

Meatball

This bank of lights along the
side of the landing area helps pilots
determine whether they are high or
low as they approach the ship to land

Length: 1,048 ft.

Port Side

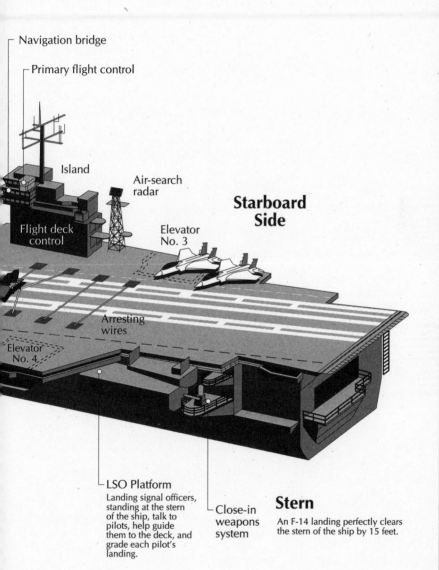

Navigation bridge

Primary flight control

Island

Air-search
radar

Flight deck
control

Elevator
No. 3

**Starboard
Side**

Arresting
wires

Elevator
No. 4

LSO Platform

Landing signal officers,
standing at the stern
of the ship, talk to
pilots, help guide
them to the deck, and
grade each pilot's
landing.

Close-in
weapons
system

Stern

An F-14 landing perfectly clears
the stern of the ship by 15 feet.

ACKNOWLEDGMENTS

M Y CHIEF ADVISER THROUGHOUT THE LONG MONTHS of writing this novel was Admiral Sir John (Sandy) Woodward, the Royal Navy's senior Task Group Commander in the South Atlantic during the battle for the Falkland Islands in 1982. There are some who consider this former naval Commander-in-Chief one of the best naval strategists of recent times. Perhaps more widely held is the view that Admiral Woodward was also one of the better submarine specialists the Royal Navy ever had. "My task for the *Nimitz Class*," he once said, "is to keep the story feasible, to keep it within the boundaries of possibility, where fiction has to be less strange than truth."

His advice was as careful as it was thorough. Somewhat miraculously, the admiral is still in my corner.

On the infrequent occasions when Sandy was unavailable, I turned for technical expertise to my friend, Captain David Hart Dyke, another retired Royal Navy officer who also faced the guns and bombs of the Argentinean Air Force in the South Atlantic in 1982.

Captain Peter O'Connor, the former Commanding Officer of the guided missile cruiser USS *Yorktown*, was my principal U.S.

Naval adviser. He has my enduring thanks for his time and patience. Another Virginian, retired Vice Admiral Robert F. Dunn, generously provided me with superb data on the day-to-day operations in a U.S. Navy aircraft carrier.

There were many other serving officers, both submariners and surface ship executives on both sides of the Atlantic, who were more than happy to guide me through the techniques of command, and I thank them all, and wish I could name them personally.

I thank, too, Alan Friedman, author of *Spider's Web*, for his careful advice about the banking tactics of the more dubious Middle Eastern regimes.

Finally, I would like to thank my longtime friend and colleague, Joe Farrell of Chadds Ford, Pennsylvania, who read the manuscript meticulously, separating American and English phrases and the military jargon which enters a book such as this. He says he was given the task of preventing American fighter pilots sounding like Winston Churchill.

Since he also arranged my introduction to Captain O'Connor, I'll forgive his irreverence.

PATRICK ROBINSON

AUTHOR'S NOTE

I MAGINE NEW YORK'S EMPIRE STATE BUILDING, TURNED flat on its side, moving across the ocean at around thirty knots, a big, white bow-wave surging over its radio tower, and you have a good approximation of a one-hundred-thousand-ton U.S. Navy aircraft carrier on patrol.

The huge $4 billion warship, is 1,100 feet long, and powered by its own private nuclear plant. This is the colossus, the Nimitz-Class carrier, named after the Texas-born World War II admiral, Chester W. Nimitz, who masterminded the ambush which destroyed the Japanese at the Battle of Midway in June 1942, sinking 4 of Admiral Yamamoto's finest aircraft carriers and 332 of his aircraft.

Today, these modern U.S. carriers rove the oceans in his name, ruling a five-hundred-mile radius of air, sea, and land wherever they move. But the Nimitz-Class giants do not travel alone. They are normally accompanied by a small flotilla of guided missile cruisers, destroyers, and frigates, and two hunter-killer submarines. Loosely arranged in classic operational disposition, this Carrier Battle Group is known in Navy shorthand as the CVBG.

The group is the undisputed master of the skies, the oceans, and the dark, menacing reaches of the kingdoms beneath the waves. Alone on his bridge, the admiral who commands it looks out on the biggest, fastest, deadliest warship ever built. He is the Warlord of the twenty-first century.

At the hub of his ten-ship surface group, there are eighty fighter/attack aircraft arrayed on the deck, with the guided missile escorts in loose proximity. The admiral's nuclear submarines ride shotgun far out in front.

Smaller countries of military wealth and sophistication—the United Kingdom, France, Germany—lack the capacity to raise even one comparable force. Not even Russia with its gigantic, moribund Navy, can match the power of the American Carrier Battle Group. The U.S.A. runs twelve of them, each carrier alone costing $440 million a year to operate.

Fifty-five percent of the money spent annually on defense by all countries is expended by the Pentagon. Each aircraft carrier sustains a gigantic seaborne staff of six thousand men, with close to six hundred officers.

Deep in the lower decks of the ship, the cooks provide eighteen thousand meals every twenty-four hours, plus a small meal for the midnight watch (MIDRATS). Three times a day the whistle blows, and they begin unpacking food from boxes on a scale almost beyond belief. Sometimes hundreds of big gleaming cans of ravioli or meatballs are being thrown, simultaneously, expertly, from the unpackers, to the kitchen hands, then on to the cooks.

A big-deck carrier stands about twenty-four-stories high from keel to masthead, with a 260-foot-wide flight deck. She draws 40 feet below the waterline. Powered by two big G.E. PWR nuclear reactors, her range and time at sea are almost infinite, limited only by the stamina of the crew. In addition there are four steam turbines, generating 260,000 horsepower. Four propeller shafts, each the size of a hundred-year-old California redwood, drive her forward.

Of her 6,000 personnel, 3,184 are concerned solely with moving the great warship safely about the oceans. There are 2,800 aircrew on board, responsible for flight operations and maintenance of the aircraft. The admiral, whose concerns are battle group strategy, tactics, efficient firepower, and surveillance of a potential enemy, travels with a staff of twenty-five officers and forty-five men. His operations center is the bottom line of the U.S. Navy's offensive and defensive charter.

The admiral can, at will, move heavy United States muscle closer to an enemy's border than any other commander in history. He can move freely through international waters. He is completely mobile, self-contained, and deadly to any opponent. In the bowels of the ship there are stored missiles with nuclear warheads.

The carrier is flanked by Aegis missile cruisers, whose computer-controlled weapons can hit and obliterate an incoming air attack traveling at up to twice the speed of sound. The Battle Group's close-in destroyers can take care of any air, surface, or underwater threats. The guided missile frigates, with their LAMPS helicopters, provide an anti-submarine dragnet which can stretch for hundreds of miles in every direction.

The nuclear killer submarines, which can stay underwater for years if necessary, patrol hundreds of miles, clearing the trail for the carrier and its consorts. Armed with wickedly accurate wire-guided torpedos and cruise missiles, they seek principally to destroy their enemy counterparts.

A vast electronics system ties the group together in a tight network of communications, relaying minute-by-minute, ops-room-to-ops room, ship-to-ship, the operational state of this moving cell of almost inconceivable power. The Carrier Battle Group is perfectly capable of eliminating, simultaneously, threat from air, surface, and underwater.

The spearhead of its attack is its bomber force—twenty deadly accurate, all-weather aircraft, archenemies to any ship hostile to the United States, plus twenty FA–18 supersonic fighter/attack Hornets. To defend the Battle Group and/or to provide cover for the bomber force, there are another twenty fighter aircraft—principally the heavily gunned missile-launching F–14 Tomcat and the supersonic F–14D Super-Tomcat. In an emergency, they can launch these aircraft with the huge steam-driven catapults, two at a time, off the five-acre flight deck— zero to 150 mph in two seconds.

In addition there are usually four EA–6B Prowlers, another heavy-hitter which possesses the unique ability to jam enemy radar completely, rendering any opponent impotent, a sitting duck for the U.S. air offensive line. The other great electronic specialist aircraft on deck is the S3 Viking, a search-and-strike torpedo-launching attack plane, which can probe underwater from the air, and destroy an enemy submarine hundreds of miles out from the main group.

On deck and in the hangars below there is usually a fleet of eight helicopters—Cobra gunships, Sea Kings, and probably one massive CH–53 transporter, which can carry, and land, either attack, or rescue, teams of up to fifty-five United States Marines.

The aircraft carrier itself is equipped with missile and gunnery capability, the Nimitz Class being the most heavily armored warship afloat. Her double hull and heavy sealed compartments along the waterline make her easily the most survivable warship in Naval history.

Every major team needs a quarterback, and in the CVBG the big plays are called by the E2C Early Warning and Control, Hawkeye.

With its great radar dome sending and receiving the electronic beams above the aircraft's computerized ops room, this heavyweight Naval warplane makes it just about impossible for any enemy to move undetected within a thousand-mile range of the carrier.

The carrier's strike aircraft are supersonic and on the surface the carrier itself can travel up to five hundred miles in a day, controlling the sea wherever she sails. With forty of America's forty-two allies residing across various oceans from the U.S. mainland, it is as well that 85 percent of all the land on this planet lies within range of an American Carrier Battle Group. And 95 percent of the world's people.

Yet few of these hundreds of millions of citizens realize their lives are lived in comparative peace and security because of the iron-fisted defense capability of the United States Navy. Most of them believe this security has been orchestrated by the United Nations, or NATO, or by some quasi-European defense project. But when push comes to shove, it is the U.S. Carrier Battle Group, the fortress at sea, that matters. This is the force that is apt to show up off the shores of potential aggressors.

Unreachable by air or sea attack, virtually unsinkable by any conventional underwater weapon, surrounded by a wall of guided missiles and tracking electronics, protected twenty-four hours a day by a sweeping, computerized radar field, home to its own fighter-attack supersonic air strike force . . .

No word in the English language accurately describes the invincibility of the U.S. Navy's aircraft carriers, save one. Impregnable.

Almost.

CAST OF PRINCIPAL CHARACTERS

Senior Military Command

The President of the United States (Commander-in-Chief, U.S.
   Armed Forces)
General Joshua R. Paul (Chairman of the Joint Chiefs)
Vice Admiral Arnold Morgan (Director, National Security
   Agency)

Carrier Battle Group

USS *Thomas Jefferson*

Rear Admiral Zack Carson (Flag Officer)
Captain Jack Baldridge (Group Operations Officer)
Captain Carl Rheinegen (Captain of the *Jefferson)*
Lieutenant William R. Howell (fighter pilot)
Lieutenant Freddie Larsen (Radar-Intercept Officer)
Lieutenant Rick Evans (Landing Signal Officer)

Ensign (Junior Grade) Jim Adams (Arresting Gear Officer)
Captain Art Barry (Commanding Officer USS *Arkansas)*

Lieutenant Commander Chuck Freeburg (Anti-Submarine
   Warfare Officer [ASWO] USS *Hayler)*
Lieutenant Joe Farrell (Navy pilot)

U.S. Navy Senior Command

Admiral Scott F. Dunsmore (Chief of Naval Operations)
Admiral Freddy Roberts (Vice CNO)
Admiral Gene Sadowski (C-in-C Pacific Command)
Admiral Albie Lambert (C-in-C Pacific Fleet)
Admiral Schnider (Head of Naval Intelligence)
Vice Admiral Archie Carter (Commander, Fifth Fleet)

U.S. Navy Personnel

Lieutenant Commander Bill Baldridge (Naval Intelligence)
Lieutenant Commander Jay Bamberg (Assistant to the CNO)

USS Columbia

Commander Cale "Boomer" Dunning (Commanding Officer)
Lieutenant Commander Jerry Curran (Combat Systems Officer)
Lieutenant Commander Lee O'Brien (Marine Engineering Officer)
Lieutenant Commander Mike Krause (Executive Officer)
Lieutenant David Wingate (Navigation Officer*)*

U.S. Navy SEALS

Admiral John Bergstrom (Commander, Special War Command,
   SPECWARCOM)
Commander Ray Banford (SEAL Mission Controller)
Lieutenant Commander Russell Bennett (Platoon Leader, SEAL
   Number Three Team)
Lieutenant (Junior Grade) David Mills (SEAL SDV driver)

Political and Presidential Staff

Robert MacPherson (Secretary of Defense)
Harcourt Travis (Secretary of State)

Dick Stafford (White House Press Secretary)
Sam Haynes (National Security Adviser)
Louis Fallon (White House Chief of Staff)

CIA Officers

Jeff Zepeda (Expert on Iran)
Major Ted Lynch (Middle East financial specialist)

Family Members

Grace Dunsmore (wife of CNO)
Elizabeth Dunsmore (daughter of CNO)
Emily Baldridge (mother of Jack and Bill)
Ray Baldridge (brother of Jack and Bill)
Margaret Baldridge (Jack's wife)

Royal Navy Personnel

Admiral Sir Peter Elliott (Flag Officer Submarines)
Captain Dick Greenwood (FOSM's Chief of Staff)
Lieutenant Andrew Waites (Flag Lieutenant)
Admiral Sir Iain MacLean (Retired FOSM)
Lieutenant Commander Jeremy Shaw (Commanding Officer
    HMS *Unseen*)

Family Members

Lady MacLean ("Annie," wife of Sir Iain)
Laura Anderson (Daughter of Sir Iain and Lady MacLean)

Senior Foreign Officers

General David Gavron (Military Attaché, Israeli Embassy,
    Washington)
Vice Admiral Vitaly Rankov (Head of Russian Naval Intelligence)

Foreign Navy Personnel

Leading Seaman Karim Aila (Dock Sentry, Iranian Navy)

PROLOGUE

D EEP IN THE MEDITERRANEAN SEA, HALFWAY BETWEEN
the Greek mainland and the long western headland of Crete,
lies the rough and rugged island of Kithira. It is a coarse rock,
twenty miles long at most, set in the middle of a shining and bejew-
eled sea.

Along the eastern end of the Mediterranean there is a pure,
transparent light which seems to flood the depths of the water.
This is a paradise for visiting scuba divers, but for local fishermen, the azure ocean which surrounds them is a harsh and
unforgiving place. There are not enough fish anymore. And life
is as hard as it has ever been.

It was 5 A.M. on a hot morning early in July. The sun was just
rising, and the fishing boat was sailing close to the rocky shore
on the south side. Up on the portside of the bow, his feet trailing
over the side, sat sixteen-year-old Dimitrios Morakis. He was in
deep trouble.

On the previous afternoon he had managed to lose the only
good net his family owned, and now his father Stephanos sat,
unshaven and grumpy, on the tiller. The man was secretly proud
of his golden-skinned son. And he stared at the boy's Etruscan
nose, a mirror image of his own, and the large hands, too power-

ful for the slender, youthful body; the boy's genetic bounty from a long line of Kithiran fishermen.

Nonetheless, Stephanos was still peevish. "We'd better find it," he said, unnecessarily. And in a light morning breeze, they slapped along, against the wavelets, while out to the east, for a few translucent moments, the earth seemed to rise up through veils of scarlet and violet.

The net showed up more or less where Stephanos thought it would be, driven into a curved outcrop of rock by the unvarying Aegean currents. Lost nets had been washing up against those particular rocks for centuries.

The problem was, it was jammed. Working in the water for almost half an hour, Dimitrios was unable to free it. "It's caught up way below the surface," he yelled to his father. "I'll get back on the boat and then dive deep with a fishing knife."

Three minutes later the boy split the water, headfirst, kicking his way downward. In the crystal clear depths, he found the bottom of the net, entwined and stuck in a crevasse between two rocks. There was no option but to cut it.

He stuck out his left hand to give himself purchase, and slashed the knife sideways. The net came free, and as it did so, Dimitrios tugged the twisted cord from the V-shaped gap in the rocks. He had been underwater for twenty-four seconds now, and he needed to surface.

But he was kicking against a weight on his shoulders. He twisted left and saw, still resting on his arm, two large black boots. Dimitrios pushed away and even in the water the weight was considerable, because these boots contained one full-sized, very drowned, human body, trapped by one arm in the ancient rocks of Kithira.

The other arm flapped free, skeletal. It had been eaten by fish and was swaying in the morning tide. Dimitrios stared at the white, bloated head, the eye sockets empty, the flesh on one side stripped from the skull, the teeth still there, the half-mouth grinning grotesquely in the clear water. It was a phantasm, straight from the imagination of the devil himself.

Choking with disgust, Dimitrios stared at the grisly cadaver as it continued performing its hideous slow-motion ballet just beneath the surface, the one arm and both legs rising and falling in the gentle swell, the body spot-lit by the finely focused under-water rays of the clear Aegean sun.

Then he turned and kicked with the frenzy of the truly terri-fied, desperate for air, driven by the ludicrous thought that somehow the specter would find a way to pursue him. He glanced down as he went, and as he did so, he noticed the sun creating a bright light on the dark blue jersey which covered the hideous white balloon of the waterlogged body—the light glis-tened upward, reflecting thinly, from a tiny, two-inch-long silver submarine badge, inlaid with a five-pointed red star.

April 22, 2002.
The Indian Ocean.

On board the United States Aircraft Carrier
***Thomas Jefferson*. 9S, 92E. Speed 30.**

T HEY HAD WAVED HIM OFF TWICE NOW. AND EACH TIME
Lieutenant William R. Howell had eased open the throttle of
his big F–14 interceptor/attack Tomcat and climbed away to
starboard, watching the speed needle slide smoothly from 150
knots to 280 knots. The acceleration was almost imperceptible,
but in seconds the lieutenant saw the six-story island of the carrier turn into a half-inch-high black thimble against the blue sky.

The deep Utah drawl of the Landing Signal Officer standing
on the carrier stern was still calm: "Tomcat two-zero-one, we still
have a fouled deck—gotta wave you off one more time—just an
oil leak—this is not an emergency, repeat not an emergency."

Lieutenant Howell spoke quietly and slowly: "Tomcat two-
zero-one. Roger that. I'm taking a turn around. Will approach
again from twelve miles." He eased the fighter plane's nose up,
just a fraction, and he felt his stomach tighten. It was never more
than a fleeting feeling, but it always brought home the truth, that
landing any aircraft at sea on the narrow, angled, 750-foot-long,
pitching landing area remained a life-or-death test of skill and

nerve for any pilot. It took most rookies a couple of months to stop their knees shaking after each landing. Pilots short of skill, or nerve, were normally found working on the ground, driving freight planes, or dead. He knew that there were around twenty plane-wrecking crashes on U.S. carriers each year.

From the rear seat, the radar-intercept officer (RIO), Lieutenant Freddie Larsen, muttered, "Shit. There's about a hundred of 'em down there, been clearing up an oil spill for a half hour—what the hell's going on?" Neither aviator was a day over twenty-eight years old, but already they had perfected the Navy flier's nonchalance in the face of instant death at supersonic speed. Especially Howell.

"Dunno," he said, gunning the Tomcat like a bullet through the scattered low clouds whipping past this monster twin-tailed warplane, now moving at almost five miles every minute. "Did y'ever see a big fighter jet hit an oil pool on a carrier deck?"

"Uh-uh."

"It ain't pretty. If she slews out off a true line you gotta real good chance of killing a lot of guys. 'Specially if she hits something and burns, which she's damn near certain to do."

"Try to avoid that, willya?"

Freddie felt the Tomcat throttle down as Howell banked away to the left. He felt the familiar pull of the slowing engines, worked his shoulders against the yaw of the aircraft, like the motorcycle rider he once had been.

The F–14 is not much more than a motorbike with a sixty-four-foot wingspan anyway. Unexpectedly sensitive to the wind at low speed, two rock-hard seats, no comfort, and an engine with the power to turn her into a mach-2 rocketship—1,400 knots, no sweat, out there on the edge of the U.S. fighter pilot's personal survival envelope.

Still holding the speed down to around 280 knots, Howell now took a long turn, the Tomcat heeled over at an angle of almost ninety degrees, the engines screaming behind him, as if the sound was trying to catch and swallow him. Up ahead he could no longer see the carrier because of the intermittent white clouds obscuring his vision and casting dark shadows on the blue water. Below the two fliers was one of the loneliest seaways on earth, the 3,500-mile stretch of the central Indian Ocean between the African island of Madagascar and the rock-strewn western coast of Sumatra.

The U.S. carrier and its escorts, forming a complete twelve-ship Battle Group including two nuclear-powered submarines, were steaming toward the American Naval base on Diego Garcia, the tiny atoll five hundred miles south of the equator, which represents the only safe Anglo-American haven in the entire area.

This was a real U.S. Battle Group seascape, a place where the most beady-eyed admirals and their staff "worked up" new missile systems, new warships, and endlessly catapulted their ace Naval aviators off the flight deck—zero to 168 knots in 2.1 seconds. This was not a spot for the faint-hearted. This was a simulated theater of war, designed strictly for the very best the nation could produce . . . men who possessed what Tom Wolfe immortally labeled "the right stuff." Everyone served out here for six interminable months at a time.

Lieutenant Howell, losing height down to 1,200 feet, spoke again to the carrier's flight controllers. "Tower, this is Tomcat two-zero-one at eight miles. Coming in again." His words were few, and again the jet fighter began to ease down, losing height, the engines throttling marginally off the piercing high-C shriek which would splinter a shelf of wineglasses. Howell, insulated behind his goggles and earphones, searched the horizon for the hundred-thousand-ton aircraft carrier.

His intercom crackled. "Roger, Tomcat two-zero-one. Your deck is cleared for landing now—gotcha visual . . . come on in, watch your altitude, and check your lineup. Wind's gusting at thirty knots out of the southwest. We're still right into it. You're all set."

"Roger, Tower . . . six miles."

All Navy and Air Force pilots have a special, relaxed, aw-shucks way of imparting news from these high-speed fighter aircraft, some say copied directly from America's most famous combat ace, General Chuck Yeager, the first test pilot to break the sound barrier in his supersecret Bell X–1 in 1947.

Talking to the tower, almost every young Navy flier affects some kind of a West Virginia country boy drawl, precisely how they imagine General Yeager might have put it, real slow, ice-calm in the face of disaster. "Gotta little flameout on the ole starboard engine, jest gonna cut the power out there, bring her in on one. Y'all wanna move the flight deck over a coupla ticks, gimme a better shot in the crosswind. It ain't a problem."

Lieutenant William R. Howell imitated the general "better'n any of 'em." And easier. Because he was not really Lieutenant William R. Howell, anyway. He was Billy-Ray Howell, whose dad, an ex-coal miner and Southern Methodist, now kept the general store back in the same hometown as Chuck Yeager—up in the western hollows of the Appalachian Mountains, Hamlin, a place of less than a thousand souls, right on the Mud River, close to the eastern Kentucky border in Lincoln County. Like Chuck Yeager, Billy-Ray talked about the 'hollers,' fished the Mud River, was the son of a man who had a shot a few bears in his time, "cain't hardly wait to git home, see my dad."

When he had the stick of an F–14 in his hand, Billy-Ray Howell *was* General Yeager. He thought like him, talked like him, and acted as he knew the general would in any emergency. No matter that big Chuck had retired to live in California. As far as Billy-Ray was concerned he and Chuck Yeager formed an unspoken, mystical West Virginia partnership in the air, and he, Billy-Ray, was a kind of heir-apparent. In his view, the old country way of life out among the hickory and walnut tree woods of Lincoln County gave a kid a tough center. And he was "damn near sure Mr. Yeager would agree with that."

The strategy had paid off too. Billy-Ray had achieved his school-boy ambition to become a Naval aviator. Years of study, years of training, had seen him close to the top of every class he had ever been in. Everyone in Naval aviation knew that young Billy-Ray Howell was going onward and upward. They had ever since he first earned his engineering degree at the U.S. Naval Academy.

No one was surprised by how good he was when he began his jet fighter training, pushing the old T2 Buckeyes around the skies above Whiting Field, east of Pensacola, in northwest Florida.

And now the voice coming into the flight-control area was nearly identical to that of General Yeager, the steady "up-holler" tone, betraying no urgency: "Tower, Tomcat two-zero-one, four miles. I got somethin' gone kinda weird on me, right here . . . landin' gear warning light's jes' flickin' some. Didn't feel the wheels lock down. But it might be somethin's jes' wrong with th'ole lightbulb."

"Tower to Tomcat two-zero-one. Roger that. Continue on in and make a pass right down the deck at about fifty feet, two hundred knots. That way the guys can take a close look at the undercarriage."

"Roger, tower . . . comin' on in."

Out on the exposed and windswept carrier deck, the Landing Signal Officer radioed instructions to the pilot and could see that Tomcat 201 was about forty-five seconds out, a howling, twenty-ton brute of an aircraft, bucking along in the unpredictable gusts over the Indian Ocean, the pilot trying to hold her on a glide path two degrees above the horizontal. There was a big swell on the surface, and the whole ship, moving along at fifteen knots, was pitching through about three degrees, one and a half degrees either side of horizontal: that meant the ends, bow and stern, were moving through sixty feet vertically every thirty seconds. All incoming aircraft would have a hell of an approach into the strong, hot wind, and timing the moment of impact would test the deftness and proficiency of every pilot. That was with landing wheels.

The LSO, Lieutenant Rick Evans, a lanky fighter pilot out of Georgia, was now standing on the exposed port-quarter of the carrier. His binoculars were trained on Tomcat 201. And he could already see the landing wheels were not down—and the flaps weren't down either. His mind was churning. He knew that Billy-Ray Howell was in trouble. Nonfunctioning landing gear have always been the flier's nightmare, civil or military. But out here it was a hundred times worse.

A fighter plane does not come in along the near flat path followed by civil jetliners, which glide, and then "flare out" a few feet above mile-long runways. Out here there's no time. And not much space. Navy fliers slam those twenty-two-ton Tomcats down at 160 knots, flying them right into the deck, hook down, praying for it to grab the wire.

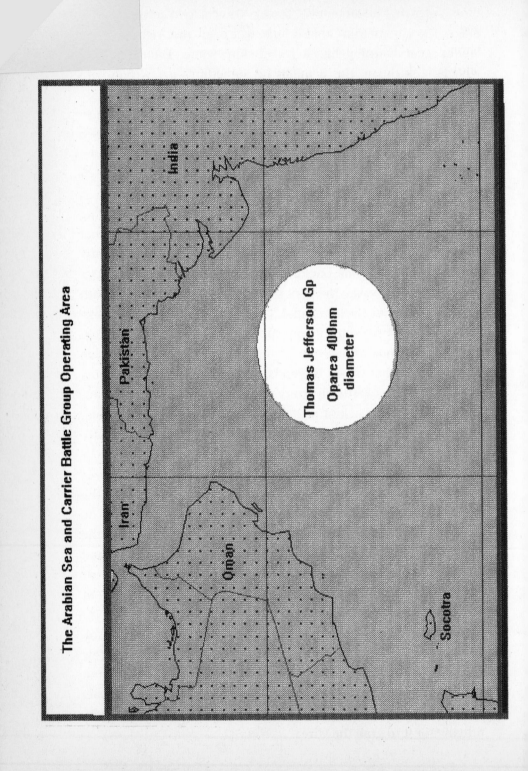

The Arabian Sea and Carrier Battle Group Operating Area

Iran

Pakistan

India

Oman

Thomas Jefferson Gp

Op area 400nm
diameter

Socotra

The downward momentum on the landing wheels is astronomical. They are monster shock absorbers, built to kill the entire onrushing weight of the aircraft. If the hook misses, the pilot has one twentieth of a second to change his mind, to "do a bolter"—shove open the throttle and blast off over the bow, climbing away to starboard with the casual observation, "Comin' on in again."

The slightest problem with the locking mechanism aborts the landing, and, almost without exception, writes off the aircraft. Because the Navy would rather ditch a $35 million jet, on its own, than kill two aviators who have cost $2 million apiece to train. They would also much prefer the aircraft to slam into the ocean, and avoid the terrible risk of a major fire on the flight deck, which a belly-down landing may cause. Not to mention the possible write-off of another forty parked planes, and possibly the entire ship if the fire gets to the millions of gallons of aircraft fuel.

Everyone on the fight deck knew that Billy-Ray and Freddie would almost certainly have to ditch the jet, and blast themselves out of the cockpit with the ejector, a dangerous and terrifying procedure, one which can cost any pilot an arm or a leg, or worse yet, his life. "Holy Christ," said Lieutenant Evans, miserably.

By now the LSO and his team were all edging toward the deep, heavily padded "pit" into which they would dive for safety if Billy-Ray lost control and the Tomcat plummeted into the carrier's stern. All fire crews were on red-alert. "Conn-Captain, four degrees right rudder. Steer two-one-zero. I want thirty knots minimum over the deck. Speed as required."

Everyone could now hear the roar of the engines on the incoming Tomcat, and the bush telegraph of the carrier was working full tilt. Most everyone had a soft spot for Billy-Ray. He'd been married for only a year, and half the personnel of the Naval Air Base on the Pax River in Maryland had been at the wedding. His bride, Suzie Danford, was the tall, dark-haired daughter of Admiral Skip Danford. She'd met the curly-haired, dark-eyed Billy-Ray, with his coal-miner's shoulders and sly smile, long before he had become one of the Navy's elite fliers, while he was completing training at Pensacola.

And now she was alone in Maryland, waiting out the endless six months of his first tour of sea duty. Like all aviators' wives, dreading the unexpected knock upon the door, dreading the stranger from the air base calling on the phone, the one who would explain that her Billy-Ray had punched a big hole in the Indian Ocean. And there was nothing melodramatic about any of it. About 20 percent of all Navy pilots die in the first nine years of their service. At the age of twenty-six, Suzie Danford Howell was no stranger to death. And the possibility of her own husband joining Jeff McCall, Charlie Rowland, and Dave Redland haunted her nights. Sometimes she thought it would all drive her crazy. But she tried to keep her fears silent.

She did not know, however, the mortal danger her husband was now in. There are virtually no procedures for landing gear failure. Nothing works, save for a touch of blind luck if the pilot can jolt down and then up, and the gears slam down and lock, putting out the warning light. But time is short. If that Tomcat F–14 runs out of gas it will drop like a twenty-ton slab of concrete and hit the long waves of the Indian Ocean like a meteorite. . . "Billy-Ray Howell and Freddie are in trouble". . . the word was sweeping through the carrier.

On the tower side of the flight deck, Ensign Junior Grade Jim Adams, a huge black man from South Boston, dressed in a big fluorescent yellow jacket, was talking on his radio phone to the hydraulics operators on the deck below who controlled the arresting wires, one of which would grab the Tomcat, slowing it down to zero speed in two seconds flat, heaving the aircraft to a halt. Big Jim, the duty Arresting Gear Officer, had already ordered the controls set to withstand the Tomcat's fifty-thousand-pound force slamming into the deck at 160 knots precisely, with the pilot's hand hard on the throttle in case the hook missed. But Jim knew the problem. . . "Billy-Ray Howell's in big trouble up there."

Big Jim loved Billy-Ray, a most unlikely duo on a big carrier, where aircrew tend to be a race apart. They talked about baseball endlessly, Jim because he believed he would have made a near-legendary first baseman for the Boston Red Sox, Billy-Ray because he had been a pretty good right-handed pitcher at

Hamlin High. Next year they planned a jaunt to watch the Red Sox spring training for four days in Florida. Right now Big Jim wished only that he could check out and fix the hydraulics on the Tomcat's landing gear, and he found himself whispering the age-old prayer of all carrier flight deck crew. . . "Please, please don't let him die, please let him get out."

Up on the bridge, Captain Carl Rheinegen was speaking to the senior LSO back on the stern. "Has he got a hydraulics malfunction? Do not land him. Hold him up and clear!"

Again the big waterproof phone clutched by Lieutenant Rick Evans crackled, and the incoming voice was still slow. "Tower this is Tomcat two-zero-one. Still got some kinda screwup here. Tried to give her a few jolts. But it didn't work. Light's still on. I can cross the stern okay and come on by, but I don't think the hydraulics are too good. I'd prefer to keep the speed at 250 and take her straight back up. Git a little air underneath. No real problem. Stick's a little tough. But we got gas. Lemme know."

And now the F–14 was thundering in toward the stern, twice as fast as an 80 mph Metroliner through New Jersey, and ten times as deafening. Too fast, but still with height. "Tower to Tomcat two-zero-one. Hit the throttle and pull right out, forget the pass. Repeat, forget the pass."

"Roger that," said Billy-Ray Howell carefully, and he slammed the throttle forward and hauled on the stick. But nothing much happened except for acceleration. She seemed to flatten out and then she was diving in toward the end of the flight deck, still with two Phoenix missiles under her wing. Enough to blow half the flight deck to bits. Still slow and easy, Billy-Ray drawled: "Tomcat two-zero-one, I'll jest take a little jog to my left and git out over the portside." And he watched through his deep-set eyes as the heaving flight deck roared up to meet him. He fought to stay aloft but the Tomcat now had a mind of its own. A bloody mind.

Rick Evans, watching the F–14 now hurtling toward the portside edge of the flight deck, snapped back into the phone: "Get out, Billy-Ray, *hit it!*"

For a split second Freddie Larsen thought his pilot might consider an ejection a sign of weakness or lack of cool. And he screamed for the first time in his flying career, "*Punch it out, Billy-Ray, for Christ's sake, punch it out!!*"

The Tomcat ripped past the carrier's mast, just as Lieutenant William R. Howell's right fist banged the lever. The compacted-charge exploded beneath his seat and blew him head-first out of the cockpit. Freddie followed, point five of a second later, the violence of the two explosions rendering them both momentarily unconscious. Freddie came around first, saw the Tomcat crash about twenty feet off the carrier's port bow, sending a spout of water fifty feet into the air, almost up to the flight deck.

But they were clear. When Billy-Ray came around, he saw his parachute canopy swinging above his head and the carrier's surging, white stern wake beneath him. And even as he and Freddie hit the water, the Sea King helicopter was lifting off the roof of the carrier, in a roaring whirlwind of air. Flight deck crew were emerging from cover. All landing and takeoff operations were suspended, and down in the heaving sea, half-drowned despite his watertight survival suit, fighting for breath, Billy-Ray Howell could hear the God-sent voice of the rescue chief yelling through the loud-hailer: "Easy, guys, take it real easy; release the chutes and keep still, we'll be right down."

The big chopper came in. A nineteen-year-old sailor jumped straight out into the water with the lines, and made for the two stricken U.S. airmen. "You guys okay?" he asked. "We're a whole lot better'n we would be still in the ole F–14," said Billy-Ray. Thirty-five seconds later they were both winched up to safety, both trembling from shock, Freddie Larsen with a broken right arm, Billy-Ray with a gashed eyebrow and blood pouring down his face, which made his grin look a bit crooked.

The chopper came in to land on the starboard side of the deck. Three medics were there, plus stretcher bearers. Lieutenant Rick Evans was also trembling and he just kept saying over and over, "Gee, I'm just so sorry, guys. I'm just so sorry."

There was a small but somber welcoming party for the two battered airmen. Big Jim Adams came rushing through the group, against every kind of Naval regulation, and he lifted Billy-Ray right out of the chopper, cradling him in his massive arms, saying:

"Don't you never damned die on me again, man, hear me?" Everyone could see the tears streaming down Big Jim's face.

The medics then took over, giving both men a shot of painkiller, and strapping Billy-Ray and Freddie into the wheeled stretchers. And the whole procession, now about fourteen strong, all a bit shaken, headed for the elevators, bound together by the camaraderie of men who have looked into the face of death together.

Freddie spoke first: "You are a crazy prick, Billy-Ray. You shoulda hit the button fifteen seconds earlier."

"Bullshit, Freddie. I had the timing right. If I'd punched out any earlier you'd probably be sittin' up there on top of the mast right now."

"Yeah, and one second later we'd both be sitting on the bottom of the fucking Indian Ocean."

"Shit!" said Billy-Ray. "You're an ungrateful sonofabitch. I jes' saved your life. And you ain't even my real problem. Do you realize Suzie's gonna have a heart attack when she hears about this? Guess I'll have to blame you."

"This is unbelievable," said Freddie, trying to smile, reaching out with his good arm to grasp his pilot's still shaking hand. "Wanna do it again sometime!"

The loss of a big Tomcat fighter aircraft is generally regarded as a career-threatening occurrence. A scapegoat is a near essential in the U.S. Navy after a foul-up which costs Uncle Sam around $35 million. Both the captain and the admiral would have to answer for this, and they had a lot of questions. Was this pilot error? Was it flight deck error? Who had checked and serviced the aircraft before it came up on deck for its last journey? Had the officer in charge of the final checkover, moments before takeoff, missed something? Was there any clue that the launching officer should have seen?

The preliminary report would be required in the Pentagon just as soon as it could be completed. And the official inquiry was convened instantly. Hydraulics experts were called in first. The officers would routinely talk to Billy-Ray and Freddie during the evening, in the carrier's brilliantly equipped hospital, after the surgeons had set the young navigator's arm.

None of the aviators believed the pilot had made any kind of mistake, and everyone knew that Lieutenant William R. Howell had hung in there until the last possible second in order to drive his two-hundred-knot time bomb safely out over the side of the ship. Senior officers would no doubt reach a sympathetic conclusion, but there would be real hard questions asked of the Maintenance Department and its specialist hydraulics engineers.

While the preliminary inquiry into the accident continued, the day-to-day business of the U.S. Battle Group at sea also proceeded on schedule. Up on the Admiral's Bridge, Captain Jack Baldridge, the Battle Group Operations Officer, was normally in charge, in the absence of the admiral himself. But right now he was in conference on the floor below, in the radar and electronics nerve center with the Tactical Action officer and the Anti-Submarine Warfare chief. As always, this was the most obviously busy place in the giant carrier. Always in half-light, illuminated mainly by the amber-colored screens of the computers, it existed in a strange, murmuring netherworld of its own, peopled by intense young technicians glued to the screens as the radar systems swept the oceans and skies.

Jack Baldridge was a stocky, irascible Kansan, from the Great Plains of the Midwest, a little town called Burdett, up in Pawnee County, forty miles northeast of Dodge City. Jack was from an old U.S. Navy family, which sent its sons to sea to fight, but somehow lured them back to the old cattle ranch in the end. Jack's father had commanded a destroyer in the North Atlantic in World War II, his younger brother Bill was a lieutenant commander stationed outside Washington with the U.S. Office of Naval Intelligence; somewhat mysteriously, Jack thought, but young Bill was an acknowledged expert on nuclear weapons, their safety, their storage and deployment.

Most people expected that the forty-year-old Jack would become a rear admiral. Naval warfare was his life, and he was the outstanding commander in the entire Battle Group, shouldering significant responsibility as the Group Admiral's right-hand man. His kid brother Bill, however, who looked like a cowboy, rode a horse like a cowboy, and was apt to drive Navy staff cars like a cowboy, had gone as far as he was going. He was not a natural commander, but his scientific achievements in the field of nuclear physics and weaponry were so impressive the Navy Chiefs had felt obliged to award him with senior rank. Bill was a natural crisis man, a cool, thoughtful Naval scientist, who often came up with solutions no one had previously considered. There were several elderly admirals who did not care for him because of his unorthodox methods, but Bill Baldridge had many supporters.

Where Jack was a solidly married, down-to-earth Navy captain of the highest possible quality, no one quite knew where Bill would end up, except in a variety of different beds all over Washington. At thirty-six he showed no signs of giving up his bachelor lifestyle and the trail of romantic havoc he had left from Dodge City to Arlington, Virginia. Jack regarded his brother with immense benevolence.

Down in electronic operations, Captain Baldridge was moving on several fronts. Captain Rheinegen, in overall command of the ship, had just ordered a minor change of course as they steamed over the Ninety East Ridge which runs north–south, east of the mid-Indian basin. Here the ocean is only about a mile deep, but as the carrier pushed on along its northwesterly course the depth fell away to almost four miles below the keel. Captain Baldridge had already calculated that the Tomcat probably hit the ridge as it sank and settled about five thousand feet below the surface.

He verified the positions of all the ships in the group, agreed with his ASW that four underwater "contacts" were spurious; he talked briefly to the Sonar Controller and the Link Operators; checking in with the Surface Picture Compiler. He could hear the Missile/Gun Director in conference with the Surface Detector, and he took a call on a coded line from Captain Art Barry, the New Yorker who commanded the eleven-thousand-ton guided missile cruiser *Arkansas*, which was currently steaming about eight miles off their starboard bow. The message was cryptic: "Kansas City Royals 2 Yankees 8. Five bucks. Art."

"Sonofagun," said Baldridge. "Guess he thinks that's cute. We've just dropped a $35 million aircraft on the floor of this godforsaken ocean, and he's getting the baseball results on the satellite." Of course it would have been an entirely different matter if the message had been Royals 8 Yankees 2. "Beautiful guy, Art. Gets his priorities straight."

Baldridge glanced at his watch, and began to write in his notebook without thinking, not for the official record, just the result of a lifetime in the U.S. Navy. He wrote the date and time in Naval fashion—"221700APR02" (the day, the time, 5 P.M. then month and year). Then he wrote the ship's position—mid-Indian Ocean, 9S (nine degrees latitude South), 91E (ninety-one degrees longitude East). Then, "Bitch of a day. Royals 2 Yankees 8. Tomcat lost. Billy-Ray and Freddie hurt, but safe." He too had a soft spot for Bill-Ray Howell.

221700APR02. 41 30N, 29E.
Course 180. Speed 4.

"Possible on 030, ten miles. Come and look, Ben. Maybe okay?"

"Thank you . . . yes . . . plot him, Georgy. He's a coal-burner, and probably slow enough. If he keeps going for the hole, and his speed suits our timetable, we'll take him. Get in . . . but well behind him, Georgy."

"Take two hours."

221852.

"They start to look for us. Time expired one hour. First submarine accident signal just in, Ben."

"Good. What have you told the chaps?"

"What we agree. Cover for special covert exercise. We answer nothing. Soon they stop. We not exist anymore."

"Okay. It'll be dark inside an hour. Now let's get organized for the transit. Watch for the light on Rumineleferi Fortress up there on the northwest headland, then go right in . . . follow the target as close as you possibly can."

"Fine. Even though no one ever done it, right? Eh, Ben?"

"My Teacher once told me it could be done."

"Ben, I do not speak your language, and my English not as good as yours. But I know this is fucking tricky. Very bad crosscurrents in there. Shoals on the right bank, in the narrows near the big bridge. Shit! What if we hit and get stuck. We never get out of jail."

"If, Georgy, you do precisely as we discussed, we will not hit anything."

"But you still say we go right through the middle of port at nine knots with fucking big white wake behind us. They see it, Ben. They can't fucking miss it."

"Do I have to tell you again? They will not see it, if you keep really close, right in the middle of the Greek's wake. He won't want to run aground anymore than you do. He won't push his luck in the shallow spots. Let's go, Georgy."

"I still not like it much."

"I am not telling you to like it. DO IT!"

"Remember it is your fault if this goes wrong."

"If it goes wrong, that won't matter."

222004.

"I want to be in our spot early, and get settled before we reach the entrance. We want a good visual night ranging mark on him. His overtaking light will do fine."

"Slack Greek prick, leave them on all day."

"I noticed. Use height ten meters on stern light."

"What about his radar, Ben?"

"He won't see us in his ground wave, and if he does, he'll think it's his own wake. This chap is no Gorschkov. He can't even remember to turn his lights off."

"What about other ships in channel?"

"Anyone overtaking will stay well to one side. Oncoming ships will keep to the other. My only real worry is the cross-ferries. That's why we want to be going through the narrowest bits between 0200 and 0500, when I hope not to meet any of them. Bloody dreary if one of them slipped across our Greek leader's bum and we rammed him."

"How come, Ben, you know much more about everything than I do?"

"Mainly because I cannot afford mistakes. Also because I had a brilliant Teacher. . . bright, impatient, clever, arrogant . . . Stay calm, Georgy. And do as I say. It's dark enough now. Let's range his light, and close right in."

281400APR02. 9S, 74E.
Course 010. Speed 12.

Eight miles off Diego Garcia the weather had worsened, the warm wind, rising and falling, making life endlessly difficult for the aviators. On the flight deck of the U.S. carrier *Thomas Jefferson* the LSO's were in their usual huddle, taking advantage of the comparative quiet, talking to the pilots of the seven incoming flights from the day's combat air patrol, four of them circling in a stack at eight thousand feet, twenty miles out.

The day-long exercises had demanded supersonic speed tests, and many landings and takeoffs. There had already been two burst tires, one of which had caused an incoming F/A–18 Hornet strike-fighter to slew left on the wire, and damn near hit a parked A–6E Intruder bomber.

Gas was now low all around. Tensions were fairly high. And before the six fighters came in, the entire flight deck staff was preparing to bring down the quarterback, Hawkeye, the much bigger radar early warning and control aircraft, unmistakable because of its great electronic dome set above the fuselage.

Jim Adams was calling the shots. Earphones on, yellow jacket visible for miles, he was racing through his mental checklist, yelling down the phone to the team below on the hydraulics. "Stand by for Hawkeye, two minutes." He knew the hydraulic system was set properly, and now his eyes were sweeping the deck for even the smallest speck of litter. No one gets a second chance out here. One particle of rubbish sucked into a jet engine can blow it out. The whiplash from a broken arrester wire could kill a dozen people and send an aircraft straight over the bow.

Jim looked up, downwind. The Hawkeye was screaming in, the arresting wires spread-eagled on the deck, ready for the grab of the hook. Down below the giant hydraulic piston was in position, set to withstand, and stop, a seventy-five-thousand-pound aircraft in a controlled collision of plane and deck.

"*Groove!!*" bellowed Jim down to the hydraulic crew. This was the code word for "she's close, stand by."

Seconds pass. "*Short!*"—the key command, everyone away from the machinery.

And now, as Hawkeye thundered in toward the stern, Jim Adams bellowed: "*Ramp!*"

Every eye on the deck was steeled on the hook stretched out behind. Speech was inconceivable above the howl of the engines. The blast from the jets made the sky shimmer. At 160 knots the wheels slammed down onto the landing surface, and, right behind them, the hook grabbed, the cable rising starkly from the deck in a geometric V. One second later the Hawkeye stopped a few yards from the end of the flight deck, the sound of her engines dying quickly away.

Suddenly there was pandemonium, as the deck crews raced out to haul the Hawkeye into its parking place. Jim Adams shouted into the phone to change the settings on the hydraulics, the LSO's were getting into position, one of them talking to the first Tomcat pilot, very carefully: "Okay one-zero-six, come on in—winds gusting at thirty-five, check your approach line, looks fine from here . . . flaps down . . . hook down . . . gotcha . . . you're all set."

Lieutenant William R. Howell was back in the game, with a new RIO, and a big plaster over his eyebrow. His pal Jim Adams was double-checking everything, as always. One by one he shouted his commands: "*Groove . . . Short . . . Ramp!*"—until Billy-Ray was down, to universal shouts of "Good job!" "Let's go, Billy-Ray!" It was always a little tense on the first landing for a crashed aviator. Up in the control tower, Freddie Larsen was permitted to stand and watch, and if his arm had not hurt so badly he too would have clapped when Billy-Ray hit the deck safely. "That's my guy," he yelled without thinking. "Okay, *Billy-Ray!*" Even the *Thomas Jefferson*'s commanding officer,

Captain Rheinegen, himself a former aviator like all carrier commanders, allowed himself a cautious grin.

And now, with a night exercise coming up, there was a change of deck crew. The launch men were moving into position, and aircraft were moving up from the hangars below on the huge elevators. All around, there were young officers checking over the fighter bombers, pilots climbing aboard, another group of engines screaming; uniformed men, many on their first tours of duty, were on their stations. The first of the Hornets was ready for takeoff. The red light on the island signaled "Four minutes to launch."

Two minutes later the light blinked to amber. A crewman, crouching next to the fighter's nose wheels, signaled the aircraft forward, and locked on the catapult wire.

The light turned green. Lieutenant Skip Martin, the "shooter," pointed his right hand at the pilot, raised his left hand, and extended two fingers . . . "Go to full power." Then palm out . . . "Hit the afterburners . . ." The pilot saluted formally and leaned forward, tensing for the impact of the catapult shot.

The shooter, his eyes glued on the cockpit, saluted, bending his knees and touching two fingers of his left hand onto the deck. Skip Martin gestured: *Forward.* A crewman, kneeling in the catwalk narrowly to the left of the big fighter jet, hit the button on catapult three, and ducked as the outrageous hydraulic mechanism hurled the Hornet on its way, screaming down the deck, its engines roaring flat out, leaving an atomic blast of air in its wake. Everyone watched, even veterans almost holding their breath, as the aircraft rocketed off the carrier and out over the water, climbing away to port. "Tower to Hornet one-six-zero, nice job there . . . course 054, speed 400, go to 8,000."

"Hornet one-six-zero, roger that."

281835APR02. 35N, 21E.
Course 270. Speed 5.

"Ben, we got rattle. Up for'ard."
"Damn! We'll have to stop, right away, fix it. We can't afford to travel one more mile with that."

"No problem. I will fix. Soon as it's dark. Very quiet here anyway."

290523APR02.

"At least the rattle's gone. But I really am very sad about your man. It sounds heartless. I don't mean it to be so. But I just hope they never find his body."

"No time look anymore. Not blame anyone. Just freak wave. I seen it before. Now we say good Catholic prayer for him."

"I should like to join you in that."

041900MAY02. 7S, 72E.
Course 270. Speed 10.

Inside the mess room of the *Thomas Jefferson,* still off Diego Garcia in the Indian Ocean, big Jim Adams was giving a party in one of the ward rooms. Four hours earlier he had received a message that his wife Carole had given birth to their first son—a nine-pound boy, whose name would be Carl Edward Adams. This, Jim explained, had been agreed two years ago, the first name for the longtime Red Sox outfielder Carl Yastrzemski, the second for the legendary Red Sox hitter Ted Williams.

And now little Carl Edward had come in to land, and the aviators on the carrier were exercising two of their other major skills—making their two cans of beer (permitted on the sixtieth day out) last for about four hours, and feeling truly sorry for other human beings on Planet Earth who were not involved in the flying of jet fighter planes off the decks of the biggest aircraft carriers in the world.

A visiting commanding officer from one of the destroyers, Captain Roger Peterson, trying to dine in peace in a far corner with Captain Rheinegen, remarked to him that it takes a crew of more than three thousand men to keep the boisterous, white-scarved, winged heroes in the air.

No one heard, and it would scarcely have mattered if they had. Because the one shining fact known to any aviator is that all other forms of life, including submariners (especially submariners), guided missile experts, gunnery officers, navigation and strategic advanced warfare staff, were, and would ever be, their absolute inferiors.

Meanwhile Big Jim was up on his feet sipping his second can of iced beer, the last of his ration, making a little speech, in which he announced that Lieutenant Howell was to be Carl Edward's godfather. This provoked yells of derision, that Billy-Ray was a godless hillbilly and poor little Carl Edward would receive no moral guidance in his whole life.

Billy-Ray stood up and told them that in his opinion such criticism was essentially "bullshit," since his dad was a churchgoing Methodist back home in Hamlin, and that he considered himself an ideal choice.

This caused Big Jim to stand up and admit that Billy-Ray was only his second choice, but that since Yaz himself had not made himself available he was happy to move the selection process from an outfielder to a hillbilly. Anyway, he had instructed Carole to give birth while he was at sea because that would allow him to be first man off the ship when the *Thomas Jefferson* finally returned home in September.

041500MAY02. 36N, 3W.
Course 270. Speed 5.

"Okay, Ben, here's island now. Can't see much, on red 40, visibility not good."

"Anyone live there?"

"Don't know. Maybe few Spanish fishermen, but empty. Maybe your Teacher say city size of Moscow there but no one notice."

"No. He told me it was empty too."

"Anyway, you have plan for straits?"

"I have no requirements whatsoever, except we do not get caught. You've driven through here many times I'm sure."

"Yes, but long time back—and Americans have better surveillance now. They got suspicion last time. Maybe satellite *photo. Now how you make another miracle, Ben? How we go through in secret?"*

"Basically, Georgy, old man, we have only one choice. Very slowly, very quietly, and hope to God no one really sees us."

"No problem with that. I agree. You expect message from boss?"

"Not yet. Not until the final phase. Possibly not till the fuel turns up. Possibly not at all."

"Okay. I make crew accept story. But this is long journey."

"They'll be well rewarded in the end. From here on, we must take extra care again. We'll stay in silent drive at five knots for forty-eight hours. Ultra quiet, please, Georgy."

061200MAY02. Fort Meade, Maryland.

Vice Admiral Arnold Morgan, Director of the National Security Agency, a short, hard-eyed Texan with grimly trimmed white hair, sat alone behind his desk. He was normally on three telephones, growling orders which would be relayed by satellite to his agencies throughout the world. The admiral's reputation was that of a voracious and dangerous spider at the center of a vast electronic web of Navy intelligence resources. Most of the time he just watched. But when Admiral Morgan spoke, men jumped, on four continents and the oceans surrounding them.

Right now the admiral was curious. Open wide on his desk was the weighty current edition of *Jane's Fighting Ships*, the British bible of the world's warships. He had not expected it to provide an answer, nor did it. Neither did three other highly classified Naval reference books which were also piled around his desk.

Late on the previous evening he had received a satellite message. It had not been urgent, or alarming, or even particularly informative. It was, nonetheless, distinctly unsatisfactory, and something about it irritated Arnold Morgan. The story was simple: "Gibraltar facility picked up very short transient contact on very quiet vessel at 050438MAY02. Insufficient hard copy data for firm classification—aural, compressed cavitation, one shaft, five blades, probably non-nuclear. No information on friendly transits relate."

Admiral Morgan understood that someone with very sharp ears on the other side of the Atlantic had heard a noise in the water, for a matter of twenty to thirty seconds, which sounded a lot like a non-nuclear-powered submarine. It was propelling on a single shaft with a five-bladed screw. It was probably well off-shore, almost certainly below the surface, and had made the noise either by speeding up somewhat carelessly, or putting her screw too shallow for the revolutions set. Perhaps she had momentarily lost trim, pondered the admiral, himself an ex-submariner, ex-nuclear commander.

In the good old days it was possible to discern a Soviet-built boat because of their insistence on six-bladed props when Western nations went for odd numbers of blades, three, five, or seven. If Admiral Morgan closed his eyes tightly, and cast his thoughts back twenty-three years to his own days in the sonar room of a Boomer, deep in his mind he could hear again the distinctive "swish—swish—swish—swish—swish—*swish*" of the blades on a distant old Soviet Navy submarine.

They used to be hard to miss but it was much more difficult nowadays to identify any submarine. Even modern, quiet fishing trawlers can make this kind of noise if they speed up suddenly and inadvertently hassle the haddock. But Admiral Morgan had no interest in fishermen. The only furtive, five-bladed fucker he would worry about was a submarine. And he could sort that out pretty quickly.

Admiral Morgan was a living, snarling, encyclopedia when it came to checking out foreign warships. He wanted to know what kind of contact it was, who the hell was driving it, and where the hell was it going. The merest possibility of a submarine had that effect on him.

It took about five minutes on the computer for the admiral to figure out that it could not have been an American or British boat. A bit longer to find out that it could not have been French or Spanish either.

Israel had one submarine of Russian origin in service that he knew of, but there was a record of it entering the Atlantic four weeks ago. So it was not them. The goddamned Iranians had three they bought from Russia, but they had all been accounted for in the Gulf recently—thoroughly enough for him to know that none of them were that far from home.

He knew the Indonesians had some old and defunct Russian boats, which were unlikely to have cleared the breakwater in safety. Even the Algerians had a couple of Kilos, brand new in 1995, but both were back in refit, he knew, in St. Petersburg. The Poles had one in the Baltic, the Rumanians one in the Black Sea, both out of action and both recently observed. The Libyan's Kilo fared no better than its six "Foxtrot" predecessors, two of which sank alongside—it had not been to sea for a year. The Chinese had quite a few, more modern designs. But none of these people had any known business in the strait.

He had already played a long shot and placed a call to his opposite number in the Russian Navy in Moscow. It was all very cheerful these days, and without hesitation, the Russians told him they had not sent any of their diesel boats through the strait for eighteen months.

In fact the only Russian diesel unaccounted for was lost in an accident in the Black Sea about three weeks ago, and was right now resting in seven hundred meters of water with everyone in it dead. They were still searching, but had found her special indicator buoys drifting, and a small amount of debris.

All of which baffled Admiral Morgan. He kept repeating to himself the same scenario. If one of the U.S. Navy's sonar wizards said he had heard a quiet propeller, then the admiral believed there had to be a suspicion in that operator's mind.

Only a few people can even *hear* these subtle, distant sound waves, and even fewer can recognize them. And if his man in Gibraltar said he had heard one shaft and five blades, then that was what he had heard. But this guy had not only bothered to report it, he had also included a veiled personal suspicion that it was "probably non-nuclear."

"I think our man suspects it was underwater," Morgan thought. "The contact was transient. And the trouble with all transients is their similarity to code-breaking . . . if you have just a small sample you don't really know much. Just enough to want to know a bit more. Like what precisely was the type of boat, and who was driving the bastard?

"But our new friends in Moscow are saying no—and why should they lie? Not only are we at peace, we could not give a rat's ass if they drove a diesel up and down the Atlantic all year, calling at all stations. If they pitched up in Norfolk, Virginia, hell we'd probably give 'em a cup of coffee."

When he had first seen the message, he did not understand. And he still didn't. The facts seemed mutually exclusive—a mental outcome guaranteed to infuriate him.

At fifty-seven, Arnold Morgan was a driven man, a ruthless demander of matching, orderly facts. Admiral Morgan did not accept Chaos Theory. This character trait had cost him two marriages, and strained his relationships with his children. The Navy regarded him as the best intelligence chief they'd ever had. If there was one single criticism of him, it was simply that he was inclined to become overinvolved in what some people considered petty details.

"I do not accept incompatible facts," he said firmly to the still-empty room. "That, gentlemen, is a matter of principle." And with that, he consigned the signal and all of the results of his many questions about the phantom contact to his highly efficient electronic filing system. His only comfort lay in the knowledge that if indeed it was a submarine, it would turn up somewhere, sometime, and the problem would be resolved.

Until then, he decided to put it down as a kind of fishy snafu. And the admiral detested all snafus. Especially underwater snafus, because those were, unfailingly, both expensive and embarrassing.

"So perhaps it was," he announced to the empty room, "just a fishing trawler. Perhaps our man was just a tiny bit overzealous. Hmmmm."

Then, visibly brightening, "Unless some bastard's lying."

271300MAY02. 6S, 73E.
Course 340. Speed 12.

SURROUNDED BY HIS MOST SENIOR STAFF, REAR ADMIRAL Zack Carson, one of the few high-ranking, seagoing officers in the United States Navy, was methodically grappling with a zillion details involving the waging of war on a scale never before witnessed on this particular planet.

He was seated in a king-sized leather chair in the Flag Operations Room on the third floor of the island, thirty feet above the five-acre flight deck of his flagship, the USS *Thomas Jefferson*.

They had moved generally WNW during the past two weeks in the Indian Ocean, and the huge aircraft carrier was now proceeding close-north of the remote tropical atoll of Diego Garcia. To the NNE, 850 miles away, stood the headland of Cape Comorin, the southernmost point of the Indian subcontinent. If, however, the *Thomas Jefferson* followed the polestar due north she would steam for 1,600 miles before entering her patrol zone in the Arabian Sea. Deep blue waters, shark-infested, some 450 miles due west of the teeming seaport of Bombay.

Admiral Carson was due on station in those tense, somewhat unpredictable seas eight days from now. His massive presence there, at the very gateway to the Gulf of Iran, served as a warning to all who might challenge the right of the world's tankers to ply their trade along the sprawling crude oil terminals which stretch from the Strait of Hormuz to Iraq. His presence would also, unavoidably, deepen the already simmering hatred toward the United States by much of the Islamic nation. But that goes with the territory of a Battle Group Commander. And the six-foot-four-inch Kansan Zack Carson, at the age of fifty-six, had long since accepted that not everyone flew a flag of pure joy when his giant ship hove into sight along the horizons of the Middle East.

At his command were cruise missiles, guided weapons of all types to attack targets above, on, and under the water, a small all-purpose Air Force, whole batteries of artillery, to send in thousands of shells per hour. And stored deep in the bowels of this great ship, and in his two nuclear submarines, other missiles—missiles of such colossal destructive force, not even Zack Carson was comfortable contemplating the consequences of deploying them. The admiral, and his masters in the Pentagon, could, if instructed, damn nearly destroy much of the world. In very short order.

That was not an actual part of his plan, but a U.S. Battle Group must, at all times, be right at the peak of the warfare efficiency curve, which heads steeply upward according to the value of the hardware. The view of the Chiefs of Staff, not to mention the hard-nosed Southwestern Republican currently occupying the White House, was, broadly, "at that price it better work, and it better work real good, right on time, no bullshit."

Thus, at this particular moment, in deep conversation with his fellow Kansan, Captain Jack Baldridge, Admiral Carson was making doubly sure that the previous month's intense battle training programs had transformed this ship, and all of the six thousand men who sailed in her, into the best it was possible to be. From the cooks to the navigators, from the sonar men to the guys in the print room, from the firefighters to the fighter pilots, the radar wizards to the missile loaders—the Battle Group commander could afford no weak link in his chain of command, no suspect system, no indecisive officer, zero inefficiency. This was the very frontier of warfare, the bottom line of the United States

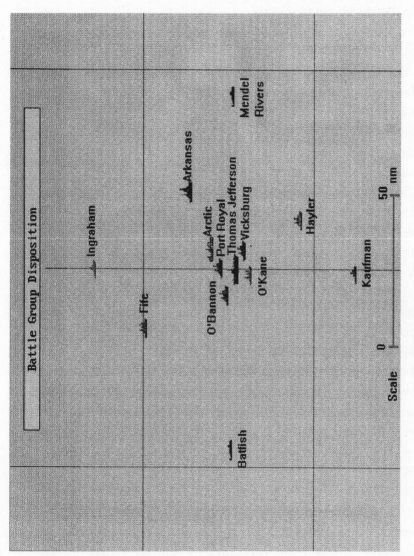

Battle Group Disposition

Ingraham

Fife

Arctic
O'Bannon Port Royal
Thomas Jefferson
Vicksburg
O'Kane

Arkansas

Hayler

Mendel
Rivers

Kaufman

Batfish

Scale

0   50   nm

21:03, July 8, 2002

offense and defensive charter. The admiral, reverting easily to the more relaxed vernacular of the prairies, often reminded his closest staff officers in the following way, "A long time before the buck comes to a stop in the Oval Office, someone's gonna shove it right up my rear end."

For weeks on end, the admiral had driven the entire Battle Group to the heights of their abilities. Twice a day he sent out communications detailing exercises which ultimately involved all sixteen thousand of the men serving in the dozen ships in the group.

There was endless training for the Aegis missile cruisers—training which ensured they really could knock out any incoming missiles, even traveling at twice the speed of sound.

The submarine commanders, ranging far out in front of the Battle Group, were made firmly aware of the admiral's special interest in their work. He believed not only in the offensive capability of these search-and-strike underwater killers—but in their critical role as the group's front-line anti-submarine weapon; the destroyer of their own counterparts. After several weeks out here, practicing and patrolling endlessly in the deep waters of the Indian Ocean, the phrase "deadly accurate" really did apply to all of their systems, but especially the lethal wire-guided torpedoes, equally effective against ship or submarine.

Zack Carson, a surface ship man and, in his youth, a former aviator, had often wished he had been a submariner. He was just never sure he could have passed the searching examination process these sailor-scientists require before taking command of a U.S. Navy SSN . . . the degree in marine engineering, the electronics, the mechanics, the hydrology, the deep navigational skills, and the nuclear engineering courses. These days the underwater commanders represented the elite of all Western navies, and Zack Carson was kind of uncertain that he possessed quite the academic grasp the submarine service required of its captains.

He had made his name as a battle line strategist, an expert in aviation, missiles, and gunnery, a tactician on the grand scale, a commanding officer who painted in broad, sure strokes, but never strayed too far from the minutiae of his trade. Everyone liked Admiral Carson, because he still sounded like some kind of a gunslinger from the High Plains of Kansas—as indeed a couple of his direct ancestors had been—and he displayed a deliberate, laid-back nonchalance under pressure that was plainly deceptive, but nonetheless an enviable quality in any ship's operational center.

All of which was pretty impressive from a Midwestern farm boy who had grown up in the little town of Tribune, in the middle of the endless wheat prairies of Greeley County, hard by the western state border where Kansas joins Colorado. These lands summon up the true meaning of the word "nowhere." Flat, sprawling Greeley County contains only two small towns in its entire 620 square miles. Both of them are set along the little local highway, Route 156, which starts 180 miles to the east near the great bend of the Arkansas River.

These are the remotest American lands, with populations of about one hundredth the average for rural U.S.A. Miles and miles and miles of wheat and grassland, flat, windswept, and, in an uncluttered way, made glorious by the sheer absence of spectacle. Out here, under the big sky, untouched by modern intrusion, names like Elija, Zachariah, Jethro, Willard, Jeremiah, and Ethan were commonplace. Zachariah Carson was the tall, lean son of Jethro Carson, who farmed thousands of acres of the prairie, as his immediate forefathers had also done.

Perhaps it was a young lifetime spent watching the wind sweep across the endless acres of gently waving wheat which gave Zack Carson his early longing for the ocean. But for as long as he could remember, he had an uncomplicated yearning to join the United States Navy. There were two other brothers in the family to carry on farming the wheat, but it almost broke old Jethro Carson's heart when his oldest boy packed his bags at the age of eighteen and set off across the country from the most landlocked state in America for the U.S. Naval Academy at Annapolis, Maryland. His entry into the historic Navy school represented the biggest teaching triumph in the entire history of Tribune High.

With his gangling walk, crooked grin, and down-home way of expressing himself, Zack Carson proceeded to stun successive Navy examination boards with his grasp of the most intricate details of warfare at sea. He gave up Navy aviation after ditching a faulty jet fighter over the side of a carrier, when he was just twenty-six, and he commanded a frigate before his thirty-sixth birthday. He had charge of a guided missile destroyer at thirty-nine, and by the time he was forty-eight, Zack was captain of the giant carrier *Dwight D. Eisenhower*—named after another Kansas boy. This was most unusual for an aviator turned "black shot"—but Zack was pretty unusual, too, and recognized as such.

They promoted him to rear admiral within four years and in the year 2000 awarded him the honor of the newest U.S. aircraft carrier, the *Thomas Jefferson*, for his flagship. Within a few months he requested as his Battle Group Operations Officer another Kansas farm boy, Captain Jack Baldridge, whose hometown of Burdett was about 120 miles from Tribune, straight along Route 156. Like Jack he was married with two daughters, and both families now lived in San Diego, California, where the *Thomas Jefferson* was based.

Baldridge was a barrel-chested disciplinarian who reacted swiftly and decisively to any possible threat or danger to his ships. Admiral Carson was more inclined to give a few "Uh-huhs." Under pressure, Admiral Carson was cautious, thoughtful, cynical, and superstitious. He was also absolutely decisive.

They made a truly formidable team. When either of them spoke, the Combat Information Center jumped. Because when Captain Baldridge issued an order, that was an order from the admiral himself. And in a big-deck carrier that was an order that was seldom questioned.

Right now the two of them were discussing the possibility of yet another heavy night-flying program, as part of the major upcoming war game against the U.S. Battle Group they would soon be replacing in the Arabian Sea. The battle lines were now being drawn, and as ever these apparent practice sessions were taken with immense seriousness by all concerned. Because this was their opportunity to hone their battle skills in a theater of almost real war.

These exercises are both career breakers and makers. They are blisteringly expensive, and represent the only way the U.S. Navy has to simulate battle conditions, and to assess various key players and how they will react to the heightened speed and danger of the exercise. In the forthcoming combat zone, the *Thomas Jefferson* would attack the resident, and now outgoing, Battle Group centered on her fellow Nimitz Class 100,000-tonner, the USS *George Washington.*

A time is set for the "attack" to begin and from then on the aggressor will use every piece of electronic guile, cunning, and naval hardware to get in close to the opposing carrier and "kill" her. No one actually fires a shell, or launches a missile, or even drops a bomb, but that's what it feels like for the defenders when they pick up the telephone to hear the fatal communication. "Admiral, we regret to inform you, our submarine is three miles off your starboard beam, and three minutes ago we fired two torpedoes, both nuclear. You are history. Good morning, we'll drop in for a cup of coffee later!"

Between the start and the completion of the three-day exercise, there are constant air "attacks" on the missile ships; computer and radar systems are tuned to record every detail, and every department throughout the fleet is monitored assiduously. The normal opening moves involve careful reconnaissance and probing, to establish the enemy group's disposition, layout, and makeup. Step two is to deduce the enemy's intentions and likely battle plan, while concealing yours from him. The normal outcome is a "victory" for the defenders because it really is *almost* impossible to get close to a carrier. And her missile men pick off the incoming attacks in pretty short order. They also "sink" a few ships and submarines while they are about it.

The Hawkeye radar station in the sky can see for so many hundreds of miles, an undetected attack above water is a great rarity. However, there are always instances of a Carrier Battle Group's outer layers being penetrated in these exercises, and the consequences are extremely uncomfortable for the "losing" commanders. No purely defensive measures are ever 100 percent effective. The occasional "leaker" will sometimes get through.

The vital question is, can he do any damage once he gets in? If he does, there will be, without doubt, a major postmortem, and there is always the unspoken threat that the exercise was in fact a high-level examination to identify future senior battle commanders. For the Navy brass there is of course the solace that it took one U.S. Battle Group to sink another. No one else could play in the same league. Nonetheless, defending commanders in these multimillion-dollar war games feel themselves to be on trial, and they expect no mercy from their opponents.

Which was, essentially, why Admiral Zack Carson and Captain Jack Baldridge were currently locked in conference with several of their senior departmental chiefs, deciding whether to order yet another night-flying exercise off the carrier, knowing how tired many of the pilots and air crews already were.

Opinion was just about divided on whether it was really necessary, but Captain Baldridge was an old acquaintance of his opposite number in the *George Washington*. "That sonofabitch will attack at night," he said. "He won't care how long he waits, he'll come at us after dark. I know the guy. He's as cunning as an old coon dog, hunts after dark, and we want CAP's up there early, about a hundred miles up-threat. Nearly every goddamned problem we've had on the flight deck these past few weeks has been at night, and I think we should spend the next week keeping the pilots sharp."

Admiral Carson said slowly, "Well, you guys, about eighteen years ago I knew an admiral who lost one of these war games to a small Royal Navy frigate group we were working with. Right out here in the Gulf of Arabia.

"The Brits lit up a destroyer like a Christmas tree, found some guy who could speak Bengalese, and made out like a tour ship. Next thing that happened they were on the line about two miles from the carrier, in clear weather, announcing they just fired half a dozen of those Exocet missiles of theirs, straight at the ole 'mission critical'—a lot of people thought it was funny as hell. But not in Washington. It turned out to be a real embarrassment for that admiral. I could get by real easy without any of that bullshit breaking out here.

"So I'll go with Jack. Start flying again tonight. Warn *Arctic* we want everyone topped up before dark."

Moments later, even as the new night-flying orders were being prepared, the ship's bush telegraph, which operates along the main upper deck where the pilots live, was buzzing. Squadrons were grouping together, pilots were razzing each other about shaky night landings, the Landing Signal Officers were checking schedules. Certain engineers and hydraulics specialists were already heading down to the gigantic hangars on the floor below—an area 35 feet high and 850 feet long, the overall size of three football fields.

This was the garage for the fighter/attack aircraft, the bombers and the surveillance planes. Also down here were the aviation maintenance departments and the jet engine repair shop. Directly above the for'ard end were the massive hydraulic steam rams for the catapults; above was the domain of Ensign Jim Adams, who would have First Watch as Arresting Gear Officer tonight.

Meanwhile the distant whine of engines being checked over was already beginning on the sweltering tropical heat of the flight deck, where the Tomcats, the Hornets, the deadly, all-weather Intruder surprise bomber, the EA–6B radar-jammer, and the ever-present Hawkeye, were being prepared once more to go to work.

271600MAY02. 15S, 3W.
Course 165. Speed 8.

"Okay, Ben, I'd say St. Helena is about a hundred miles off our starboard beam now. We better start looking for the tanker. Getting real low on fuel. He better show up."

"He'll be there, Georgy, in about two to three hours I'd guess, just before dark. We have not seen a ship for a week—so we'll have the place to ourselves, I'd think."

"This is a big ocean, Ben. Something go wrong down here, take six months to find us."

"If something goes wrong down here, we don't want anyone

to find us. Better to swim to Africa. Remember what I told you about St. Helena. That's where the English locked up Napoleon for six years after Waterloo. He died there. We might end up in his old cell. Keep going as quiet as you can."

"I'm quiet, Ben. You have to admit that. No mistakes, eh?"

"One minor one, Georgy. Just that one, in the straits. Remember? I almost jumped out of my skin."

"You jump more if we hit that tanker. I had to speed up, you know."

"I'm not complaining, Georgy, but in that area the Americans are very, very thorough. Someone might have heard us."

"For only twenty seconds, Ben."

"That'll do for the Americans. They are very alert to any mistake by anyone. Just hope no one noticed."

"If anyone did they gave up a long time ago. Not even see aircraft for a week."

"Well, that's true. We'll just take care, hold this speed and start looking for our fuel about two hours from now."

"Okay, Ben, you're the boss."

290900MAY02. USS *Thomas Jefferson*. 5N, 68E.
Course 325. Speed 30.
Midway between the Carlsberg Ridge and
the Maldives. 2,500 fathoms.

"Okay. Start time 1200 confirmed. *George Washington* about five hundred miles due north. That means her SSN's might be as close as three hundred miles already. Order both our submarines into sectors northeast and northwest ASAP. And have everyone else on top line from 1000. I don't trust their Group Ops Officer any better than he trusts me. He might just go ahead and start this thing right away, and no one will give a shit if we bleat. We take no chances."

Captain Baldridge was glaring out over the Admiral's Bridge, which was in pretty stark contrast to his boss, who was grappling with the crossword from the Sunday edition of the *Wichita*

Eagle someone has sent up to him. "Easy, Jack," he muttered. "They won't close in on us before the start time. This is a heavy overhead area. Everyone would see. How about another cup of coffee? We're ready."

"Well, I don't look for an incoming air strike till after dark, but I just don't trust their submarines. I don't trust any submarines except for the ones directly under our control. Those guys are brought up to be the sneakiest shits in the Navy. They can't help themselves. And they know roughly where we are. So we might as well have a full active policy, every one of our sensors needs to be up and running, active and passive."

Admiral Carson looked up, and said laconically, "Eight-letter word, starting with 'T'—Devious Roman Emperor."

"Mussolini," growled Jack Baldridge, unhelpfully.

"Close. But I guess Tiberius might fit a bit better. He was a tricky old prick in his time."

"Shoulda been a submariner," said Baldridge, hiding his constant amazement at the obscure facts the admiral stored beneath that farm-boy thatch of straw hair. "Anyway I'm still taking no chances with the enemy's submarines, and with your approval I'll thicken up the ASW effort for the first thirty-six hours."

"Go ahead, Jack, we don't wanna get caught with our shorts down. But of course you won't forget to bias it a bit west because we'll be flying in that direction. Their SSN's are always gonna be our major threat. You got that right."

010430JUN02.

Billy-Ray Howell and the newly fit Freddie had already led the eight Tomcats home after "wiping out" the entire attack force of the *George Washington*—caught them 250 miles out, off the Hawkeye's radar, but held their fire until they were sure. Both the enemy submarines had been located and "torpedoed," one still a hundred miles from the carrier. The other was dispatched by a couple of anti-submarine helicopters when it was detected on radar, at periscope depth, twenty miles out.

"Too fucking close," growled Captain Baldridge, somewhat

ungraciously to the operators. Then turning to the admiral he said, "Sneaky pricks, submariners. Told you. Never take a chance with those bastards."

"You don't need to remind me about 'em, Captain," replied the admiral. "They've been a preoccupation of mine for years. I'm always darn glad to get 'em out of the way in these exercises. I'm almost like you. I don't trust 'em. But I admire them, and you plain hate 'em."

"Bastards," confirmed Jack Baldridge.

And now the exercise was over, and the *Jefferson* had scored an overwhelming victory. Radar beams had crisscrossed the sky and ocean throughout the hours of darkness, and below the surface, the underwater men in the SSN's had searched tenaciously for each other. Both of Admiral Carson's submarines had survived the night intact, and the big Kansan had called the operation off just before dawn. He was within one hour of taking out the opposing carrier either with missiles or torpedoes. The *George Washington* had only one live escort left.

"Shoulda sunk 'em all," muttered Baldridge.

"Not necessary," said the admiral. "The record will be clear enough. I thought our guys, specially the pilots, were damned good tonight."

The weather had turned bad shortly after midnight. There had been a lot of wind, and low, heavy clouds were making the landings more perilous than usual. One by one the fliers had brought them thundering into the deck. The hooks grabbed and connected every time.

With the wind on the increase and rain sweeping straight down the angled deck, they waited for the arrival of the last one—the Hawkeye, lumbering in from its high-altitude tour of duty. Ensign Adams, on another night watch as Arresting Gear Officer, was at his post on the pitching deck, watching for the dim navigation lights of the big radar aircraft.

The Landing Signal Officer standing right out on the port-quarter was in phone contact with the Hawkeye's pilot, Lieutenant Mike Morley, an ex-Navy football tight-end, out of Georgia. Morley was good in any conditions, but he was at his best under real pressure, at night, in difficult weather. Right now he was following nighttime low-visibility landing procedures. He was coming in at 1,200 feet, six miles out.

The LSO attempted to instill confidence in the incoming crew. "Okay, Mike. Four-eight-zero, you're looking great . . . watch your altitude . . . check your lineup . . . "

One mile out, the big E–2C Hawkeye was still right on the landing beam, and the LSO heard Morley say quietly: "Okay, I've got the ball. Nine thousand pounds." They could now see the powerful beams of the landing lights on the aircraft's wings, rushing in toward the stern of the carrier, rising and falling with the buffeting headwind. Everyone was on edge as the last of the *Jefferson*'s nighttime warriors came charging home.

Jim Adams shouted into the darkness, "*Groove!*" And now they could hear the howl of the props on the Hawkeye's eighty-foot-wide wingspan as it bore down on the ship, an angry, glowing alien from space, made tolerable only by the design on its rear fuselage, the old familiar white star in the blue circle, the red stripe, and the single word: NAVY.

"*Short,*" yelled Adams, then seconds later, "*Ramp!*"—and Mike Morley flew the *Jefferson*'s battle-line quarterback fifteen feet above the stern, then hard into the deck, poised to open the throttle as the wheels slammed in, but hauling it closed as he felt the hook grab and the speed drop from 100 knots to zero in under three seconds. The scream of the engines drowned out the spontaneous roar of applause which broke out from several corners of the flight deck. There were beads of sweat on the forehead of Mike Morley, and he would never admit his heart rate to anyone. "Came in pretty good," he drawled in his deep Southern voice, as he walked away from the Hawkeye. "Y'all did a real fine job gettin' me down. Thanks, guys."

171430JUN02. 26N, 48E.
Course 040. Speed 8.

"You sure we go outside the big island, Ben? Gets real rough out there."

"Not, I assure you, as rough as it would get if we got caught between the island and the mainland. The Pacific Fleet patrols those waters these days. I do not think there is overhead surveillance, but I cannot risk being spotted by a U.S. warship. They are extremely jumpy at best. If they did see us, they would be very curious."

"Yankee motherfuckers, hah? We stay away from them."

"Yes, Georgy. For the time being we stay away from them—and everyone else for that matter."

"What about next refuel? Under half left."

"Well, this thing will go well over 7,000 miles at this speed. We're around 1,750 from the Carlsberg Ridge. Then another 250 to our final refueling point. We're fine, Georgy."

"Okay, what's that, another ten days before we look for tanker?"

"Exactly. Are the crew all right?"

"Not bad. It long and boring, but we change that soon, eh?"

"Remember your chaps, all fifty of them, understand they are conducting a critical mission on behalf of Mother Russia. You should perhaps remind them of that."

"High risk though, Ben. I don't think I ever see home again. Either way."

"Maybe not home. But you will have a new one in another place. We will take care of everything."

261200JUN02. On board the *Thomas Jefferson.*
21N, 64E. Course 005. Speed 10.

Three weeks into their on-station time, Admiral Carson's Battle Group was four hundred miles southwest of Karachi and six hundred miles southeast of the Strait of Hormuz, home of the Iranian Naval base of Bandar Abbas. To the West lay the coast of Oman, to the north, the deeply sinister mountain ranges which reach down to the coast of Baluchistan.

On the direct instructions of the admiral, Captain Baldridge had called a conference of the main warfare departmental chiefs. They were all there, sitting around the boardroom-sized table in the admiral's ops room—the key operators from the Combat Information Center, the senior Tactical Action Officer, the Anti-Submarine Warfare Officer, the Anti-Air Warfare Officer, the Submarine Element Commander, Captain Rheinegen, the master of the carrier itself, Commander Bob Hulton, the Air Boss. From the rest of the group, there were six senior commanders, including Captain Art Barry, of the guided missile cruiser *Arkansas*, New York Yankees fan and buddy of Jack Baldridge. He had flown thirty miles, from the western outer edge of the group.

For several of them it was a first tour of duty in the Arabian Sea, and Zack Carson considered it important to let them all understand why they were there, and to impress upon their various staff officers the critical nature of this particular assignment. "Now I know it's real hot out here, and there doesn't appear to be that much going on," he said.

"But I'm here to tell you guys that this is an extremely serious place to be right now. The tensions in the Middle East have never been a whole hell of a lot worse, not since 1990. And as usual ownership of the oil is at the bottom of it all—and I don't need to tell you that every last barrel of the stuff comes right out past here—Jesus, there's more tankers than fish around here as I expect you've noticed.

"The policy of the State Department is pretty simple. As long as we are sitting right here, high, wide, and handsome, no one is going cause much of an uproar, no one's going to monkey around with the free movement of the oil in and out of the Gulf. However, should we not show a U.S. presence in these waters, all hell could break loose.

"The Iranians hate the Iraqis and vice versa. The Israelis hate the Iraqis worse than the Iranians. The Iraqis are plenty crazy enough to take another shot at the Kuwaitis. The Saudis, for all their size and wealth, are damned badly organized, and they control the most important oil field on earth—the one brother Saddam was really after in 1990.

"I guess I don't need to tell you how dangerous it would be for world peace if anything happened to take that big oil field out of the free market. I can tell you the consequences if you like—the United States and Great Britain and France and Germany and Japan would be obliged to join hands and go to war over that oil, even if we had to take the whole damned lot away from the Arab nations. And that would be kinda disruptive. I expect you recall that in 1991 the U.S.A. sent five Carrier Battle Groups into the area, enough to conquer, if necessary, the entire Arabian Peninsula.

"But, gentlemen, while we are here parked right offshore, and making the occasional visit inside the straits, no one, but no one, is going to try anything hasty. And if they should be so foolish as to make any kind of aggressive move, I may be obliged to remind them, on behalf of our Commander-in-Chief, that for two red cents we might be inclined to take the fuckers off the map. Last time I heard a direct quote from the President on this subject, he told the CJC he wanted no bullshit from any of the goddamned towelheads, whichever tribe they represented.

"Our task is to make sure that these areas of water where we are operating are clean, that the air and sea around us are sanitized. No threat, not from anyone. Not to anyone. That's why Hawkeye stays on patrol almost the entire time. That's why we keep an eye in the sky twenty-four hours a day, why the satellites keep watch, why we must ensure the surface and air plots are, at all times, clean and clear of unknowns, and hostiles.

"Because this, gentlemen, is real. Without us, the whole goddamned shooting match could dissolve. And our leaders would not like that—and, worse yet, they'll blame us without hesitation. In short, gentlemen, we are making a major contribution to the maintenance of peace in this rathole. So let's stay right on top of our game, ready at all times to deliver whatever punch may be necessary. The President expects it of us. The Chiefs of Staff expect it of us. And I expect it of you.

"I consider you guys to be the best team I ever worked with. So let's stay very sharp. Watch every move anyone makes in this area. And go home in six weeks' time with our heads high. I know a lot of people will never understand what we do. But we understand, and in the end, that's what matters. Thank you, gentlemen, and now I'd be real grateful if you'd all come and have some lunch with me, ordered some steaks."

Each of the men at the admiral's table understood, perfectly, all of the political ramifications of the Middle East. And the potential danger to all American servicemen in the area. But they still required, occasionally, some personal confirmation of their prominent positions in the grand scheme of things. Which, given their relatively modest financial rewards, was not a hell of a lot to ask. And Zack Carson's hard-edged, aw-shucks way of delivering that confirmation made him a towering hero among all of those who served under his command. Not most. All.

271500JUN02. 5N, 68E.
Course 355. Speed 3.

"I can hold this position three hours, Ben. But I sure hope tanker shows up soon. Fuel's low, and crew know it. Not too good, hah? They get worried."

"Not so worried as if they knew our precise mission, eh, Georgy? Tell 'em not to worry. The tanker will arrive inside four hours and she'll show up right on our starboard bow—she must have cleared the Eight-Degree Channel early this morning, making a steady twelve knots. We'll be full by 2100 and on our way north."

280935JUN02. 21N, 62E.
Course 005. Speed 10. Ops Room.
Thomas Jefferson.

"Anyone checked the COD from DG? It's supposed to have a 'mission critical' spare on board for the mirror landing sight."

"I checked at 0600, but I'll do it again before he takes off. They used another spare last night. It was the last one."

281130JUN02. 9N, 67E.
Course 355. Speed 8.
200 miles from refueling point.

Officer of the Watch: "Captain in the control room."

Georgy's voice: "What is it?"

"Just spotted twin-engined aircraft, around thirty thousand feet—probably turboprop. Identical course to our own. I'm guessing U.S. Navy. He's no threat. But you say secret journey."

"Well done, Lieutenant. I come and look . . .

". . . Hi, Ben, just taking a look at aircraft—he very high and going north, but my Officer of Watch thinks it U.S. Navy, and he probably right. That's an American military turboprop for sure."

"Well, what are you going to do about it?"

"Me? Nothing, Ben. That pilot just a truck driver. No threat to us."

"That is the advice, Georgy, of a man whose nation has never fought a war in submarines. I'm going to tell you something, which I do not want you to forget. Ever. At least, not as long as you are working for me.

"It was taught to me by my Teacher . . . in this game, every man's hand is against you. Assume every contact, however distant, has spotted you. Assume they will send someone after you. Usually sooner than you expect. Particularly if you are dealing with the Americans."

"Let me take quick look again, Ben."

"Do nothing of the kind. I already assume we have been sniffed by a U.S. Navy aircraft. We must now clear the datum. We take no chances. Georgy, come right to zero-five-zero. We're going northeast toward the coast of India. Then, if they catch us again in the next couple of days, they will see our track headed for Bombay, and designate us Indian, therefore neutral, as opposed to unknown, possibly hostile.

"This detour will cost as one and a half days. But we'll still be in business. Hold this course until I order a change."

281400JUN02. 21N, 64E.
The *Thomas Jefferson*.

On patrol in the Arabian Sea, the Battle Group is spread out loosely in a fifty-mile radius. Up on the stern, one of the LSO's is talking down an incoming aircraft, the COD from the base at Diego Garcia. It contains mail for all of the ships, plus a couple of sizable spare parts for one of the missile radar systems, plus two spares for the mirror landing sight. The pilot is an ex-Phantom aviator, and the veteran of three hundred carrier landings.

With an unusually light wind, calm sea, and perfect visibility, Lieutenant Joe Farrell from Pennsylvania thumped his aircraft down onto the deck and barely looked interested as the hook grabbed and held.

They towed her into a waiting berth beneath the island, and opened up the hold, while Lieutenant Farrell headed for a quick debrief, and some lunch after his four-hour flight. Right at the bulkhead, he heard a yell: "Hey, Joe, how ya been?"

Turning, he saw the grinning face of Lieutenant Rick Evans, the LSO who had talked him in. "Hey, Ricky, old buddy, how ya doin'—come and have a cup of coffee, it's been a while—they made you an admiral yet?"

"Next week, so I hear," chuckled the lieutenant. He and Farrell went back a long way, to the flight training school at Pensacola, seventeen years previously.

The two aviators strolled down toward the briefing room, and, as they did so, almost collided with Lieutenant William R. Howell, who was walking backward at the time sharing a joke with Captain Baldridge. "Hiya, Ricky," said Billy-Ray, "We about done for today?"

"Just about. Hey, you know Lieutenant Joe Farrell, just arrived from DG with the mail and a couple of radar parts?"

"I think we met before," said Billy-Ray cheerfully.

"Sure did," replied Farrell. "I was at your wedding with the rest of the United States Navy."

Everyone laughed, and Captain Baldridge stuck out his hand and said, "Glad to meet you, Lieutenant. I'm the Group Operations Officer, Jack Baldridge. Have a good flight up here?"

"Yessir. A lotta low monsoon cloud back to the south, but some long clear areas as well, no problems. Ton of tankers below."

"Well, I'll leave you guys to shoot the breeze . . . catch you later. . . "

"Oh, just one thing, sir," said Farrell suddenly. "Would you think it odd if I told you I saw—or at least I thought I saw—a submarine—about a thousand miles back, somewhere west of the Maldives."

Captain Baldridge swiveled around, his smile gone. "Which way was it heading?"

"North, sir, same way as I was."

"Why do you think it was a submarine?"

"Well, I'm not certain, sir. I just happened to notice a short white scar in the water. But there was no ship, just the wake. I only guessed I was looking at the 'feather' of a submarine. I couldn't really be sure."

"Pakistani I would guess," replied Captain Baldridge. "Probably about to swing over to Karachi. But you're right. You don't often see a submarine in these waters—unless it's ours, which this one plainly wasn't."

"Anyway, sir. Hope you didn't mind my mentioning it."

"Not at all, Lieutenant. Sharp-eyed aviators have a major place in this Navy. I'm grateful to you."

"One thing more sir . . . I thought it disappeared, but then about coupla minutes later, just before I overflew it, I noticed it again. I suppose it could have been a big whale."

"Yes. Possibly. But thank you anyway, Lieutenant," said the captain. "Before you have lunch, put a message into the ops room and give your precise position when you spotted her, will you? You say she was heading slowly due north?"

"Yessir. I'll give them that information right away."

291130JUN02. 11N, 68E.
Course 050. Speed 7.

"Okay, Georgy, I'd say we've gone far enough. If they haven't come looking for us by now they're not coming.

Besides, our little detour took us right off the line of flight of that U.S. aircraft, if, as I suspect, it's on its way back to Diego Garcia."

"You want me steer left rudder course three-three-zero."

"Three-three-zero it is."

012000JUL02. The *Thomas Jefferson*. 21N, 63E. Course 215. Speed 10.

The *Thomas Jefferson* headed into the wind. Standing by for the first launch of the night-flying exercises, Jack Baldridge and Zack Carson shared an informal working supper in the admiral's stateroom.

"Well, I wouldn't get yourself overexcited, if I were you, just on account of the uncertainties," Admiral Carson said, grinning. "First, we don't even know it was a submarine. Second, we don't know who it belongs to; third, we do not know either its speed or its direction at this precise moment. Fourth, we have no idea what his intentions are. Fifth, just how much of a shit do we give? So far as I know, we aren't even at war with anyone. At least not today. And the only Arab nation which even owns a submarine in this area is Iran, and our satellite says that all three are safely in Bandar Abbas.

"At least it did, three days ago, and you can be dead sure we'd know if they'd moved one of 'em. There are two other nations bordering this part of the Indian Ocean. They both own submarines, but are both more than friendly with the U.S.

"So unless that good-looking broad with the big eyes and tits who runs Pakistan is suddenly turning nasty on us, I don't think we have a lot to get concerned about. Jesus, she went to Harvard, didn't she? She's on our side. Want another cheeseburger?"

Baldridge, laughing, "Well, Admiral, if he's a nuke, and he's coming our way, we'll catch him for sure when he gets real close. The last exercise has just shown we can catch the quietest in the world. Good idea, let's hit another one of those burgers."

* * *

051700JUL02. 19N, 64E.
Course 045. Speed 4.

"Well, Georgy, this is just about it. Aside from our little trip to India, we are here on time. The monsoons are also on time and the weather seems excellent for our purposes. I do not believe we have been detected, and right now she's around 120 miles to the north. We have tons of fuel, and if we aren't caught going in, there's no great likelihood they'll get us on the way out. It's entirely possible they won't even realize we exist."

"I guess you right, Ben. You always are. But I worry . . . why they so busy?"

"Not really, Georgy. We're hearing just normal ops on station so far as I can tell. We just stay under five knots, dead silent, and keep edging in. Let's check the layers, see if we can improve the sonars a bit. The weather's getting so murky we can't see much anyway."

071145JUL02.

In the ops room of the old eight-thousand-ton Spruance Class destroyer USS *Hayler*, positioned twenty-five miles off the starboard beam of the *Thomas Jefferson*, Anti-Submarine Warfare Officer Lieutenant Commander Chuck Freeburg was contemplating the rough weather. In this cavern of electronics warfare, the darkened room, lit mainly by the amber lights on the consoles, was pitching and rolling with the rising sea beyond the kevlar armor-plated hull. A new track appeared suddenly on his tactical screen, 5136 UNK.

Turning to the Surface Warfare Compiler, Freeburg said quickly, "Surface compiler, ASWO, what is Track 5136 based on?"

"Desk Three reported disappearing radar contact. Four sweeps. No course or speed."

"ASWO, aye. Datum established in last known. Datum 5136. Put it on the link."

071146JUL02. On the Admiral's Bridge of
the *Thomas Jefferson*, 22N, 64E.
Course 035. Speed 12.

Big seas have caused the cancellation of all fixed-wing flying. Captain Baldridge is speaking on the internal line.

"Admiral, I had this disappearing radar contact fifty miles southeast. Datum established on the last known."

"How many's that today, Jack?"

"That's the fifteenth I think, Admiral. Must be the weather."

"Well, we can't afford to ignore them. Keep the PIM out of the ten-knot limited line of approach. Get a sonobuoy barrier down, this side of the datum. If it's a submarine, we'll hear him as he speeds up. If he stays slow, he's no threat. If it's not a submarine, who cares? Don't wanna waste assets on seagulls."

"Aye, sir. We always get 'em around here. I guess there may be some kinda current or upwelling causes it."

"Still we don't want to run scared over four sweeps on a radar scan. Let's proceed, but keep watching. Lemme know, Jack, if something's up."

071430JUL02. 20N, 64E.
Course 320. Beam to sea. Speed 3.

"Shit! You see that? Jesus Christ! I just seen sonobuoy, starboard side. We nearly hit the fucker. They must have heard us. Holy Christ!

"Ben! There's a sonobuoy right out there forty meters. They must have anti-submarine aircraft in the air. Jesus Christ! Ben, we don't fight U.S. Battle Group, they kill us all."

"Cool it, Georgy. Cool it. *Keep the speed down to three knots, which means we are silent, and keep listening. Also try to keep that somewhat hysterical edge out of your voice. It will make everyone nervous, even me. Keep creeping forward. And for Christ's sake cool it. Now let's have a quick chat in your cabin . . . "*

"You say cool it! Jesus Christ! Ben, they bring in frigates and choppers, surround us, we caught like rat in a trap. Oh fuck, Ben. Yankee bastards—they kill us, no one never know. Oh fuck."

"Georgy, shut up! Let me remind you we have as much right to be in these waters as they have. They will do nothing to us unless they are sure we are going to do something to them. Anyway, I could pass for an Indian officer. I can speak passable Urdu, but my Anglo-Indian is certainly sufficient to confuse an American commander.

"They have no right to search this ship, and we have committed no offense against anyone. So kindly refrain from panic."

"You are a hard man, Ben. But you forget. Americans can do anything. They trigger-happy cowboys. They call everyone to find out about us. We never get out of jail. Like that French bastard Napoleon."

071600JUL02. 21N, 64E.
Ops Room *Thomas Jefferson*.

"Yeah, I heard the Sea Hawks are back, found nothing. Which at least means there's not some spooky nuclear boat following us around."

"Probably means there's nothing following us around. They got nothing on the barrier. Hardly surprising in this god-awful weather. Bet it was just a big fish. If there was an SSN snooping around we'd hear him. We'd hear him for sure."

"We would if he was nuclear. But I don't think Captain Baldridge is very happy. He's been down here in the ops room three times in the past two hours, asking questions."

072300JUL02. 20N, 64E.
Course 340. Speed 3.

Back and forth on a four-mile patrol line. "We just wait here, Georgy, and stay silent. No need to go anywhere near the sonobuoys they dropped. I think the big ship will come back to us in the next day or two.*

"Right now we have time to get a good charge in. We're just about in the middle and I doubt they'll be looking for us here. Then we'll be okay for two or three days, smack in the right place at roughly the right time. Crew happy? What did you tell them?"

"Just what we agreed, Ben. They still think we are on special exercise, making covert test of new nuclear weapon. I tell them Indians get the blame for breaking test ban treaty. Once it gone, maybe trouble from crew. But too late then, and they not know what happen. Even Andre, he not know, but I tell officers quick, right after. They control crew. Maybe worry for first minutes, but okay I think. No choice for them anyway."

081758JUL02. The *Thomas Jefferson*. 21N, 62E. Course 220. Speed 10.

Weather foul. Very strong monsoon gusts. On the Admiral's Bridge, Zack Carson and Jack Baldridge were peering through the teeming bridge windows, and all they could observe was a couple of miles of murky, rain-swept sea. All fixed-wing flying had been canceled for the night.

"Strange weather, Admiral. You'd kinda expect a chill when it's so gray and wet. When it looks like this in Kansas, it's usually as cold as a well-digger's ass."

"This is the southwest monsoon, Jack. It's a warm wind blowing right across the equator, and it brings with it all the god-damned rain India is gonna get this year, from now till about next spring. Mustn't that be a bitch if you happen to be a farmer?"

They stood in silence for a while, and the carrier was curiously quiet, with the flight deck almost deserted. Only the occasional squall slashing against the island of the carrier disturbed the peace, as the giant ship pitched heavily through the long swells, 130 feet below the two officers. They were heading back upwind, across the carrier's 120,000-square-mile patrol zone.

If he squinted his eyes, Zack could just make believe he was looking at a great field of Greeley County wheat in the gray half-light of a rainy summer evening. He'd hardly ever been in hilly country in all of his life. His landscapes were strictly flat, the

High Plains and the High Seas. He thought about his dad, old Jethro Carson, still going strong at eighty years of age, ten years widowed now, but still the master of those hundreds and hundreds of acres. And Zack resolved to take the entire family out to visit in the fall, when the warm, sweeping grasslands of his youth were, to him, so unbearably beautiful.

"You don't think there really is anything out there snooping on us, do ya, Jack?"

"No, Admiral, I really don't. But when you get a contact, you gotta run the checks. It's not my job to take anything at all for granted. Especially with those sneaky pricks. But I do believe if some goddamned foreigner was sniffing around our zone, we'da got him by now."

"I guess so, Jack. But those Russian diesels were just about silent under five knots."

"Yeah, but they weren't that good. And even in this weather we'd be sure to hear them snorkeling."

081800JUL02. 20N, 64E.
Course 155. Speed 3.

"She's out there, Georgy, off our port bow, coming back from the northeast."

"I guess three to four hours. You sure about this, Ben?"

"I am sure, my nation is sure, and my God is sure. I expect your bank manager would also be sure."

"I want distance five thousand meters—not closer. This thing very stupid, very big. Work on time only. Run four minutes. We might get a more accurate distance visually. But we might not."

"Check all systems, Georgy. For the last time. We've come a long way for this. I just wish we could have done it four days ago. More poetic somehow."

082103JUL02.

On board the nine-thousand-ton Ticonderoga Class guided-missile cruiser *Port Royal*, operating close in to the carrier, Chief

Petty Officer Sam Howlett decided to take a breather. As he stepped out onto the portside deck the murky sky suddenly lit up. A deafening blast followed seconds later. As Howlett instinctively grabbed for the rails, a thunderous rush of air took him by surprise flinging him sideways and downward, his skull fracturing as he hit the deck. Before losing consciousness, Howlett looked up to see the towering SQ28 Combat Data Systems mast rip clean out of its moorings and crash onto the deck. The great warship heeled to starboard and the giant mast rolled with it, crushing a young officer on the upper deck outside the bridge.

Astern, on the flight deck, the blast flung the LAMPS helicopter off its moorings onto the missile deck, killing two flight deck crew. Its ruptured rotor, spinning in the rush of air, snapped in two, decapitating a twenty-three-year-old aircraft mechanic. Two other men were blasted one hundred yards out into the sea.

Below, the force of the smaller for'ard radar mast slamming into the port edge of the deck split it in two. As it caved in, the deck crashed into a fire main, rupturing it. The split fire main crashed down into a companionway, trapping two sailors while it pumped out hundreds of gallons of compressed seawater, drowning them both. A twenty-year veteran Petty Officer, with blood streaming down his face and three broken ribs, wept with rage and frustration as he tried unsuccessfully to free them.

Up on the bridge there was carnage. The top of the main mast had broken off completely, and it plummeted down, smashing through the roof of the bridge and killing the Executive Officer, Commander Ted Farrer. Every portside window shattered in the blast, one of them practically severing the right arm of the young navigator, Lieutenant Rich Pitman. The face of the Watch Officer was a mask of blood. Young Ensign Ray Cooper, just married, lay dead in the corner. The cries and whispers of the terribly wounded sailors would haunt Captain John Schmeikel for the rest of his life.

The suddenness of the disaster from nowhere temporarily paralyzed the *Port Royal*. No one knew whether they were under attack or not. Captain Schmeikel ordered the ship to battle stations. All working guns and missile operators sought vainly for the unseen enemy, a task rendered impossible with no radar, no communications, no contact with any other surface ship in the Battle Group.

082103JUL02.

On board the eight-thousand-ton Spruance Class destroyer *O'Bannon*, also working close in to the carrier, no one had time to move. The blast of air roared through the ship, heeling her over almost to the point of broaching, hurling sailors into the bulkheads. But it was the following near-tidal wave which did the damage. The ship had not quite righted herself when the mountain of water hit the *O'Bannon* amidships. This time she almost capsized, and down in the galley, where cooking oil was now streaming across the floor, a terrible fire swept from end to end. Two oil drums exploded, and all three of the duty cooks were shockingly burned in the ceiling-high flames—twenty-four-year-old Alan Brennan would later die from his injuries, and his assistant, nineteen-year-old Brad Kershaw, lost the sight of both eyes.

Eight men were catapulted overboard when the wave struck. Three of them were hammered into the bulkhead and were unconscious when they hit the water. These men would never regain consciousness, despite swift and heroic rescue attempts by the crew.

The engine room was a catastrophe. Chief Petty Officer Jed Mangone suffered terrible facial burns in a flash from an electrical breaker, and two young engineers were crushed by a huge generator they had been repairing. Neither of them would ever walk again. Up on the bridge the scene was almost identical to that on the *Port Royal*. Flying glass from the blown windows had reduced the area to a war zone, a grotesque scarlet and crystal nightmare, in which no one had escaped injury.

Captain Bill Simmonds, who would later need sixty-three stitches in his face, took over the blood-soaked helm himself, ordered his ship to battle stations, cursed the communications failure, and roared at the top of his lungs for someone to access the Flag.

082103JUL02. 20N, 64E.
Course 230. Speed 25.

Twenty-four miles northeast of the carrier, the USS *Arkansas* was changing course, closing to her former position in the inner zone, as decreed by the admiral's policy of frequently altering the disposition of his group to hide the carrier on any foreign radar screens.

"Captain . . . Conn. Just saw a *weird* flash in the murk to the south. Coulda been lightning, but it don't seem right somehow."

"Captain, aye. Coming to the bridge."

"Conn . . . CIC. Sonar reports massive underwater explosion. Bearing two-four-five. . . "

"Captain, sir, sonar reported massive underwater explosion . . . two-four-five . . . I'm turning toward."

"Got that. What's going on?" But even as he spoke, a thunderous explosion split the night, and a blast wave of solid air crashed through the bridge windows.

The rest was lost in the roar of the wind and the unexpected chaos on the bridge, as the Watch Officer tried to restore order in the dangerous shambles of broken glass and wounded sailors.

And now behind the first blast, another wind was rising, a grotesque unnatural wind, warm and vicious, like the height of a typhoon, sweeping across the ocean, blasting now across the upper works and radar installations of the big Aegis missile cruiser, slowing the eleven-thousand-ton bulk of the warship in her tracks.

"*Jesus!* What's going on out here? Is this an earthquake?"

"Captain, sir. That was one hell of a blast—Jeez! You feel the ship stagger? And why has the wind backed a whole twenty degrees? Even the sea feels strange, rolling in from the wrong angle."

"Beats the hell out of me . . . but it has to be one hell of a disturbance. I think we will . . . wait a minute . . ." To himself, "Take no chances, Art." Then, "*Okay* . . . Go to General Quarters, Officer of the Deck."

The captain stayed on the bridge, but down in the sonar room

they were replaying their record of the apparent subsurface eruption which had occurred several miles away just moments before.
At least they did not hear the dreaded noise of tinkling glass that
always echoes and echoes, back through the underwater, and
then through the mind, when a big ship goes down. Instead there
was just a strange continued rumbling, slowly dying away to eerie
silence. No one had any answers. None whatsoever.

Whatever had caused the violently freakish conditions had
also caused a certain amount of chaos in the operations center
of the USS *Arkansas*. Communications were down everywhere.
The big round radar screen that showed the surface picture of
the Battle Group was out altogether, and the Air Warfare Officer
was trying to coax it into life. It seemed darker than usual
because so many screens were blank.

Captain Barry headed for his high chair and hit the UHF radio
phone on the inter-ship network, direct to the carrier's Combat
Information Center. The line was a dead end. No one in the command ship replied. But he heard an erratic transmission voice
from one of the outlying frigates, almost seventy miles away to
the south, apparently calling the carrier. "*Jefferson* . . . this is
Kauffman . . . Radio check . . . Over." But faraway *Kauffman*
was getting no answer either. Art Barry tried the encrypted line
to the admiral's ops room. No reply.

Then he tried the direct line to his baseball pal, Jack Baldridge.
There was total silence on his phone too. Captain Barry asked
Comms for a satellite link to the carrier . . . "Sir, we're having a
real problem with satcom . . . aerial stabilization, intermittent
malfunction. Been trying for several minutes . . . achieved occasional access to the satellite, but there's no contact from
Jefferson. As far as I can tell all normal comms with the Flag have
died on us."

"Someone try to raise the CIC in the *O'Kane*. She's operating
close in today, a couple of miles off the carrier's port bow.
They'll know more than we do . . . "

"No communication there either, sir, we were just trying."

"Okay, try *Hayler*, she was about twenty miles out when we
lost the surface picture. Get their captain . . . yes, regular UHF."

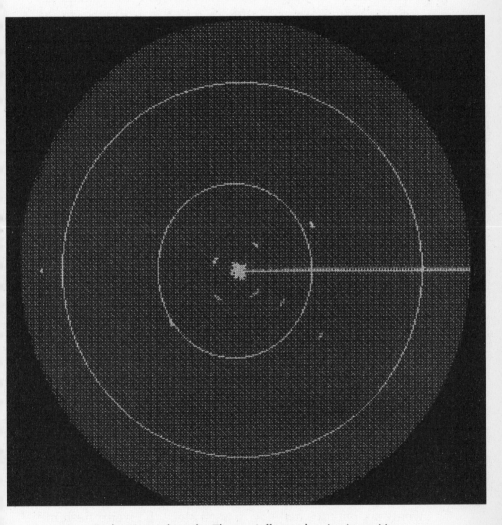

Radar picture from the *Thomas Jefferson* showing its position
within the Carrier Battle Group, July 8, 2002.

"*They're on, sir!* Commander Freeburg, encrypted."

"Hey, Chuck . . . Art Barry. Can you tell me what the hell's going on around here . . . we can't raise the carrier, most of my comms are down, and we couldn't raise *O'Kane* either . . . neither could you . . . ? Jesus . . . ! Who? . . . You got one of the SSN's in comms? It was a big bang all right. . . God knows . . . ! You're heading in to meet the carrier? No . . . don't do that. Hold station on formation course and speed. I am approaching *Jefferson*'s last known to investigate . . . Meantime, I've gone to GQ and I'm gonna turn on my radiation monitors . . . you better do the same. There's something weird goin' on here . . . I will keep you informed."

"Captain, sir, look out. The biggest wave I've ever seen is coming . . . !"

As the Watch Officer shouted, almost in slow motion, a sixty-foot-high wall of ocean seemed to rise up from nowhere. It hit the *Arkansas* head-on, breaking right across the fo'c'sle, and up over the superstructure—thousands of tons of green water crashing across the guns and missile launchers, submerging the entire ship it seemed, and roaring through the broken bridge windows.

But like all modern warships, she righted herself swiftly, seeming to shake the ocean from her decks, and shouldered her way forward with seawater still cascading down the hull. The Officer of the Watch could see the colossal wave rolling on, like that strange wind, toward the northwest and the shores of Arabia.

The next wave was not quite so big, but it swamped the ship again, and the one after that did the same. Slowly the waves diminished, and as the seas returned to the normal swell, the Officer of the Watch set about checking that no one had been swept or blown overboard.

Twenty-six minutes had now passed since the weird flash in the southern sky had barely been sufficient for the Officer of the Deck to bother his captain. But now only four of the possible ten other Battle Group surface warships were coming up in comms with *Arkansas*. Art Barry found himself apparently in charge of the group until the carrier came back on line. He established that both guided missile frigates, the four-thousand-tonners

Ingraham and *Kauffman*, appeared intact, as did the four-thousand-ton Spruance Class DDG *Fife*. The other Spruance, *Hayler*, appeared in similar shape to the *Arkansas*, wind- and sea-swept, but almost back to full working order.

Both SSN's, *Batfish* and *L. Mendel Rivers*, reported themselves unharmed at periscope depth. Both submarine captains gave their intentions, to remain on original station fifty miles out from the carrier, west and east respectively, on formation course and speed, maintaining constant comms. "Outfield beautiful," muttered Barry. "Where the fuck's the pitcher?"

Everyone in comms was now reporting the same violent underwater upheaval. *Ingraham* and *Kauffman* were first hit by a smaller forty-foot wave. Both of them were fifty miles out from ZULU ZULU (the Group Center) at the time. *Hayler* and *Fife*, however, had been about twenty-five miles out, and like *Arkansas*, had taken a sixty-foot wave. Unlike *Arkansas*, *Ingraham* had taken it right on the beam and very nearly capsized.

Of the missing six ships, not yet in comms, there appeared to be only five surface radar contacts close to ZULU ZULU. These were all stationary, or nearly so. By 2145 *Arkansas*'s surface picture was back in business, which partly clarified the situation for Captain Barry.

He could now see twelve other contacts from his link picture, including himself. There were two SSN's and five surface warships in good to reasonable shape, five others were floating, but unidentified, and still making way to the southwest, but out of comms.

One was missing.

At 2150, the ship's broadcast of the *Arkansas* blared: "Radiation alarm! Radiation alarm! Clear the upper deck. Assume condition 1A. Activate pre-wetting. Decontamination parties close-up." This official imperative ended with the traditional U.S. Navy roar of no-questions-asked, do-it-now urgency . . . "*No shit!*"

Within seconds all ventilation fans were crash-stopped. It took ten more minutes to get the ship properly isolated from the outside air, from the radioactive particles, which had set off the monitors. She was now like a huge, sealed cookie tin.

Every hatch, every flap, every external bulkhead door, every opening to the outside air was clipped hard home. Only then was it safe to bring in the gas-tight "citadel" ventilation to provide fresh air via special filters which would sift out all the radioactive particles. The system raised the pressure inside the citadel to slightly above atmospheric, and thus prevented any inward leakage of the lethal radioactive outside air. All drafts were headed OUT.

As the ship swung away across the monsoon wind, and cleared the radioactive plume to the north, the upper-deck working parties began to power hose the decks with saltwater and bleach, standard procedure for clearing radioactive particles from every area in the path of a nuclear explosion. Monitoring parties accompanied the hose crews, checking every corner.

By 2155, Captain Barry was ready to take a break. He needed thinking space to assess what had happened. There had plainly been a nuclear detonation, and he desperately needed to find out which ship was missing. Six would not, or could not, answer, and only five were on his radar.

For a couple of minutes he stared at the screen, *willing* it to produce the sixth contact at the center of the group. But his space-age electronics were unable to tell him what he needed to know: who was missing?

He knew he would have to go back to basics, to what sailors call the "Mark I Eyeball." He ordered a course change: "Conn . . . Captain . . . come left, two-three-five . . . flank speed . . . I am closing to make visual contact on the most northeast contact of the group ahead . . . that is track 6031 . . . he may have no lights burning . . . check visual signaling lamps."

By 2309, Captain Barry had seen what he needed to see with his own eyes, searching the dim, shadowy seas, probing the darkness to come alongside each of the four ships that showed up on his radar.

He was able to identify the huge 49,000-ton full-load fleet

oiler *Arctic*, minor casualties only, radar and comms out, but 70 percent operational. He found the formidable 9,000-ton Ticonderoga Class guided-missile cruiser *Port Royal*, with ten dead, twenty injured, severe aerial damage, major structural damage in the stern area, including her harpoon battery and one helo, severe flooding in the hangar area.

He also found her sister ship, USS *Vicksburg*, which had taken the big wave fine on her starboard bow, no serious casualties, severe aerial damage, no significant structural damage. The *O'Kane*, as she lay stopped and listing in the water, was a floating wreck, in desperate need of aid. And he found the Spruance Class DD, sister ship to *Hayler*, the *O'Bannon*, many casualties, number not yet known, ship nearly capsized in the tidal wave, able to make way through the water but little else, severe damage topside and internal.

Captain Barry stared at his screen again, in shock, at the space where the carrier must have been. The radar made its familiar, emotionless, circular sweep. And still there was nothing where once the mighty warship had been. No one could see her. No one could speak to her. And no one could hear her. The *Thomas Jefferson* was gone.

As the senior officer in charge of the second most important warship in the Group, Captain Barry now ordered his communications office to access the satellite's direct line to the U.S. Navy headquarters in Pearl Harbor, to Admiral Gene Sadowski, Commander-in-Chief, Pacific Command (CINCPAC).

The two men spoke for less than three minutes. The sentences were terse, two lifelong Naval officers communicating in the economical language of their trade. Within moments Admiral Sadowski had opened his private line to the Pentagon. It was 1318 local in Washington, D.C., as the Chief of Naval Operations, Admiral Scott F. Dunsmore, picked up his telephone.

"I regret to inform you, sir," said Admiral Sadowski, "that the carrier *Thomas Jefferson* has been lost in what looks like a nuclear accident. All six thousand men on board appear to have perished."

1320 Monday, July 8.

ADMIRAL SCOTT DUNSMORE HAD BEEN AN OFFICER IN the United States Navy for nearly forty years. He had served in warships all over the globe. His last command was of a Nimitz Class carrier in the Gulf War, facing the missiles of Saddam Hussein.

He occupied his present position as the professional head of the Navy with the utmost distinction. The son of an illustrious Boston banking family, he was regarded as the successor to the present Chairman of the Joint Chiefs of Staff.

Yet nothing, in all of his years as a warship and fleet commander, nothing in all of his years of examinations, degrees, and diplomas, nothing in all of his recent years rubbing shoulders with America's most eminent politicians, had prepared Admiral Dunsmore to grasp the enormity of the words being uttered to him by Admiral Gene Sadowski . . . *"All six thousand men on board appear to have perished."*

For ten seconds, maybe twenty, he said nothing, and tried to assemble his thoughts. The silence was so prolonged, Admiral Sadowski thought it might be another line of communication down. Dunsmore cleared his throat, searched for words, and just then there was a sharp tap on the door to his office and his senior assistant, a young lieutenant commander, burst in.

"Admiral, I got NSA in Fort Meade on the line—Morgan in person—we got one big problem in the Arabian Sea. I have to talk with you. You want me to transfer that call to someone else?"

"Not for the moment," replied the admiral. "Tell Admiral Morgan we'll call him back as soon as I finish with this." And then he addressed Admiral Sadowski for the first time, "Do you have a degree of certainty on that, Admiral?"

"I would not have called unless it was 100 percent, sir. One of our guided missile cruisers, *Arkansas*, has entered the area around the last known position of the carrier.

"He did so because his Combat Information Center was observing five contacts on the radar screen when there should have been six. He came alongside the five ships, all of which had sustained damage in an obvious nuclear explosion. There's a lot of radioactive fallout.

"Captain Barry's *Arkansas* has already compared his findings with other ships in the Battle Group. Their findings are identical. The *Thomas Jefferson* has vanished, in an area heavily contaminated with nuclear fallout. No one has seen any sign of wreckage, but the sonar operators were extremely concerned by the impact of an explosion, which took place at 2103. We have further loss of life, sir, possibly twenty to thirty men. But nothing comparable to the catastrophe involving the aircraft carrier."

"So. Into the valley of death rode the six thousand," intoned the admiral, an edge of disdain in his voice, suggesting he held CINCPAC responsible for the entire outrage.

Gene Sadowski betrayed no irritation. He fought back his sorrow at the loss of several personal friends, and replied. "Yessir. I suppose they did."

Admiral Dunsmore was not able to discern the shock in his voice, for the two men were strangers, and their priorities were different. The Washington-based Naval Chief now faced one of the most onerous tasks ever visited upon a peacetime commander—within thirty minutes he must face the Chairman of the Joint Chiefs, and then, possibly, the President of the United States. To each of them he would be required to explain how his Navy had managed to lose more than twice as many serving officers and men as had been killed at Pearl Harbor on December 7, 1941.

"Thank you, Admiral," he said. "I'm grateful for the promptness and the privacy of your call. Please stand by for further instructions. Inform the Battle Group to close down all communication circuits except within the fleet, and to Pearl Harbor HQ. And thank you once more for the clarity of your call."

"Holy shit!" he shouted as he replaced the receiver.

The admiral pressed the button to summon Lieutenant Commander Jay Bamberg back into his office. The young officer moved faster than the admiral had ever witnessed before. He cleared the big room in two bounds and blurted out the chilling but four-minute-old news that Admiral Morgan, over at the National Security Agency, was "damn near certain we've lost a big warship in a nuclear explosion somewhere in the northern half of the Arabian Sea."

Jay Bamberg was visibly shaken. He was too well trained to allow his sentences to become confused, but he kept talking. "Morgan has evidence on the satellite, sir," added the CNO's assistant. "They picked it up on one of the KH–11's which was still photographing all of the approaches to the Gulf after that last panic. They have a clear picture of an obvious rise in temperature in the water, consistent only with a nuclear test, right in the middle of the Battle Group surrounding the *Thomas Jefferson*. He thinks we may have lost the carrier. Says he cannot think of any other solution to such a major explosion. Wants you to call him right back. He's hoping to have more for you. Jesus Christ! Can you believe this! . . . er . . . sorry, sir."

Admiral Dunsmore shook his head and said resignedly, "That last call was from CINCPAC. We've lost the carrier, almost certainly in a nuclear accident. They believe there are no survivors."

"Good God, sir."

"Yes. Good God . . . Now let's touch base with Admiral Morgan . . . then with CINCPAC. Tell NSA we do know, and find out if they have anything significant I should hear. Then suggest Admiral Morgan contact CINCPAC directly, and meanwhile please arrange for me to meet the Chairman in the next ten minutes as a matter of the highest possible priority."

Lieutenant Commander Bamberg left the room, and Admiral Dunsmore tried to prevent his mind from conjuring up a picture of a U.S. aircraft carrier containing six thousand of the finest men in the nation being instantly vaporized ten thousand miles from home. It was always fatal to focus on individuals, but for the moment he could not believe he would never see Zack Carson again, and the death of Jack Baldridge was almost more than he could cope with.

He stood up and walked across the room, put on his jacket, and paced back and forth for a few minutes. Then there was a tap on the door and Jay Bamberg put his head around the corner and said quietly, "The Chairman will see you immediately."

Scott Dunsmore had rarely, if ever, looked forward less to a meeting. "Come down with me," he said, and the two men strode out into corridor seven, turned left, past the salute of the young Naval guard, and onto E Ring, the great circular outer throughway of the Pentagon, where the High Commands of all three services operated, the Army on the third floor, the Navy and Air Force on the fourth. The office of the Chairman of the Joint Chiefs was located on the second floor, immediately below that of the Secretary of Defense. Each of the five outer corridors which traverse the Pentagon, on all five upper levels, was over three hundred yards long. The world's largest office building contained more than seventeen miles of passageway, and was three times bigger than the Empire State Building.

It is said that no two points in this monstrous military labyrinth are more than seven minutes apart. As far as Admiral Dunsmore was concerned, seven hours would have been much better. The short journey down the elevator and into the office of the senior military figure in America seemed to him as if it took only seven seconds before he stood in the outer office of the beefy five-star general who ran the place, fifty-five-year-old Joshua R. Paul of New York, Vietnam veteran, Gulf War tank commander, possibly the best running back ever to play football for West Point.

"I am not," muttered Admiral Dunsmore, in the general direction of Jay Bamberg, "terribly looking forward to this. Wait here, will you? I may need assistance."

"Morning, CNO," said the Chairman. "Siddown. Wanna cup of coffee? I'm having some." He grinned cheerfully, his bright blue eyes peering over the top of his half-spectacles, noticing instantly the look of undisguised concern on the normally composed face of the tall, patrician Chief of the Navy. "What's up?"

"Well, sir, first of all, I might recommend we both give serious consideration to the possibility of a bottle of brandy rather than a couple of mugs of coffee."

"Oh shit. Trouble?"

"Very, very big trouble, sir. I am almost certain we have lost an aircraft carrier."

"Well I suggest you get your guys to find it, real quick."

"Nossir. I am talking about the total destruction of a U.S. Navy aircraft carrier, along with all six thousand men on board. Nuclear accident in the Arabian Sea."

General Josh Paul sucked his breath in, hissing through his teeth. "Jesus Christ! Tell me you're kidding me. You could not be serious. You are sitting there telling me that we somehow have to deal with the biggest single peacetime crisis in American history? You sure that as Joint Chiefs we're not having some kind of a Joint Dream."

"Do I look as if I'm dreaming, sir?"

"No, Scott," he said gently. "No you don't. You look as if you have just seen a fucking ghost."

"Six thousand of them, actually, sir."

"Jesus Christ! Okay. Now give it to me slowly and carefully."

"Right, sir. The one-hundred-thousand-ton carrier *Thomas Jefferson* is on station in the Arabian Sea about four hundred miles southeast of the Strait of Hormuz.

"She is loosely surrounded by her Battle Group, you know, cruisers, destroyers, half a dozen frigates, a couple of SSN's. Not to mention her entire air force on deck and in the hangers. 'Bout eighty-four aircraft.

"Around twenty-five miles away, they see a sudden flash, sonar operators all over the fleet would have had their ears blown out but for the audio cut-off system. A series of damn great waves come through and almost sink four ships, the wind from the blast causes some damage, all communications go out, and within twenty minutes or a half hour it becomes obvious to a couple of the big outer warships that the carrier has vanished.

"There's no communication. And when the radar systems start working again, she's definitely vanished. And the entire downwind area is covered by radioactive particles. CINCPAC hears from Captain Barry on board *Arkansas*. He's the senior captain. He searched the last known area of the carrier personally, and has now assumed command. He gives his degree of certainty as 100 percent. Admiral Morgan over at NSA has a satellite picture showing the kind of increase in water temperature consistent only with a nuclear test."

"I guess I don't need to ask whether the carrier was carrying substantial nuclear missiles, do I?"

"No, sir. You do not."

"Okay. You get back upstairs and begin compiling in the next ten minutes all the information we can get. I'll contact the White House, and request a personal, immediate meeting with the President. He can decide if anyone else sits in. My instinct is the less people who know about this for the next two hours the better. Get back down here fifteen minutes from now; we'll go down in my elevator, and I'll have the car waiting for us."

"You want me to come as well, sir?" asked Admiral Dunsmore somewhat lamely.

"You don't think I'm gonna deal with this one on my own," replied the Chairman wryly. "Besides, the President is probably going to hit the ceiling. I'd prefer he was furious with both of us, than just me."

"Yes, I do see that of course," said the admiral. "He will have to broadcast to the nation. Which he is not going to love. How long before you announce it to the press?"

"Well, we'll liaise with the White House on precisely what time *you* are going to announce it to the press."

"I was rather afraid you might mention that, sir."

"There is a certain kind of real heavy tackle I have always taken great care to avoid. Brace yourself, Admiral. We're heading for the roughest seas either of us have ever seen."

The somewhat bludgeoning nature of the conversation had the effect of shifting the admiral's mind into a higher gear. The entire hideous scenario was moving rapidly from a grim, distant, unreal accident into a stark and immediate nightmare which required urgent, drastic attention. He must bring clarity to the disaster, he must find a way to lay this out before the President of the United States in a form which was lucid, reasonable, and above all manageable. Everything is manageable to the full-sized intellect, he was telling himself.

"But God help me if I'm not up to it," he said aloud. "Because if I screw it up, the President will hang me up by the thumbs, or worse. Within about six minutes of this announcement there will be people demanding that the Navy *never* be permitted to drive around the world armed with such shocking, self-destructive weapons."

The CNO and Lieutenant Commander Bamberg headed back to the fourth floor, carrying with them the gargantuan secret which all too soon would cause the media to ask the kind of dread questions service chiefs detest . . .

"Was this accident avoidable?" "Should big-deck aircraft carriers be carrying these kinds of weapons?" "Should *anyone* be carrying these kinds of weapons?" "With the nuclear threat of Russia now diminished, why are we doing this?" "Isn't this what the anti-nuclear lobby has been warning us about for thirty years?" "Did it take the death of so many young Americans to finally show you what the liberal Democrats have known for years?" "Are you a fit person to be running this country?" "Should the Pentagon be abolished since everyone in it is plainly crazy?"

The real question was one he was not yet ready to face.

The admiral did not look forward to the forthcoming press briefing, which would almost certainly be staged at the White House. But he knew the President himself would be in for a far rougher ride this evening.

Back in his office he ordered Jay Bamberg to reopen the line to Admiral Sadowski, and he called back Admiral Morgan at NSA. The intelligence chief was steady and controlled, and advised that the CNO make a public announcement very quickly.

He had already fielded a call from the Russian Naval intelligence commander and feigned ignorance. In his opinion something needed saying officially, inside the next ninety minutes, or someone else would break the news for them.

The CNO wound up the call swiftly and spoke briefly to CINCPAC. The news was sparse. It was still pitch dark and the weather was worsening. The frigates felt it dangerous to reenter the contaminated "last known" position. There could be no further doubt about the fate of the *Thomas Jefferson*. The great ship had gone, in a nuclear fireball, made less blinding by the low clouds, fog, and rain which annually blanketed the Arabian Sea during July and August when the southwest monsoon swept in.

Scott Dunsmore gathered up his final reserves of self-control, and instructed Lieutenant Commander Bamberg to speak once more to CINCPAC and inform Admiral Sadowski that in his opinion the remainder of the *Thomas Jefferson* Battle Group should return to Diego Garcia, regroup, make temporary repairs, and head as soon as possible for their home port of San Diego.

Then he walked back out into the wide corridor of E Ring and set off for the meeting which had the potential, in his opinion, to begin an insidious political reduction in U.S. Navy firepower—firepower which had grown relentlessly from the early days of the Polaris submarines to the modern era of Trident and the carrier Battle Groups. No one walking along E Ring noticed him brushing the forearm of his dark blue suit across his weather-beaten face.

Dunsmore joined General Paul in the second-floor office and the two Chiefs, accompanied by two military aides, made their way down in the elevator to the subterranean Pentagon garage. The staff car was parked four strides from the door. Only General Paul and Admiral Dunsmore embarked, and the Army driver, briefed in the urgency of the journey, drove swiftly out into the sweltering humidity of a Washington summer afternoon, air-conditioning at full blast, right foot ready to hit the gas pedal as they headed for I–395.

"Did you tell the President what has happened?" asked the admiral.

"No. I interrupted some meeting in the cabinet room and told him I was on my way to see him on a matter of such grave consequences, I would not even trust the White House switchboard to overhear the conversation.

"You know how quick he is? He just said, 'Fine. Get over here. I'll be waiting. Do I cancel appointments?'

"I told him in my view he ought to clear his schedule for at least two hours. If I'd been completely honest I probably shoulda said two months, or years."

"You go through the White House Chief of Staff for this kind of appointment?"

"No. With this President, there's a direct line between CJC and the Chief Executive. Someone else answered the call and I said: 'This is the Chairman of the Joint Chiefs speaking from the Pentagon. I need to speak to the President on a matter of extreme urgency. Right now.' That's all it takes. He was on the line in seven seconds."

The staff car sped across the Potomac, and the tires squealed as they swung off 395 at the Maine Avenue exit, heading west along the waterfront, and then hard right, straight up the short wide highway which cleaves across the top end of the Mall, past the Washington Monument and onto Constitution Avenue.

As they threaded their way up through the government buildings, Admiral Dunsmore asked two questions: "Will he be alone? And who speaks first?"

"Yes, to the first. At least initially. I do, to the second. Then I'm passing the ball right into your safe hands."

"Where are you going to be during my explanation?"

"I am afraid to say, right next to you."

"West Executive Avenue entrance coming up, sir," announced the driver as he hit the brakes. And it was already clear they were expected. The guard waved them straight through, and at the door they were both instantly issued security passes handed to them by Secret Service agents.

Two of them escorted the military Chiefs straight into the West Wing, directly to the southeast corner, to the Oval Office. The senior agent tapped just once and opened the door. He and his colleague walked through first, beckoning the general and the admiral to follow. The President stood up, nodded to the agents to wait outside, shook hands gravely with his visitors—both of whom he knew well—and asked them to sit down in the two sturdy wooden armchairs set before his desk.

The admiral glanced briefly at the portrait of General Washington, admired the beautifully scalloped arch above the bookshelves, and stared out onto the sunlit southern lawn of the White House. He could hear General Paul speaking.

"Mr. President, it is my very sad duty to inform you that we have lost a U.S. Navy aircraft carrier in some kind of a nuclear accident in the Arabian Sea, about three hours ago. There were six thousand men on board and you may assume there are no survivors."

The President hesitated, grappling with the immensity of the words. "I may assume there is absolutely no possibility of a mistake, General?"

"You may, sir."

"*God Almighty! Six thousand dead? Six thousand American servicemen dead? How could such a thing possibly happen?*"

"Mr. President, I just wish I knew. But we were all ten thousand miles away from the Arabian Sea. There's never been anyone killed in a nuclear *accident*. I just cannot offer any explanation. But Admiral Dunsmore may be able to clarify the situation a little better than I."

"Okay. Okay. Now let's just stay calm, despite the fact that the United States is about to earn both the ridicule and the sympathy of the entire world during the next twenty-four hours. Come on, Scott, any clues? Any excuses? Any ray of light? Can you give me a rough outline of what transpired? I guess we'll have to announce something real quick. But talk me through it first. Then I'll call in some help."

The admiral ran swiftly through the facts—the position of the *Thomas Jefferson* and the Battle Group, the sudden underwater eruption, the huge waves, the nuclear fallout, the lack of sonar confirmation of a big ship breaking up. The sudden, inexplicable disappearance of the carrier. The devastating, irrevocable conclusion that the USS *Thomas Jefferson* had been vaporized in some kind of a nuclear holocaust.

The big Oklahoman behind the presidential desk was still for a moment, resting his chin upon his hands. Then he asked suddenly, "Who was the Flag officer?"

"Zack Carson, sir."

"I was afraid you were going to say that," he said. "He and I are from the same part of the world."

Both the military Chiefs already knew that. Everyone in America was acquainted with the President's rural background in the Oklahoma Panhandle, close to the Kansas border, where his family's cattle ranch was well known. He later had a dazzling academic career at Harvard Law School.

"Sir, I think the announcement should be made from here, given the scale of a national disaster. I would recommend that the CNO makes a formal statement to the White House Press Corps in the next forty-five minutes. Then you should address the nation at around 2100 this evening. Or before."

"I agree with that," replied the President. "But I have one question. You sure this was an accident?"

Admiral Dunsmore looked up sharply, surprised by the directness of the question he knew must be asked sooner or later. He paused for a moment, staring past the President at the flags of the Marines, Navy, and Air Force which flanked the tall windows. Then he answered, "No, sir. I cannot be sure of that. At this stage no one can. We cannot rule out an attack from an unknown enemy. Nor can we rule out some act of sabotage. However, until we have some kind of suggestion to that effect, sir, I see no reason to cause that kind of alarm to the public."

The President looked thoughtful. "It's kinda hard to know which way to swing," he said. "An accident makes the Navy look incompetent, which I would dearly like to avoid. A successful attack on an American aircraft carrier, possibly by some guy essentially dressed in a sheet, would spread great consternation, possibly even panic. The fucking liberal press would absolutely love it. I guess we are talking about the lesser of two evils. And either way the Navy looks bad."

"The way I see it," said General Paul, interrupting the Navy-Presidential conference, "is this. If that ship was attacked, then I guess we'll find out in the end. But I see no need, at this stage, to suggest the possibility to the press or the public. As things stand, we must deal with a huge outpouring of grief, recrimination, scorn, and derision. There is no need to add public fear to an already lousy equation."

"I agree," said Admiral Dunsmore. "Let's not add to our woes. At this point, despite some natural reservations, I think we should announce a shocking accident on one of our carriers. There is no advantage whatsoever in suggesting a U.S. Battle Group came under attack and a $4 billion carrier was obliterated by foreign persons unknown. My God, if you're not safe in a carrier, protected by a private strike/attack air force, guided missile cruisers, and two nuclear submarines, how on earth can anyone, anywhere, ever feel safe?"

"My thoughts precisely, gentlemen," said the President. Then, smiling wryly, "And I trust you will forgive me for bringing up the unthinkable?"

Scott Dunsmore nodded courteously. But he was thinking, "Every time I meet you, I understand better why you are sitting in that chair. If you'd been in the Navy, you'da been sitting in mine. Or more likely the General's."

In the next thirty minutes, the White House staff geared up for the press conference. The two military Chiefs adjourned to President Reagan's old Situation Room in the West Wing basement, with the Press Secretary, Dick Stafford, and two writers.

The general sat in on the statement, while Admiral Dunsmore sat in the corner with an open line to the Pentagon, summoning top Navy brass to a conference on the fourth floor, E Ring, which would begin at 2200 right after the President's address to the nation.

He placed his number two, the Vice CNO, Admiral Freddy Roberts, in charge of this, and a Navy jet was already refueling out at the San Diego Navy base in readiness for the flight to Washington. On board would be the C-in-C Pacific Fleet, and the Commander of the Naval Surface Fleet in the Pacific. The

Commander of the US Naval Forces (Central Command and Middle East), who was visiting San Diego, would also be on board. The Commander of Space and Naval Warfare Systems was being traced on a visit to an electronics corporation in Dallas and would be scooped up by the same aircraft.

Admiral Dunsmore also requested the presence at the meeting of Admiral Morgan, and of a young lieutenant commander from Naval Intelligence, Bill Baldridge, the best nuclear weapons man in the service, whose brother had been lost on the carrier. As the monstrous Naval crisis began to take shape in the White House, he was gunning his 1991 Ford Mustang up the Suitland Parkway at around 87 mph, chatting on his mobile phone to the raven-haired wife of a notoriously uninteresting Midwestern senator. "Yeah, I don't know what it's about yet, but we don't start till 10 P.M. I could be at the Watergate by 2:30. I still got my key. Yeah, I knew he was in Hawaii, read it in the paper."

Meanwhile the President was in conference in the Oval Office with his National Security Adviser, Sam Haynes, his White House Chief of Staff, Louis Fallon, and the Secretary of Defense, who had just arrived by helicopter from Norfolk, Virginia. The problem was how to distance the President from any kind of responsibility, protect the Navy, and make political capital from being seen to be concerned to the point of distraction.

By now Dick Stafford was shuttling between the Situation Room and the Oval Office, trying to mastermind the confident phrases which would allay the terrible damage the press were about to inflict on the U.S. Navy and the Presidency.

The one being written for Admiral Dunsmore was much the easier of the two, and at 4.30 P.M. he stood before the packed White House press briefing room and read his prepared statement. "It is my sad and unfortunate duty to announce the loss of the U.S. Navy aircraft carrier *Thomas Jefferson*," he began. The statement concluded with the words: "There were six thousand men on board, and there are no survivors."

For perhaps ten seconds there was a stunned, disbelieving silence in the room, as if no one wanted to accept the paralyzing news as real. But when pandemonium finally broke out, it very nearly registered on the Richter Scale. It seemed that every journalist in the room, all two hundred of them, leapt to their feet at the same time waving notebooks and microphones, yelling for information.

Admiral Scott Dunsmore wisely refrained from answering the questions which rained down on him from all areas of the room.

"When exactly did it happen?"

"When do we get a list of the dead?"

"How do you know there were no survivors?"

"Is this the biggest peacetime disaster in U.S. military history?"

"Will the Chief of the Navy resign?"

White House aides moved instantly to the admiral's side, the press secretary appealed for order . . . "Gentlemen . . . *gentlemen! This is a day of great tragedy . . . please! Try to act in a dignified manner!*"

Too late. This was beyond a press conference. This was a feeding frenzy; the sharks of the media scented blood. Anyone's blood. And they were circling Scott Dunsmore as if he were Adolf Hitler come back to life. Flashbulbs lit up the room, cameramen fought for position, trying to photograph the devastated CNO. No one could be heard clearly above the frenzy, which eased only marginally as the wire service men from UPI, Associated Press, and Reuters dived for quiet corners, mobile phones vibrating with the sheer magnitude of the story they were imparting to their city desks.

The White House Chief of Staff ordered the Marine guards to move forward between the front row and the dais and the press secretary ordered the room cleared.

Even as Admiral Dunsmore was being escorted from the room by four U.S. Marines, tomorrow's tabloid headlines were already being drafted . . . "6,000 U.S. SERVICEMEN DIE—NAVY NUKES ITSELF". . . "NUCLEAR HOLOCAUST ON U.S. CARRIER". . . "U.S. FLATTOP SELF-DESTRUCTS". . . "NAVY NUKES 6,000 AMERICANS."

It would be up to the President to check the balance, to try to convince a by-then hysterical public that the U.S. Navy was not in fact being run by a group of homicidal maniacs. He had about four hours to perfect his words. Dinner for the ten participants involved in the drafting process—which included Scott Dunsmore and Josh Paul—consisted of ham sandwiches and coffee. By the time the last sandwich had gone, the American public was being blitzed by news, news of death and destruction in a faraway ocean, news of massive incompetence by the U.S. Navy, news of evasion by service Chiefs, news implying a cover-up, news designed to spread consternation, uneasiness, and, above all else, news to make the public want more. Much more.

Meanwhile, the two service Chiefs left for the Pentagon at 8:30 P.M. At just about the same time the Navy jet from San Diego and Dallas touched down at Andrews Air Force Base. There was a Navy helicopter on the runway, waiting to fly them in, direct to the Pentagon.

Twenty-five minutes later, the President, wearing a perfectly cut dark blue suit and a jet-black silk tie, left the Oval Office with Dick Stafford, and walked down the long corridor to face the media; Stafford for the second time that day, the President for the first time in six weeks. His mood was one of wary contempt. His party might dominate the Senate. But it did not dominate the awaiting pack. He would have to face them alone, with all of his formidable intellect, and all of his renowned rattlesnake cunning under pressure.

Stafford announced there might be a limited "questions and answers" at the conclusion of the speech. But too little was yet known by the Navy's investigating professionals. There would however be a major briefing at the Pentagon at 1100 hours tomorrow morning. Then he requested silence for the President of the United States, who walked steadily to the dais and stood before hundreds of microphones. The cameras whirred. The lighting was dazzling, the mood pseudo-reverential.

The President spoke carefully, in the thoughtful tones that unfailingly mesmerized a big audience. And right now he had one of the biggest television audiences in history. Maybe *the* biggest.

"My fellow Americans," he began.

"I address you this evening on one of the truly saddest days in the entire history of the United States—a day when we have lost several thousand of our finest men in what appears to have been a freak accident, a one-in-a-billion chance, which is baffling our most senior military scientists.

"There has never been a nuclear accident in our armed forces—and the sheer scale of this one, which this afternoon devastated the great aircraft carrier, the *Thomas Jefferson*, has brought to each one of us a sense of shock; of grief for the anguished families of the men who served in her; of sorrow for colleagues and friends.

"This most appalling event will in the coming days touch every corner of our country, because the scale of this disaster will spread its sorrow into communities for which death has usually been of intimate local importance, brushing only those lives which came close to a lost friend or relative.

"The bereavement we all face now is of another dimension. I too had friends serving on board the *Thomas Jefferson*. And I am all too aware of the sadness their deaths will bring to lonely farming communities in the High Plains of the state of Kansas. One of them was a beloved senior admiral, another a first-class captain, destined for the very highest office in the service.

"I know there will be personal sorrow too in little towns along the coast of Maine, in New Hampshire, Massachusetts, Rhode Island, New York, New Jersey, Maryland, Virginia, West Virginia, and the Carolinas . . . the traditional recruiting grounds for some of our finest Navy commanders.

"In Georgia and Florida, too. In the South and the Midwest, and perhaps most of all, up and down the coast of California . . . in particular in the great port of San Diego, which was home to the *Thomas Jefferson*, and to so many of those who sailed in her.

"At this time I would ask your forbearance in what I am about to say. For I come only to praise them, these finest of American patriots, who have made the final sacrifice of their calling in the most unforeseen way. But death to them, in the split-second unconscious heart stop of a nuclear fireball, was not quite what a similar death might have been to us—we, whose risks are so minimal, whose lives are mostly led without fear and ever-present tension.

"*For these men who died on the* Thomas Jefferson, *death, and its unseen threat, was a perpetual companion.*

"Because peacetime to us did not mean peacetime to them. We have a perception of peacetime *only because of them*. They were not part of its blessing. They were the *cause* of it; they were its guardian and its savior. No more in life than in death. They were not *ordinary* men. They were men who went down to the sea in ships; who patrolled the world's oceans beneath the flag of this great nation. They were men who *demanded* peace. *Pax Americana*—peace on the terms laid down by the great steadying hand of the United States of America. Peace because *we say* there's going to be peace, because *we say* the world's free trade must *always* be permitted . . . in peaceful waters. *Peace because we say so.*

"How many times, in moments of international strife, have you read the words: 'The United States has warned . . . '? The United States can issue warnings *only because of the men who died on the* Thomas Jefferson. They were not like other men. They even have a joke about facing death in battle: "You shouldn't have joined if you can't take a joke." The words of our military men down the ages.

"Each man who sailed in the great warship knew that deep in her bowels there were weapons of destruction that did not merely pack sufficient punch to blow up *any* enemy; they formed the barricade behind which *all of the free world lives in peace*. The men on the *Thomas Jefferson* knew that. As they gazed out at the awesome fighter/attack bombers that flew from her decks they saw the fire and the fury we could use against *any* aggressor. They knew that.

"But these men had joined the United States Navy. And they knew something else. They also knew that in their most dangerous calling they might be asked to make the final sacrifice, in war, or in peace, at any time. They always *knew* that. For them, few days passed without reminders of the proximity of death.

For their workplace was lethal—filled with mach-one fighter aircraft screaming in over the stern of the carrier; with guided missiles; with great Navy guns and bombs; with nuclear submarines. These men, the men of the *Thomas Jefferson* Battle Group, *knew* the frightening responsibilities of their profession. And they knew the great honor that profession bestowed upon them, and *all of their families—every day of their lives*. They died with suddenness, all of them in the prime of their being . . . these were the men for whom we sing, "For those in peril on the sea . . . "—the sailor's hymn.

"Which brings me, as it brought many other occupants of this office, to the lines written by the English poet Laurence Binyon:

They shall grow not old, as we that are left grow old.
Age shall not weary them, nor the years condemn,
At the going down of the sun and in the morning
We will remember them.

"And now I would like to ask each one of you to reflect, in the memory of these men, upon an issue which each one of them held dear until the end. Should the United States continue to police the world's oceans? Is the danger, the shocking danger of it all, just too much to ask? I know my answer, and I believe I know the answer we would have received from the admiral who commanded the *Thomas Jefferson*—down all six thousand men, to the most junior rating, to the youngest of the missile officers. Is it worth it? That the U.S.A. should take on such onerous obligations and risks in order that we as a nation, and most of the world, may live without fear from *any* enemy?

"Is it worth it? Is it right? *Should we go on doing it?* Each time in the future, whenever that question is asked, the beloved memories of the men of the *Thomas Jefferson* will *stand before us all.*

"And each time we should consider what *their* answer would have been, the answer of those six thousand men. Fellow Americans, these were military men. These were the greatest of Americans. Patriots. Men of honor. Men of duty. They were not *ordinary* men. And their answer would have come without hesitation. Is it right? Yes. *It would always have been, yes.*

"And so, in this darkest of our nights, let us harbor no betrayal of their ideals. Let us not even consider that they died in vain. Let us consider only that they died for us, in the course of their most dangerous duties—duties that they loved and, above all, believed in.

"Let me ask, most humbly, for your prayers for them, and for their families, on this most terrible night. Let me assure the bereaved that no one is alone this evening. For tonight we all stand together. As we always have. For what it is worth, the prayers of my family, and of course my own, are with you not only now, but for all of my days in this place.

"May I now wish all of you whatever peace there may be tonight—and pray that a new dawn will bring a ray of light and hope, to everyone who loved and admired the Americans who served in the *Thomas Jefferson*."

His voice finally broke as he spoke. And he said quietly: "I am afraid I am not up to questions." And he walked from the dais, with immense dignity, leaving the world's media, and much of the nation, awestruck by his words.

By the time Dick Stafford reached the lectern to declare the Presidential address formally over, the White House switchboard, which fields forty-eight thousand calls a day, was literally jammed with thousands more, as were the switchboards of all the network television stations. Thousands of ordinary Americans were calling, not only to express overwhelming support for the United States military but also to inquire about where donations and wreaths should be sent.

Dick Stafford, an old Harvard buddy of the President's, hurried back to the Oval Office. He spoke in the dialect of Nebraska, for he originated from Valentine, up there in the gigantic sprawl of Cherry County, north of the Snake River. "Mr. President," he said, "considering the circumstances, I thought that went reasonably well."

The reply came out of deep, northwest Oklahoma. "Dick, thanks. I'm grateful for your help. I just wish I could have announced something for the families," said the President.

"Not yet. Not yet. We have to pace this. I know what you want. And I believe you are correct in all of your instincts. But you must trust mine. Give it at least four days, then make another announcement. Let the inquiry get under way. Let the Navy take the flack until the weekend. Then we'll have some time at Camp David to plan three new, separate Presidential initiatives, the special pensions for the families, the day of National Mourning, and a Presidential edict that will require all U.S. Navy ships and shore bases to hold an annual service and wardroom dinner in memory of the *Jefferson*—for all time. People will speak of attending the *Jefferson* dinner, like the Royal Navy over in Britain has always held a Trafalgar Night dinner in all of its warships and bases."

"Hey, I like that. Hope I get invited. You don't think it matters that Trafalgar was a huge victory for the Brits, whereas the *Jefferson* was not a triumph for us?"

"No, I do not. Gallantry is gallantry. Dying in the service of your country has a glory of its own. And I feel very certain that the American people understand that, and appreciate what our armed forces do. I actually think the liberal press and all liberal democrats have been wrong in their dismissal of the military for years. Remember President Reagan, from this very office, increased our military spending by damn nearly 40 percent and was reelected in one of the biggest political landslides in our history.

"We should remember too that Reagan's big military spending ultimately shut down the Soviet Union as a serious military opponent for us—smashed the Iron Curtain. I happen to believe that the ordinary common sense of the people tells 'em the U.S. Armed Forces are *always* on the right track, and ought not to be tampered with, not by left-wing assholes."

The President smiled at his short, stocky press secretary. His combination of Harvard intellect and shameless use of words like "assholes" were irresistibly appealing to him. And clarity. He loved Dick Stafford's crystalline clarity.

"What now?" asked the press secretary.

"Well, I think we should let Admiral Dunsmore get his act together for the next hour, then I think you and I and Sam Haynes should ride over to the Pentagon and sit in on the meeting for a while. We need to follow this thing every step of the way. Let 'em know we'll be there around midnight."

General Paul decided that the forthcoming debriefing scheduled for 2200 hours should be held in the heavily guarded private conference room used by the Chiefs of Staff for their weekly discussions with the Defense Secretary. Situated off the ninth corridor of the second-floor E Ring, this inner sanctum of the U.S. military was big enough and grand enough to accommodate all of the Navy senior management. It would also be a suitable high-security room for the President and his closest advisers should they put in an appearance. Both Admiral Dunsmore and General Paul believed this was a distinct possibility.

Awaiting the President would be five four-star admirals, two vice admirals, and one rear admiral. In addition there were two lieutenant commanders, one from Admiral Morgan's National Security office, plus Bill Baldridge from Navy Intelligence. General Paul had requested Scott Dunsmore chair the meeting, and at the far end of the table six armchairs had been placed for the Chairman of the Joint Chiefs, the President, the Secretary of Defense, and senior White House staff members.

The Committee of Inquiry had already been formed by the time the President arrived. It would be based in San Diego while the preliminary data were established and damage to other ships was assessed. The C-in-C Pacific Fleet would be its chairman and he had already asked that Captain Art Barry be flown home to California at the earliest possible time from Diego Garcia. Captain Barry had replied via the satellite and requested that he bring his Watch Officer with him, since he had witnessed most of what little there was to see. All such requests were given an immediate go-ahead.

The President was briefly introduced to those around the table, and he took considerable care to greet everyone he knew by name. When he was introduced to Lieutenant Commander Baldridge he walked right around the table and clasped the hand of the young nuclear weapons expert. "My God, Bill, I can't tell you how upset I was to hear about your brother. I guess you know our parents have known each other for many years . . . please remember to pass on my deepest sympathy to everyone."

Baldridge was keeping his emotions under iron control. This was without doubt the most important gathering he had ever attended. Probably the most important he ever would attend, and he was trying to concentrate while haunted by the fact that he would never see Jack again.

He was listening to Admiral Dunsmore explain how far they had come. New information trickling in from the Middle East was confirming what was already suspected. More nuclear particles detected on the ships, no detection of sound on the sonars of any impact, or of a ship breaking up or sinking. Just the great muffled thunder of an underwater eruption. Everything pointed to the fact that the source of the explosion was *inside* the great ship, somewhere deep below the waterline where the big nuclear warheads and missiles were stored. One weapons storage area right above the keel was about a hundred feet for'ard from the twenty-two-foot-high propeller. It was five stories high, the size of a large apartment house.

"If one of the warheads in there went off, that would be sufficient to vaporize the entire carrier," said Admiral Dunsmore. "I'm inclined to think that our accident occurred in that particular part of the ship."

"What could make a nuclear warhead explode like that?" asked the President, suddenly. "How do these damn things work?"

"I think Lieutenant Commander Baldridge might be the best person to answer that," Admiral Dunsmore replied.

"Well, sir, it takes some kind of an electrical impulse. The parameters for impulse need to be set deliberately. The simplest of them work on a timing device with a small, rather sophisticated clock. They are not designed to detonate on impact, not like a regular bomb.

"For instance, a nuclear warhead used in a torpedo would be set to explode at a certain time, precalculated from the torpedo director's best predictions of the position of the weapon and its target. All intended to ensure the warhead goes off in the approximate direction of its quarry.

"Quite honestly, sir, I have a real hard time trying to think of a way one of them could ever explode without some very heavy man-made assistance."

"Does this bring us to the possibility of sabotage?" asked the President quickly.

"Well, sir," replied Baldridge, assuming the question was still directed at him, "I have an even harder time dealing with that. Those weapons are under the most unbelievable strict guard. Even to get into the area you need a special pass signed by God knows how many people. Then you have to get past the two Marines who guard the entrance, and then you would be escorted into the area you are visiting by about three ordnance men including one officer. Anyone tried to get in there illegally, well, my guess is those two Marines would shoot you down like a prairie dog. No questions asked."

"Does *anyone* have access to go in there alone?" asked the President.

Admiral Arnold Morgan interjected. "Nossir, no one may enter alone, ever. It would be unheard-of for anyone, the Captain, the Admiral, whoever, to visit the ordnance area without at least one, or maybe even more, accompanying officers who are formally cleared for access. It would be like you wandering around the boiler room in the White House by yourself.

"Kind of too bizarre to contemplate. And anyway it would require two real experts to prime a warhead, and they would need signed passes. Unless there was a lunatic conspiracy among the top brass of the ship to blow themselves and all of their colleagues to pieces, I would personally regard the entire notion of sabotage as out of the question."

"So would I," said Admiral Dunsmore. And there was a murmur of agreement from all around the table.

"There is no evidence of anything really," added Dunsmore.

"Just the deep eruption and the disappearance. I do not think we need pursue the sabotage theory. But I suppose we should consider the possibility that the ship was hit by an unknown enemy."

The table went completely silent, until, after twenty seconds, Lieutenant Commander Baldridge broke it. "Well, we know the carrier was sunk by nuclear forces, of a magnitude that produced so much heat, the atoms of the ship just vaporized, leaving very possibly no trace. So if you would like to deliberate that theory it might be wise to work out just how that warhead arrived."

"There are only three ways it could have arrived," said Admiral Dunsmore. "In a guided missile delivered from an aircraft; in a sea-skimming guided missile delivered from a ship; in a torpedo delivered from a submarine."

Admiral Albie Lambert, C-in-C Pacific Fleet, himself a former Carrier Battle Group commander, now stepped into the discussion, somewhat to the relief of the CNO. "I would consider it impossible that a missile could have come in from an aircraft, and utterly unlikely that it could have come in from a surface ship or a submarine.

"To blow the aircraft theory out of the water, as it were, we need only to know that there were at least five guided missile warships sweeping the skies with their radar at the time, and three and a half hours before, Hawkeye had reported nothing within three hundred miles in any direction. No one can hide from *him*. In the event of an incoming long-distance missile, the ships could not have missed it. They would have taken it out in thirty seconds. Besides, who could have fired it? No one in that part of the world has such a capability."

"I actually think the likelihood of a ship-to-ship missile is even more out of the question," said Admiral Dunsmore.

"We know there was not another warship within hundreds of miles of the group. If there had been, Zack Carson and Jack Baldridge would have warned it off. Even if it had been completely invisible, they would have spotted an incoming missile on five different screens. Those guys detect seagulls, never mind nuclear warheads."

"Well," said the President. "What about a submarine?"

"Bill?" said Admiral Dunsmore, referring to the Lieutenant Commander, who he knew had spent all of his early career as weapons officer in a nuclear subsurface boat.

"Possible, but highly unlikely unless you have been trained here, or in Britain," said Baldridge. "Torpedoes are famous for their stupidity. They are very hard to program and it is not that easy to fit them up with nuclear warheads. When you do, you have a great chance of missing the target. You have to prime them, make a real accurate guess as to when it is going to arrive at the target, then set the clock for the exact correct time. You've gotta get in close for accuracy, real close, around five thousand yards, but no closer because you have a very good chance of blowing yourself up as well.

"In my judgment it's near to impossible to get it right, unless you are very highly trained. The issue is getting an attacking submarine in close enough to the Battle Group without being seen. I'd say about a million to one, but there will be gentlemen at this table far better qualified than I am to talk about the likelihood of getting in that close. I wouldn't want to try it myself."

"As an ex-Battle Group commander," said Admiral Albie Lambert, "I believe the carrier to be just about impregnable. She is surrounded by so much detection, surveillance, and radar. And yet we do know of instances of other boats, during exercises, getting in much closer than we would have thought possible. I once knew a Royal Navy submarine admiral who told me one night he *could* get into the defenses of a U.S. battle group. And probably sink the carrier.

"Actually he was the same chap who bamboozled a Carrier Battle Group in the Arabian Sea by pretending to be a goddamned Indian. He was commanding a surface ship then. But I believe he was the best submariner the Royal Navy ever had. Ended up in charge of Her Majesty's submarine service. Just shows though. Nothing's impossible."

"I think for the purpose of this meeting," said the CNO, "we should reserve judgment on the possibility of a nuclear hit against us until we receive the full surveillance reports from the other ships in the group. We should get the damage report of the other ships first thing in the morning. I suggest we reconvene at 1400, right here if the Chairman agrees. And meanwhile we continue to pursue the most likely, and by far the most convenient, theory, both politically, and professionally, that we are dealing with a major nuclear accident, the cause of which our top scientists are still deliberating."

The President looked up and nodded his assent. Dick Stafford leaned over and said, "Let's not encourage these guys to look for anything sinister when there probably is nothing. One leak of such a discussion would send the media berserk."

The President nodded again, and added, "Right now we don't even have a serious enemy. I'm glad Scott wants to stay with the accident scenario."

And so the meeting dispersed. Cars awaited the visiting brass ready to whisk them to hotels. Bill Baldridge glanced at his watch before heading to the garage, and then set off along the endless corridor accompanied by Dick Stafford, the President, and Sam Haynes. The President fell into step with the younger scientist from Kansas. "Well, Bill, as accidents go I consider that one about as bad as any of us will ever know," he said.

"Matter of fact, sir, I consider the accident theory to be pure, copper-bottomed bullshit."

"You what?" said the President, startled, stopping in his tracks.

"That warship was hit, by a big missile with a nuclear warhead," he said. "Nuclear weapons don't go off bang all by themselves, by accident. That is not just unlikely, sir. That is *impossible*. Someone, somehow, hit your ship, Mr. President. No doubt in my mind."

0210 Tuesday, July 9.

Confirming the deaths of all 6,000 men on board, a
Navy spokesman at the Pentagon admitted late
last night that no one had any solid theory as to
what had caused the explosion inside the giant
aircraft carrier.

—*New York Times*

DICK STAFFORD COULD SEE THE PRESIDENT IN CON-
versation with Lieutenant Commander Bill Baldridge. They
were walking quickly, just out of earshot. Stafford saw them stop
momentarily—causing everyone else to stop as well, backing up
the otherwise deserted E Ring second floor. Then the President
turned around. "Dick, I want to talk to Lieutenant Commander
Baldridge some more," he said. "He can ride back with me. You
and Sam come with us. Have someone bring Bill's car over to the
White House, will you?" Baldridge tossed the keys high, and
Stafford caught them expertly left-handed way over his head.
"Shortstop, University of Nebraska Huskers '61," he said.

Five minutes later, the Secret Service led the three-car
Presidential motorcade back through the night, east toward the

Potomac. "Okay, Bill. How can you be so certain the nuclear blast was *not* an accident?" the President insisted.

"I'm not 'so certain,' Mr. President. I am 100 percent certain. Someone has to prime those weapons and set up an electric impulse to start the explosive process. It's a very delicate operation, setting off a chain reaction involving atoms, neutrons, and electrons.

"These weapons are specifically designed to *prevent* the process happening by accident. We've had one dropped in the deep ocean from a crashing aircraft, and it *still didn't go off*. You could throw a small bomb into the weapons storage area, and that wouldn't do it either. The entire ordnance area of the ship is again *specifically designed* to be able to take quite severe damage, without dealing itself a nuclear death-blow.

"If you launched a torpedo with a nuclear warhead in it, and the detonation system failed, for whatever reason, it would fail-safe . . . just keep on running until its fuel was finished. Then it'd sink to the bottom and remain entirely safe indefinitely. Once we actually *recovered* a nuclear bomb the Air Force dropped in the sea by mistake.

"When those babies go off, it's for one reason only—because someone fixed 'em to go off. That's why you never ever hear of nuclear bombs going off by mistake. They go off when they are told to go off."

"Jesus," said the President. "And you rule out sabotage?"

"Sure do, sir. You can't get in the ordnance area, for a start. And if you did, you sure as hell could not be alone. And it would take two men and some very sensitive equipment to prime a nuclear warhead. It could not happen, unless everyone in the High Command was deranged and made a conscious decision to kill everyone in the ship. And even if that did happen . . . my brother Jack would have stopped it . . . I know he would."

For the first time, the Lieutenant Commander's control seemed to be slipping, and the President patted him on the shoulder. "No doubt of that, Bill," he said. "He was a great man, and I cannot tell you how sorry I am." Baldridge was glad of the dark because he did not want anyone to see him this upset, but the tears streaming silently down his cheeks were almost as distressing for the President as they were for him.

They rode in silence for a few minutes until the President said softly, "Bill, is there a nuclear warhead powerful enough to vaporize an aircraft carrier that would fit into a torpedo?"

"Oh, no trouble, sir. Remember that hunk of semtex that blew up the Baltic Exchange, plus a couple of streets, in London a few years back?"

"Uh-huh. IRA terrorists, right?"

"That's it. Well, I'd guess that small hunk of semtex was the equivalent of ninety tons of explosive. A nuclear warhead inside a twenty-one-inch torpedo of the size that sank the *Belgrano*—an old Mark 8 two-star—might be the equivalent of sixty thousand tons of explosive, enough to knock down New York City."

"Jesus Christ."

The cars swung into 1600 Pennsylvania Avenue. It was a little after 2:30 A.M. The President asked Dick Stafford to arrange a breakfast meeting for 8 A.M. in the White House. "This is political. I want you, Sam, the Secretary of Defense, Secretary of State, Admiral Morgan, and no one else from the Navy . . . except for Bill here for technology assistance. And get a couple of CIA guys in who know something about the Middle East."

The President went inside to his bedroom on the third floor, and Bill somewhat thankfully climbed into his faithful Mustang and headed down the drive, back out onto Pennsylvania Avenue. He drove up to Washington Circle and made a left for the short run down to Senator Chapman's apartment at the Watergate. As he did so he felt the car slow uncharacteristically. There had been very few occasions in his life when he had resisted the opportunity of hours of sexual diversion in the skilled hands of Mrs. Aimee Chapman. Tonight was going to be one of them. He just didn't want to be alone. He hoped she'd understand. About Jack and everything, and the huge gap in his life his lost brother would leave.

The senator's wife turned out to be a model of understanding. She led him into her husband's study, and then left him, while he called Jack's widow Margaret in San Diego. No one would be sleeping anywhere in the Baldridge family. Not this night. Bill was on the phone for almost a half hour, and Aimee could only guess at the trauma with which he was dealing on the other end of the line. She heard his voice rise only once, and she caught his muffled words . . . "Mags, you've gotta get outta there . . . as soon as you can . . . San Diego's gonna be like a ghost town . . . please call Mom . . . she'll fix everything. *Mags . . . you must take the girls to Kansas.*"

Aimee saw the light flicker on the phone as Bill made a second call, to his mother. And when he finally emerged, she noticed his tearstained face. She poured him a drink, and that night she did not bother to coerce her longtime lover into anything less chaste than a good-night kiss. She held him in her arms until he slept, just as she had done in the nights after his father had died, years previously.

Aimee had been Bill's girlfriend at seventeen, when he first went to Annapolis, his mistress through the years when he had very nearly married Admiral Dunsmore's daughter. And his lover again after she had married her wealthy but somewhat disinterested politician, who quickly rose to the Senate, but not to much else.

Jack Baldridge had always thought Bill should have married Aimee. She was very beautiful, petite and dark like her French mother, and she had adored the tall, lean Midwesterner since they first met at a party at the U.S. Naval Academy. Like many other young Washington undergrads she found him irresistible with his deep and thoughtful intellect, his athletic frame honed by long summer months wielding a sledgehammer, mending fence posts out on the ranch.

As a Navy midshipman, that cowboy toughness served him well. He could outrun, out-train, and out-think most of his class. He probably could have played wide receiver for the Navy if he had taken football seriously.

But he never did. He was always too unorthodox, too likely to shrug it all off, decline to compete, as if being an outsider to all men was his mission in life. It had prevented him from getting on the "captain's ladder" in the Navy. And it had prevented him from making a lasting commitment to any girlfriend. He was still single, risking God knows what, by sleeping in the Watergate, in the apartment of a wife of a United States Senator, a few hours before he was to have breakfast with the forty-third President of the United States.

Nevertheless, Bill Baldridge was a fairly remarkable young officer. His personal background put him on a first-name footing with some of the highest in the land. His professional Naval knowledge and high academic achievements made him stand out among his peers. And his personal characteristics enabled him to bring these two advantages together, to punch a high weight, far beyond his rank.

In the final reckoning, Bill Baldridge was a renegade. He looked like a younger, thinner Robert Mitchum, with the kind of piercing blue eyes you often find with deep-water yachtsmen, or plainsmen. But it was still hard to categorize him. In uniform he cut the relaxed figure of a six-foot-two-inch Naval officer. But back home in Kansas you would place him as a lifelong cowboy who had never left the Plains.

The morning newspapers seemed to contain nothing but the story of the stricken aircraft carrier. The *Washington Post* ran its front page ringed in a black border—U.S. AIRCRAFT CARRIER LOST IN NUCLEAR BLAST—6,000 DEAD—NAVY MYSTIFIED.

Bill Baldridge merely glanced at the story, straightened his tie, and fled for the Mustang, slinging his bag in the backseat, and heading back to the White House.

Both of the senior officers on board the lost aircraft carrier *Thomas Jefferson* were from western Kansas. Admiral Zack Carson, the Battle Group Commander, was born and raised on the family wheat farm near Tribune, Greeley County. His Group Operations Officer, Captain Jack Baldridge, was from Burdett on Route 156, southwest of Great Bend. Mr. Jethro Carson, the eighty-year-old father of the admiral, was said to have collapsed when told of the news, and was last night under sedation.

—*GARDEN CITY TELEGRAM*

Breakfast had been prepared for the ten men in a White House West Wing conference room. The President said he wanted no serious note-taking, just a very private chat with very trusted people.

He sat at the head of the table flanked by the Defense Secretary, Robert MacPherson, and the Secretary of State, Harcourt Travis. Dick Stafford, Sam Haynes, and Admiral Morgan completed the left-hand side of the table. There were seats on the right for Admiral Schnider, the head of the Naval Intelligence Office, the two CIA Middle East experts, and Bill Baldridge, who arrived just ahead of Sam Haynes.

Bill's immediate boss, Schnider, seemed somewhat surprised to see him. Even more so when the President looked up and said cheerfully, "Hi, Bill. Sleep okay? Good to see you."

With the two waiters dismissed, the President began, "Gentlemen, this is an off-the-record discussion. And I want to put my cards on the table even before we think of talking to the Chairman of the Joint Chiefs. I believe it is possible that the *Thomas Jefferson* was actually hit by an enemy torpedo armed with a nuclear warhead."

He paused, let his words sink in. Then he said, "In Bill Baldridge here we have one of the best nuclear physicists in the country—a Naval officer with a doctorate from MIT. Bill has told me he believes it is *impossible* that a nuclear warhead could ever detonate accidentally, much less while it is stored, dormant, in the ordnance area of an aircraft carrier. So what's left? Only the possibility of a hit against us. And for the purpose of this discussion, I want you to tell me, by whom, how, and why?"

"Well," said Secretary MacPherson, "not many of the nations in that area have such a capability. Our intelligence says no terrorist group could make such an attack without significant help from a nuclear weapon state."

"Bob, I'd be happier with elimination. Start by telling me who could have, but probably wouldn't want to."

"Forget the Brits. Forget France. Forget Pakistan. Forget Israel. They all have nuclear weapons, but would not use them, nor make them available to anyone else. Forget India. Their weapons are pretty basic, and they are not particularly fanatical about protecting their oceans. That only leaves the Russians, who are a possible source of weapons, and the Chinese, who we dismiss for several reasons. We are not of course sure about nuclear-weapon security in Russia and the Ukraine.

"But the weapon which may have destroyed the carrier had to be compatible to the system which launched it. That means the Russians would have to have supplied both.

"How about little guys with submarines—Algeria, Rumania, Poland," interjected Admiral Morgan. "Not to mention Iran."

"Yeah, how about those guys?" said Dick Stafford. "I guess they count as potential enemies of the U.S.A."

"May I have first who, then how and why?" asked the President.

"Sir," said Harcourt Travis, another tall, steel-haired ex-Harvard professor. "The *Jefferson* was operational in the Arabian Sea, and she was probably going to enter the Gulf at least once. We should look at which nations would like America out of the Gulf, for whatever reasons. I suggest the answer must be both Iran, which wants to dominate the area, and Iraq, for more obvious reasons—insane regime, plus known animosity toward the U.S.A. I cannot think of any other nation which hates us sufficiently to try to pull off something close to genocide, which the sinking of a carrier is."

Admiral Morgan interrupted. "I am assuming you all consider this must have been achieved by a submarine, rather than a surface ship."

"I guess that would be the Navy thinking right now," said the President, recalling the previous night's discussions. "They believe the Battle Group would easily have stopped, and at the very least reported, any incoming missile delivered from an aircraft or surface ship. We'd know."

"I am certain that is true," said Admiral Morgan. "Also, sir, I checked this morning—no foreign ships were anywhere near the carrier on any of the radar screens. We have those reports in-house, sir. Captain Barry is in the air himself now, on his way to

San Diego. He should be in Washington by tomorrow afternoon."

"Okay. No advances on the submarine theory?"

"Well, sir, if I may speak as an ex-weapons officer in a Boomer," said Baldridge, "I would think an incoming warhead would have been delivered in a torpedo rather than an air-flight missile. Fired from a range of say five thousand yards. I think I mentioned last night, get much closer to the bang, you got a real shot at blowing yourself up, as well as the target.

"Also it's impossible for a big nuclear submarine to get anywhere near the center of a CVBG without being detected. We've tried. At high speed we pick 'em up passive in the deep field. If they're slow—our active sonars pick up all big hulls. Period. In fair conditions the CVBG'll get 'em at around thirty miles, no sweat. It wasn't a nuke. It must have been a really quiet, modern, oceangoing diesel boat."

"So, who has 'em?" asked the President.

"Several nations," said Baldridge. "The British, the French, the Russians, the Chinese. God knows who else. But I'm betting Admiral Morgan knows where every one of them is right at this moment."

The admiral looked up and did not smile. "We gotta pretty good handle on them," he said. "And as for feasibility, the only nation I could suggest might have tried, successfully, to pull off something like this would be Iran. First of all, they want us out of the Gulf. Their government is filled with Islamic Fundamentalists.

"And they do own three Russian-built Kilo Class submarines, all stationed down at their Naval base in Bandar Abbas, only around four hundred miles from where the *Thomas Jefferson* was operating.

"The Iranians have been struggling to buy and organize a submarine fleet for several years now. They bought two secondhand Kilos from the Russian Black Sea Fleet, then they got their hands on a third, much newer one in 1996. We spotted all three of them on the satellite five days ago in Bandar Abbas. The latest pictures are in the Pentagon right now. I have checked. No one saw any one of them move. So I guess the latest pictures will still show all three in the same place."

"And if they don't? If one of them is missing?" asked the President.

"Then we have a live suspect," said Admiral Morgan. "They have the motive. And the submarine."

"How about Iraq?" said the President. "Could they have one of these Kilos?"

"They could, I suppose, in theory. But they have a serious problem with harbors. They have no infrastructure to run submarines. If they had, we'd have seen it. There's nothing. If we assume they did somehow buy or rent such a boat from the Russian Black Sea Fleet, then they must have driven it out through the Bosporus, right under the eyes of our satellites, and the Turks.

"Then they must have driven all through the Med, past our surveillance at Gibraltar, then five thousand miles south, right around Africa, finding a way to refuel, then up into the Indian Ocean, north to the Arabian Sea, dodged through all of our Battle Group defenses and blown up the carrier with a nuclear-headed torpedo.

"At the conclusion of which, gentlemen, they would have no home port. They'd have to get rid of the submarine. In which case we, or someone else, will find something, or at least someone."

The audience sat fascinated. Finally Defense Secretary MacPherson said, "Arnold, does this mean you write off the possibility of Iraq?"

"Well, not quite. I suppose they *could*—just—have pulled off what I just outlined, but I seriously doubt it. Submarines are very complex machines. For a long operational run, you need a real expert. I can't see an Iraqi masterminding something like this. You see, we're not talking even about the very best of the breed. We're talking fucking genius. I hope we could produce one or two such commanders. The Brits probably have a couple too. After that you got yourself an empty cookie jar. Iraq? Forget it."

"Stated like that, I guess so," said the President. "It would have to be a million to one. What are the odds about Iran?"

"Well," said Admiral Morgan. "I'd say if all three of their known submarines are still safely in port when we get the latest satellite pictures—then they probably did not do it. Because they would have needed to pull off exactly the moves I described for the Iraqis—and I cannot imagine an Iranian captain in the control room of a submarine on such a mission."

"Okay," said the President, through a mouthful of scrambled eggs. "Then what happened to the *Jefferson?*"

The City of San Diego was in shock last night as news of the lost aircraft carrier became known. The Naval base was stunned—more than 3,000 families were suddenly without fathers, some without sons, wives without husbands. For many it will be a night without end. The Navy's worst ever peacetime disaster took a toll on this city from which it may never recover. San Diego alone has four times more bereaved families than San Francisco had in the earthquake of 1906.

—*San Diego Chronicle*

"It must have been an accident. There is no other explanation," said Harcourt Travis.

"Agreed . . . no other explanation . . . must have been an accident . . . nothing else fits." The men around the table were edging toward a conclusion, the sound political conclusion. The sensible conclusion. There was no dissenting voice, save for one. The most junior voice in the room.

"It was not an accident," said Baldridge softly.

The President looked up. But it was MacPherson who spoke. "Bill," he said. "I appreciate your concern, and everyone here appreciates your opinion and your knowledge of the technology. But you must see that we cannot go around making wild accusations against another nation, without one scrap of evidence. Nor even a feasible scenario that actually might fit a potential aggressor's intentions. We'd look absolutely ridiculous."

"True," replied Baldridge. "But not quite so ridiculous as you might look if the sonsabitches hit us again."

The President of the United States sat very still, and stared at Lieutenant Commander Baldridge. Then he turned away and said, "I did hear that. But every ounce of my political instincts tells me to ignore the nonaccident theory."

"And remember, gentlemen," said MacPherson gently, "This is a political discussion. We are trying to decide what to *say*, not what to do. Every sentence we utter will have enormous repercussions, both here and around the world. We must speak with the utmost prudence. We have to protect the President, the government, the Navy, and the morale of the nation. Not to mention the defense of the nation—one word from us, that we may have been vulnerable to attack, any attack, and it might give someone else . . . er . . . encouragement."

"I don't have a problem with any of that, sir," chipped in the lieutenant commander. "But I am here as a scientist, and my trade is to distill many known facts into one major fact. It's nothing to do with me what anyone *says*. The question I assume you want me to study is, did someone blow up our carrier? And if they did, Who? And *how*? And, after that, I guess we need to assess whether they might do it again. If you guys want me to, I'm real happy to work in total silence, deep in the background. If someone hit us, we *must* find that out, even if we never admit we're checking."

"I think that is straight," said Admiral Morgan. "Right here we are moving into two separate spheres of operation. In my book too, Bill's correct. We *must* find out if there is something going on, and I want to volunteer my services to head up that investigation, perhaps as a coordinator, answering to Scott Dunsmore.

"I would like to work closely with Admiral Schnider, and I would like to have Bill Baldridge in the field. He's junior enough not to matter, and smart enough not to be easily fooled. He's also arrogant enough to be a real pain in the ass, which is not that bad—since we don't much want to hear what he finds out. In this way the main players, the President, Dick, Sam, Bob, and the Defense staff can devote their time to the formal investigation, keeping the public informed, and the careful management of the news—I hesitate to say manipulation because it's not my business. But I understand the importance of how this catastrophe is presented to the world.

"Meanwhile, we can quietly get into the 'down and dirty' without telling anyone. That way, with a bit of luck, we might find out what these scumbags are really at."

"From my point of view, I cannot stress too strongly that it is better for us to take ridicule from the media over an accident, than to admit we were hit," Dick Stafford said. "That's about a hundred times worse, because it would allow the media to slam us from every direction. There is an unspoken public sympathy for an accident, on the basis that we are all, generally speaking, human.

"But the press and television can whip up public fury at blind incompetence; and they can make a hit look like just that, blind incompetence. Then they will go for the President, every Republican senator, members of the Armed Services Committee, not to mention the Navy, and the Pentagon. I can only suggest that you never even consider making it public that a U.S. Navy carrier was hit by a missile. If you want to teach someone a real serious lesson, go do it, with my blessing, but please . . . don't ever admit why you did it."

"How about, *if* we did it?" asked the President.

"Say nothing," said Stafford. "Look after the interests of this nation as you all think fit . . . you want to scare someone to death, fine . . . you want to beat the shit out of someone, still fine. But remember the media would not hesitate to urge the government to start dismantling the Navy, even though such a course of action borders on insanity. They will hang anyone in power at the slightest chance."

In the terrible catastrophe which happened on the aircraft carrier *Thomas Jefferson* yesterday, the town of Hamlin lost one of its finest sons—Lieutenant Billy-Ray Howell, a U.S. Navy fighter pilot, aged twenty-eight, was one of the 6,000 dead. He had been flying an F–14 Tomcat off the deck of the carrier throughout her tour of duty. Lieutenant Howell's parents, Mr. and Mrs. Bobby Howell, proprietors of the Village Store, right off Main Street, were too upset to comment last night. They were awaiting the

arrival of their daughter-in-law, Mrs. Suzie Howell, who was on
her way from her home in Maryland.

—HUNTINGDON HERALD-DISPATCH

"One thing about a Republican administration," said the
President, "you get a lot of very wise, very erudite guys hanging
around the White House. I think we are on the right lines, but
there is one danger I want to point up. And I want each of you
to have this in mind in all of our actions in the coming weeks. I
do not want the Navy fucked over. I do not want these assholes
telling the nation that nuclear weapons ought to be banned. The
only freedom there is, on this troubled goddamned planet, is
courtesy of the enormous power of the American Carrier Battle
Groups. Even the Russians at the height of their own power
were afraid of us. And I don't want us to be undermined by a lot
of left-wing bullshit and bleating. Bear that in mind, will you?"

Around the table there were sounds of agreement, and the
President moved to wrap up the meeting. "I agree with Admiral
Morgan's proposal that he head up a deep background investigation, answering to Scott Dunsmore. And I would be grateful for
the close support of Admiral Schnider for as long as it takes.
Commander Baldridge will be seconded to the group as the man
in the field. Please tell General Paul I would like to sit in on the
military meeting at the Pentagon late this afternoon for an hour
or so. I will probably broadcast again tomorrow evening. Thank
you, gentlemen. Keep it tight."

It was 10 A.M. when the breakfast group adjourned, and
Admiral Morgan suggested that Baldridge and the two CIA men
accompany him to the Pentagon for a talk before the afternoon
meeting. The four of them piled into the big Navy staff car waiting at the door of the White House. Admiral Morgan told the driver to take them to the Washington Navy Yard.

It was just a few minutes' drive, and Admiral Morgan told the
driver to head for the submarine area at the Navy Memorial
Museum, where the public can look through periscopes at the
Washington skyline.

By this time the two CIA men, Jeff Zepeda, a Brooklyn-born

expert on Iran, and Major Ted Lynch, one of the Agency's leading financial and Middle East experts, were beginning to wonder
what kind of a mystery tour this was. The suspense was short-
lived. Admiral Morgan had whistled up a senior guide and they
were escorted to one of the big periscopes in an area cordoned
off by thick red velvet ropes. "You guys ever looked through a
periscope before?" he said cheerfully.

"Not me," said Jeff. "Nor me," said Ted.

"Good," replied the admiral. "Now I'm gonna get this thing
focused. And then I'm gonna hand it over to Jeff. And I'm gonna
tell you what you're seeing."

He adjusted the periscope himself, with the grace of someone who knows a lot about the subject. Then he said, "Okay,
now take a look." Jeff Zepeda stepped forward, grasped the handles, and stooped to peer at the Washington rooftops.

"You see the Capitol building?" he asked.

"Yup, got it. Hell, it looks pretty big through this thing, but
somehow far away."

"Now I'm going to ask you to imagine something . . . I want
you to imagine that huge building is the USS *Thomas Jefferson*,
okay? And I want you to imagine that you are about to punch a
nuclear missile right into its guts and obliterate every single person in there. Thousands of them . . . "

All four men were absolutely silent. "I want you to understand that you are about to destroy the lives of thousands of
decent people—perfect strangers to you . . . wives, children,
mothers, fathers, and young men at the peak of their careers.
The view you have now is the view he had when he called out
his last order . . . 'Bearing one-three-five—range seven thousand
yards now . . . *fire!*'

"Do you know how evil you have to be to pull off something
like that, Jeff? If I'm right, and if Bill here is right, we are looking
for one of the most ruthless assassins in the history of mankind.
And I am afraid he's also goddamned clever. Whatever they are
saying at the White House and the Pentagon, we must find him,
because, like Bill, I actually think the bastard might do it again."

When Jeff Zepeda stepped back from the periscope he was

plainly shaken. This was a man who had served in the embassy in Tehran until it fell to the Revolutionary Guards in 1979. A man who had gone undercover, in Arab dress, riding the Tehran railroad out to Damascus and back for three years. Jeff Zepeda had watched from doorways, from safe houses, as the massed thousands of the Ayatollah's followers had raised their banners proclaiming, "*Neither East nor West—Islamic Republic.*"

He knew about trouble on the grandest possible scale, having struggled for months, making contact with the Hezbollah, trying to befriend one of the Mullahs, trying to free hostages. Yet few times, in his long career as a deep-cover CIA operative, had he listened to words which chilled him quite like those of Admiral Arnold Morgan. He just nodded curtly, but it was the nod of a professional who understood the stakes.

Admiral Morgan adjusted the view, then he said quietly, the menace gone from his voice, "Okay, Ted, please look through the periscope. That's the top of the Washington Memorial in front of you. Imagine it's the big radio mast on top of the bridge of the *Thomas Jefferson.* Right below, there is one of the Navy's most accomplished professionals, Admiral Zack Carson.

"Standing right next to him is the President's buddy, Captain Jack Baldridge, Bill's brother. Both of them are just trying to keep the peace in those godforsaken seas around the Gulf. But they have just seconds to live, because you are about to issue your order—you're going to blow everyone to smithereens.

"Keep staring for a moment, Ted. Try to imagine the sheer evil of this motherfucker in the submarine. He's out there somewhere, Ted. And if it's the last thing any of us ever do, we're going to find him, and we're going to destroy him. I want us to be clear on that. The sinking of that carrier was not an accident. We know it, the President knows it, and Scott Dunsmore definitely knows it. I just wanted to make a quick visit here to keep us on the ball, to clarify the magnitude of our present situation."

One of the key officers who died on board the *Thomas Jefferson* was Ensign Junior Grade Jim Adams, the Arresting Gear Officer. His wife Carole gave birth to their first son in

Boston two months ago. He was christened Carl Edward, after
the Red Sox hitters Carl Yastrzemski and Ted Williams, but the
South Boston Naval officer had never seen his son. Last night a
Red Sox spokesman said that every member of the 2002 team
would attend the memorial service for Ensign Adams at the Old
North Church, the church of the patriots, later this month.

—BOSTON GLOBE

The four men drove swiftly across the bridge spanning the
Anacostia River, and onto the parkway. Then they swung due
west across the Woodrow Wilson Memorial Bridge and into the
historic old eighteenth-century tobacco port of Alexandria,
hometown of two great American generals, George Washington
and Robert E. Lee.

Admiral Morgan told the driver to take them down to the harbor area, where he located a waterfront restaurant bar. Their
reserved table, overlooking the broad expanse of the Potomac,
was catching a nice southerly breeze, beneath the canopy of the
screened porch. Their booth was separate, at least fifteen feet
from any prying neighboring tables.

"It's kinda quiet here," the admiral said. "No one will see us,
no one will recognize us, and no one will hear us. It's swept
every week. When we leave, we go straight through that door
there, the one marked 'No Entry,' down a flight of wooden outside stairs and the car will be waiting."

Admiral Morgan ordered coffee, and called his team to order.
"Right, guys, now let's just chew this over one more time. If
someone hit us, it was with a torpedo from a submarine, right?
And we're agreed it was probably fired by Iran."

Both Bill Baldridge and the admiral had heard in the opening
reports from the Arabian Sea that the *Thomas Jefferson* had
been steaming on a southwesterly course when she vanished. If
the submarine had been waiting in the area the carrier could
have come up on his port bow. The submarine would have
steered southeast in order to aim its torpedo at a ninety-degree
angle to the course of the huge ship—straight at the heart of the
carrier as she passed, well below the surface.

Bill had noticed that Admiral Morgan called out an imaginary final command of the submarine, "Bearing one-three-five. Range seven thousand yards."

"He even allowed for the two thousand yards the carrier would have traveled while the torpedo was on its way in," Baldridge said aloud to himself. "This ole bastard's smarter'n I am."

"Okay," said the admiral. "Let us assume we are Iranian. And our plan is to blow up a U.S. carrier in some kind of attempt to get Uncle Sam out of the Gulf. We have three Kilo-class submarines, two of them constantly in refit, one of them in good shape. First, do we have torpedoes armed with nuclear warheads on board? Answer, no.

"We might have torpedoes which came with the boat from Russia, but they would not supply nuclear warheads, even though they do possess such things, already assembled. They might be found guilty of an injudicious sale, but they would not want to be found guilty of arming another nation to conduct a preemptive nuclear strike against the U.S. Navy. Even they are not that slow-witted.

"So where do they get the nuclear warheads?" asked the admiral.

"China," replied Ted Lynch. "They could get 'em there, and bring 'em back by sea."

"Very risky, that," said Morgan. "There is such a thing as the Non-Proliferation Treaty. Our Navy and our satellites watch these matters very, very closely. In any event Chinese weapons would be most unlikely to fit a Russian export Kilo. That way the Iranians would need to be in some Chinese dockyard for a couple of months. And that we know hasn't happened.

"So let's assume the Chinese weapons were suitable, without any modification to the Iranian boat. There are two ways to get them aboard the Kilo . . . one, send 'em by Chinese freighter to Bandar Abbas . . . A nonstarter. We check that out. Two, a clandestine transfer at sea, from a freighter to the submarine. Another nonstarter because we *know* their submarines were all safely in Bandar Abbas last Friday.

"Even the Iranians would not much want to try shipping nuclear warheads right under our noses into their Navy yards, with the U.S. satellites watching above, and our guys on the ground. That, they know, might just cause us to get downright ugly."

"Yeah," said Jeff Zepeda. "I agree with that. I don't think they would have risked the China deal. It's too complicated, too far away, and too chancy. Plus the fact they are a nation that lives with screw-ups on almost every level. I can't see them even attempting something that tricky, not with such a big margin for error, and, potentially, a huge downside to their own interests."

"If I were an Ayatollah and I wanted to hit the American Navy," said Baldridge, "I know what I would do. I'd reopen my lines to Soviet Russia. I'd either buy or rent a fourth Kilo Class submarine from out of the Black Sea, I'd pay for it in cash, U.S. dollars, and it would have to contain a full outfit of torpedoes, at least two of them armed with nuclear heads.

"I'd send my team there to deal directly with one of those Russian captains who haven't been paid for about two years. And I'd suborn him with a sum of money beyond his wildest, and then my very best commander would move in and bring the submarine out secretly through the Bosporus, underwater, with some amazing cover story to keep the crew in line. Remember a hundred million bucks might be a lot of cash to the Mafia, but it's peanuts to the government of a major oil-producing nation. Anyway, that's what I'd do."

"So," said Admiral Morgan, "would I."

"One minor problem," said Ted Lynch, who was one of those Army officers who had spent several years attached to U.S. embassies and consulates in the Middle East. "It's not legal. You have to give the Turks two months' notice if you want to bring *any* warship through the Bosporus. That's Turkish territory on both banks.

"If you hit the bottom and got stuck, the Turks could quite legally claim salvage rights, throw up their hands and say, 'But you had no right to be there, especially with nuclear weapons, unannounced in Turkish waters.'

"There's an old military saying which has stood the test of time since the Ottoman Empire. Actually I can't remember it, but it means, translated from the Greek or Latin or something, 'Fuck not around with brother Turk. Because he gets real pissed off, real quick.' Trust me. Hit a shoal in the Bosporus, you'd never get your ship back."

"Yeah, but the towelheads are fanatics," said Admiral Morgan. "They believe in their God, Allah. They believe his kingdom beckons for the righteous, and that it would be a privilege to die in such a cause. Death means less to them than it does to us. Much more, spiritually. They *would* try something like this, if they really wanted to cast a monster blow against 'The Satan U.S.A.'—because broadly that's what they think of us."

The four men were silent for a moment, each one of them pondering the possibility of anyone daring to run the gauntlet of the Turks. "The other thing you do have to remember," said Baldridge, "is that such a journey would take you straight through the middle of Istanbul harbor! Can you imagine that? Plowing through the ferry lanes—the periscope leaving a huge white wake?"

"There are ways around all of that," said Admiral Morgan.

"Yeah," said Baldridge. "But not when you're fucking around in about a hundred feet of water, with old wrecks and God knows what else on the sea bed."

"Yes, there are," said Morgan again. "The key question is, could Iran, or any Arab nation, come up with anyone good enough even to start such a mission? There are damn few submarine officers anywhere in the world who could pull it off. And they are probably British . . . the U.S. Navy hasn't operated small diesel submarines for years."

"There's a lotta blind alleys here," said Zepeda. "And they all lead us to a very clever Arab, who we don't think exists."

"Well, it'll please the Pentagon guys this afternoon," said Lynch. "You just know the brass wants to stick to the accident theory. And the politicians will not waver from it. You could tell the President does not believe it. But he really has no choice. An accident is a bitch and all that. But a nuclear hit on a U.S.

ship . . . Christ! That could be war, and the populace might panic. The media would definitely panic. Or at least they would look as if they were panicking."

"I think that is correct," said Morgan. "And in a way that's good for us. Because we are going to be asking a lot of questions. I'll coordinate all the data on where every submarine in the world has been in the past three months. We'll get a long way by elimination—I'll pull up all the files on all detections. A lot of 'em will be whales, but we just might hit something. There was something a couple of months ago which kinda baffled me. I'd like to find out some more about that.

"But before that I'd like to talk to Ted about tracing large amounts of cash."

"That gets harder each year. So many foreign banks, wire transfers, with no one paying attention."

"Yup," said Morgan. "But I think we might be talking about 10 million bucks minimum, in greenbacks. That lot had to come from somewhere."

"Sure did, Admiral. I can't promise record speed. But I think we get can some kind of a handle on that."

"How do you start, Ted?"

"Well, we'll make a few discreet inquiries in the Naval ports around the Black Sea, particularly those where we know there are submarines. Big sums of money in small close-knit communities tend to become pretty obvious pretty quickly. But, if we are correct in our assumptions, it won't be that surprising to find a few recipients. The hard part will be finding where that money came from, and precisely who distributed it. But it's a whole *bundle* of cash, and it's hard to hide a whole *bundle* of anything."

Jeff Zepeda said he would get busy with various Iranian contacts and agents to see if he could smell out any such plot to demolish an American carrier.

Bill Baldridge seemed preoccupied with the problem of the mysterious Arab commander. "My view is this," he said. "I may be wrong, but I really do not think the Iranians would have used one of their very public submarines—the three Russian-built Kilos in Bandar Abbas—to attack an American Battle Group.

"I mean, Jesus, that's not terrorism, that's like trying to start a goddamned war. I think it is so much more likely they will have gone for a fourth boat, purchased or hired from the Black Sea, and crept quietly around the globe until they found the *Thomas Jefferson*.

"I do realize that thereafter the problems become *almost* insurmountable, on a sheer technological basis. But there is one problem that refuses to budge from the very front area of my brain. You know what it is? They must have had *someone*—a brilliant Arab submariner, a guy who could creep through the Bosporus, the Gibraltar Strait undetected, past all the U.S. surveillance, on and under the surface, in the sky, and on the ships.

"This is a truly brilliant guy. Who could it possibly have been? They must have had someone in charge and that someone must have been one of their own, in the submarine, in the control room, calling the shots. But who trained him? Was he an American traitor? A British traitor? It is *almost* impossible to believe such a man could exist. But not, guys, *as impossible* as trying to establish that fucking uranium went off by mistake."

The more Admiral Arnold Morgan heard from Baldridge the more he liked him. Actually he liked all of the men sitting with him in the corner booth of this little restaurant on the waterfront of colonial Alexandria. But it was Baldridge he really warmed to. Baldridge was a terrier, with a clear mind, and he was after a rat, and he was very, very focused, wrestling with the problem himself, assuming the responsibility was his.

"Einstein with a red-and-white dishcloth on his head," Baldridge mused. "That's who I'm after."

Admiral Morgan chuckled, noting the Kansas scientist said "I" not "We."

"Don't let this eat you up, son," he said. "Might affect your judgment."

Lieutenant Commander Baldridge made no reply, gulped his coffee, and muttered absently, "The thing is, so far as I can see, the fucker's still out there."

What the American people are entitled to know is the precise odds against such an accident happening again. While self-satisfied Pentagon staffers—particularly in the Department of the Navy—walk around making up absurd excuses for the catastrophe—there are fathers and mothers out there with boys trying to make it through the Academy at Annapolis. And those American parents want to know the risks of further accidents. Indeed they may rise up and *demand* to know the risks. It is one thing to make a statement talking about "a one-in-a-billion chance," as the President did—but what is the reality? For how many more of our boys does the U.S. Navy represent a nuclear death trap?

EDITORIAL PAGE
SAN FRANCISCO TIMES

Admiral Morgan, without getting involved in a debate, ordered a big bowl of Caesar salad and French bread for the table. "Let's hit this and get back to the Pentagon," he said. "Then we can spend four hours listening to the highest military brains in the country discuss an accident not even they believe happened."

Everyone laughed. And an uneasy silence took over as they chomped their way through about four acres of beautifully dressed lettuce, munched the hot bread, and sipped the coffee.

Afterward, they slipped through the "No entry" door, down the stairs, into the staff car, and were gone within fifty seconds, racing north up the Washington Parkway toward the Pentagon.

Inside the Chairman's conference room, the meeting had not yet been called to order, but Admiral Dunsmore was reading out a report filed from Hawaii by Captain Barry, detailing the death and injury toll on the other ships. By far the worst of these was *Port Royal*, which had been operating within four miles of the carrier. Ten of her crew had been killed in the general carnage of flying glass and steel which occurs when a big warship is nearly capsized. Twenty more were injured, nine of them seriously. Only the freak angles of the waves had somehow flung *Port*

Royal back onto her keel, otherwise she would have gone to the bottom, in short order. Right now she was limping back, toward the American base at Diego Garcia.

There were only minimum injuries on board the *Vicksburg*, but the *O'Kane* and *O'Bannon*, which had also been operating close-in, now had four men dead and another forty hospitalized, with severe burns, cuts, bruises, broken ribs, arms and collarbones, sustained when the destroyer broached in the deep trough of the first huge wave from the blast. They too had cheated death, but like *Port Royal*, were making painfully slow progress back to Diego Garcia.

According to Captain Barry, the nuclear contamination had moved in the classic manner, down range, opening up into a fifty-mile-long trumpet shape. Several ships had not been in the path of the lethal radioactivity. Nonetheless, it had been an extremely difficult night, with Captain Barry operating in the pitch dark and fog, with unreliable communications.

Somehow he had managed to round up a couple of working helicopters to fly surgeons to the stricken ships, two of which were operating on small emergency lights only. There had also been a shortage of nursing staff, since the main hospital facilities had been on the carrier herself. None of the senior officers in the Pentagon envied Captain Barry his task that night.

Admiral Dunsmore called the meeting to order and briefly recapped the preliminary report from Captain Barry, which confirmed that a nuclear blast had destroyed the carrier, and very nearly taken two other warships with her. The report also contained information from the CIC of USS *Hayler*, in which the Anti-Submarine Warfare Officer had recorded the fleeting event of 11.45 A.M. on the morning of July 7, the day before the explosion, when one of his operators had come up with a new track, 5136, a disappearing radar contact, picked up on four sweeps but with no opportunity to discern course or speed.

As the CNO spoke, Admiral Morgan looked up sharply. "Did they put it on the link?" he asked, almost brusquely.

"Sure did," replied Admiral Dunsmore. "Captain Baldridge acted on it too. Sent up two Seahawks, scanned the area to the stern of the carrier, dropped a sonobuoy barrier into the water—according to this, eighteen active buoys went down. All our ships in the area were alerted, but the line was never broken. Nothing came through, which suggests it was probably a whale."

"Unless it was a diesel-electric submarine on battery power, at periscope depth," interjected Baldridge. "A little further astern than we thought, and they actually saw one of the buoys, then turned away. To wait."

"Surely, if they'd been at periscope depth, we would've picked them up on radar?" said Jeff Zepeda.

"We did," replied Baldridge softly. "Track 5136, I believe."

A profound silence suddenly enveloped the huge table deep in the Pentagon. There was something unreal about the young lieutenant commander's words. How on earth could any submarine have got this close to the carrier and not been nailed? The two CIA men glanced at each other grimly. The commanders from the Pacific Fleet stared at their reports. Admiral Morgan glowered, and Scott Dunsmore frowned.

The CNO was about to speak when a Marine guard opened the door, slammed his heels together, and announced, "The President of the United States." The Chief Executive entered accompanied by his security chief, and the Secretary of Defense. This particular President was in and out of the Pentagon more than any of his immediate predecessors. Not since Eisenhower had an occupant of the White House taken such a fervent interest in military affairs. And none of them had ever faced a more nerve-racking crisis than the one unfolding right here in Washington in the high summer of 2002.

"Sorry to be a couple of hours early," he said. "But right now this thing is taking over. I may broadcast again either tonight or tomorrow, and I want to stay right on top of the situation. Fill me in, please?"

"Well, sir," said Admiral Dunsmore. "We were just going over Captain Barry's report, which mentions a radar contact on the previous day, spotted by one of our destroyers and checked out by our helicopters. Nothing very strong. The operators picked up on only four sweeps."

"That's about what you'd expect with a top guy," said Baldridge, with a sudden urgency in his voice, and absolutely no regard for protocol. The President, however, was getting used to the careless but calculating manner of Jack Baldridge's kid brother.

All eyes were now on the lieutenant commander. But the President spoke first. "Elaborate on that, Bill?"

"Well, sir, any submarine, on such a mission, is going to operate in a very clandestine way. I'd guess she would be moving at no more than three knots, at which speed a Russian Kilo is totally silent. Picture this: she is listening to the sounds of the U.S. Battle Group. She can hear the networks, pick up the sounds of the propeller shafts, especially the giant one which is louder than the rest, and belongs to the carrier."

Right here, Admiral Morgan, the ex-nuclear submarine commander, interjected, "The submarine knows in which direction the surface ships are, but not precisely how far away the carrier is. With time, he will develop a fair idea of their course and speed. But only when he thinks he might see something will he slide up to periscope depth.

"The captain takes a good look down the sonar bearing in less than seven seconds. In the monsoon conditions, visibility's poor. He probably sees nothing. He may then try the ESM to see if there's radar *anywhere* on the bearing, but only for three seconds. This is very dangerous for him, because he might be spotted. He lowers the mast, real fast, and goes deep again, at which point the submarine has vanished without trace.

"Remember, if you will, her radio masts were *never* exposed for more than seven seconds; which translates, roughly, to four sweeps on *Hayler*'s radar. That's when she picked up just two feet of the submarine's big search periscope jutting out of the water. Then nothing . . . but she's still there."

"Shit," said the President.

"Yeah, and that's not all," added Admiral Morgan. "Remember how slowly she's going, silently at three knots, probably in a racecourse pattern over about four miles. If her commander is as smart as I think he is, he will just position himself upwind of the carrier, always upwind . . . because if the carrier is flying aircraft, she must be heading upwind for takeoff and landings. If the submarine stays upwind, the carrier will eventually come to him.

"When Captain Baldridge ordered up the choppers and dropped the buoys, the submarine commander may have heard them. He may even have seen them doing it. But more likely he came back in, a couple of hours later, came to periscope depth and actually saw one of the buoys, or even heard it transmitting. He just turned away again. And waited, perhaps for twenty hours, while the buoys ran out of steam and sank to the bottom. Then he came in again, moving closer to the carrier."

"Jesus Christ," said the President.

"Yessir," said Morgan, adding, "I am not describing anything magical. I am just describing advanced operational procedures by a top class submarine commanding officer. The problem, at the beginning of this thing, was the same as it is now. Where the hell did the goddamned Arabs get such a man? I'm just afraid he might be American. Or British. No one else could possibly be that good."

Admiral Dunsmore interrupted. "Thank you, Arnold. I am sure the President would prefer now to get into his own agenda, since we are all agreed that for the purposes of public announcement, this was an accident. I do not want anyone to forget that."

"Actually, Scott," said the President, "I am finding this all very instructive. If there are any technical points you think should be aired, please go ahead. For the moment, I would like you to run the meeting as you think fit."

"Okay, sir. Anyone else have anything relevant to this meeting regarding procedures and actions on the ships?"

Admiral Dunsmore's deputy, Admiral Freddy Roberts, had thus far been silent. But now he spoke up. "Sir, just this . . . I have been glancing through the list of radar contacts picked up that day, and transmitted on the link, as laid out in Captain Barry's report. There were a total of fifteen, some of 'em big fish, maybe flocks of birds. Five of 'em from one ship, four from another. But there was nothing else from *Hayler*.

"Ships which report *everything* have historically jumpy ops rooms. Nothing wrong with that. Better safe than sorry. But I know the ASWO in *Hayler*, real good man, very experienced, Lieutenant Commander Chuck Freeburg. The point is, he thought it was something. That's why he mentioned it and put a report on the link. I think we should definitely assume there was *something*. Chuck's a very unjumpy guy."

"Okay, Freddy. Thank you. Mr. President, I am, of course, bearing in mind that we are announcing *only* an accident. But, on the other theory, there is just one other point I would like Admiral Roberts to put forward, and it has to do with the time and weather."

"Okay, sir. As you know I served some time out there myself in a destroyer, and I can tell you that by the end of June, the southwestern monsoon is beginning to sweep in from the African coast and throughout July and August you get a lot of real sticky weather conditions in the northern Indian Ocean and the Arabian Sea.

"There's often rain, and a dense, warm sea mist being carried along on a strange kind of wind, always feels too hot, but plays hell with the visibility, and pulls up a heavy sea.

"Now if I was going to take out an American warship I'd definitely do it in July or August. If I was a real fundamentalist who hated the U.S.A., I'd probably go for the Fourth of July. In my view they were four days late.

"But their timing was otherwise perfect. Dark falls quickly in the Middle East—by around six-thirty in the evening. The submarine would have come in close then, checking on the carrier every twenty minutes, at periscope depth, for maybe two hours. At around eight-thirty they were in position, waiting off her starboard bow.

"At nine o'clock local, we know they struck. At this time they were aware that there was still eight or nine hours of pitch-black darkness to come, making pursuit out of the question, 'specially with the predictable fog. Perfection makes me nervous. And these guys, whoever the hell they are, got a lot of things dead right."

The President was thoughtful. "I would like someone 1
me in on exactly why the accident theory is so hard f(
expert to accept. Admiral Morgan . . . ?"

"We're back to Commander Baldridge on that. Bill, run the
technology past the President, would you?"

"Sir, let me start by assuming you have only limited knowledge of how a nuclear warhead works. Basically we are dealing
with two hunks of radioactive material, probably uranium 235.
Like all metals this is made up of atoms—this is a very little guy,
about one four-hundredth of a millionth of an inch in diameter,
which operates like a tiny solar system. Its core is the nucleus,
made up of neutrons and protons. It is this nucleus which concerns us.

"The trick is to upset the basic balance of the atom's nucleus,
and somehow split it. We do it by helping extra neutrons to hit
the nucleus which causes the whole thing to become unstable,
and start to split apart. In turn, this generates energy, releasing
more neutrons to bombard all the other nuclei, starting off a
lethal chain reaction, with the bombardment process occurring
400 million million times in a split second.

"While all this is happening, the whole thing is being held
together by the mechanism of the trigger, just long enough for a
massive buildup of energy, and then a gigantic explosion."

"We achieve this in a warhead by placing two hunks of highly
radioactive uranium 235 a safe distance apart on the edges of
the warhead. The idea is merely to slam them together with sufficient force to hold the material together in one supercritical
piece, while the chain reaction goes completely and explosively
out of control.

"To do this we have two explosive charges which must be detonated at precisely the same time, accurate to within one-thou-
sandth of a second, in order to slam both hunks of uranium into
head-on collision with each other, with precise force. If even one
of the charges does not explode on time, or fails to explode correctly, the warhead will simply not function. The electronic
impulse must activate the explosive on both sides, at the exact
same moment. One half hitting the other is not sufficient for full

force. They must be blasted into each other precisely as designed.

"There is a lot of room for error here, and the trigger device is very delicate. It must be set and activated with absolute precision. The radioactive material must be fabricated and assembled with immense care.

"You guys really think all this happens by some kind of a fluke . . . an accident . . . ? Forget it. It could not, and did not, happen."

"Thank you, Commander," said the President. "I'm grateful for the explanation. Nonetheless, I know that everyone here understands the gravity of the implications. We will not be deviating in any way from the accident theory. Neither, of course, would any other nation in our position."

For a moment, the great man hesitated, then he looked up and half-smiled. "It's a funny thing, but from the moment Bill here mentioned he thought we'd been hit, I'd had it in my mind that there was some kind of an enemy submarine stalking our giant carrier and finally getting to the right range for the torpedo shot. But it's not like that at all, is it?"

"Nossir," said Admiral Morgan. "He did not do it like that. That submarine commander *knew* the two-hundred-mile by two-hundred-mile area of ops for the carrier. He got in there while she was far away—and then he just waited and waited . . . for the carrier to come to him . . . running silently at his lowest speed . . . with all the time in the world to set up and make his one shot count. A cool professional approach. I guess you'd call it military terrorism, an ambush on the grandest possible scale."

"Yeah, I guess you would," replied the President. "And right now there is only one thing that really matters. We must make someone pay . . . someone, somewhere, is going to pay a terrible price. The people of this nation did not elect me to preside over the destruction of the Navy—at the hand of some fanatic.

"If it should come down to two, or even three, suspects . . . I'll hit the whole lot of them before I'll let anyone get away with it."

He glanced up at Admiral Dunsmore, who seemed to be shaking his head. "Scott? You have some kind of a moral problem with that?" the President said.

"Absolutely not, sir. I was just thinking about the irony of the situation—Admiral Chester Nimitz was the master of the trap. At Midway, he ordered the American fleet to wait and wait for Yamamoto's carriers to come to us—and then we struck, hard and fast, sank four of them with dive bombers from right off the decks of the *Enterprise*. Now, all these years later, we may have lost the finest carrier of the Nimitz Class, sailing in the name of the great man, in precisely the same way, ambushed by a stealthy enemy."

"Hmmm," murmured the President. "We lost a carrier too, didn't we, at Midway?"

"Well, sir, the *Yorktown* was severely bombed and burned, but she survived the onslaught."

"Oh, I thought she sank."

"She did, sir, but that was three days later."

"More bombs?"

"No, sir. They got her with a submarine."

1900 Wednesday, July 10.

THE PRESIDENTIAL PARTY ENTERED THE PRIVATE ELE-
vator used by the Chairman of the Joint Chiefs and
descended to the Pentagon garage accompanied by two U.S.
Marine guards and two Secret Service agents. The other Navy
brass remained in conference, except for Bill Baldridge, who
arrived in the garage four minutes later. He reached the Mustang
just as the three-car White House motorcade moved off through
the lines of parked vehicles toward the bright light of the
entrance.

As the big limousines swept past, Lieutenant Commander
Baldridge stood back and saluted his Commander-in-Chief. The
President, sitting alone in the rear seat, involuntarily returned
the salute. And he glanced back at the Kansas officer, who was
still standing quite still, a lonely, defiant figure among a thousand
cars. "So long, Bill," he muttered. "God go with you . . . and me."

It was a little after seven-thirty in the evening when Bill
finally left Washington and set off for Virginia, recrossing the
Potomac and heading south along the west bank of the river.
The traffic was still heavy and it took him thirty minutes to
cover the sixteen miles to the Mount Vernon turnoff.

In another dozen miles he ducked left off the parkway onto a
small country road, and in the glow of the July sunset he sped

through a woodland drive into the precincts of a majestic, white-columned colonial house, built on a bluff overlooking the upper reaches of the Potomac estuary, with views across to the heights on the Maryland shore. By any standard, it was a spectacular piece of property, and it had taken the entire proceeds from the sale of one of the grandest houses on Boston's Beacon Hill to buy it. The pity was, its owner now had a job of such magnitude, his time here was very limited. These days he lived almost exclusively in the official residence in the Washington Navy Yard, with its electronic security, and staff. But never a day passed without the great man thinking wistfully of this place.

A U.S. Navy guard, on duty in the foyer, opened the huge front door for Bill, took his bag, and led him into a high, bright summery room full of joyous, rose-patterned English chintz. But the slim, blond fifty-five-ish lady who advanced toward him wore a plain dark green silk sheath dress, with a single strand of pearls. Her smile seemed tired, and she held out her arms to him as if welcoming a little boy. Suddenly, the iron-clad discipline he had exercised for two entire days, fell from him as a dark mantle, and he rested his head on her shoulder and wept uncontrollably. "Darling Billy," she whispered. "I'm so very, very sorry."

It took him several minutes to regain his composure, and when he did he just kept repeating over and over, "Jesus, Grace . . . It just seems so unfair. . . so goddamned unfair . . . why Jack . . . why the hell did it have to be Jack . . . ?"

At that moment, Grace's husband entered the room carrying a small silver tray and three glasses of scotch and club soda. He handed a glass to his wife, selected one for himself, and gave one to their guest. Then he put his arm around Bill Baldridge's shoulder and said gently, "I thought you might need this, Billy. You've been very, very brave."

"Thanks, Pops," said the lieutenant commander to Admiral Scott Dunsmore.

The three of them sat in easy companionable silence; three old friends, bound together during the long years of the early nineties when everyone had hoped Bill would marry the tall, fair-haired Elizabeth Dunsmore, the light of her father's life.

Their seven-year affair had been fraught with all of the problems of Navy romances—mostly the long absences by the young
officer, especially while Bill was trying not only to become a
submarine commander but also to obtain his doctorate.

The U.S. Navy is traditionally cooperative when any of its
more promising officers seeks the highest academic qualifica-
tions. But for Elizabeth, who was only a couple of years younger
than her fiancé, it meant that Bill was either groping around the
bottom of the Atlantic Ocean, or sitting behind a twelve-foot-
high pile of books in a granite-walled library in Boston.

When he occasionally broke free, she would invariably apply
for a few days' leave of absence from her Washington law firm,
and accompany him to Kansas, where they would spend days
riding the endless horizons of the Baldridge ranch. From time to
time, the admiral would join them. He and Bill's father would go
out shooting quail together, attend cattle auctions, and drink
beer out on the veranda. They had all been together when old
Tom Baldridge had died after a short, brutal bout with cancer.
They had all attended Jack's wedding, and variously been
together through the normal family triumphs and disasters.

When Elizabeth Dunsmore had suddenly announced five
years previously that she had tired of waiting around for her
sailor-cowboy, and was marrying a fellow Georgetown lawyer,
the members of both families were saddened beyond words.
Bill's mother pleaded with her, Grace pleaded with her, Admiral
Dunsmore pleaded with her, and Jack Baldridge pleaded with
her. Bill did not plead with her, neither did he offer to marry her.
He told everyone he guessed she knew her own mind. To Jack
he confided that she'd never be happy with anyone except him.
Which caused Bill's big brother to get right back on the phone to
Grace and tell her there was hope after all.

But in truth there was none. Bill Baldridge was not about to
make the grand commitment. Elizabeth married her attorney,
and Jack ended up by calling Bill a "pure-bred country asshole."
And he and his wife and Grace Dunsmore spent many a long
dinner in Washington and San Diego bemoaning the absurdities
of the youngest of the Baldridge sons.

But the family ties between the Dunsmores and the Baldridges remained strong. These days, the admiral still made the journey out to Kansas and shot quail with Jack and Bill, while Grace took long, leisurely horse rides through the big country with various Baldridge sisters and cousins.

Inside the U.S. Navy, however, the well-established, rigid standards of protocol and seniority remained unbroken. Bill called Admiral Dunsmore "Sir" or "Admiral" on all occasions. The admiral addressed him as "Bill" extremely rarely. But their friendship was so long and so lasting that the Chief of Naval Operations never batted an eyelid when the lieutenant commander called him "Pops" in the intimacy of either of the family homes.

And now the three of them sat quietly in this great house overlooking the Potomac, united in a shared grief over the loss of Captain Jack Baldridge, beloved brother to Bill, and beloved friend and surrogate brother to the admiral and to Grace. The captain had been such a huge presence in all of their lives because he was, although only the second son of Tom, the assumed head of the family. The eldest brother, Ray, who had never left the ranch and was married with four children, took it for granted that one day Jack would return from the high seas and take on the responsibility for the sprawling cattle empire.

Had he lived, Jack would have become the fourth Baldridge in as many generations to have served as an officer in the U.S. Navy and returned to run the complicated financial operation of a huge Kansas ranch. As old Tom had once announced, "None of us owns this place. We have just been given its custody, for each of our lifetimes. And like my great-grandfather, and my grandfather, I'm designating the future head of the corporation. And that's obviously gonna be Jack. So don't no one think of discussing it anymore."

No one ever did. And outside the family, no one would ever quite comprehend the shocking sense of loss all of them now felt. And no one would ever feel Bill Baldridge's sense of desolation quite like Grace Dunsmore.

They sipped their scotch in silence for a while, until finally the phone rang in the hall and Grace went to answer it. She was just gone for a few minutes, and when she returned said, "It's Elizabeth, and she wants to speak to you, Billy. You don't have to, if you don't feel like it."

"Oh no, that's okay, I'll be happy to speak to her." He was gone for some time, and was smiling when he returned. "She just wanted to talk about Jack for a while," he said. "Aside from that she seems fine." He did not of course report her parting words: "Good-bye, Billy. I love you, and that's never going to change." Before he could reply, she had put down the phone. Bill Baldridge's smile was the smile of a man who had been required to make no commitment.

Grace Dunsmore's smile was that of a mother who had guessed anyway precisely what her beautiful headstrong daughter had said. But now she excused herself, explaining that there was a light supper for the two men in the admiral's study, a decanter of Johnnie Walker Black Label, a decanter of Château Haut-Brion, and half a decanter of port. "Select your poison," she smiled, leaving them to it for the rest of the evening.

"Well, Billy, you tell me what's on your mind. As if I don't know."

"Can I assume you agree with me that our carrier got hit? No accident. No sabotage," Baldridge asked.

"Assuming you understand that this conversation, as with all of our private conversations, goes no further than these four walls."

"Of course."

"I *know* the carrier got hit. I knew it got hit about an hour before you nearly gave the President a heart attack on E Ring the other night. There's no other explanation, as you well know. But I may not say so except in deadly private, and the President may never say so, whatever he thinks. But he knows, make no mistake about that. So does every member of the Navy High Command. We all know, and it happens to suit everyone real well for you to be the eager young officer saying it. Your opinions, advice, and judgments are all useful, but not irreplaceable, young Bill, so don't get too pleased with yourself.

"It is your position in the whole system that is so useful, indeed, it is possibly irreplaceable. You can do and say things we, who operate nearer the top, can never do or say. Happily your voice is not senior enough to incite the populace to riot. But be damned careful if you ever get within a mile of a journalist."

"Yessir. No one ever made that situation clear to me before. Not that clear anyway. But what I want to talk about is something that has been on my mind right from the start. Everyone agrees there are only two real suspects here. Iran, which has the wherewithal. Just. And Iraq, which probably does not, on account of its lack of deep water. Right?"

"Ye-e-es," said the admiral. "Although privately I have wondered about Pakistan."

"You have? You never mentioned it."

"I'm too important to risk saying things about which I am uncertain. I expect you have noticed, people have a tendency to rush off and act on my merest suggestion. I call it the 'Yes, Boss Syndrome.' That's how it is in the military. That's why we have lieutenant commanders to serve up ideas, and admirals, in the light of their much greater experience, to make decisions."

Bill Baldridge grinned. There were times when the old boy seemed so avuncular, but get him alone and you quickly understood why he occupied the chair at the very head of the U.S. Navy, and why he would undoubtedly become the next Chairman of the Joint Chiefs.

"Why Pakistan?"

"Well, back in January of 1993, two CIA agents were gunned down outside the Agency's headquarters in Virginia. The man wanted for those murders for a long time was from a tribe in Baluchistan. The guys who bombed the World Trade Center, one month later, were also from Baluchistan. All had connections in the capital city of Quetta. In March 1995 three American consulate officials were ambushed and their van sprayed with gunfire on a busy street in Karachi. The CIA thinks there is a connection between all three attacks.

"Baluchistan is set in a triangle where Pakistan, Iran, and Afghanistan meet. It's a desperate place, damned nearly lawless, for centuries ruled by rich and powerful tribal chiefs. There was a lot of CIA activity in the area after the Soviet Union invaded Afghanistan in 1979. Thousands of tribesmen from Baluchistan found themselves working for the CIA, running arms and ammunition north to the resistance fighters, the *mujahideen.* And with that came some kind of a backlash. Students burned the American flag, and a strong nationalist movement grew up among the Pathans—that's the most militant of the local tribes. A lot of them call themselves "the children of the CIA *jihad.*" The World Trade Center guys were some of 'em.

"I personally examined the possibility of this crowd trying to pull off something like an attack on an American warship. But in the end I drew a blank. Even as a nation, Pakistan does not have the capacity.

"Their entire Navy has only seven somewhat suspect submarines capable of firing torpedoes. Most of them are French, and pretty old . . . although they have been recently operating a program to build a couple of new ones under license from France, Hashmat Agosta Class.

"And anyway, the whole history of submarines being built by foreign powers, under license, is very shaky. They either don't work, or they keep going wrong. If you asked me if the Pakistan Navy could have sunk the *Thomas Jefferson,* I would have said most probably not. Could a group of Baluchistan tribesmen have commandeered a submarine from Karachi and done it? Absolutely not. We would have caught and destroyed them before they came within a hundred miles of the Battle Group, no ifs, ands, or buts. That is, if they hadn't all killed themselves first.

"Zack Carson's group could have put away the entire Pakistani Navy, never mind a couple of creaking Gallic submarines. It's one thing to blow a hole in a garage in the Trade Center, rather sneakily setting fire to a few Cadillacs. But quite another to *obliterate* the world's most powerful warship—not while it's on full battle alert.

"My conclusions are thus identical to those of Admiral Morgan. It was Iran. Or Iraq. Most likely Iran."

"That," replied Bill Baldridge, "brings me to my next point. Whichever of the two nations it was, they must have had at least one, possibly six, senior Naval officers on board, all nationals. One of them must have been an outstanding submarine commander—a man with experience of a modern diesel-electric, and a high level of tactical expertise. Let me ask you the key question: who trained him? Answer that."

"God knows," said Scott Dunsmore, giving away nothing.

"I know as well," said the lieutenant commander slowly.

"You do?"

"I do."

"Surprise me."

"The Brits. The man we seek was trained in Faslane, Scotland, at the Royal Navy's submarine base on the Clyde."

"How could you possibly know that?"

"Because there is no other alternative. Look, it is likely that this guy somehow got a submarine out of the Black Sea, through the Bosporus, and then took it on a journey of thousands of miles. Through the Med, down the Atlantic, around Africa and up into the Arabian Sea. He must have refueled at least twice, possibly three times, which is a highly technical, dangerous, and demanding exercise in the middle of a rough ocean. Just finding the goddamned tanker wants a bit of doing.

"And all the while, he kept that machine running, sometimes below the surface, sometimes at periscope depth, sometimes snorkeling to recharge his giant battery. Always traveling at, I'd guess, around eight knots, slowing to under five if anyone came near. Probably traveling at around two hundred miles a day. As far as we know right now, he made very few mistakes, if any.

"And then came the really tricky part. This bastard actually got in among the Battle Group. He got through our defenses, and, if he hit the *Jefferson* with a torpedo armed with a nuclear warhead, he got that dead right too. We have no indication that he fired more than one . . . but he did put a nuclear-tipped torpedo in exactly the right spot to blow away our carrier. All this without our people getting one single clue, because if they had it would have been on the link faster than you could say 'towel-head.' That's a clever sonofabitch we're dealing with here. Because no one gets to be that lucky. And I ask you one more time, Pops, *who trained him?*"

"I don't know, Bill. I really don't. You tell me."

"Okay. Well, it was definitely not Ali Shamkhani or whatever that guy's called who runs the Iranian Navy. Jesus, those guys couldn't get a submarine through New York Harbor without hitting the Statue of Liberty.

"It *could* not have been any of the smaller nations with submarines. Most of 'em can't even keep one submarine in good working order for longer than about a month. And the French never like telling another nation anything. They didn't even train their best customers, the Pakistanis, very seriously.

"Nossir. This man was trained either by us, or by the Brits. I doubt it was us for several reasons. One, we have not used diesel-electric boats for years, and I doubt we still have the skills. And two, we do not train foreign nationals to drive submarines which may be used against us. So if the guy was trained here he must have been a traitor.

"The Brits, however, have trained foreign nationals. And their command qualification course is the best in the world. *And* they use diesels. I did hear they trained a couple of Saudi Arabian officers a coupla years ago when they were considering selling submarines to old King Fahd. I am not certain about this, but I think they also trained a few Israelis and Indians for the same reason. We should talk to the Brits, in my opinion."

"I suppose you are right, Bill. I'll admit I have been trying to avoid the subject. Because once we take the massive step of confiding in another government that we are possibly searching for the greatest terrorist in history, then we lay ourselves open to press leaks and God knows what else. You can imagine, damaging speculation by 'specialist' journalists, who always know just sufficient to be downright dangerous, but brutally unhelpful."

"Yeah, sure."

"Nonetheless, I am afraid we are going to have to step up to the problem, just as you have done. By the way, why did you select Faslane in Scotland as being the site of the dirty deed?"

"Ah, now I was just coming to that. Shall we go next door and get into some supper and another drink? Then I'll tell you my theory."

"Good call, Bill. Want another scotch or a glass of wine?"

"Wine, I expect, if it's a selection from your cellar."

The two men walked across the big downstairs hall of the great house, where the guard was still on duty and snapped, "Sir!" as the admiral and the lieutenant commander walked by, both in uniform. "Evening, Johnny," replied the CNO. Inside the red-walled, book-lined study—known as the Scarlet Nightclub to friends of the Dunsmores—Bill Baldridge picked up the empty, decanted wine bottle, and muttered, "Jesus! Haut-Brion '61. The favorite wine of your fellow-Virginian Thomas Jefferson. Pretty special."

Admiral Dunsmore poured them each a generous glass, declined to remind the younger officer that it was he who had first told him about Jefferson's love of Haut-Brion, and just said, sadly, "I don't think we should drink to Jack's memory in anything much less, do you?"

"Nossir. Nothing less."

And so, they touched their glasses lightly, and the admiral said solemnly, "To the memory of a great Naval officer, Captain Jack Baldridge." And for both of them the room was filled with a thousand memories, and they drank the forty-one-year-old, deep purple wine from the Graves district of Bordeaux. "And," said Lieutenant Commander Bill Baldridge, "I am going to run to ground the guy who presumed to take away the life of my big brother."

Scott Dunsmore was about to mention, "Faslane?" when the private telephone line next to his armchair rang. Bill could hear only snatches of the conversation and he could see the CNO scribbling notes on a pad. "Hi, Arnold, everything shipshape?"

"They what? . . . Where? . . . Was he dead? . . . Well, yeah I guess he would have been. Did you talk to anyone yet? . . . Oh yeah, four in the morning . . . What correlates . . . ? . . . Maybe the guy was on vacation? . . . Yeah . . . yeah . . . Damned interesting . . . Call me first thing, willya . . . Yup . . . Great . . . Bye, Arnold.

"Billy boy. The plot thickens."

"What's happened?"

"That was Admiral Morgan, still in his office. He just received a call from one of the monitoring guys at the intelligence office in Suitland, who has heard from one of our guys in Athens. There's a small story running in the Greek papers. The body of a Russian seaman has washed up on the southern shore of a small island called Kithira, which sits around sixty miles northwest of the eastern end of Crete.

"According to Arnold, the papers are saying the body had been in the water for a couple of months—they actually thought the man had been dead for around ten weeks. God knows how they work these things out. Anyway, the guy still had his dog tags on. The Naval attaché in the Russian embassy in Athens has apparently confirmed that he was a submariner.

"They didn't really have much choice—the cop on Kithira had made a notation of the rank and number, and photographed the guy's metal submarine insignia, which was still attached to his jersey.

"Arnold says it was pretty amazing anyone found him. The body was apparently in a really lonely spot jammed between a couple of rocks—some fisherman found him while they were looking for a trawl net which had got away and fouled the same rocks."

"I'm not absolutely certain how this ties in with us," said Bill. "The Russians have submarines all over the place, don't they? It's not all that unusual for a man to be washed overboard in that particular Navy, is it?"

"Not really. But Arnold's guys in Gibraltar believe they heard a mystery diesel-electric boat in the Strait of Gibraltar in the small hours of May 5. They have an accurate record of the contact. Only transient. But in their opinion a solid detection of a non-nuclear submarine. Arnold's just dug it all up on his computer. At the time he was sufficiently mystified to contact Moscow.

"But the thing that's getting to him now is this: Gibraltar is a little less than sixteen hundred miles from Kithira. Ten weeks ago, when the pathologist says the Russian sailor drowned, was somewhere between the twenty-sixth and twenty-eighth of April. According to Arnold, if that Greek physician is more or less accurate, and that submarine was making eight knots, or two hundred miles a day, the guy who fell off the boat, fell off the same boat our surveillance guys heard eight days later in the strait. He's checking it all out, and talking to Moscow first thing."

"Holy shit!" said Bill Baldridge.

"Yes. Well stated," replied the admiral, pouring another couple of glasses of Bordeaux. "Meanwhile we can't elaborate much more until we hear from Arnold again in the A.M. Now, tell me about Faslane."

"Right. Now, I expect you already know exactly where it is— on a lonely Scottish loch, west of Glasgow, with access to the Clyde Estuary, and then, beyond the Western Isles, to the Atlantic.

"Faslane is just a short ride across the water from Holy Loch where we ran a Polaris Squadron for thirty years. This area is serious submarine country, with the most exacting standards of excellence in the world—and that includes all of our own bases here in the U.S. Of course both the U.S. Navy and the Royal Navy were as thick as thieves up there. There's a lotta respect.

"Faslane is also home to the toughest training on earth for officers who wish to become underwater commanders. It is known formally as the Submarine Commanding Officers Course, usually shortened to 'The Periscope Course.' Actually, the Brits always call it 'The Perisher.' And they jog the word around a bit. They say, 'Failed his Perisher' or 'He did a bloody good Perisher.' The guy in charge is called the Teacher, and he would refer to 'One of my best Perishers.'"

Baldridge took a long and appreciative swig of his Haut-Brion. He savored the deep vintage wine, took a long breath, and said, "Pops, the man we want was a Perisher, and an exceptional one, in that he was both foreign and brilliant.

"I am nearly 100 percent certain about that. And I want you to fix it for me to go over there and find out who he was. Get me some clearance, and I'll leave in a few days."

"Given the scale of the damage inflicted upon us, I'm tempted to suggest the Brits think of a new name for their Periscope Course," replied the CNO.

"No need, the whole program was ended in the Tory government's defense cuts of 1994. A lot of people think it will never be adequately replaced. It had a 20 percent failure rate. Gave some guys nervous breakdowns it was so tough and dangerous. There is no place else in the world our Arab commander could have learned his trade the way the Royal Navy taught it in Faslane."

The admiral pondered for a few moments. Then he said briskly, "Done. I'll have someone call the British submarine chief in London and get you some cooperation. I'm just trying to avoid going too high on this. You know what happens, the Brits bureaucracy is worse than ours. I call the First Sea Lord, he touches base with the Minister of Defense, he talks to the goddamned Prime Minster, he clears it with the monarch, who presumably checks with the Archbishop of Canterbury, and he with God, whom they all assume to be British.

"Before you know it, the whole place will be seething with chatter—everyone trying to find out what we are doing. Then someone will. Better to keep this relatively low level. I will tell them little, just enough for you to get in to the submarine boss. He'll be Admiral Sir Someone or other. Then I want you to tell him the absolute minimum, if you can. The Brits are inclined to be very cynical, and you will be pressed for information. But in the end, their hearts are always in the right place. And they're always on our side. They'll help."

The two men talked on, rehashing the ground they had already covered. It must have been Iran, and whoever commanded the submarine had most likely been taught in Scotland.

Shortly before midnight they had a glass of port, and Bill Baldridge made one final request. "Pops, do you think you could arrange me a ride to the airport in the morning, and let me leave my car here? I'm going out to Kansas, just to see Mom and Ray and the family. Then I'll go straight to London. No sense leaving on Friday. I'll go Sunday night, get a full week in with the Navy if I need it."

"No trouble, Billy. Let's just see what Arnold Morgan has for us first thing in the morning, then you get on your way. You got enough stuff with you?"

"Yup. Suitcase packed. I kinda expected to be gone awhile when I first came to Washington."

"Cash?"

"Arnold's wiring it to Kansas. I told his office I thought I might be on a transatlantic trip before I arrived here."

"Good. Travel on scheduled airlines as unobtrusively as possible. I will ask the Royal Navy to meet you at Heathrow—just enough concern to let 'em know you're my man, but not enough to arouse suspicions of top-level secrecy. Just play it nice and low key, and tell 'em nothing unless you have to."

"Check. Arnold's office will let your guys know my flight number. I'll leave Sunday night, arrive Heathrow early Monday morning."

The two men walked across the hall together. "We'll meet at 0800 on the terrace," said the admiral, and Bill Baldridge prepared to walk up the old familiar staircase to the big bright spare room on the third floor, the one where he always slept, the one in which he and Elizabeth had spent so many nights together. It seemed like a long time ago.

Before he went, he turned once more to the admiral, and said formally, "Sir, for one final time. Are you, personally, absolutely certain in your own mind that none of the other somewhat hostile Middle East nations could have pulled this off?"

"Certain. Syria and Libya had both decommissioned their Soviet submarines by the end of 1995 because of a chronic lack of spares and technical support. According to the Mossad, there was a total of thirteen Arab boats deactivated at around that time. Most of 'em lost their 'safe to dive' certificates. One of the Syrians sank on its moorings!

"Right now Syria is trying to buy three Kilos, but you need hard cash these days. There's no military credit in Moscow. The Libyan situation with submarines has always been a bit like a Chinese fire drill. They haven't dived below the surface for eight years, according to Fort Meade—despite owning six boats. The fact is they are all tragically inefficient."

"Good night, Admiral," said Bill. "There is no doubt really that it was Iran, is there?"

"Just a little bit," replied Scott Dunsmore. "But not enough for you to concern yourself with."

And so the lieutenant commander climbed the stairs wearily, and went to bed all alone in his lovely room overlooking the broad river. But he dreamed his worst dream that night, the one where the giant black submarine pursues him along the seabed, trying to pin him and engulf him in evil. Evil under the water. He awoke sweating and breathless. Those kinds of dreams are commonplace among the submarine fraternity, caused, according to Navy psychiatrists, by years of suppression of terror, trying to avoid imagining the worst fate that can befall a submariner: death below the surface in a submarine that will no longer obey commands—death by suffocation or drowning. The imagination finds it almost impossible to shake away the ever-present proximity of death, which is the lot of the submarine officer.

101000JUL02. 18N, 59E. Speed 7.
Course 224. Depth 150 meters.
260 miles southwest of the datum;
due east Suqrah Bay, Oman.

"Ben, we suffer many small problem, but big leak on main shaft hull gland getting very bad. Engineer say pumps not holding—wants to stop, then surface, and repair packing. Water pouring in."

"You tell your engineer, Georgy, that he may think he has problems down here, but they would probably be ten times worse on the surface."

"Ben, pumps working flat-out. A foot of water in the bilge. Spray everywhere. Crew very worried. Some younger ones very scared."

"I don't care how much water is coming in as long as it's not sinking us. Right now I am trying to balance the risk. You just have to answer one question. Are the pumps getting rid of as much water as we are shipping?"

"Working flat-out, Ben, just. But draining battery."

"Then we stay submerged, but come above the layer, slowly to periscope depth. That will reduce the leak rate by nine tenths. If we stay shallow, we can stay out of sight without killing the battery. I'd like four hundred miles between us and the datum. Because, if we surface, and they catch us, we are dead men. All of us."

"How long, Ben? I must tell them something."

"Look, Georgy, this problem is mathematical. One hour from the datum there is a search area, in which we could be lurking, of around 150 square miles, roughly 12 miles by 12, a small patch for a dozen ships all looking for one submarine. But after six hours, running at seven knots, it becomes 5,500 square miles. When we have gone 400 miles the square becomes impossible, and that's when we know we're going to live, understand?

"Go to the surface and we may be finished. The American surveillance is good when they are relaxed. Today it may be superhuman. If they suspect anything. Tell the crew, Georgy. We stay at periscope depth, and we keep running at seven knots, until either we are sinking, or our battery's dying on us."

"Okay, Ben, you win. Your superman Teacher again, hah?"

"As you say, Georgy. But restrict yourself to Superbrain Teacher."

Two hours after the eastern sun had fought its way above the Maryland horizon, Bill Baldridge and Scott Dunsmore sipped orange juice and ate toast and preserves, the younger man silent, while the admiral apprised him of Admiral Morgan's findings.

"He's been on to Moscow, who are not admitting the drowned sailor was a member of the crew of the Kilo they thought had sunk in the Black Sea in April. Morgan's men reckon it would just have been possible for a bottle to have washed through the Bosporus, across the Sea of Marmara, and down to the Greek Islands—but not a body, which would have been eaten. Doesn't tally.

"The Russians say they told Admiral Morgan the submarine had sunk when he made his inquiry back in May because they honestly believed it had. There was some debris, but nothing significant, and they searched for a month. But they never found the hull. The body of their crewman *ought* to confirm what they must have suspected, that the Kilo broke out of the Black Sea with its crew and has not been seen since. However, for reasons only they know, Moscow is not ready to confirm what Morgan now believes is the obvious truth."

"Holy shit!" said Baldridge.

"Furthermore, if it was making eight knots through the Med it could very easily have been the boat one of Arnold's men heard in the Gibraltar surveillance post in the early morning of May 5. The dates fit accurately with the Greek pathologist's assessment of the time of death."

"How come no one else ever heard the damn thing?"

"I would guess they were being very stealthy and then made a mistake. Arnold says our man heard them for less than thirty seconds—single shaft, five blades, sudden sharp acceleration. Then silence. He was damn sure it was a submarine. That's why he made the report. He even said it was probably non-nuclear. He thought it was a diesel. Admiral Morgan thinks he was dead right."

"Sounds pretty decisive to me," said Baldridge.

"Things usually do when they fit as we want them to fit," replied the admiral, thoughtfully. "But there is yet another piece to this jigsaw."

"Which is?"

"The satellite pictures are showing only two of Iran's three Kilos in residence at Bandar Abbas. That's been so since Friday, July 5."

"Well, if one of 'em left, how come we did not see it immediately, and then track it?"

"Good question. The fact is no one did see it leave. No one has seen it at all."

"Do you think it could have just crept out without anyone knowing, and then blown up the carrier?"

"Search me. The experts say not a chance. But it's still missing."

"If you ask me, that makes the Iranians doubly suspicious. They could have just moved the submarine to throw us off the scent of the one they hired in the Black Sea—the real culprit."

"Possibly. But Admiral Morgan's men believe it would have been impossible for them to have got the Kilo out through the Strait of Hormuz without us knowing. We have the KH–11 satellite camera trained on that stretch of water night and day. Every day. I think they just moved it or hid it to confuse us. Either way they are beginning right now to look very, very guilty."

"No doubt about that."

"Go see your mom, Billy. Then hit the gas pedal for Scotland. Let's get busy."

They walked around to the front of the house, climbed into the rear of the Navy staff car, and headed north up the parkway to the Pentagon. Admiral Dunsmore jumped out in the garage and was met by a Marine guard, who escorted him into the private elevator and to General Paul's office.

The car swung around with a squeal of tires and headed to the airport. There Bill Baldridge grabbed his bag from the front seat and went to find his ticket. He had only an hour to wait before boarding, and he slept most of the way to the great sprawling city on the Missouri River which straddles two separate states. He would need to shuttle down to Wichita and then pick up a small local Beechcraft to Great Bend. Bill called his brother Ray from the airport, asked him to come pick him up, a journey of about thirty-eight miles.

Kansas City International Airport is positioned in the top right-hand corner of the state, to the north of the river. It never felt much like home to Bill Baldridge. In fact he never felt anywhere near home until he buckled up his seat belt in the aircraft on the flight southwest to Wichita and heard that old down-home accent again. Today, flying through the clear cobalt-blue sky of the Midwestern summer he could see the great billiard table of his home state, millions of acres of wheat and the wide prairies of bluestem grass, the finest cattle-rearing pasture on this earth.

Because he would not have presumed to have breakfast with the Chief of Naval Operations without wearing full uniform, he was still dressed as an officer in the United States Navy.

The deeper he flew into the heartland, the more he yearned for his high-quilted boots, spurs, and chaps, and for the feel of his hard bay workhorse between his knees, his long whip and his Stetson. In the next ten minutes he knew he would see one of the great geographic phenomena in the U.S.A.—the sudden rise from the plains of a series of rounded dome-shaped hills. To a stranger looking down they looked like some ancient Indian burial ground, like the Valley of the Kings up the Nile from Cairo.

These were the strange Flint Hills, rising one behind the other in a gently sculpted symmetry, now in July a deep green, but out in the distance, pushing against the horizon, a misty blue, sometimes almost purple. From the air they seem desolate, a place where a man could find true solitude.

They were flying due east of Wichita now, over the interstate highway east to the Missouri border at the old Cavalry outpost, Fort Scott. Below, Bill knew, was the huge sprawling acreage of Spring Creek Ranch, owned by the Koch family, the principal employers in the state of Kansas—Koch Industries, of Wichita, the greatest privately owned oil-pipeline empire in the world.

Old Fred Koch and Tom Baldridge had been quite good friends back in the 1960s, but Fred died young, and Bill Baldridge knew a bunch of brothers owned the company now. The youngest, and, Jack always said, the nicest, and the cleverest, was Bill Koch, who won the America's Cup off San Diego in 1992. Jack had gone out to watch as a guest of his fellow Kansan a couple of times while he was in port. Jack had been saying for several years that Bill Koch should run for governor.

They were finally descending, dropping down into Wichita Mid-Continent Airport, which coped on a daily basis with an armada of private jets bearing executives to the big oil and air-craft-building corporations.

Nonetheless, when Bill stepped out into the hot plains after-noon, the air, as ever, tasted better. Three times on his stroll to the baggage area he was interrupted by people who recognized him and wanted to offer their condolences. Lieutenant Commander Baldridge was gracious and polite to them all, and as he picked up his bag, he heard another familiar voice: "Hey, Billy, comin' on up to Great Bend with me, there's just three of us. They told me you'd probably show up." Out here, matters like short-hop air flights were strictly routine. The big Kansan families never even bothered with tickets. A highly reasonable monthly bill just came in to the Baldridge spread, and the ranch office paid it.

And now Rick Varner, the pilot, picked up the Naval officer's bag and began walking out to the Beechcraft. "I ran your ma out to Tribune yesterday," he said. "There's a little airstrip just to the southeast of the town. She wanted to visit poor old Jethro Carson. She said Zac's death has broken the old boy apart. Hasn't uttered but one word since he heard the admiral was gone. Apparently the whole of Greeley County is in mourning. Jethro was pretty old, but he was in great health till this. Your ma thinks it might finish him. She says you can get a broken heart at any age."

"Guess so, Rick. I'm not feeling that great myself. Mom seem okay?"

"Stranger mighta thought she was. But I've known Mrs. Baldridge a lotta years. She was putting on a brave face. I never saw so many people so upset as they were last Tuesday when we heard about the carrier, and that Jack was on board. There were four of our office people in tears. My goddamned copilot was in tears. I was in tears. We did not see much of Jack recently—but it just seemed so real to all of us, you know, to have known someone for so long, and suddenly he was gone."

"He's gonna leave a huge gap in our family, that's for sure."

They rode in silence for the rest of the twenty-five-minute trip across the central plains before Rick finally dropped down and flew low over the huge bend in the wide, jade-colored Arkansas River. This is the famous swerve which gave birth to the city of Great Bend, right on the north bank, where the flow of the water switches from its northeast course to southeast across the low fertile plains to Wichita. After that it still runs wide and onward, almost due south into Oklahoma. The Arkansas is one of the great American rivers, flowing out of the Colorado Rockies for fifteen hundred miles across the western high plains of Kansas, then through the lush lowlands of southwest Kansas, right across the Oklahoma panhandle, into Arkansas. It hits the Mississippi fifty miles shy of the Louisiana border.

Despite its massive interstate journey, all Kansans thought of it as their private river and anything it did before or after leaving the state was regarded as strictly irrelevant. Bill Baldridge considered that river his home waters.

They put down at Great Bend's small commercial airfield, where the lean, tanned figure of Ray Baldridge stood tall in a short-sleeved cotton shirt, light trousers, and a Stetson, waiting to welcome his younger brother home. "Good to see you, kid," he smiled, but the loss of Jack was too overpowering and they walked out to the Cherokee pickup in silence.

Ray broke the ice. "Mom don't seem too bad, but I guess she's fighting it," he said. "So'm I, really. I just can't believe we'll never see him again."

"I don't think I'm ever gonna get used to that."

"Well, the ranch is running fine. Making a ton of money this year, profits still going into the trust Dad set up. I'm just hopin' you'll leave the Navy soon and come out here and take it all over. I'm fine running the herds, overseeing the breeding, hiring and firing the guys, making it all happen. But I guess we all thought Jack'd take over the heavy-duty stuff, buying and selling land, budgeting for repairs, investing in new herds, watching the markets, deciding when to sell and all. Ain't no one can do that for us really, 'cept for a member of the family. We got accountants to look like they're doing it but not like it was you or Dad or Jack. I just wanna pure-bred Baldridge out here in charge."

"Yeah, Ray. I know. I just have one last job I'm gonna do in the Navy, then I'm resigning, mainly because I'm not going to be promoted any higher. I'd rather get out than stay a lieutenant commander for the rest of my career. I'd planned on coming home anyway this year or next. But, shit, I wasn't really counting on taking over the whole operation. That's one hell of a commitment. That's a lifetime."

"You got it, Billy. But it's your lifetime . . . and mine."

By this time, they had crossed the Pawnee County line, driving westward across the old Indian lands along a flat, near-deserted prairie road as straight as a gun barrel. To the left and to the right the landscape was identical, miles and miles of uncluttered farmland, sometimes wheat, less often ripening corn, and, much more often, great swathes of prairie, endless grass, waving in the ever-present whisper of the south wind.

This was the Big Country, the land of Wyatt Earp, the Dalton Brothers, Bat Masterson, Wild Bill Hickok, the Comanches, the Pawnee and the native Kanza, the plains Indians, who once rode out here behind herds of buffalo twenty-five miles long.

The Baldridge Ranch, with its distinctive B\B brand, set in wrought iron on the high gateway to the house, was actually across the Pawnee border in Hodgeman County, built in a rich alluvial plain in the fork where the Pawnee River and Buckner Creek finally converge before meandering on down to the broad Arkansas. But the Baldridge land begins before the border, straddling two counties, and Bill could see part of the white-faced family herds of Herefords long before they came in sight of his mother's house.

He cast an expert eye over them. "Looking good, Ray," he said. "A real credit to you. Like always."

"Thanks, little brother. We've been pretty lucky this year. Lotta rain in the late spring, brought the grass on—you know the story, the better the pasture, the less they wander, and the more weight they put on."

"Yup," said Bill. But then he fell silent again. And once more the vision of the sinister black Russian Kilo stood stark before his mind's eye, as it had done just about every two hours for the past five days. He knew exactly what it looked like, just as he knew the minutest detail of the conformation of a Hereford steer. Right now he seemed to occupy two worlds, each one several million light-years from the other—the soft winds and homely cattle out here, grazing on what a Kansan poet once described as the Lawns of God. And far away, the villainous, menacing, malevolent arena of international, militarized terrorism, into the black heart of which he must journey before the next week was done.

Ray drove the Cherokee up to the door of the big white clapboard house, with its long Doric columns, surrounded by great maple trees planted by generations of Baldridges.

Inside, across the high timbered hall and through the arched doorway to the sunlit living room, sat the tall, white-haired matriarch of the family, Emily Baldridge, aged seventy-five. She was nursing a cup of English tea, a copy of the state magazine, *Kansas*, and Bill guessed, a broken heart.

She rose as he walked through the door, smiled and hugged her youngest son. "And how's my Navy officer today?" she said, holding him appreciatively at arm's length.

"Pretty good, Mom," he said, secretly marveling at her control, so soon after the shocking death of the male head of the family. "My own news is varied. I've been appointed to an investigation into the accident on the carrier, and I've pretty well made up my mind I'm resigning from the Navy right after it's over.

"Ray and I had a chat on the way out here. I'm coming home within the year."

"Oh, bless you, Billy. I so hoped you would. It's too much for Ray and me. I was always worried it may have been years before Jack could come back but now he's not coming back and I was beginning to consider reducing the land and livestock. It's too big for us."

"I'd say it's a good thing neither Dad nor Jack heard you say that, both of 'em hated selling anything. I don't like it much either, so let's not do anything. And, Mom, you were right. It would have been a long time before Jack got back home. They were going to make him an admiral for sure. He'd have ended up right at the top. In the Pentagon. He was the best potential battle commander I ever met. Everyone knows that. Scott always said he was just keeping the ole CNO's chair warm for Captain Baldridge. And he didn't mean me!"

"Ah, my darling, but he couldn't ride a horse like you, could he?"

"No, ma'am, that he couldn't. But he coulda taken on the Russian fleet. Coupla times I heard him say he'd a been real happy to do just that. Wasn't he something?"

Bill knew he had to change the subject quickly. But there was something compulsive about the subject of Jack Baldridge. Bill gazed at his mother with profound affection, but he was too late. She was trying to tell him that Margaret and her two granddaughters were arriving from San Diego next week. But there were tears streaming down her face—hopeless, helpless, desolate tears for her lost, beloved second son, the only one of the three who looked just like his father. The one she had loved most of all.

"I'll get him, Mom," he blurted, incomprehensibly to her. "You can put the ranch on that. I'll get him."

But Emily Baldridge was too preoccupied regaining her own self-control to worry about Bill's. She gratefully accepted the big white linen handkerchief he offered, and fled toward the door. "I'll just go and rejoin civilization," she called. "Go and have a rest. Let's all meet on the veranda at seven."

Bill stood and watched her go with huge sadness. She was such a handsome woman, still clinging to her starchy East Coast manners, still aware of the old taboo about showing emotion, still bearing the stamp of Wellesley College, plain as if someone had put a **W*** branding iron to her just before graduation. She and Tom Baldridge had seemed a slightly out-of-step couple to strangers, she so much more polished than the broad-shouldered Kansan rancher.

Bill followed his mother up the long oak staircase, through the arch set with the big longhorns and Indian regalia. He wandered along to his old room, the heavy, brightly covered Sioux blanket slung over the bed, the crossed Comanche lances beside the mirror, the big framed sepia picture of Crazy Horse gazing sternly across the room. It was the headquarters of a schoolboy scout, a veteran of a hundred battles in this historic plains Indian country. At the bottom of the bed were two pairs of cowboy boots, one with spurs. Inside the big pine wardrobe there were four Stetsons, and a selection of cowboy shirts and trousers, befitting the youngest son of one of the big ranchers in the area.

Ten minutes later he strode out over the veranda, dressed now in the only clothes in which he felt truly at home, the lightweight white Stetson pushed back a bit, just enough to take the glare off his eyes. Tonight he would ride alone for a while, heading west into the gigantic Kansan sunset. Bill's spurs clanked lightly as he headed out to the stables.

He lingered for a while talking to Freddie, the big bay horse, which only he and Ray ever rode. Then he hoisted the big western saddle, with its Indian markings and wide saddle horn, up and across the horse's back. He tightened the girths, moving easily around the quarters, gently smoothing Freddie's tail, unafraid of the hind hooves which could launch a man with the wrong touch twenty yards through the air.

When Bill rode out past the cattle pens, tipping his hat toward a couple of ranch hands mending a fence, no one would have guessed he had ever left this place.

"Hey, Billy, welcome back . . . terrible 'bout Jack. Everyone's very sad out here right now."

Bill Baldridge rode slowly westward, out between the two rivers. Forty miles to the southwest lay Dodge City, their nearest sizable town—his mom was a trustee of the museum there. Dead ahead lay more or less nothing, mile after mile of prairie, the wind making patterns on the bluestem. In this late afternoon light, the pasture seemed greenish gold in color. But as the south wind gusted the grasses bent before its gentle force and bluestems showed in long patches like the ripples on water. Bill stared, watching the blue patterns as he once had as a boy, dreaming of an ocean he had never seen.

Freddie's hooves were almost silent on the prairie, so deep and lush was the grassland. The only sounds were the occasional soft crushing of the taller stalks, and the endless chirping of the cicadas. Glancing down, Bill could see bare patches where all of the grass and wildflowers appeared to have been the victims of a giant lawn mower, and the wind blew no patterns here.

The great Baldridge herds had passed by very recently. So recently none of the wildflowers had shot new blooms. Bill knew the cattle must be close, but he had to get back to meet his mother and Ray. Another mile or so and he must turn around, maybe let Freddie have a gallop home, blow him out a little, keep him young.

They kept going for a bit, now at a light canter through this lonely American outback, which renders its natives lifetime prisoners of a vast and silent beauty.

Bill gazed out in front of him, to a bank of high cloud building on the horizon. He squinted his eyes into the lowering sun, which was already becoming the color of spent fire. He could not see the herds yet, and he turned his horse around and began the ride home, with the last of the day's warmth now upon his back. A mile from the ranch, riding now close to the creek where the ground was a little softer, he spurred Freddie on, urging him to gallop.

Up ahead he could see two cowboys rounding up the last of a half-dozen stray steers, down by the water. They nearly had them bunched now, riding with one man to the rear and one out on the left. Two steers kept wheeling away back toward the river. Instinctively Bill Baldridge urged Freddie forward, drawing his long whip from the left side of his saddle. He came up on the right, on an easy stride, just outside the leading runaway. The famous Kansan brand, B\B, was clear on their hides.

Bill Baldridge let out a yell, cracked the whip high over his head, and drove Freddie into the steer's right flank, and turned the brute away, back to his pals in the bunch. Bill grinned at the look of stark relief on its bovine white face.

He rode in to the group, guarding the right-hand escape route. "Hey, thanks, Bill," said the older of the two men, another tall cowboy, with a big tobacco bulge in his left, nut-brown cheek. "Ain't lost your touch any, have you?"

The two men had not spoken for a couple of years, but there are some places where time stands, more or less, still.

Bill grinned. "No problem, Skip. These hot days they can get real determined to stay near the water."

"Sure can. Staying long?"

"Uh-uh. Leaving Sunday."

"Miss havin' you around. We was thinking you might come back now . . . Jack and everything."

"Next year I'll be back. For good."

They rode in silence for a little way, before Skip McGaughey spoke again. "Know what I hate most about the Navy, Bill?"

"Lay it on me."

"I hate the way there are no gravestones for most men who die in big warships. You know, my grandfather was killed in the Pacific in World War II. Never found him. And my grandma always said how she wished there was just somewhere she coulda seen his name."

"Yeah. Course in the *Jefferson* there were no bodies, not even any wreckage. Nuclear blasts don't leave much behind."

"At least it was instant."

"No doubt about that."

"We gonna have a memorial stone for Jack?"

"Guess so. Hadn't really thought about it much. Mom's kinda upset right now."

"Hell yeah. Still I think there should be something. You know, ever since yer dad passed away, we've always called Jack, 'the Boss', even though we didn't see that much of him."

"Yeah. I know you all called him that. I called him that myself. You already know, I guess, he was serving as the Group Operations Officer on the carrier, the admiral's right-hand man. They were gonna make him a rear admiral for sure."

"Guess then we'd never have seen him."

"Not for a few years anyway."

"That's even more reason to have a memorial, eh?"

"What kind of thing? It'd have to be pretty low key. Jack hated anything showy."

"Well, some of the boys were thinking. You know how Jack

used to go fishing down by those rocks on the creek. 'Bout four hundred yards from the main house. One of them rocks is pretty big, twelve feet tall, pure granite, like that strata over in the Flint Hills. How 'bout a memorial tablet in bronze set right in that rock, by a stonemason. Something kinda quiet, and impressive . . . like him."

Bill pondered for a moment, thinking again of Jack, of the great U.S. warship, of the black Russian Kilo he knew had sunk the Americans. Then he spoke. "Skip, I love it. Jack had fished down there all his life. He woulda liked that. Really liked that. Right next to the water. Tell you what. I'll draft the words, Ray'll get a photograph, and we'll have a bronze relief done of him in uniform. Head and shoulders. 'Bout a foot high, above the plaque. Lemme leave the casting and the mason up to you and Ray, can I? Then we'll get it fixed up, and have a little service out here in the spring. Surprise Mom . . . get a few of the Navy High Command out. That little glade will be full of sailors and cowboys. When the priest blesses the stone, I guess Jack's spirit will have come home, from half a world away . . . at least it will to all of us."

"Beautiful, Bill. That's gonna be real nice. And we'll all be close to the boss every time those goddamned steers stray down by the river."

"Hey, I'm glad we met up. That gate open at the pens?"

"Yup. I got young Razor right there, ready to close it soon as they go in."

The three cowboys tightened their grip on the six strays, each man now with a drawn stockwhip. The horses squeezed in tight, edging up to the gateway. Then Skip broke loose, wheeled around, and came in behind fast, with a loud yell and a crack of the whip. The steers never even looked back, just bolted for the safety of the corral. Razor banged the gate shut behind them. "G'job, Skip," drawled Bill Baldridge.

"Jest about gittin' the hang of it now."

And then Bill rode over toward the stables, calling back, "G'bye, boys—till next time, eh?"

"Yes, so long, Bill—don't let 'em get you down."

Then, somewhat mischievously, the young master of the

big ranch called back, "Water trough's a little empty."

"Goddamit, I bin filling it for thirty-five years, I don't guess any of 'em gonna die of thirst tonight."

"Guess not. Just wanted to keep you sharp," shouted Bill, laughing.

"Git owta here, willya?" chuckled the veteran cowboy.

Bill waved back, steered Freddie into the stables, where the fleet-footed Razor was now ready to hose him down, feed and water him. "Thanks, buddy," said Bill, pressing a twenty-dollar bill into his hand. "Look after him while I'm gone."

In the next-door stall he could see Jack's old cow pony, Flint. To Bill he looked a bit forlorn, like everyone else around here. The sadness was everywhere, and Bill walked out into the bright sunset still thinking of Jack, and of the shocking unreasonableness of his death.

Before he showered and changed for dinner with his mother and Ray's family, he sat briefly at his old schoolboy desk and wrote on an old legal pad the following words:

CAPTAIN JACK ETHAN BALDRIDGE

(1962–2002)

Beloved son of the late Tom Baldridge
and Emily Henderson Baldridge.
Lost at sea in the USS *Thomas Jefferson*
disaster, July 8. Captain Baldridge,
the Battle Group Operations Officer
on board the aircraft carrier, perished
in the Arabian Gulf along with all 6,021
men of the ship's company. A fine cattleman,
a brilliant Navy officer, and a great Kansan.
Never Forgotten. By All at the B\B.

Dinner with his family was too sad for levity, and the discussion involved mainly the future of the fifty-thousand-acre

Baldridge ranch. Emily Baldridge told Bill that when he returned he would move into the big house as the master of the operation. Ray and his wife and family preferred to remain in the more beautiful, but smaller, six-bedroom River House, a quarter of a mile away, beyond the horse paddocks.

Should Bill return with a wife, Emily would take up residence in the "Boot"—the three-bedroom ranch house across the front lawn, built by Bill's grandfather, and never fully occupied since he died. The Boot, named because of its shape, was normal in every respect except that it had one huge room with a beamed cathedral ceiling hung with Indian regalia, including a painted kayak suspended from the rafters.

On every wall there were mounted moose heads, bison, even a wildcat. Indian blankets were thrown on the big handmade sofas. Three mighty bearskin rugs covered the polished wooden floor. The yawning stone fireplace made it probably the best room on the property for a winter evening.

Bill always thought it a pity they never used the Boot except for parties. He also thought that if his mother ever moved in, the bison and the wildcat had about ten minutes before she replaced them with paintings of what she would call "a more agreeable ambiance." Emily herself was already planning a beautiful new house, to be constructed further along the river, for Jack's widow, Margaret, and the two girls.

Like most Navy wives, Mrs. Jack Baldridge was accustomed to living on either the East Coast or the West Coast. But within hours of the news from the Arabian Gulf, Margaret had expressed a firm wish to bring her family deep into the rural heart of the United States. Deep into the rural heart of the Baldridge family, the closest place in all of the world to the memory of her lost husband.

Emily had been magnificent. She had dispatched two ranch hands and a lawyer to San Diego to supervise an immediate move east for Jack's family. She had tried to point out that the quiet, secure pace of life out in Burdett might not be quite what Margaret imagined. But Margaret had been insistent that she intended to make a new life here.

Now Emily was preparing to welcome them all, with arms open as wide as the prairie, right into the bosom of the Baldridge cattle empire. They represented a new generation, and they were arriving to perpetuate what was already there. Emily could not resist a feeling of joy beyond her own tears. She adored Margaret, and her granddaughters, and had often been saddened by the fact that they would be too grown up by the time their father was ready to return to the ranch.

Jack's death had cost them a natural-born leader, and a loving father, but in the eyes of Emily Baldridge, it had also made her family more complete. Tom would have loved that, all of the young Baldridges together at the B\B.

The following days passed quickly, and Bill spent much of them closeted with the family lawyers in Dodge City straightening out the trust in the aftermath of Jack's death. He toured the ranch a few times with Ray and left written instructions for the accountants to try and buy five hundred acres more down near the creek, further west. There was some unproductive land to the north Ray wanted to sell, but the trust decreed no land could be sold without being replaced. The Baldridge acreage had thus never been reduced in three generations.

On Sunday morning, July 14, rested and dressed again in his newly pressed Naval uniform, Bill headed out to the Cherokee where Ray was waiting. Just as he opened the door, his mother hurried down the veranda steps. "Billy," she called. "Before you go, just one thing . . . try to remember . . . to take care of yourself," she said, reaching to embrace him.

"Don't worry," he reassured her.

Bill had told her nothing of where he was now going, but she was aware of his uneasiness. She sensed something sinister would accompany her last Naval officer, on his last mission, and Emily Baldridge watched in silence as the Cherokee drove out to the prairie in a cloud of dust.

1730 Sunday, July 14.

LIEUTENANT COMMANDER BALDRIDGE ARRIVED AT Boston's Logan Airport late Sunday afternoon. Outside, the temperature was still 92 degrees under clear skies. He picked up his suitcase, headed for the American Airlines counter, and handed over his economy-class ticket and passport. A slim dark brunette from Customer Service approached him. "Mr. Baldridge?" she inquired.

"That's me."

"Come this way, and I'll take you down to the Admiral's Club. I'll bring your ticket and passport."

Baldridge shrugged and walked down the wide corridor, through the security check, and crossed the concourse to the big oak door guarding the first-class lounge. His escort pushed the door open, gave a cursory nod to the attendant, and led him to a private corner table marked "Reserved." A telephone was positioned next to his deep armchair, and someone was asking him whether he preferred a drink, or perhaps coffee.

"Coffee, please," he said. "Black, two sugars. Thanks, ma'am." Someone in high authority had cleared his path, he had no doubt of that.

No one at American Airlines, nor indeed at the Royal Navy's

headquarters, had the remotest idea of the young American officer's mission.

When the flight was called, Bill was escorted to a first-class seat. There was no one in the seat next to him. He had a couple of large glasses of fresh orange juice, an early dinner of steak fillet and fruit salad, and slept for the rest of the night. The six-hour journey passed quickly, and the flight attendant awakened him with a pot of fresh coffee. He drank it, disappeared for a shave, and stepped down the jetway into London's Heathrow Airport at 7 A.M. refreshed but in a somber mood.

He was escorted through passport control, his bag was brought to him in the customs hall, and he walked straight out through the "Green, nothing-to-declare, lane," into the safe custody of a Royal Navy staff driver and a female officer.

He sank quietly into the backseat, and left it to the driver to fight his way through the rush-hour traffic out onto the M4, and from there onto a circuitous route through the western suburbs to the tree-lined, unprepossessing military base in Northwood, some fifteen miles from central London. From a bunker beneath these bland modern buildings, Margaret Thatcher conducted the Falklands War in the company of her generals, admirals, and air marshals. Only the forest of radio and satellite communications which protruded from a half-dozen roofs betrayed this place as a secret citadel of Great Britain's military defenses.

They passed through the guards at the gate, drove on down the hill, and stopped outside the main building. "I understand you will be here for most of the day, sir," the driver ventured. "Leave your bag. I'll be waiting."

Bill was escorted up the steps, through the glass doors, and up two additional flights to the offices of Admiral Sir Peter Elliott, the Royal Navy's Flag Officer Submarines. He was greeted by the Flag Lieutenant, Andrew Waites, who shook hands and hustled him next door to meet the admiral's Chief of Staff, Captain Dick Greenwood, The place left an impression of battleship gray, steel desks, slightly tired carpets, cluttered tabletops.

It was the people who set it apart, as indeed they set apart the Navy offices in the Pentagon. Here in England each man was dressed in his "number twos," dark blue trousers, white shirts and black ties, navy sweaters with high round necks and lapels. A small insignia on the shoulders indicated rank. All the faces, the manners, the attitudes were those of highly trained, confident, fit men.

The Royal Navy appeared to Bill to have misplaced a submarine of their own, judging by the conversation—a couple of "Oh shits," three "Jesus Christs," and a loud "Well, send him another fucking message." Baldridge grinned. It was the same in every top submarine service. The sheer difficulty of communication with an underwater warship, which couldn't hear a goddamned thing most of the time, was the most frustrating aspect of the job.

The COS was brisk and to the point. "I don't see any reason to hang around. Tell me how you like your coffee and we'll pop straight in and see the boss."

The Royal Navy's Flag Officer Submarines (FOSM), Admiral Elliott, stood up behind his desk and shook hands with the American. He was not as tall as Bill, but he was slim and stood very erect—unmistakably a military man. The eyes were piercing blue, the dark hair graying at the temples, the skin still tanned. The expression wide open, but wary. A man who has spent a lot of years at sea, Bill thought. What he did not know was that Admiral Sir Peter Elliott had been an outstanding submarine captain, commanding a Polaris in the 1970s, and a nuclear hunter-killer in the Falklands. He had also been the Teacher at Faslane. So indeed had Captain Greenwood, another nuclear boat commander.

The three men sat down and chatted briefly about the hot summer, both in England and the United States, and then the Royal Navy's submarine Flag Officer asked Bill Baldridge precisely what he wanted.

"I have been given no briefing from the Admiralty, save a message to suggest I cooperate with you within my discretion. It may also be within my discretion to report our conversation to the Ministry of Defense, and I think you should understand that before we proceed."

"I understand perfectly, sir. However, I have been asked by the CNO to make all of my inquiries here as discreet as possible."

With the playing field now clear of minor obstacles, and the slow Kansan drawl of the American settling easily on his ears, the British admiral smiled and said quietly, in an impeccable English accent, "Well, Mr. Baldridge, how can I help you?"

"Sir, I would like to request your permission to review your files of foreign officers who passed through the Commanding Officers Qualifying Course at Faslane during the period from 1982 to 1992."

Admiral Elliott shot a glance at Captain Greenwood, who imperceptibly shook his head—a shake of such infinitesimal motion, Bill was glad he caught it.

"Impossible for several reasons, I am afraid, the most obvious being that the material is highly classified."

"Hmmm. Can I get around that?"

"Well, perhaps if you were to tell me what you're looking for, that might be a start."

"I don't think so, sir." And then, "I am not really empowered to do so," he lied.

"You must understand one thing. Even if I gained the necessary permission to show you the documents, I would have to clear each one with the respective embassy of the officer concerned. Before I showed you one word."

Bill now knew he was in a serious game of poker. "Well, sir, I would remind you that I am here on the highest possible authority."

"I do not really have proof of that. I would most certainly require you to verify it. How far up can you go—I mean to a U.S. official we can contact right now."

"Quite high, sir. The Chief of Naval Operations at the Pentagon, if necessary. If that won't do, the Secretary of Defense. Failing that, the President of the United States. Even at this early hour of the morning."

"Yes," replied the Admiral, slowly. "You really do want to see those records, don't you?"

"Yessir. Yes I do."

"Okay, Bill. I am going to ask you formally, now, and I want you to answer me, otherwise I shall have no alternative but to refer your inquiries to Whitehall, which has a way of holding things up for several weeks . . . sometimes years!"

"Sir, if I have to, I'll have the President call the Prime Minister . . . "

"I know you can, and I know you will. But all of that may not be necessary. Answer me. Tell me why you want to see my records."

"Because I'm looking for someone, sir."

"Yes, I have worked that out. Who are you looking for . . . ?

"I can't say, sir . . . well, not really."

The admiral stood up, smiled down at Bill, walked over to a table, and poured three cups of coffee, two sugars for Bill. "Very well," he said. "Let me ask you a question. And I require you to answer it honestly."

"Okay, Admiral," said Bill.

The admiral swung around, stared straight at Bill, and said sharply: "You think some bastard blew up the *Jefferson*, don't you?"

"Yessir. I do."

"So do we. Matter of fact we've been waiting for you to show up for several days now."

Lieutenant Commander Baldridge's face expressed pure relief. For the first time he knew he was among friends.

"May I assume, Commander, that you are working on the theory that the carrier may have been hit by a torpedo delivered from a submarine?"

"Yessir."

"What kind of a submarine?"

"Small, sir. Non-nuclear."

"Built where?"

"Either here, sir, or Russia."

"Exactly."

"You don't suspect us, do you?" interjected Captain Greenwood, a trace of indignation in his voice.

"Nossir. That's why I'm here."

"Suspects?" snapped the admiral.

"Oh, Middle Eastern, I suppose. The usual identity parade, Iran, Iraq, Syria, Libya . . . possibly Pakistan."

"Hmmm. Well, Bill, let me put my cards on the table. I don't need to have higher clearance to give you access to the records. But I was required to hear from you exactly what you were investigating. I guessed anyway. Now we both have what we want—and I would like you to inform your CNO, and your government, that you will have, as always, the complete cooperation of the Royal Navy and, I am quite certain, of Her Majesty's Government."

"Thank you, sir. Could I ask you a question?"

"Shoot."

"When did you first realize the *Jefferson* had been hit?"

"Well, I heard about it toward the end of the ten o'clock news on the evening of the disaster. They showed live film of Scott Dunsmore making the announcement. I suppose by about 2235. I was pretty leery about an accident. I always considered sabotage a possible but rather silly theory. I spoke to the First Sea Lord at about 2245. He agreed with me. I spoke also to Dick here, which made three of us nearly certain there was a bit of skulduggery. Been waiting to hear from you ever since."

"You were a bit quicker than we were, sir."

"Oh, I shouldn't worry, Bill. It's sometimes easier to be clear when you are far away and not so embroiled. Anyway, we've been at it a bit longer. Admiral Nelson would have opened fire on Baghdad by now, if he could have got *Victory* up the river!"

Bill looked up. He considered discussing the Iraqi theory with this very hard-eyed British submarine chief, but decided to say no more than he had to. For the moment.

"Yeah, I guess he would at that. Meantime, to get back to my assignment, perhaps I could spend a few hours looking at the records, and then come back and discuss the best way to proceed."

"Perfect . . . Dick, take the commander out to Andrew's office and then find him a space where he can work in private. Andrew should stay with him, and with the files, as a matter of security."

The admiral offered another handshake, smiled, and observed that he had enjoyed their brief meeting.

But as the American reached the door, the admiral called out, "Oh, Bill. Good luck, old chap, we'll find him. I was told your brother was on board. I am very sorry."

"Thank you, sir. Thank you very much."

As he left, Bill heard the admiral call out, somewhat informally, "Have we found that fucking submarine yet? . . . Good . . . what was it? . . . radio mast . . . bloody things are always going wrong."

And now he followed the Flag Lieutenant downstairs to the basement. They entered a very private room, with a long table, no windows, many telephones, a television, and the kind of upholstered armchairs arranged around the table which suggested this room was sometimes occupied by persons of high standing.

"Sit down here, sir," said the lieutenant, respecting the American's rank, "and I'll nip upstairs and collect the files. It's just the foreign Perishers, sir, right?"

"Right," said Bill, grinning. "Just the foreign Perishers."

"Oh, sir, are you interested in the ones who failed? There's a few of them."

"No, Lieutenant. My Perisher passed. I suspect with flying colors."

"Quite so, sir," said the lieutenant, with a slightly knowing grin, and bounded back up the stairs. He returned quickly, with a surprisingly small file. "I think most of 'em are in here," he said. "But there may be one or two others. I'm going to run through the whole list again. Back in ten minutes. No hurry. The admiral wants you to have lunch with him—three hours."

Bill Baldridge opened the file. There appeared to be about four sheets of paper on each man, clipped together in a red cardboard folder with MOD stamped on the front. He glanced first at the format without bothering to read the details. The top of page one gave the man's name, rank, and nationality. It also gave his home base and a brief summary of his experience as a Naval officer. It then carried a succession of reports charting his progress, his examination marks, with comments. There followed a detailed assessment of his personal and professional character, his strengths and weaknesses, on what was clearly an official report. It was signed on the last page by the Teacher.

Also on the table in front of him was a big Navy writing pad, yellow pages, lined. Bill tore one out and folded it neatly in two. He decided to open each file and then clip the folded paper to the top of page one, covering the part which gave the details of the man's background. That way he could read the report carefully, with an open mind. No prejudices, no preconceived ideas. If the report showed a potentially outstanding submarine officer, then he would go back and uncover the personal details. And the nationality.

The first file was a bit of a joke. A young commander from Saudi Arabia. Passed the course, just, but in the opinion of the Teacher possessed "no flair, no inspiration, and little imagination."

"That man," muttered Bill, "did not blow up an American carrier."

The next three files were more promising, but again there was no evidence of flair, nor inspiration, nor even daring. Their marks were not bad, and having read four reports now, Bill realized the key passages were those written about each man by the Teacher. So far he had read reports by three Teachers, but two of the reports, both completed in 1987, were penned by the same man. They were signed, Commander Iain MacLean. "Now there is a tough ole sonofabitch," murmured Baldridge. "Trying to get a compliment out of him must be like climbing mountains in Pawnee County. Maybe he just doesn't like foreigners."

He read two more reports. By this time Lieutenant Waites was with him, reading as well, keeping the files straight.

"Andrew," said Bill, "can you get hold of another couple of files on good English guys who passed? I'd like to compare how the Teachers write about nationals as opposed to foreigners."

"Sure. I'll just get it cleared by the boss, and bring 'em down. There's two more foreign reports also coming down in a minute. They were in a separate file."

"Okay. I'd just like to get a feel on how harsh these Teachers are. I'm telling you . . . this guy MacLean, what a tyrant. Glad he didn't mark my stuff at MIT. I'd still be there."

"I've never met him, sir. But he certainly does tell it like it is."

The final two foreign reports arrived, and the young Flag Lieutenant checked them in, and then went back upstairs to retrieve a couple of the English documents. Bill Baldridge opened the first of the newly arrived files and carefully placed his folded paper over the identity section on page one. He skimmed the results, noting the highest marks he had seen on any of the foreign papers. He skipped quickly to the Teacher's comments, and his heart pounded as he read just six words. "The best Perisher I have taught yet."

In his haste to see who had signed it, he turned the page, dropped the file, and managed to knock everything onto the floor. He shoved back the chair and stuck his head under the big table, as Andrew Waites arrived.

"What the hell are you doing down there?" he asked. "Trying to tunnel your way out?"

"No. I just knocked all the stuff over. Got kinda overexcited. But I think I have something."

Bill stood up and reopened the critical file. He carefully turned to the last page. The signature was clear. Commander Iain MacLean. "Holy shit!" said Bill Baldridge. "I think we might have him."

They sat down together to read the full report. "This man was quite outstanding in every respect. He might have been even better if he had listened more carefully to my refinements. He was, however, a maverick by nature, and when I told him anything he was always trying to improve it before testing it.

"A perfectly remarkable mind . . . with the best memory of the periscope picture I ever met, never mind taught . . . iron nerves in the face of the oncoming frigates . . . icy sense of command under pressure . . . strange preoccupation with self-preservation . . . but a natural-born streak of daring.

"If I had to name one officer with whom I had to stand shoulder-to-shoulder in any submarine warfare situation it would be without question this lieutenant commander."

Officer's Confidential Report (See BR 8373 Chapter 12)   Revised 6/86

1. Personal Details   Date of report: 28 July 1988   Occasion for report: COQC

Date of birth	Rank	Seniority	Forenames	Surname
4/4/60	Lt Cdr	1/1/88	Benjamin	Adnam

Age	List	Commission	Spec/subspec	Ship/Establishment	Command
28	n/a	n/a	SM	Israeli Navy	n/a

Period of report   Date joined   Acting Rank   Decorations/degrees/Quals

From 2/2/1988 To 28/7/1988   4/4/88   n/a   Nil

Duties Student on Submarine Commanding Officer's Qualifying Course

2. Specialisation/Department Report   **Professional ability**   9

Adnam is the best memoriser of the surface picture through a periscope I have ever met, never mind taught, he seems to have total recall after even the briefest look. His judgement of the tactical situation is unerring, his timing immaculate and his estimates of target course and range very accurate even in poor visibility. His understanding of technical matters is as good as any I have yet seen and suggests a solid engineering background training as well as quality training in the operational skills. Professionally, Adnam is the best Perisher I have taught yet.

Signature *I.B.R.MacLean*   Name I.B.R.MacLean   Rank Cdr RN

3. General report

Of high moral standards, Adnam is an first class example of the Jewish faith without being noisy or explicit about it. Fit and quick but not easy to like or enjoy, Adnam is serious, reserved and quiet, sometimes enigmatic, but always ready with the percipient comment. He has tremendous stamina and determination. Obviously highly intelligent, he applies himself to all problems and difficulties with dedication and and diligence, finding good answers with little apparent effort. What he lacks in humour, he makes up for in sheer intellect. He displays courage, iron nerves and precise judgement in the face of oncoming frigates, indeed in face of any problem set him. He has an icy sense of command pressure, yet there remains a feeling that he has a strange pre-occupation with self-preservation. These two qualities could seem to conflict but a natural-born streak of daring carries him quickly forward where others would turn away. Although a man of many contradictions and difficult to get to know personally, if I had to name one officer with whom I had to stand shoulder-to-shoulder in any submarine warfare situation it would be without question Lt. Commander Adnam.

4. Characteristics

Attribute	Marks
a. Zeal	8
b. Reliability	8
c. Common Sense	9
d. Intelligence	9
e. Initiative	8
f. Leadership	7
g. Power of expression	7
h. Organising ability	8
i. Tact/Co-operation	6
j. Personal qualities	7
Total	77

5. Future Potential

For selective Promotion

If in zone

Now	n/a
Not yet	n/a
No	n/a
IK	n/a

If not in zone

Early	Yes
Normal course	
Late	
IK	
Not at all	

Signature *I.B.R.MacLean* Name I.B.R.MacLean   Rank Cdr RN

6. Remarks of Senior Officers   Date of Entry (Re-entry) n/a

From the little I have seen of Adnam, I am entirely confident that his Teacher is correct. His final attack on the "fast" day was a tour-de-force. I could wish the Royal Navy had a few more like him.

J.S.Breckenridge   (J.S. Breckenridge) Captain, Royal Navy.

Bill gazed anew at the signature. It was identical to three others—the handwriting unmistakably that of Commander MacLean.

He turned back to the opening page, unclipped his covering sheet, and tried to stay calm while he read through the personal details, hoping to discover a Muslim fundamentalist. But the officer was an Israeli, and a Jew.

"Fuck," Baldridge muttered to himself.

And yet a sixth sense was telling Bill Baldridge that he had found his man. This brilliant Israeli submarine officer, who had passed the course in 1988, must now be around forty-two years old. Lieutenant Commander Adnam was his name—Benjamin Adnam.

He and Lieutenant Waites glanced through the final report, another Saudi, who was not in the same league. "No natural instincts for warfare," the Teacher had written.

"Hey, we gotta go. I'll take the main file, and we'll ask the admiral if you can have a copy of the bits you want to take. I'll tell him I checked 'em through with you."

They hurried back up to FOSM's offices. Bill recounted his findings to Captain Greenwood, who sent him directly to the admiral.

The great man listened carefully, and gave permission to copy the document and allowed the American to take it with him. "It's a bit irregular," he said. "But when our closest Naval allies have taken the body-blow you chaps have . . . we'll usually bend a few rules to help out . . . now let's go and have some lunch . . . celebrate a satisfactory morning's work. Mr. Adnam, eh? Clever little bugger, by the sound of it."

The admiral and his Flag Lieutenant accompanied Bill down the stairs, and into the large officers' mess hall. The communal tables sat twelve people, and admirals mingled freely with captains, commanders, lieutenants, and lieutenant commanders. The Navy is more democratic than other services—possibly because when the bugle sounds the call of battle, senior officers do not send anyone anywhere. They all go together.

Bill Baldridge sat next to the admiral with Andrew on his

other side. Bill thoroughly enjoyed chatting with fellow officers from the Royal Navy, reveling in their wit and laughter, as they fought their way through gigantic portions of fried cod and chips. After lunch he asked Admiral Elliott if he could see Commander MacLean. "He's retired now," the admiral replied. "I relieved him in this job. Admiral MacLean lives in Scotland, quite near Faslane. But yes, certainly you may . . . might as well take the three-forty British Airways flight up to Glasgow. I'll have someone meet you. Andrew'll fix up your ticket. All we ask in return is that you keep us informed."

"Thank you, sir. I am certain we will stay in close cooperation. I really appreciate all your help."

Bill Baldridge collected his file, and a return ticket to Glasgow, which had appeared somewhat miraculously. He then said good-bye to his new friends, and the Navy driver got him to the airport with a half hour to spare. And once more the American was escorted to a double seat, with no neighbor, for the eighty-minute flight to the great shipbuilding city on the Clyde.

They touched down at Glasgow airport a little after five o'clock. The weather was much cooler, and a Royal Navy driver was again there to meet him. The man behind the wheel, Able Seaman Reginald White, turned out to be a submarine rating known to his friends as Knocker, whose home was in east London. The journey was slow, through rush-hour traffic and out across the River Clyde onto the busy A82 highway up to the Highlands. Road signs pointed to a place called Dumbarton, and quite suddenly the busy, urban character of the A82 gave way to an entirely different landscape. Where, just a few miles previously, the banks of the Clyde had been lined with shipyards, and the river itself an obvious, but rather deserted, commercial estuary, there was now a vast, glorious expanse of lonely water.

Out to his left Bill could see the Clyde become wider. To his right were low mountains which he guessed were likely to get a lot higher. He also sensed the car turning north. Quite suddenly, it seemed, the clouds vanished and he was surprised the sun was still so high.

"What's the big white building on the far shore?" he asked Knocker. "The one right at the edge of the land."

"That's the Cloch Lighthouse, sir," the man answered. "It's over at Gourock. A landmark for submariners returning to base. Just past there we make a long starboard turn toward Helensburgh—in a few minutes I'll show you our markers at the Rhu Narrows. Faslane's about four miles up from the entrance.

They sped through a little town, still hugging the shore, and Bill could see now how narrow the entrance to the great submarine loch really was. There were several channel markers and navigational buoys around, but without the chart, Bill could make little of them. As a place to bring home a damned great submarine, he considered it would present a bit of a challenge.

"Christ!" said Bill. "That is narrow. You come through here at any time of the day?"

"Yes, sir," he said. "It's a lot easier now. They widened it quite a bit for Trident—that's a really big bastard—ever seen one?"

"Uh-huh," said Bill. "Matter of fact I've been on one of our own. You're right. It's a big bastard. Where's Faslane from here?"

"Further up on the right, sir. You'll see the 'ole complex over this next 'ill."

Bill kept gazing at the peat-dark stretch of water. He was thinking how strangely deep it must be. And in his mind he envisioned one of the Royal Navy's diesel-electrics sliding through here with just her periscope showing above the surface. "Too narrow," he thought. "Can't be more than about four hundred yards across."

Staring through it was the dark-skinned, anonymous yet cruel face of Lieutenant Commander Benjamin Adnam. "You'd want to be very good indeed to command a submarine in these waters," he said slowly.

"Yessir, very good. They don't have anyone 'ere who's *not* very good. At least, not in command of a submarine, thank Christ! And the best 'ere are the best there is. Trust me."

"I believe you," said Bill Baldridge, staring again at the dark waters of the Rhu Narrows. For a while he just stared in silence. And then he said, absentmindedly, "I wonder what he looks like."

"Who? Admiral MacLean?" said Knocker cheerfully, continuing before his passenger could gather his thoughts. "He'd frighten the bloody life outta you. He was the toughest Teacher who ever served 'ere. Everyone knows that. He failed more Perishers than anyone had ever done before. They fail one in five anyway. They say ole MacLean failed about one in two.

"For some that would mean he wasn't nothing more than an ole bastard. But they say he was the best submariner there's ever been."

By now they could see the submarine base up ahead. It seemed to nestle down on the foreshore beneath the mountains. To the layman it might have looked like a sprawling factory complex. To a submariner it was unmistakable as a Navy base. Behind, to the north was a rugged Scottish mountain, the highest they had seen, jutting up into the clear blue sky, a summery green in the late sun of a July day.

"That's called 'The Cobbler,'" said Knocker helpfully. "Our main landmark comin' home. You can see it for a long way, but you get used to the shape of it, as you turn up into the Gareloch. It's got snow on its peak for about five months of the year. Must be bloody cold up there even in summer."

Bill looked up at this great natural backdrop to Europe's most sinister submarine base. It seemed to get bigger by the minute. But then suddenly they were at a guarded gateway. There was a small painted sign to the left: "ROYAL NAVY SUBMARINE BASE. FASLANE." And then, underneath, "UNAUTHORIZED PERSONS NOT ADMITTED."

Bill thought it might just as easily have said "UNAUTHORIZED PERSONS WILL BE SHOT," judging by the vigilance of the armed MOD Police guards. They must have known this was a staff car, and they must have recognized Knocker. But they treated him as a perfect stranger. One asked politely for his pass, and then handed it back with another document, for Lieutenant Commander Baldridge. Only then did the second guard step away from the front of the car.

Knocker drove through. "Bloody guards everywhere," he said. And he added, "I dunno who the 'ell would wanna break in here. Load of ole cobblers, really." Bill assumed this was a mark of general deference to Faslane's private mountain.

They pulled into a parking place outside one of the low buildings above the waterfront. Bill could see a huge nuclear submarine at the jetty, and another much smaller one about a hundred yards further along the quayside. He was still surprised by the height of the sun, and even more surprised by the sudden, damp chill in the air. Knocker led the way into the reception area and told the duty guard he was in possession of Lieutenant Commander Baldridge from America, who was here to see Admiral Sir Iain MacLean. He then told Bill that it had been nice meeting him, and he would leave his suitcase with the guard as he understood he would not be required further.

Bill shrugged, followed a guard down a short corridor into what he guessed was a private room for senior officers. Around the walls were some excellent marine paintings and on two long tables were scale models, under glass, of Royal Navy submarines. The furniture was comfortable, like a men's club— leather armchairs, polished side tables, and a leather and brass fender seat around a large fireplace, in which a big, rather garish electric fire glowed falsely at him.

To the left of the fireplace was another deep leather armchair with a slightly higher back than the others, the kind of stately chair in which one might expect to find Admiral Lord Nelson himself. Instead, there sat the unmistakable figure of Vice Admiral Sir Iain MacLean, wearing a dark gray Savile Row suit, sipping China tea, and reading the *Financial Times*.

"Lieutenant Commander Baldridge, sir," said the guard. The admiral peeped over the top of his half-spectacles, and stood up slowly. He was a tall man, all of six feet two inches, with pale blue eyes, and the kind of lined face which tends to settle upon those who have spent a lifetime at sea. His expression was one of mild amusement, and his handshake rock solid. Bill put him at around sixty. "Good afternoon, Mr. Baldridge," he said. "I understand you are interested in one of my Perishers."

Bill smiled his most disarming Midwestern grin. "Hello, Admiral," he said. "It's kind of you to come and meet me."

"No question of kindness," he replied, a bit brusquely. "I was ordered here. On what I suspect was the highest possible authority. Thought I'd done with all that. Now, sit down and let me get you a cup of tea, and I'll outline what you might describe as my game plan."

Bill sat, sipped his tea, and enjoyed the slightly perfumed taste of the Lapsang Suchong. Civilized. Relaxed. He was beginning to admire some aspects of the British way of life.

"Right," said Admiral MacLean. "Now it will be inconvenient for me to stay at the base for long. My daughter and her children are coming from Edinburgh for dinner tonight, so I propose that we finish our tea and drive over to my house in Inveraray. As the crow flies it's only about seventeen miles, but we have to go right round the lochs, which will make it thirty-five miles.

"It's not a bad road. We'll make it in just over an hour. We can go straight up the west bank of Loch Lomond, which you might find interesting. The sun does not set here until about 10 P.M. and it stays light for at least another hour. You can stay at the house for a couple of nights. And I thought we'd pop over to the base tomorrow and I'll show you around."

"Sounds good to me," said Bill. "In fact that all sounds great."

"Good. Well, it's almost six-thirty. We may as well shove off."

The admiral drove a nearly new, dark green Range Rover. In the backseat were a huge bag of golf clubs and three fishing rods. Behind the backseat, a metal grill prevented three large, exuberant, barking Labradors from crashing forward to proclaim their idolization of their master. "Fergus! Samson! Muffin! SHUT UP!" commanded the admiral.

They swung south, turned left in the middle of Helensburgh, ran for four miles back to the A82, and immediately headed north. Off to their right was the spectacular Loch Lomond, the largest lake in Great Britain, twenty-four miles long from Ardlui in the north to Balloch Castle. The admiral pointed out the big island in the middle of the five-mile-wide southern reach of the loch. "That's Inch Murrin," he said. "There's a big ruined castle right in the middle of it—the Duchess of Albany retired there back in the fifteenth century after King James I slaughtered her entire family. I always thought he was the most frightful shit, you know."

Bill Baldridge remarked that Loch Lomond, with its sensational backdrop of rolling mountains—like the coast of Maine off Camden—was just about the most beautiful stretch of water he had ever seen.

In the south, the giant loch is dotted with picturesque wooded islands, one of them, Inch Cailleach, the site of the ancient burial grounds of the ferocious MacGregor clan, whose most famous son was Rob Roy, the fabled Robin Hood of Scotland. Admiral MacLean kept his guest amused with local history as they headed on up the loch. It was not until they reached the narrow northern waters, within the three-thousand-foot shadow of the great mountain of Ben Lomond, that the Scottish officer broached the subject of his finest Perisher.

"It's Adnam you're interested in, isn't it?" he said. "I was not told why, but I was asked by FOSM to give you total cooperation. What do you want to know? And, if it's not too awkward a question, why?"

"Well, sir, we think it is just possible that the *Thomas Jefferson* was taken out by a foreign power."

"Yes, that was a thought that had crossed my mind. And you think Adnam may have been responsible?"

"I think we must assume someone was, since there was no other way to hit the carrier apart from a nuclear-tipped torpedo from a submarine."

"Yes. I see that. But why Adnam?"

"Who are our enemies around the Arabian Gulf? The list is small. Iran. Iraq. Libya. Maybe Syria. A couple of rather shaky factions in Egypt and Pakistan. Not really Russia anymore, nor even China. You would then have to say that Libya and Syria simply would not have had the right skills. Nor would Egypt, nor Pakistan. Which leaves Iran and Iraq."

"And what's that got to do with Adnam?"

"I was rather hoping you might elaborate on that for us," said Baldridge.

"That's an easy one."

"It is?"

"Yes. You've left out one of your prime suspects."

"We have? Who?"

"Israel."

"*Israel*! Christ, we finance 'em, don't we?"

"Gratitude, Bill, is like beauty, usually in the eye of the beholder. There is a very strong right-wing faction in that country—its most extreme branch took out the Prime Minister seven years ago. They have never forgiven the Americans for allowing Saddam Hussein to bombard them with those Scud missiles during the Gulf War.

"America, remember, made a promise to Israel. Bush told them that if they would not retaliate for the Scuds, he would take care of Saddam once and for all. Well, I know that in the end the Americans decided, perhaps wisely, to leave Saddam alone. But there are some very angry people in Israel. People who believe, fervently, that no enemy should be allowed to attack Israel in any way whatsoever without paying the most terrible price.

"These are people who believe, like Margaret Thatcher, that at the very least, Saddam's military equipment should have been either confiscated or destroyed, *and* that his bloody Army should have been made to surrender in complete humiliation. Well, President Bush funked it. Saddam actually claimed victory . . . no amount of American financial cooperation is ever going to erase those events from a true Israeli's mind."

"Well, I know that, sir. But what possible mileage could there be for them in wiping out a U.S. Carrier?"

"Oh, that's another easy one. They know Iraq would get the blame, and that America would exact a fierce and predictable military revenge. If not Iraq, Iran would get the blame, and suffer the consequences, which the Israelis would almost like more, because Iran, at present, is rather more dangerous. Better yet, you and I both know that this particular American President would not lose one wink of sleep if he had to hit both of them, just to make certain the right one copped it."

"Jesus. That's pretty devious."

"There are many devious regimes, Bill Baldridge. But there are no more devious people on this earth than those who work in the Hadar Dafna Building."

"The what?"

"The Hadar Dafna Building. A big tower block in King Saul Boulevard, central Tel Aviv. The home of the Israeli Institute for Intelligence and Special Operations. Known to us outsiders as the Mossad."

"You think those guys would dare to blow up a U.S. Carrier with six thousand people on board merely to get Iraq or Iran into the deepest possible trouble?"

"Oh, without doubt," said the admiral. "First of all, you have to understand the deep and abiding hatred there is between Iraq and Israel to get the full picture. Remember Saddam Hussein only once possessed a really serious nuclear reactor—that was back in 1981. He got it from the French . . . it was his most pre- cious possession—Osirak One. It worked in harmony with two other of Saddam's cherished nuclear plants. Of course he said it was for nuclear power to make electricity, but what he really wanted was the residue from the process, the end product, plu- tonium, with which he could manufacture nuclear warheads."

"Didn't the Israelis attack one of his plants?"

"Attack?" said the admiral. "Six of their fighter-bombers streaked in from the north and blew the entire operation to smithereens. In under five minutes, Osirak One was history. The Mossad takes no chances."

"Yes . . . I remember reading about it."

"The Mossad is full of people who believe that Israel has no friends. Just enemies, and those who are neutral.

"I expect you have read in recent months there have been fears about Iraq beginning a new germ-warfare program. Well, in my view, it would not be beyond the wit of the Israelis to blow up a U.S. Carrier, secretly, in the fervent hope Iraq would instantly get the blame, and that America would do their dirty work for them."

"Yes, but we think Iran is more likely."

"As I mentioned, it would delight the Mossad if America

chose to take out the Iranian submarines at Bandar Abbas. They have long felt Tehran was getting a lot too big and aggressive for its own good, and might even be capable of another major strike at Iraq . . . and if they pulled that off, it would give the Ayatollahs almost total control of the Gulf. The Israelis would not like that, not one bit."

"I'm not sure we would be mad about it either."

"Nor we."

By now the Range Rover had swung left across the northern end of Loch Long, and was making fast time through the Argyll Forest. Up to the right was the 2,700-foot peak of The Cobbler, the same mountain Bill had seen as he had approached the Faslane base.

"We're about ten miles out now," said the admiral. "In a moment we will circle around the narrow end of one of the big sea lochs. It's called Loch Fyne, runs right past our back door, but causes us to make a huge detour whenever we go anywhere. The lochs and the mountains up here are touchingly beautiful, but they add miles and miles to every journey because you always have to go around them. Down at the base, people used to dread having to drive over and see the Americans at Holy Loch. By sea it's about seven miles—twenty minutes in a fast boat. By road it's more than forty miles, right around two lochs, down the side of another, and through a range of mountains."

"Sir," said Bill suddenly, "did you develop the Israeli theory just because you knew I was interested in Lieutenant Commander Adnam? Or had you always considered it a real possibility?"

"Bill, when you are as old as I am, you will have learned that when anything really shocking happens in the Middle East, then you must look very carefully at the Israelis. Consider always their motives, how events will affect them, and remember always they are much cleverer, much tougher, and much more efficient than every other nation in the area.

"Also do not close your eyes to the fact that both their government and their Secret Service are crammed full of people with very long memories.

"Inside the government alone, there are women who just over twenty-five years ago stood on the slopes of the Golan Heights, under terrible fire from the Syrian tanks . . . they struggled through a night of sheer terror, in lines of frightened girl-soldiers passing artillery shells up to the gunners, helping the Israeli 7th Armored Brigade claw back the land, with heart-breaking courage, yard by yard, up those mountains.

"Take Benjamin Netanyahu, the most eloquent of the senior Israeli politicians in recent years. Remember his brother Jonathon was the only Israeli killed when the Israeli commandos went into Entebbe Airport to rescue the hijacked airliner. Benjamin never got over that, that's why he is such a fierce nationalist.

"There are departmental chiefs in the Mossad who fought shoulder to shoulder with General Avraham Yoffe when they smashed their way through the Mitla Pass, with unbelievable bravery, in the Six-Day War in 1967—six days in which the Israelis destroyed four armies and 370 fighter aircraft belonging to four attacking nations.

"There are men in the Mossad who stood alongside my great friend General Sharon in 1973, men who were wounded as their comrades fought and died in the desert, trying to throw back the armies of Egypt. None of them ever forgot the hand-wringing response of the West after their costly and frightening victory . . . accused them of bullying—bullying after the Egyptians stormed across the canal with five hundred tanks, just as the entire Israeli nation knelt in prayer, on their most holy day of the year.

"I don't want to sound like a retired Israeli general, but I am warning you, and your colleagues, to take a damn close look at anything which might involve the Israelis. I believe it is perfectly possible they might have taken out your carrier—just to watch the U.S.A. exact a fierce revenge on either Iraq or Iran, or for that matter, knowing your President, both of them.

"Ask me who drove their submarine? I should say without any hesitation—Benjamin Adnam. There are very few commanders who have the talent for such an operation. But he had it. Did he ever."

"How good was he, Admiral? What was it about him?" asked Baldridge.

"I think there was a fanaticism about him. There was something that drove him. He did not just want to be the best in his class, he wanted to be the best there had ever been. He had the most phenomenal memory . . . the first time I ever tested him on the periscope . . . you know, giving him a thirty-second all-around look at the surface picture, he could recall every single detail. The submarine commander's greatest asset is his ability to store a photograph of that view in his mind. Ben Adnam could hold that picture better than anyone I ever taught.

"He had an instinct for a submarine, for what it would do, and what it wouldn't. We have one exercise where we send three frigates away, and then have them turn around and come back toward us.

"The frigates often come straight at the Perishers, so they have to dive to safe depth underneath. They are instructed to do so with exactly one minute to go before collision. Even then, the noise of the frigates' propellers rumbling overhead is damned nerve-racking. There are always chaps who fail the course right there. You can see them with their eyes shut, praying the overhead warship will not slam into the conning tower.

"Adnam was absolutely fearless. Consciously so. He knew the distance, he could make all the calculations in his head, quickly and effortlessly. It would never have occurred to him that a frigate could hit his ship. He would have made bloody certain it didn't.

"He had his own private sixth sense. I remember standing with him one lunchtime while the frigates were going away. Suddenly, for no reason, he said, 'I believe the frigates have turned, sir.'

"Now I knew they had turned. I had discerned the faint change in the Doppler of the sonar. That comes with about twenty years of being a submarine officer and commander. I plainly knew they had turned, but God knows how he knew. Nonetheless, he did. I tested him on it. He was always correct. He was a submarine genius. Of that there is absolutely no doubt.

"He had a sound grasp of all the workings of the ship underwater . . . hydrosystems, mechanics, electronics, weaponry, missiles, torpedoes, and gunnery. He could navigate as well. I once lectured them on the art of the classic sprint-and-drift submarine attack. At the end of it he came and had a chat with me about the finer points.

"No Perisher in my entire experience ever demonstrated a more thorough grasp of the subject. Even at that comparatively young age—around twenty-eight—he was safe. He was steady. And he could handle his machine as a weapon of war.

"He just had an instinct for underwater warfare, and he was, technically, its master. But there was something more. He had a gift. And I always knew he was ruthless. I can tell you this, if he had been British, and if he had stayed in the submarine service, he would have become FOSM—and if we had ever had to send the Submarine Flotilla to war, Ben Adnam would have been a very good man to command it."

"Aside from that, I guess he was pretty average all around?" chuckled Bill. "Did he have any weakness at all?"

"Only one."

"Oh . . . what was it?"

"He was in love with my daughter."

The laid-back Kansan manner of Bill Baldridge fell from him in an instant. He turned quickly to the admiral and asked, "Is she still in touch with him?"

"She is now a highly respectable lady, married to a wealthy Edinburgh banker. Two children."

"Yes, but is she still in touch with Adnam?" Bill persisted.

"I've always been afraid she might be," replied Admiral MacLean. "You can ask her yourself in a minute. She ought to be arriving with the children at about the same time as we do.

"I always wondered whether their affair went on after she was married, long after he returned to Israel. She once left mysteriously for a short vacation, and my wife found an entry to Cairo in an old passport. However, I shall deny I ever said those last sentences. You'll have to ask her."

"You wouldn't mind if I did?"

"Certainly not. If my daughter has a line of communication to perhaps the most ruthless mass murderer in recent history, I will insist she recognizes her duty."

At this point the car pulled into the drive of a white Georgian house on the outskirts of Inveraray. Bill guessed that the admiral had not purchased it on the proceeds of his Navy salary, any more than he himself could have purchased the Baldridge Ranch out in Pawnee County. He either inherited this, or else Lady MacLean is loaded, was his considered opinion, as he climbed out of the Range Rover.

The admiral seemed to read his thoughts. He loosed the three Labradors who charged around the house toward the loch. He grabbed Bill's suitcase, and said, "Inherited this. It belonged to my father and my grandfather. Family have lived around here for generations. I retired a couple of years ago—they weren't going to make me First Sea Lord, but they would have offered me Commander-in-Chief Naval Home Command.

"I considered it . . . but decided I didn't much want a desk job in the bloody dockyard in Portsmouth. Preferred to come home really, and spend my declining years playing a bit of golf, fishing, sailing on the loch, and doing a bit of shooting. An admiral's pension is perfectly adequate for living in Scotland, and Annie and I have a lot of friends up here. When they didn't offer me the top job, it just seemed the right time to go. So I went."

They walked through the front door to be greeted by the same three Labradors, who had charged right around the house, and were now skidding over the big Persian rug in the hall, being yelled at by a trim, elegant, blond lady in a tartan skirt, white shirt, and camel-colored sweater.

"I'd be so grateful if you could control these bloody animals," she said to her husband, as all three began leaping up on the American visitor.

Then turning to Bill, she introduced herself. "Commander Baldridge? Good evening. I'm Annie MacLean. I'm delighted to meet you. Leave your case right there. I'll get Angus to take it upstairs in a minute."

She must, thought Bill, have been the perfect admiral's wife.

Very like Grace Dunsmore in manner. Brisk, confident, and friendly. High-ranking Navy officers usually have wives of that type; poised and highly skilled at making people feel at home. It goes with the territory. Years of nursing young officers and their wives through daunting social occasions, knowing they are terrified of one's husband. Meanwhile Bill leaned down and managed to greet Fergus, Samson, and Muffin all at once, patting them with a practiced, friendly roughness, the way Labradors expect to be treated.

"You a countryman, Bill?" asked the admiral, observing his ease with the boisterous dogs.

"Yessir," replied the Kansan. "I'm from the Midwest. Family raises cattle out there."

"They do? Then you're a real countryman."

They chatted for a while about the High Plains, and then the admiral said, "Now, why don't you go upstairs and move into your room, and then meet me in there in fifteen minutes." He pointed to a white-painted door on the left side of the hall, and added, "I'll pour you a decent glass of malt whisky. Don't dress."

Bill correctly assumed this meant no need for uniform at dinner, so he climbed the stairs hoping the unseen Angus had dealt with his suitcase. He had. Everything had been unpacked and placed in a tall Sheraton tallboy, dirty clothes removed, washing kit laid out in the bathroom.

The bedroom itself overlooked Loch Fyne. And although it was still light, there was a thin beeswax-colored mist laying low across the water. The room was decorated with English chintz, bluish and pink in tone, but the main window was a bay, with a little antique desk and chair. There was no shower in the bathroom, so he tipped half a jar of fragrant blue crystals into the tub, filled it with hot water, and hopped in. When he emerged five minutes later, he dressed in dark gray slacks, white shirt and tie, with a dark blue blazer. Downstairs the admiral had poured the promised malt whisky. "Water?" he asked as Bill came in the door.

"Thank you, sir," replied the American.

"I am no longer a serving officer," Admiral MacLean said.

"Please call me Iain. My wife expects you to call her Annie. My daughter, when she shows up in a minute, is Laura."

Because Bill Baldridge had grown up with a certain amount of deference, as the son of one of the biggest ranchers in central Kansas, and later as a highly respected submarine weapons specialist in the Navy, not to mention his entitlement to be addressed as "Dr. Baldridge"—certainly within the hallowed confines of MIT—he never gave a thought to the sudden intimacy he now enjoyed with this very grand Scottish family.

He was unaware of the rigidity of the British class system, how by some unknown radioactivity, Admiral Sir Iain MacLean and Lady MacLean both knew instinctively that he was, despite the huge distance apart of their worlds, of their class.

But before either the wife or the daughter arrived, there was one question Bill wanted to put to the admiral. He sipped his whiskey, interested in its deep smoky flavor, and said, "Admiral, tell me something. Which nation do *you* think hit the *Jefferson?*"

Iain MacLean smiled and said quietly, "I do not like answering a question with a question. But you've obviously checked whether all three of the Iranians' Russian Kilos were still anchored at Bandar Abbas?"

"Yes, we have. There were three of them on the Friday before the hit. But only two on the following Wednesday."

"Then I make Iran my number-one suspect. It is possible to hide a Kilo. And if they have done so, then I would consider they had made the hit from another source. Maybe a fourth Kilo we do not know about yet. Either way I would consider their behavior suspicious in the extreme.

"Also we should remember the unprecedented activity there has been from the Iranian Navy in recent years. Back in 1993 they conducted thirty-six exercises in the Gulf. They have now conducted more than sixty. They have conducted joint exercises with Pakistan. And they are making closer and closer ties with Oman, with whom they control the Strait of Hormuz.

"They are the only Gulf state to have a known, workable submarine capability. I expect you remember three years ago, when there was a delay in the U.S. Carrier Battle Group arriving on station in the Arabian Sea, the U.S. put eighteen F–16 fighter air-craft on Bahrain as a precautionary measure. Remember also, the Iranian Navy operates under a single command—that of the Islamic Revolutionary Guards Corps.

"This is only a personal opinion from an old, fairly unimportant submarine driver. But if I were the President, I should consider that now would be a very timely opportunity to frighten the living daylights out of them. And I'd be inclined to do it very, very soon."

Baldridge, who, since leaving Faslane, was receiving the best lesson in modern warfare history he had ever had, was loving this talk. But he kept his eye firmly on the ball. He smiled and nodded in agreement. Then he said: "Who would be your second choice, sir?"

"Well," he said, "I'm not sure where Iraq would put a submarine after the mission. No one has seen it, and they plainly have not scuttled it, otherwise someone would have found wreckage. So I would have to say, Israel would be very high on my list. As things stand I imagine the Americans are anxious to get rid of Bandar Abbas as a submarine base, which of course is precisely what the Mossad would love."

"One more thing, sir. Where do you think the submarine came from—the one which destroyed the *Jefferson*?"

"Well, I am certain it's not British. So it has to be Russian. I'd say it came from the Black Sea."

"But how did they get it? Did they buy it? Rent it? And how did they get it out?"

"I'm not sure how they got it. But those Naval ports are full of the old Soviet Navy personnel, who rarely get paid. Men from the Middle East bearing gifts, like millions of dollars, would doubtless get a proper welcome in poverty-stricken communities like those."

"But how did they drive it out?"

"Oh, straight through the Bosporus," said the admiral crisply. "A deal with the Turks."

"Admiral Morgan says the Turks say emphatically not."

"Hmmmmm."

"Admiral, could they have got it out underwater through the Bosporus?"

"I doubt it. No one ever has."

"Could Ben Adnam have done it?"

But there was no time for an answer. The door pushed open, and a voice said softly, "Hello, Daddy . . . Commander Baldridge."

Bill turned and saw a slender woman in her mid–thirties. She had long dark hair that fell below her shoulders, and her face was gentle as well as striking. She gazed at Bill with a mildly amused expression. "I haven't met many Americans," she said.

But the Kansan seemed slightly lost for words. He just stared into a perfect pair of calm, green eyes—perhaps, he thought, belonging to the lover of the man who had murdered his brother Jack.

2030 Monday, July 15.

D INNER AT THE GRAND LOCHSIDE HOME OF SIR IAIN and Lady MacLean was not, Bill thought, too shabby. It was served by the white-coated and red-bearded Angus, in a fifty-foot-long dining room with southerly views toward Strachur and the Cowal Hills. Annie had seated them, as a four, on a long, highly polished antique table, she and her husband facing across to Laura and Bill. Behind the American was a magnificent Georgian sideboard where a two-foot-long, perfectly cooked Scottish salmon had been laid out with a dish of new potatoes and another of fresh peas. In the center of the table were two silver dishes filled with mayonnaise.

Bill guessed, correctly, that the admiral had caught the salmon. "Would you like me to serve everyone, sir?" asked Angus.

"Oh yes, a bit of everything for everyone." Then to Bill he added, "I never bother with a first course with salmon. Everybody would much rather have another bit of fish if they're still hungry. Landed this one up on the Tay two days ago."

"That's a heck of a fish, sir," said Bill. "My brother was a fisherman, but he never caught anything like this on our local rivers in Kansas."

The admiral looked up sharply. "You said 'was'—you mean he's given up the greatest art of the sportsman?"

"No, Admiral, I thought you knew. My brother Jack was the Group Operations Officer in the *Thomas Jefferson.*"

"Good Lord, Bill. I am sorry. No one told me, and they should have."

"How absolutely awful," said Laura, speaking for the first time. "Is that any connection with why you are here? Conducting some sort of investigation?"

"Well, in a way I am. But it's nothing to do with Jack. There are hundreds of people in the Navy who had relatives on the carrier, and thousands more outside."

"I don't suppose it makes it any easier though," she said. "Shared grief never lessens it."

"No, ma'am. It does not."

Laura looked at the sadness in his face. He really was, she thought, a very captivating man, not obviously married, and with the conspicuously cavalier air, and wayward eye, of so many submariners. Especially one other. Married mother-of-two or not, Laura assessed Lieutenant Commander Baldridge as a potentially dangerous presence in her life. Only once before had she met anyone with such instant allure.

She was surprised when he smiled at her. "I'm beginning to adjust to the tragedy now, after a week. But I'll never get used to not seeing Jack . . . not ever. He was one hell of an officer."

"I suppose it'll be up to you to carry on the family tradition now."

"Not really. I'm leaving the Navy after this investigation. Going home to Kansas."

"Will you miss all the excitement?"

"No. I don't think so. I've gone about as far as I'm going in dark blue. They are not going to give me a full command."

"Upset one too many old admirals," she laughed. "That's a good way to conclude a promising career. At least it is here."

"You might be right at that."

"Bill," said the admiral, "if you would like to ask Laura a few questions, I am afraid we are going to have to confide in her. But don't worry. She's spent quite enough of her life in and around the Navy to know what can be repeated and what can't."

Bill tried to wheel the conversation out of its corner. He turned to her and smiled. "Now where are these two children I've been hearing about?"

"Oh, they're with Brigitte on their way to bed. They're very young, three and five. After the long drive over here from Edinburgh I've just about had them for the day. I said good night before dinner. Their grandma is going up to see them in a minute—I hope."

"I guess Brigitte would be the nanny. I never met a proper English nanny."

"You're not going to tonight either," replied Laura. "Brigitte is from Sweden. She's an *au pair*."

Then her face clouded over, and she said suddenly, "It's Ben, isn't it? That's who you've come about."

Bill glanced at the admiral, who skillfully changed the subject. "Now, what would you all like to drink? There's a bottle of cold Meursault here, and I opened a bottle of claret a while ago . . . Annie always drinks white wine with fish, so I know what she will have. But I don't think white wine is mandatory with all fish. Matter of fact I prefer Bordeaux with salmon and that's what I'm having."

Bill was really growing to like the admiral. "If it's Bordeaux for you, it's Bordeaux for me," he grinned.

"And me," chimed in Laura.

"What can I tell you about Ben Adnam?" Laura asked after the wine had been poured.

Her father interrupted. "Laura, if it's all right with you, I was proposing to leave you here with Bill for half an hour, after dinner, so you can answer his questions, or not, as you wish, in private. I think your mother would prefer not to have old memories . . . er . . . rekindled."

"But, Admiral, there's something I did want to ask you," said Bill. "Why does everyone nearly have a heart attack at the mere thought of going through the Bosporus underwater? I don't get it. It can't be that dangerous, can it?"

"Yes. Yes, it can," said the admiral, slowly. "Which is presumably why no one has ever even tried, never mind failed."

"But why? What's so dangerous about it? It's pretty wide, isn't it? It's a kind of bay, right?"

The admiral smiled patiently. "In a way you are asking precisely the correct man," he said. "I have been following various reports of Russians exporting ships to Middle Eastern nations for a couple of years. There's been nothing but trouble over the submarine sales, especially to Iran, and some months ago I got Droggy to send me his latest chart of the Bosporus. Just to familiarize myself with the sheer difficulty of *anyone, ever* getting out through there, in a submarine, dived . . . just an academic exercise for an elderly retired officer with time on his hands."

"Then I have two critical questions," said Bill. "First, who the hell's Droggy? Second, can you tell me about the Bosporus?"

"Certainly I can. Droggy is our jargon for the hydrographer of the Navy. As for the Bosporus, I have been extremely anxious about this for some months . . . thought no one would ever ask me to drone on about my new favorite subject . . . do you have a couple of months to spare?"

"Sure I do, but I guess the Pentagon might wanna hear from me before September, Admiral."

They both laughed, but the admiral was serious. "The trouble with modern submariners like you," he said, "is that you think the entire world runs on computers, that your search-sensors and electronic technology will give you everything you need. But you, Bill, and your fellow American submariners, these days are essentially big-ship, deep-ocean men. And all of your kit is designed for that.

"Tackling the Bosporus requires inshore skills, which your Navy has largely thrown away. You haven't trained for them for years, and, if we're not bloody careful here, we'll be doing the same.

"Shallow water work involves a complete culture change, because so many things are completely different. For a start, your long-range sensors are useless, so you often receive no warning of approaching danger. As you know, charts and surveys get out of date. You must have the best and the latest, and make full use of them. Because, when you are operating close to shore, you are no longer sweeping like the cavalry across a wide uncluttered plain, you are groping about in the forest, like a bloody infantryman. So you have to know your ground.

"That entails extremely accurate navigation—to five meters vertical, and fifty meters horizontal. Inshore, you've got to use your eyes. And remember, above all, you've lost the advantage of high speed, particularly to escape, if you've been careless. You simply can't go fast, with the bottom that close.

"And something else you may not know, Bill—you make twenty knots at two hundred feet, and you'll leave a clear wake on the surface for all to see.

"Only stealth, stealth and cunning, above anything you have ever done before, will keep you safe."

The American officer had never heard anyone speak like that. The admiral who faced him came from a different culture all right. A different world, and one which might ultimately lead to the master's finest pupil, perhaps to the man who had found a way to destroy the *Thomas Jefferson*. Admiral MacLean no doubt told the young Adnam to use his eyes. "But," thought Baldridge, "he sure as hell must have done a lot of listening."

Laura sighed gently. Her mother smiled the smile of the deeply tolerant. Unlike the American, they were very familiar with this particular lecture. And the admiral, visibly warming to his theme, pressed on, his focus now on the dark, swirling waters of the Bosporus.

"It's a nasty little stretch," he muttered. "Not very wide for much of the way. And not very deep. There are parts which are very, very shallow for a submarine, right on the limits. Also it's busy, almost all of the time, with deep-draft freighters going each way.

"The channel is divided into two lanes, and of course you keep right. Overtaking is prohibited. And running south it's often bloody difficult to stop. Imagine a seven-knot current in the narrowest bit.

"Err to starboard, and you're on the putty. Err to port, and you're likely to have a head-on collision. In the most dangerous part, it's too shallow to go deep, under an oncoming freighter. Also there's a problem with a couple of wrecks, and I have my own doubts about the charting of the bottom. The soundings are a bit far apart for my taste."

At this point, the senior submariner began adjusting the dessert spoons and forks into a zigzag shape next to a mayonnaise dish.

"Remember," he said, pointing to the tablecloth with his knife. "You are navigating underwater, in the pitch dark, and there is a big S-bend about one third of the way down from the Black Sea . . . right here . . . parts of that are especially narrow. On either side there are shoals less than fifty feet deep." He tapped the mayonnaise dish sharply with his fish knife. "If you stray out of your channel, which is less than a couple of hundred yards wide, you'll hit the bank, and find yourself stuck on the surface, hard aground, in full view of everyone. And that would be very moderate news indeed.

"Assuming you get through the S-bend, the south-going channel really closes in, immediately afterward, to its narrowest part, less than two hundred yards across. And that's obviously where the current is at its worst, as the water surges through the bottleneck.

"Running on down under the second bridge, there's a damn great sandbank, bang in the middle of the south channel. The bottom comes up to eighty feet, which makes it impossible to duck under anything larger than a motorboat. And, to make it worse, there are already two bloody wrecks on that bank—one of them only forty-five feet down.

"Looking at the chart, I would prefer to pick my moment, to hurry down the deeper north-going lane, if I could time it between the oncoming freighters and tankers. But that's bloody dangerous, as you know.

"Also the entire exercise is illegal. Under the Montreux Convention, the Turks don't allow it. For any warships, of any nation. And they have a perfect right to stop any warship of any nation which has not given due notice, weeks in advance, of their intention to transit the Bosporus.

"You still want to know why people have heart attacks at the very notion of going through the Bosporus underwater? Because, it's not just bloody difficult and bloody dangerous, but if Johnny Turk catches you he'll be bloody-minded, to say the least."

"Are you telling me it really is impossible?"

"Not quite, Bill. But you need a master submariner for the job. Of my generation there are probably three, Admiral Elliott, whom you met. Me, just. And possibly Captain Greenwood, who's apt to get overexcited, but he might make it."

"And how about your best-ever Perisher?"

"Yes, of course."

"That's Ben, isn't it?" asked Laura.

"That's Ben."

"But why are you asking about him?"

"Later," said her father. "Bill will explain to you."

Laura smiled, plainly not considering that particular prospect akin to a sentence of death. "Very well, then," she said. "Mrs. Laura Anderson, mother of Flora and Mary, will reserve her answers for private interrogation by the United States Navy sometime after ten o'clock in the admiral's study."

"That, by the way, means that my daughter thinks you and she are going to sit by the fire and drink my best vintage port," said the admiral. "Like the Turks with the Bosporus, I like to keep a firm hand on the stopper."

"Guess so," said Bill. "You could get your cattle rustled real quick from what I can see."

Laura debated giving the American a cozy nudge with her elbow, but decided against it, on the grounds that her watchful mother would regard such an action as flirtatious for a married lady.

The admiral himself moved the subject forward, inquiring whether Bill had time for a day at sea. "This is one of the best submarine training areas in the world, particularly for shallow waters."

"Admiral, I'd really appreciate that. It's funny how insular our profession can be . . . we all share the same goals . . . but we get so far apart."

"Fine. I fixed it yesterday. We'll need an early start. Get on board by nine."

The remainder of dinner passed quickly. The Kansan glanced at his watch and saw that it was after ten, and Laura caught him doing so. "I think the U.S. Navy may be tiring," she said, pushing her chair back. "I'll just help Mum for a few minutes, then I'll be in to face my cross-examination. There's a decanter on the drinks trolley, pour a couple of glasses of that port, before Daddy confiscates it."

Bill Baldridge did as he was told. He thanked the admiral for a delicious dinner, and wished his hosts a good night. They arranged to meet for breakfast at 0715 the following morning.

Inside the book-lined study, Bill found the port, poured two glasses, and sat by the fire. Laura arrived after ten minutes, her hair freshly combed, and wearing fresh lipstick. She sat elegantly in the opposite armchair, crossed her slender legs and said, a bit too softly, "Okay, Lieutenant Commander, I'm all yours."

Bill found himself wishing, profoundly, that this was indeed so. But before him sat the lady who might help him find the man who might have vaporized the *Thomas Jefferson*. Laura might be, he knew, the only line of communication they would ever have to the world's most lethal terrorist.

He decided to tell her the reason for his visit, and he began carefully. "Laura," he said, "as you know there was a most terrible accident on one of our aircraft carriers a week ago. We do not, however, think it was quite that simple. We think a Middle Eastern power blew up the carrier. We think the missile which destroyed it was a torpedo, tipped with a nuclear warhead, and fired from a submarine. There are very, very few men who could have accomplished that. I think Commander Benjamin Adnam may have been the driver."

"Ben! But he's an Israeli. His home is in Tel Aviv. America is the great supporter of Israel. Why would anyone wish to attack their own most loyal ally?"

Bill shook his head. Then he said, "Tell me about him, Laura. What kind of man was he?"

"Well . . . he was only five feet nine, more heavily built than you, with jet-black curly hair, trimmed pretty tight. His eyes were dark, almost black. He did not have that swarthy Middle Eastern complexion; his skin was coffee-colored, soft, looked as if he never needed to shave.

"When I first met Ben I thought he was the best-looking man I had ever seen. I was in love with him, you know. He was my first love . . . my only love really."

Bill sipped his port. "But what about Mr. Anderson?"

"Mistake. Serious." Laura spoke with shuddering frankness, perhaps feeling more assured under the warm, age-old spell of the most opulent ruby wine from Portugal. "When Ben left Faslane for Israel after two years, I believed I would never see him again, whatever he said. And I thought I would die of a broken heart. I did not go out for eighteen months. My mother thought I was having a nervous breakdown. She hated Ben for what he had done to her darling daughter. But she was bloody glad when he left, and she would have died if I'd married him. But that was never going to happen, we never even discussed it.

"Anyway I used to go shooting with Dad from time to time, and I met Douglas up near Jedburgh on the borders. He was the son of a local landowner, and we used to have lunch together. Everyone else was much older. He made few demands on me, I had no interest in seeing anyone else, and after a couple of years I agreed to marry him. Everyone was delighted and my mother arranged a huge wedding.

"Then it happened. Ben phoned me the night before I was to marry. He told me he still loved me and wanted to see me. Of course I could not agree to that, and I told Ben so. But it nearly broke my heart all over again, and at the time I became Mrs. Douglas Anderson, I could not have cared less if I'd never seen my new husband again. He was very sweet and kind. And rich. But I should never have gone through with the wedding because I felt nothing for him."

Laura Anderson did not have the slightest idea why she was pouring out her soul to this near-stranger from Kansas, and she could hardly justify it by telling herself it was probably in the national interest.

Bill Baldridge shook his head in bewilderment, and turned the subject back to Ben, which was not a great test of ingenuity. "Did you ever see the Israeli again?"

"Twice. Once I went to meet him in Cairo while Douglas was away at some financial conference. And once about a year ago when Ben came back to Faslane with three other Israeli officers to train on the Upholder Class submarine their Navy had purchased. He was a full commander by this time.

"It was strange, but the sheer overpowering nature of the deceit . . . we drove up to a hotel in the Highlands . . . It had a bad effect on both of us. I was worried stiff that either my mother, my father, or even my husband was going to walk right through the door and catch us.

"When we parted I had a funny feeling I really would not see him again. And so far I haven't. He has called me a couple of times. But I don't think either of us feels the same as we once did. The long, long separation, and the duplicity of the relationship, has proved a bit too much for both of us. He is serving in the Navy, God knows where, and I am left with poor Douglas, a good-looking, highly respected forty-year-old banker who leaves me stone cold. He knows it too, I am afraid. I wouldn't blame him if he ran off with his secretary!"

"Do you have an address or phone number for Ben?"

"No. I have never had that since he left here after the Perisher. He was a bit secretive as a matter of fact. I asked him many times if there was anywhere I could just send him a letter, or even a postcard. But he always said it was a bit too complicated."

"Laura, are you sure he was an Israeli?"

"It's never occurred to me that he was anything else. He was here as an Israeli Naval Officer. How could he have been anything else?"

"Dunno," said Bill. "But the Middle East is a strange place. A few days before the Gulf War began, Saddam Hussein swore to his fellow Arab, near neighbor and apparent friend and ally, President Mubarak of Egypt, that he would not attack Kuwait. The truth is an elusive commodity once you move east of the Greek islands.

"Was there ever anything, in all the time you knew Ben, that might suggest he could have been originally from another nation?"

"No. Not really. The only thing I ever wondered about was his sympathetic view of the Arabian nations, even over terrorism. You never would have described him as fanatically anti-Arab—and he was not at all religious.

"But now I look back, there is something else. I saw him only that one time in Cairo. But there were several other times when we discussed meeting, and he always wanted it to be Cairo. Never anywhere in Israel. Is that a bit odd? I don't know. But I never thought he might be an Egyptian."

"Did he ever tell you anything about his very early life?"

"Yes. He went to school here in England—a boarding school in Kent, so I suppose his parents must have had some money. But he did not go to university here—he went back to Israel at the age of eighteen, after his A-levels—they're English exams—and from what I gathered, joined the Navy right away. He told me when he arrived in Faslane it was his first visit to the U.K. since he left school."

"Was there anything else, other than being an Israeli, which set him apart from the rest of his Perisher class?"

"Not really. But he did bring over a nice new car. A small red BMW."

"Was he popular, being cleverer than everyone else?"

"Not really. Ben had no interest in anything which he judged to be trivia. He had no polite small-talk—which my mother detested about him. If there was a birthday party, he would attend, and bring an expensive, thoughtful present. But he seemed always to be on the sidelines. Slightly preoccupied."

"Why did you love him so much?"

"Because to my young eyes he looked like a God. I was only nineteen. He was twenty-seven, the outstanding young commander of his group, rich enough to take me to nice places, the only one with a new car, and a man who could fascinate me with stories of Middle Eastern countries I had never seen. He was charming. What he lacked was vulnerability. To a woman, I suspect that is deeply unattractive. But to a nineteen-year-old girl, just out of a London secretarial college, it was very, very special. I don't suppose I would react in anything like that way if I met him for the first time now."

"Could you imagine him being sufficiently ruthless to blow up an aircraft carrier with six thousand men on board?"

Laura hesitated. Then she said, "No, Bill. Not when you put it like that. But there was a coolness, an efficiency, a determination. There was a strength about Ben, if he thought it was his duty, to sink an American aircraft carrier . . . he'd do it.

"On the other hand, he had a very engaging smile. And he could be witty about things. You might even think he was a relaxed and confident man.

"But when I really got to know him I noticed his eyes were seldom still. There was a certain wariness there. And sometimes I would catch him casting his eyes around some fancy restaurant. And then he would smile his gleaming smile at me, and make some joke. I never really thought he was interested in other women, it was just that he was so watchful, of everything.

"I used to call it his Periscope habit, taking an all-round look every few minutes. Even a Naval genius like Ben had to keep practicing, I suppose."

"Did he ever mention his parents?"

"Not really. Just that they lived in the country somewhere in Israel. I think they grew fruit, melons and things . . . but he sometimes mentioned that he had business with his family's bank in London. He went there about once a month, usually on the train from Glasgow."

"Did he have any other close friends in England, or Scotland?"

"No one here. He was not that popular. And he never mentioned anyone he even knew, in London or anywhere. I don't think he ever introduced me to anyone."

"When did you last hear from him?"

"I had one phone call about two months after he left the Upholder Class course. I was away, with Douglas and the girls, just for a weekend. When he got no reply from our house in Edinburgh, he phoned me here. Mummy was absolutely furious, but she said she was polite. Anyway I have not heard one word since—which is a bit unusual . . . the longest time he has ever been out of touch . . . Mummy probably told him he was the biggest bastard she had ever met, or something equally subtle. But she says not. I think Ben may finally have vanished from my life."

"Will you tell me about Egypt?"

"That was after I had been married for about four years—about fourteen months before Flora was born. Douglas was going to a bankers' seminar in Montreal. I had six days to myself. We planned it three months in advance. I flew all the way from Glasgow, changed planes at London Airport for Cairo. Ben arranged for me to pick up the Egypt ticket at the KLM desk."

Bill sat listening to her, thinking how much like a schoolgirl she still sounded; thinking about Ben Adnam, the big Mercedes in which he had met her at Cairo Airport, the uniformed driver, the long evening ride out to the plateau of Giza, the suite in the fabled Mena House Hotel, with its balcony view looking out to the mightiest of human achievements, stark against the desert skyline since the dawn of history.

"I'll never forget seeing the pyramids for the first time," Laura said. "I stood there, staring through that balcony window. I was alone, gazing out at five thousand years of the past, hearing in my mind the voice of the desert . . . Ben had gone downstairs to send a fax or something. It was the most romantic place in the world for an awestruck Scottish girl, and a rather cold, unromantic Navy officer. But I suppose he must have had some romance in him, otherwise he would not have brought me there. Anyway, when you've had a sheltered upbringing like mine was, your first lover can't usually do much wrong, so I suppose I had a wonderful time."

"Try to think, Laura. Was there anything that happened in Egypt that you thought was in any way unusual? Anything you can think of?"

"I don't think so . . . except we went one afternoon to a mosque."

"You did what?"

"We went to a mosque. We were sightseeing in Cairo and Ben had his driver take us down to see the Citadel, an amazing castle built originally by Saladin, I think. We then walked up to the Mohammed Ali Mosque—the most beautiful building, one of the great landmarks of Cairo. You can see it for miles because of the twin minarets, so slim they look as if they might break off. They rise high above the huge dome of the mosque itself."

Bill kept very quiet. He just said, "Go on."

"Well, it wasn't much really. I did want to go in. But Ben said he thought that might not be appropriate, for two infidels to enter a holy place of Muslim prayer. There was a little bookshop there, and I said I was going to see if I could find something to buy, to remind me of this place when I was back in Scotland.

"He said 'okay,' he'd meet me back by the entrance, because he wanted to see a view across the city. Well, I went to the book-shop, and spent about twenty minutes there, talking to the old man who ran it . . . I remember he told me he had been in the Egyptian Air Force during the Six-Day War with Israel.

"Anyway I was just walking across the courtyard to meet Ben, when I saw him slip out of a side door to the mosque, I thought a bit furtively. I stopped dead and watched him put his shoes on again. I've never thought much about it really, but I suppose you don't get many Israelis at prayer in an Arab mosque."

"Nope, I don't guess you do," said Bill Baldridge. "Did he say anything . . . make an excuse maybe?"

"Yes. He just said he thought he saw someone he knew, but turned out to be mistaken."

"I suppose he might have been telling the truth, but it doesn't really add up—an Israeli officer in a mosque, even seeing some-one he knew in the mosque, all seems a bit unlikely. And also, a brief holiday in the Mena House—that's pretty rich living for the son of a melon grower, especially one who is apparently living on the famously low salary of an Israeli serviceman."

"Yes, it was a very lavish hotel—and Ben seemed very at home there, as if he knew some of the staff. At the time I thought he had just been there a couple of days before I arrived, but there was one night when we had a drink in the garden with the manager, who seemed awfully important."

"Laura, it seems with hindsight such a bizarre place for an Israeli to be—in the heart of the Cairo establishment . . . Christ, that was where Jimmy Carter met President Anwar Sadat. Kissinger met the Egyptians there. I was reading a magazine article the other day about Nixon's Middle East policy. He stayed at the Mena House, and it mentioned that it was President Roosevelt's favorite hotel. God knows how many foreign kings have stayed there. It's an Arab institution. What's Benjamin Adnam doing there, unless he was really an Arab?"

"I can't answer that. But you have reminded me of a strange conversation we once had at the Mena House. I can't remember any of the exact words, but I do remember him saying something like, 'My masters probably would not approve of my being here so publicly with an English admiral's daughter. They might think it a bit indiscreet.'

"I asked him why, and he just went rather thoughtful, and very steely. He said something like, 'But my masters can be replaced anytime. I, on the other hand, cannot be replaced.'

"It was not the arrogance that surprised me. Ben always had a touch of arrogance, even bravado, just under the surface. I'm a bit ashamed to say how attractive I found it at the time. But it was the use of the word 'masters' that should have given me just a touch of suspicion. I've just never heard any Naval officer use those words before, not in that context. I've always remembered Ben saying it."

"Funny that, Laura. I've never heard a U.S. Naval officer use it either. I continue to wonder precisely who Ben really was."

"You really do think he was not what he said he was?"

"I do. Not least because your father thinks there are less than half a dozen men on earth who could have blown up our aircraft carrier. And he thinks Ben might have been one of them. And an Arab is a much better bet than an Israeli."

"Just after I was married Ben phoned and asked me to meet him but I couldn't. He said Cairo that time as well."

"Strange. I wonder where the hell he is now."

"Can't help much with that one. It's been several months since I last heard. I might not hear again. And I never had an address."

"Would you agree to let me know if you ever did hear from him?"

"Yes. Yes, I would. I am the daughter of a senior Navy officer, and I do understand about this, and how serious it is. I will contact you if I hear."

Laura stood up wearily and passed a hand through her hair. "Would you like to listen to some music?" she asked. Crossing the room, she flicked on the CD player and placed a disc on the sliding tray. The massed violins of the Vienna Philharmonic Orchestra playing the rhapsodic overture to one of Giuseppe Verdi's most memorable operas filled the room.

"*Rigoletto*," said Bill.

They sat in silence for a long while, listening to the divine, heart-rending arias being sung by Ileana Cotrubas as Gilda, and Placido Domingo as the Duke of Mantua.

When the soprano sang "*Caro nome*" Laura was surprised to hear the American Naval officer mutter, "It's almost unbearably beautiful, don't you think?"

She turned the sound down a shade, and asked him, "You really like opera, don't you?"

"I do at times like this," he said somberly. "My mother's brother was on the Board of the Metropolitan Opera in New York. He used to throw her a few tickets now and then. She took me a few times when I was at Annapolis, paid for me to fly up from Washington, let me hear the great maestros at work.

"I never got much further than the easier ones, like *Bohème*, *Figaro*, *Rigoletto*, *Madame Butterfly* . . . *Carmen*, *Aida*, and *The Pearl Fishers* . . . but I've always loved the music—it's like havin' someone cast a spell on you. I'd rather go to an opera than a rodeo. That's the truth."

He glanced at his watch. "Hey, it's midnight, and I haven't slept in a bed since I left Kansas on Sunday morning. I have to meet your dad real early. I'd better turn in, before I collapse on the rug."

"All right. I'll just clear these glasses and fix the fire screen. Good night, Bill. I hope I've helped."

"Yes, ma'am. I appreciate it." He debated the propriety of giving her a quick kiss on the cheek, but decided against it. Mrs. Laura Anderson considered the omission a lot more peevishly than she ought to have done.

Bill climbed the stairs and slept like a rock. He knew his second day at Inveraray was not strictly necessary but he wanted to tour this submariner's Mecca with Admiral MacLean. And he wanted to ask him a few more questions about Israel and its Navy. He justified his time with the certain knowledge that this British admiral was without doubt the most learned submariner he had ever met. He was also the man who had personally taught Commander Ben Adnam, whatever grave implications that might now have.

152357JUL02. 11N, 53E.
Speed 7. Course 192. Periscope depth.
Position, 1,070 miles southwest of the datum,
170 miles due east of Cap Guardafui, Somalia.

"Okay, Georgy. We're closer to the shipping lanes than I'd like, but let's get up to the surface, and get the main shaft locked ASAP. And tell him to fix that hull gland permanently. Right here. While we're dead-stopped. It's been a worry on and off for a week."

160124JUL02.

"Watch Officer to captain, Watch Officer to captain . . . that racket on the ESM mast thirty minutes ago . . . I'd say she's a big merchantman from the southwest. Fifteen miles, three-five-zero, twenty knots. Danger level in five minutes.

"Captain to Watch Officer, how far will he miss us?"

"Bearing steady for forty minutes."

"Christ! *The shaft's locked.* Ben! Ben! We could get run right over and we can't maneuver."

"Steady, Georgy, you're going to make a 'stopped dive.'"

"Jesus Christ! I never done one before."

"Well, I've done dozens of them. We have no options. We must dive. I do not want to be seen by anyone. And I certainly do not want to be in a collision. I did think this could happen. That's why I wanted you to catch a 'stopped trim' before we surfaced.

"Now, do precisely as I say . . . open main vents and kingstons. *Watch the angles . . . We're stern down ten right now, but that's okay. It's always a bit uneven . . . What are we? Thirty meters?*

"Christ! Ben, we sliding backward to the bottom!"

"Shut up, Georgy old boy, will you? Keep those vents open, it's just air bubbles. We've got tons of compressed air. Pull yourself together, for god's sake. I know the angle's bad . . . what are we? Sixty meters? Okay.

"The stern is down forty degrees, Ben. Crew will panic if any more."

"Well, tell them not *to panic, will you?* Shut five main vents . . . blow five main ballast . . . okay, stop blowing. *Georgy, we're heavy aft. Get ten men up to for'ard. Tell 'em to climb uphill.*

"Okay, Georgy . . . the angle's coming off . . . open five main vents . . . *That's good . . . better . . .* shut five main vents . . . *where are we? Eighty meters?*

"Let's catch trim on the layer at one hundred meters . . . open five main vents . . . shut five main vents . . . *that's good."*

"One hundred meters, sir."

160154JUL02.

"There you are, Georgy. We're just floating here quietly, a hundred meters below. She'll come over the top in the next ten minutes, none the wiser. And when she's gone, we'll just float very quietly back to the surface in the dark and finish our repair. No problem. Oh, Georgy, sorry about the angles, it's always a bit like that on a 'stopped dive.'"

"You give me humiliation. If I ever get out of here I kill your fucking Teacher, Ben. But thank you."

The following morning, Bill Baldridge and the admiral left while the great house on the loch was still asleep, speeding through the forest and turning south before the main road down the side of Loch Lomond. They took a shorter route which hugged the winding eastern shores, running on down to Faslane from the opposite direction.

"Do you think it would be easy for anyone to penetrate the Israeli Armed Forces, and work on the inside for many years?" Bill asked.

"I gave it some thought overnight, and curiously, Bill, I do. It is a country of such interracial change. When Israel first came into being, there were so many strangers arriving in the vast exodus from underprivileged European countries, I am surprised they ever sorted anything out. But somehow they created a nationality, from Jews who had journeyed from Russia, Poland, Germany, from all over East and West Europe, even from the U.S.A. What followed was that thousands of newly settled Jewish people could pass at any time for Muscovites, Londoners, New Yorkers, Berliners.

"The entry into Israel from Arab countries was no less—they came from Egypt, Libya, Syria, Algeria, the Yemen, and of course Iraq, and Iran. No one has ever known for sure about the absolute loyalty to Israel of these families—indeed some of them have since left. But Israel has always found it dead easy to recruit very successful spies to operate in almost any Middle Eastern or European country, because they had so many original foreign nationals to select from.

"It follows that the reverse would also be true . . . that in the great human influx into Israel between 1948 and, say, 1968, there were also people who had other interests, for other governments, which might find it extremely convenient having people already 'inserted' into the Armed Forces of a new nation, which may one day become an enemy.

"Or do you find that altogether too far-fetched?"

"Admiral, I don't find that far-fetched at all. Makes sense to me."

"So while I do think Commander Ben Adnam was probably an Israeli, I also recognize the possibility that he may not have been, especially as he went to school in England—a strong, eighteen-year-old, well-educated boy from a good English school, with apparently Israeli parents . . . very easy to place in almost any walk of life in the Holy Land. I'm not saying he was an Iranian, or an Iraqi . . . but it's not by any means impossible."

"No . . ." said Bill slowly. "I guess the most I can do at this moment is to keep my mind open. To be aware of the man who could have done it, and to be aware that he may not have been Israeli, and that he could have been working for someone else."

"That's it. I believe modern theorists would describe that as lateral thinking. I normally call it logical research and a bit of common sense."

By this time Bill could see across the water to the point of land where the Argyll Forest peters out between the two great fiords of Loch Goil and Loch Long. They swung away from the water and over the top of the hill, plunging straight down into the little town of Garelochhead. "Faslane dead ahead," said the admiral, and again Bill Baldridge found himself looking at the cold, black waters of the Scottish loch.

The formality of the armed guards was no less than chillingly normal, even for the entry of the greatest submariner the Royal Navy had ever known. Passes were scrutinized, and they were handed over to a lieutenant commander with a submarine badge on his left shoulder.

He showed them where to park the Range Rover, and asked Admiral MacLean whether he and his guest were ready to board. "Yes, please," replied Sir Iain, and then to Bill, "I thought I'd show you a few of the places where I taught your man to drive one of these things. By good fortune there's a Perisher boat going out this morning, actually for about a month, but they'll fly us off, down near the Isle of Arran. Back by about four o'clock."

They walked down to the quayside where a three-hundred-foot-long, five-thousand-ton hunter-killer submarine, HMS *Thermopylae*, awaited. Stored deep within this menacing instrument of underwater warfare was a battery of brand-new Tomahawk land-attack missiles with a lethal range of 2,500 miles. The balance of her weapon load, stored adjacent to the bow tubes, was made up of Marconi Spearfish wire-guided torpedoes, each of which could travel seventeen miles through the water at almost fifty knots before blasting the backbone of an enemy warship in half.

The old boy had taught Ben that part pretty well, no doubt about that. As Bill had explained to the President, a nuclear-tipped torpedo does not have to smash into the hull of its target, but it still has to run fast, straight, and accurate. Peaceful modern oceans do not provide much opportunity for hands-on practice sessions.

To Bill's surprise, they piped him aboard with traditional Navy ceremony, but not the admiral. Salutes were crisply exchanged, and the captain led the way down through the hatch into the claustrophobic, Formica-paneled companionways, to the wardroom where the six Perishers were waiting to start their first day at sea. It was strange how the name "Perisher" had stuck, even though the old "Periscope Course" was now the Commanding Officers Qualifying Course. Folklore has decreed that trainee submarine commanders will be, forever, "Perishers."

Commander Rob Garside, the 2002 Teacher, wished the admiral "good morning, sir," extending a proper courtesy to the man who had taught him thirteen years previously.

"Hello, Rob—I'd like you to meet an American officer who is going to be our guest today, Lieutenant Commander Bill Baldridge from Kansas via the Pentagon, I believe. Commander Rob Garside."

"A privilege to have you both aboard," smiled the Teacher, and, looking at Bill, said, "You will find I am not quite such an ogre as your host was back in the eighties."

"He's just being modest. Rob's one of my very best Perishers."

Admiral MacLean smiled, patted his old pupil on the shoulder, and said, "What about some coffee while they're getting this steamer to sea?"

"No time, really, sir. Not if you want to be on the bridge going down the Gareloch."

"Right. Come on, Bill. I'll show you the way."

"Permission for the admiral and his guest on the bridge, sir?"

"Yes, please."

"Okay, Bill, up we go."

Two minutes later the hunter-killer was under way. From the top of the fin, the views of the loch and surrounding landscape were so striking that Baldridge hardly spoke for several minutes. Running south before the backdrop of the great mountain, with mists still hugging the shoreline on both sides, and the long heathery hillsides of Glen Fruin up to the left, made it very easy to forget the true purpose of this mission.

It was a typical July morning; no rays of sun had yet lit up the eastern slopes of The Cobbler, as HMS *Thermopylae* slipped silently down the middle of the loch at around eight knots toward the Rhu Narrows. The sky was overcast. It looked like rain.

"Is it deep enough to run down here at periscope depth?" asked Bill.

"Yes, it is," replied the admiral. "But we don't do it these days, and certainly not in a nuclear boat. It's considered an unnecessary risk . . . I mean, if something went wrong, no one would thank us for dumping a nuclear reactor on the floor of a Scottish loch in which it would remain active for probably a hundred years."

"No. I guess not. Has anything ever gone wrong in this loch?"

"Not for a long time. Not seriously since World War I when someone managed to leave a funnel-hatch open by mistake in one of the old K-Class submarines. The water filled the boiler room and she plunged to the bottom of the loch, drowned thirty-two men. They are all buried up in Faslane cemetery."

"That's one of the big troubles with these damn things . . . one mistake and you may never get a second chance," said Bill quietly. "I guess that's why we all think that a submarine CO is superior to any other."

"What d'ya mean, *think*?" said Commander Garside. "We know it."

Everyone laughed at the boss's joke. But the seriousness of this mission had put all of them on edge. They were going out for a month, into great waters, west of the British Isles. They would take this submarine into the depths of the Atlantic, working as much as one thousand feet down, in water which was two miles deep, out beyond the Rockall Rise, five hundred miles offshore, well off the continental shelf.

This is the area known in the trade as the GIUK Gap, the deepwater patrolling ground of the most powerful nuclear submarines in the Western world. It is the "choke point" formed by the coastlines of Greenland, Iceland, and the U.K., through which all Russian submarines must pass from their principal northern bases on the Murman Coast, which forms the southern shore of the Barents Sea. This was the old Soviet submarine way to the transatlantic trade routes, should it come to war.

In those days there was no way they could navigate through the GIUK Gap without the Americans or the Brits knowing precisely who they were, how many there were, and the direction in which they were headed. From that point on, no Soviet submarine was ever alone for long.

It was the strategic importance of these deep waters which made the submarine bases in the Scottish lochs so important, and so efficient. It was easy to bottle up the Russians in the Black Sea, because the Turks were in charge of the *only* way out, through the Bosporus. And, beyond there, the Strait of Gibraltar offered another "choke point."

The difficult area was the GIUK Gap, and to that potential theater of submarine warfare both the Pentagon and the Royal Navy historically sent their best men and their best equipment.

Admiral MacLean chatted to Bill about the forthcoming program the Perishers must face as *Thermopylae* threaded through Rhu Narrows and on south past the Tail of the Bank. For fifteen miles they ran on the surface, and then, three miles south of the Cumbraes, the captain took the submarine to periscope depth.

The admiral kept Bill apprised of the activities, as they continued southwesterly toward the southern coast of the Isle of Arran, which stands in the eastern lee of the Mull of Kintyre.

Once past Arran, they surfaced again, and the admiral again took Bill to the bridge for a perfect ride across the unusually sunlit fifteen-mile channel to Campbeltown, where a Navy helicopter would pick them up and fly them back to Faslane.

All the way to Kintyre, Bill found himself wondering about the Perishers down below, working away at their notes and diagrams, listening to the sonars, consulting with the surface picture compiler, talking to the AWO, conferring with the weapons officer, discussing the systems which governed the missiles and torpedoes.

It had been in this very area where Commander Ben Adnam had learned the specialized techniques of modern submarine warfare. But there was no longer one shred of doubt in Bill's mind—for any potential terrorist, this was the place to learn the tricks of the trade. He guessed, too, that if he nailed Adnam, the Royal Navy would never again train a Middle Eastern submariner.

But now they could hear the distant clatter of the Navy chopper, flying down Kilbrennan Sound between Kintyre and Arran. For a few moments it hovered twenty feet above the fore-casing, while the winchman pulled Baldridge and the admiral unceremoniously into the cabin, before it swept away for Faslane.

On landing, there was an urgent message for Bill. "Call Admiral Arnold Morgan on his private line in Fort Meade." A waiting lieutenant escorted him to a small private office, which had a private phone line, bypassing the main switchboard. "Just dial straight out, sir, 001 then the U.S. area code, then the number."

Bill dialed, private line to private line. Within seconds he heard the permanently irritated growl of Admiral Morgan come down the line. "Morgan . . . speak."

Bill chuckled. "Lieutenant Commander Baldridge. Ready to speak."

He heard the admiral laugh. "Hey Bill, good to hear you. What's hot?"

"Howd'ya find me?"

"Old buddy. Admiral Elliott. New buddy for you, right?"

"Yessir. A real good guy. Paved my way."

"I hear you may be onto something."

"I sure am, sir. About as near to certain as I ever could be—if someone hit our carrier, I got the guy who did it."

"Give it to me."

"Israeli officer. Commander Benjamin Adnam. A-D-N-A-M. The best trainee commanding officer they ever taught up here. I've just spent a day with his Teacher, Admiral Sir Iain MacLean. He reckons there's about five people on this earth who could get out underwater through the Bosporus. Him and Elliott . . . a couple of other possibles . . . and Adnam."

"Shit! Is that right? Where is this sonofabitch?"

"Not sure. But I suppose either at the Israeli Navy Base in Haifa, or in one of their submarines. He was up here less than a year ago, working up an Upholder Class submarine his Navy had just bought."

"No chance he might be an Arab, eh?"

"Yessir. I think there is such a chance. Several quite suspicious aspects of his life. I've been talking to a close friend of his . . . he's been completely out of touch for months and months, which is apparently unusual."

"You got all you need?"

"Yessir. I was planning to come back either overnight or first thing tomorrow. I've a ton of things to tell you."

"Lemme know when you're arriving in Washington. I'll have someone meet you. Then come straight on down to Fort Meade. Between you and me, the President is getting trigger-happy. He is determined to smack someone's Navy right in the mouth, ASAP. Hurry home." The line went dead, a disconcerting habit of the admiral's. He just didn't bother with good-byes. Didn't have time. Scott Dunsmore said old Morgan did it to the President once. Not this President, the one before.

Bill glanced at his watch. It was five forty-five in the afternoon. What he needed was the Concorde flight to Washington, first thing in the morning. That meant he must leave for London this evening. He left the office, explained his situation to the admiral, who picked up a telephone and spoke to someone in Northwood. Then he spoke to someone on the base, and finally said, "Okay, that's it, Bill. We'll drive home right away. The chopper will pick you up at eight o'clock at my house and whip you into Glasgow in time for the nine-thirty flight to London. Your ticket's at the British Airways desk. If I were you I'd find a bit of supper in the airport, and catch some sleep in the Concorde lounge. It's pretty civilized and that new Washington flight boards at 0700."

The journey back around the loch to Inveraray passed quickly. Back at the house, Bill rushed upstairs, packed his bag, jumped in the bath, shaved, changed out of uniform into a civilian coat and tie, and headed downstairs. The admiral was on the phone, Lady MacLean was out with the children, and Laura was awaiting him in the hall.

"So soon," she said, quietly. "I would have enjoyed another dinner and chat."

"Duty calls," Bill replied awkwardly.

"If I hear from Ben, how do I find you?"

Bill handed her a piece of paper. On it was written the number of his apartment in Suitland, Maryland, with its answering service, and his number at the Navy Intelligence office. For good measure he also included the number of the ranch in Kansas. Ray's number, not his mother's, in the interests of security. He also included both his personal addresses. "I was kinda hopin' you wouldn't lose track of me," he said.

Laura laughed at the pile of information, handwritten on the "Inveraray Court" writing paper. And as she did so, they could hear the roar of the Royal Navy helicopter thundering down onto the lawn outside. Both of them knew they had about five seconds before the admiral emerged from his phone call.

"I wish you weren't going," said Laura, helplessly.

"So do I," said Bill. "But I must. Can I speak to you, somehow, somewhere?"

Laura pressed a piece of paper into his hand. It contained a phone number and several time frames.

Admiral MacLean came out of his study. "Okay, Bill, I hope we meet again. Come on . . . "

The roar of the chopper's engines drowned out all further conversation. Laura followed them out, and Bill instinctively ducked his head as he headed for the helicopter's door. The loadmaster was already out, and helped him aboard, strapping him into his seat. Bill latched the door shut, gave a thumbs-up to the pilot, who took off instantly, as if conducting an evacuation from a battle zone.

Bill looked out of the window at the two figures standing on the lawn, waving. He thought of the admiral's amazing kindness, and quite remarkable grasp of the situation. And he felt he had not thanked him nearly enough. And then he smiled, waved back from about four hundred feet, above the gleaming waters of the loch now. But he felt a twinge of guilt that he was not really waving at Admiral Sir Iain MacLean.

1030 Wednesday, July 17.

ADMIRAL MORGAN WAS PACING HIS OFFICE DEEP IN the heart of Fort Meade. The short, stubby, fiercely glowing cigar, jutting out like a 40mm Navy shell from between his teeth, betrayed his impatience. It was ten-thirty in the morning, and the admiral never smoked before sunset unless he was profoundly irritated.

Before him stood a young lieutenant who had been charged with the relatively simple task of contacting Captain Carl Lessard at the Israeli Navy HQ in Haifa to check whether it would be possible to speak to Israeli submarine commander Benjamin Adnam.

The lieutenant had returned to say that the admiral's request was not being complied with.

"Did you speak to Captain Lessard?"

"Yessir."

"Did you tell him you were calling for me?"

"Yessir."

"Did you tell him it was just routine, nothing serious?"

"Yessir."

"What did he say then?"

"He said he did not think he could help but would put me through to someone who might."

"Whadya mean, he couldn't help? They only own four working submarines. He must know where his fucking commanding officers are. What the hell's he talking about?"

"Not sure, sir."

"I know you're not sure! Try not to keep aiming a glaring light at the totally fucking obvious."

"Nossir . . . er . . . yessir."

"Who did you speak to next?"

"An officer in the personnel department."

"The *what!*"

"The personnel department. And he said he did not keep records of submarine commanders' whereabouts."

"Then what?"

"Well, I called back and got put through to the submarine operations center. They said they were not empowered to tell anyone the whereabouts of their commanders."

"Jesus Christ! We paid for their fucking Navy!"

"Well, sir, you did not give me instructions to get heavy with them, you just said speak to Captain Lessard."

"I know what I said, for Christ's sake. Get Lessard back on the phone. I'll speak to him personally."

That had been thirty minutes ago. Three minutes ago, a perfectly charming Israeli secretary had come onto the line and said that she was afraid that Captain Lessard had just boarded a warship and would not be available for at least three weeks.

"Some bastard's lying," Morgan fumed. And the furnace on the end of his cigar radiated with vicarious fury.

"Okay, Lieutenant, I guess I'm going to move to Plan B."

"Could I ask what might that be, sir?"

"The hell you could. I'm still working on Plan A."

Morgan chuckled at himself, at last. But it did not disguise the indignation in his face. And he decided to put the matter on hold, until Bill Baldridge arrived an hour from now.

He dismissed his lieutenant, and paced. Then he put in a call to the Shin Bet in Tel Aviv, Israel's secret interior Intelligence service, equivalent to America's FBI, and Britain's MI5. Morgan had enjoyed considerable access to the organization since the appointment of the former Navy Chief, Rear Admiral Ami Ayalon three years ago as its head.

They were old friends, and the ex-Israeli commando had been unfailingly cooperative with the Americans. Arnold Morgan knew that Ami would not be in, but trusted his assistant to connect him with someone who would be more helpful than Captain Lessard had been.

Morgan's ensuing conversation with a very senior Israeli intelligence officer had been short and brief, culminating with a promise to arrange something through the Washington embassy. At that point the admiral knew something was afoot. He picked up his direct line to the CIA in Langley, and was put through to Jeff Zepeda, who was surprised and pleased to hear from him.

Zepeda agreed to contact the Israeli embassy and get someone who would speak to the admiral in straightforward language. He spent a few minutes explaining that he was drawing a large blank so far in his inquiries in Iran, but there was something stirring in Iraq. Meanwhile the admiral should stand by for a call from one of the Mossad's representatives in Washington.

Admiral Morgan checked his watch. He did not want to be in the middle of something when Baldridge arrived. He paced, and was debating the possibility of lighting another cigar, when the phone rang. "Admiral Morgan . . . good morning . . . this is General David Gavron, at the military attaché's office in the Israeli embassy. I have been advised by Tel Aviv and by your own CIA, that it would be wise for us to meet . . . "

"Well, General, I'm kinda surprised at the momentum my very simple inquiry has generated."

"Admiral, if you do not mind my saying so, men such as yourself do not make very simple inquiries."

"And, General, men such as yourself sure as hell don't spend much time answering 'em."

"Then perhaps we should agree in advance our subject is less than simple."

"General, that goes without saying."

"Well, I did speak to Captain Lessard about an hour ago . . . "

"On a warship," interjected the admiral, an edge of skepticism in his voice.

"Of course. That's where he is. And he did tell me you were a very straight and decent man to deal with."

"Can we meet this evening say around seven o'clock?"

"I'll be where you say."

Admiral Morgan gave him precise directions to the restaurant in Alexandria and told the general to come alone, as he would.

Meanwhile he abandoned the second cigar, and settled down to wait for Bill Baldridge. The lieutenant commander came through the door bang on time, still wearing civilian clothes.

"Bill, I'm glad you're here. Let me get us some coffee." He pressed a number on the phone, ordered the coffee, and then continued, "I've scheduled us to talk until about 1400, then we're due to meet Admiral Dunsmore at the Pentagon. Before we start, look at these . . . "

He pointed to a table at the rear of his office where about one week's worth of *Washington Post*s were arranged. The papers detailed what was known about the sinking of the *Thomas Jefferson*. Bill had never seen such exhaustive coverage. But he had not yet been born when President Kennedy was assassinated.

The sinking was still the lead story nine days after the event. Bill quickly scanned the week's headlines, and was quite surprised to see that no one had posed the only question worth asking. The question he and the admiral were trying to answer. There was not one story suggesting that the nuclear fireball which vaporized the great warship had been the act of a foreign power.

The incident had placed the Navy under heavy attack, no doubt about that. Tabloid journalists were swarming all over the country looking for memorial services being held for the lost men. They were hurtling from one end of the country to the other, coaxing photographs from stunned and grieving families, interviewing the mothers, wives, and children, whose lives would be forever edged with sorrow.

Meanwhile, the press had gone berserk, slamming the Pentagon, the Service Chiefs, the President, and the policy of arming U.S. warships with nuclear weapons.

"Are you looking at that horseshit about not letting the Navy go to sea properly armed against every eventuality that could befall this country of ours?" snapped Morgan, watching Bill pause on a big inside-page article.

"Yessir."

"Can you believe those bastards? Asking us to go out and face any enemy without big weapons in case someone gets hurt. That fucking newspaper should be closed down."

"Yessir," said Bill. "I'm with you on that. But this President will never stand up for any of that crap. Would you like to hear my report, sir?"

"Shoot."

Lieutenant Commander Baldridge had half-filled a notebook during his flight from Heathrow. He regaled Admiral Morgan with every fine detail on Commander Ben Adnam, and his Perisher training at Faslane. He recounted his long conversations with Admiral Sir Iain MacLean. He had carefully recorded the admiral's precise words in describing how, and why, so few people in the world could have made a successful underwater passage through the Bosporus.

He was equally precise in recounting the firm opinion the admiral had presented to him that Commander Adnam could have done it. Of that Admiral MacLean had been very sure.

Bill startled Morgan when he reported that Israel must be regarded as a very real suspect. Whatever they might perpetrate against the U.S.A., he explained, they could be certain that Iran or Iraq would be blamed. He informed Morgan of Admiral MacLean's view that the position of Israel's extremist right wing must always be examined in any unusual occurrence in the Middle East. He pointed out MacLean's reasons, his historical assessment of some high-ranking officers in the Mossad, and the conservative factions of the Israeli Government.

Admiral Morgan, who already knew much of what the younger officer was saying, sat and listened silently. Only once did he interrupt to compliment Baldridge. "That's a beautiful job you've done, Bill. Real information. Real research. Real judgment," he said appreciatively. "Guess you found yourself on a kind of crash course in modern history. Some of those senior guys in the Royal Navy . . . damned impressive, ain't they? I love 'em. Never underestimate a top British Naval officer just because they talk funny. They don't think funny. Sorry, Bill . . . go on."

At this point Bill decided to impart the intelligence from Laura, and he built a case—not that Ben was an Arab in disguise but that he could have been a Muslim. He never revealed his exact source, but told Admiral Morgan about the mosque in Egypt, Commander Adnam's preference for Cairo, and his occasional sympathy for the Arab cause, no matter how great an atrocity had been committed. He told him too about his wariness, his coldness, his new car, and his monthly trip to London.

Admiral Morgan interrupted again. "Was she pretty?" he asked.

"Who?"

"The lady who told you all of this."

Bill smiled at the perceptiveness of the Intelligence chief, and then replied, crisply, "Yessir. She was Laura Anderson, the admiral's daughter."

"And Adnam's girlfriend?"

"Yessir, while he was at Faslane."

"She on our side now?"

"Yessir."

"Does she think Adnam would have been capable of committing such an unbelievable act of villainy?"

"Yessir. Yes she does. Not quite so firmly as you just said it. She described him to me as an ultimate professional, a guy who would carry out his duty no matter what."

"Well, if that is the considered opinion of the daughter of Iain MacLean, we'd better take that on board with due seriousness, because I'm going to tell you something about that Scottish officer you did not know, and I am quite sure he did not tell you."

"Sir?"

"You remember when the Royal Navy fought the Falklands War against Argentina back in 1982?"

"Sir?"

"What do you remember most about it?"

"That night they blew away that damned great Argentinean cruiser and drowned four hundred people . . . what was it called? "The *General Belgrano*."

"That's it, Bill. Changed the course of the war. Frightened the Argentinean fleet away for good. Iain MacLean was the submarine sonar officer who helped Commander Wreford-Brown stalk that cruiser for two days, and then blow it apart with three old Mark 8** torpedoes. Two of 'em hit, right under the bow, and the engine room. It was a perfect example of persistent tracking, followed by a careful, logical attack.

"Remember too, the *Belgrano* was accompanied by two old but pretty well-equipped guided missile destroyers, American-made, like the cruiser, very fast and carrying plenty of depth charges. Having made a textbook submarine attack, the Royal Navy made a textbook getaway. No one got a sniff.

"They vanished into the South Atlantic, and were next sighted rolling up the Clyde—where you've just been—sporting a darn great skull-and-crossbones over the tower—the traditional Royal Navy signal for a kill. I guess that's where MacLean's career started to take off. But as Teacher, and then FOSM, he became a legend. Virtually rewrote the book on submarine warfare. I met him a few times in Washington, and if I hadn't known he was retired, he would've been my first suspect on July 8!"

"Jesus! He never told me anything about the South Atlantic."

"They don't, do they? Not those Brits. So when we get warnings from such a man, even such a man's daughter, we listen with respect.

"I'm not saying Miss Laura ought to be made an honorary admiral or anything. But do not write off the possibility that the apple may not have fallen far from the tree . . . and now we wanna find out where the hell is Commander Benjamin Adnam, right?"

"Yessir. And we'd like to take a careful look at the activities and motives of Israel. So far as we know for certain, Adnam is an Israeli submarine commander."

"Yeah, but we have accounted for the Israeli submarines. As we have almost accounted for the Iranian submarines. And the Iraqis don't have any."

"Unless one of them has one we don't know about," said Bill. "An unknown boat they sneaked out of the Black Sea with an unknown commander. Because we surely know now who that commander might be. Especially now you've put a branding iron on the man who taught him."

"Bill, you'll get no argument from me on any of that. Now, let's have a few gulps of this coffee, and then I'll tell you my news."

The admiral finally stopped pacing the room. He sat down behind his desk and told Bill the salient points of his investigation. "Dealing with the rogue submarine first, we have two facts. One, we think we heard him in the strait, two, a Russian submariner went overboard and drowned off the Greek islands. The dates of the two incidents fit, which would make it, almost certainly, the same ship, and the Russians are not denying the dead man was a submariner.

"However, they are being a bit cagey about one thing. When I contacted them the day after we picked up the acoustic contact in the strait, they admitted they had lost a Kilo Class submarine in the previous three weeks in the Black Sea and were searching for the hull. But when I asked whether the drowned man was a member of that ship's company, they clammed up real fast, and refused to confirm whether they had found the hull of the Kilo. I'm working on it right now. Talking to Rankov when he gets back Friday.

"Meanwhile the Turks confirm they received no application from the Russians to bring any submarine through the Bosporus on the surface during the months of March, April, or May. So what's that goddamned Russian submariner's body doing on a Greek beach?"

"Well, he couldn't have washed right through from the Black Sea, and then the Dardanelles, not all that way," said Baldridge.

"So that's all very significant for us. How about Israel—will they tell us about Adnam?"

"Bill, I thought they would, been trying to talk to them since we spoke on the phone, but they are being even more cagey than the Russians. I'm meeting one of their guys tonight, after we finish with Scott Dunsmore."

"What's the latest on Iran?"

"Hell, that's just the usual hotbed of intrigue. We think one of their submarines vanished from off its moorings in Bandar Abbas three days before the *Jefferson* was hit. But it could be in the Iranians' big floating dock. The water's very shallow all around the approaches to the main Navy harbor. I can't see how they could have driven a submarine out of there on the surface without being picked up by the 'overheads.'

"If, however, they did, and somehow got back in again, and then parked the submarine in a covered dock, that makes them very clever, very dangerous little guys. Too goddamned clever."

"I'll tell you what Iain MacLean says. He reckons the Iranians are our number-one suspects by a long way. He says if all three of their Kilos are still in Bandar Abbas, then they either got a new one—which is still at large—or they got out of Bandar Abbas, and then got right back in again. Either way he says Iran is the likely culprit."

"He's right. They have the strongest motive, they are at least as careless about human life as the Iraqis. And they have three Russian Kilos which we know about.

"I'm telling you, Bill. The President is very concerned about them and their goddamned submarine fleet and their increases in Naval exercises in the Gulf. Right now, without a CVBG in the area, we are preparing to put at least twenty-four FA–18's on the airstrip in Bahrain, like we did before, until the new carrier arrives in October. The Emir of Bahrain is a very good guy, and we are expecting permission this week.

"I'm not sure how the CNO and the President see it, but right now, it's gotta be Iran, and Israel, probably not Iraq. Your information about Adnam is obviously critical, but we have to get the Israelis to tell us the truth. If they did do it, they'll tell us Adnam is gone. If they did not do it, Adnam probably has gone! It's a matter of getting Israeli Intelligence to tell us the truth. Then we'll know what to do."

The two men talked for another hour before leaving for the Pentagon. Once there, they apprised Admiral Dunsmore of their inquiries, told him about Commander Ben Adnam, and Admiral Morgan promised to be in touch as soon as he had finished with the Israeli general later in the evening. Admiral Dunsmore called General Paul and suggested that he meet with the President as soon as Morgan "has wrung the truth out of the Mossad."

Bill Baldridge got a ride with Morgan to the Dunsmore estate in order to retrieve his car. Which would give the Intelligence chief ample time to drive back to Alexandria and prepare for the arrival of General Gavron.

Before leaving, he asked his office to dig up some background on the man he thought might pinpoint the precise whereabouts of Commander Adnam, and told his staff he would call at around six-thirty in the evening. Thereafter the time sped by rapidly. Admiral Morgan, driving himself as usual, joined the stream of south-running traffic on the western shore of the Potomac, and, with Bill Baldridge's navigation, swept into the CNO's residence.

Bill knew Grace Dunsmore was out, and anyway he was anxious to get home to Maryland, in his own car. He thanked Admiral Morgan for the ride, and arranged to speak to him either later that night or first thing in the morning.

Admiral Arnold Morgan turned north once more and made for the quaint little seaport of Alexandria. There was however nothing quaint about his business this evening. The Israeli would be very tough, and very uncooperative at first. The admiral considered it highly likely that he might have to impart a few home truths to this particular opponent.

He reached the bar, chatted for a few moments with the landlord, and asked him to put a pot of coffee in his usual booth. Then he disappeared through a door, into the proprietor's private quarters, and called Fort Meade where his lieutenant was waiting. The time was 1830.

General Gavron's details were sketchy but interesting. He was a pure Israeli of the blood, a true Sabra, born and bred in the fertile Jezreel Valley, southwest of the Sea of Galilee, between Nazareth and Megiddo. Like his old colleague General Moshe Dayan, he had been brought up by his parents to grow fruit and vegetables but ended up spending most of his adult life in the military. His family was from Germany, and had emigrated to help plant forests in the northern half of the country and thereby increase Israel's rainfall. The Gavrons were devoted to enabling the young country to feed itself. Their eldest son, David, born six months after their arrival in 1947, elected to adopt another critical course for a Sabra, to help establish and defend Israel's boundaries.

He was called up as a conscript, like every Israeli, when he was just eighteen. By 1973 he was a promising young captain in an armored brigade. The Yom Kippur War of that year established him as an officer of much potential. He fought in the front rank of General Abraham "Bren" Adan's hastily assembled tank division as they drove out to face the army of Egypt, still swarming in across the canal, on that terrible early morning of October 8.

Face to face across the desert, heavily outnumbered, not quite prepared, still amazed by the suddenness of the surprise attack, Bren Adan drove his men into battle with reckless courage. The Egyptian Second Army, dug in and backed up by hundreds of tanks, almost lost their nerve at the ferocity of the Israeli onslaught. But after four hours, they forced the Israelis back.

At that point the entire country was in the hands of the largely teenage Army in the front line, whose task it was to hold the Egyptians at bay for forty-eight hours, until the reserves arrived. The death toll among Israel's youth in those two days was staggering. Even Adan's more experienced tank men died by the hundreds in the sands of the northern Sinai. David Gavron, fighting within twenty yards of the general, was shot in his left arm trying to drag a wounded man clear of a burning tank. Then the blast of an exploding shell flung him twenty feet forward into the sand.

But Gavron got up, and a field surgeon patched his arm, stitched his face, and, unhappily for Egypt, the same thing happened to the bloodstained Army of Israel. And when finally Bren Adan's armored division regrouped, and again rolled forward eight days later, Captain Gavron, arm bandaged, his face deeply cut and seared from sand-burn, was in one of the leading Israeli tanks, directing fire coolly, to devastating effect.

He actually heard General Adan roar the motto of his beleaguered Army—"*After me!*"—as the Israeli guns opened fire once more. David Gavron never forgot that, never forgot the sheer nobility of the man, standing in the turret of his tank, right fist clenched, while he led the battered division forward, shelling their way into the heart of the Egyptian Second Army, which cracked and then gave way in panic.

At midnight on October 17, Bren Adan and his remaining officers reached the Suez Canal and established a bridgehead. At 0500 on October 18 they crossed the canal into Egypt, driving south to the Gulf of Suez, playing hell with the Arab defenses wherever they fought, and isolating Anwar Sadat's Third Army in the desert.

The Israelis were never going to let David Gavron go back to growing fruit after that. He was decorated for gallantry, promoted to become one of the youngest colonels in the history of the Israeli Armed Forces. He became a valued friend of both Bren Adan and Arik Sharon for all of their days. And his move to the secretive, sensitive military area of the Intelligence Service meant he had been singled out for the highest calling Israel can bestow upon a battlefield officer. David Gavron was one day going to head the Mossad.

By the time the Israeli general walked into the waterfront bar in Alexandria, Admiral Arnold Morgan knew he was awaiting a man who was a towering hero in his own country, where senior military figures are held in enormous esteem. He was not disappointed.

General Gavron, at the age of fifty-five, was a tall, lean Army officer, with hair shaved even more closely than the admiral's. He had deep-set blue eyes, a hawkish nose, and a wide, thin, even mouth. A jagged scar on the left side of his face bore testimony to a distant tank battle in the Sinai. He was tanned, but fair-skinned with freckles around the nose and eyes. He wore no tie, and a gray, lightweight civilian suit, which could disguise neither the military walk nor the officer's bearing. He looked coiled, as if he could break your neck with a single blow, and he stood smiling while Arnold Morgan climbed to his feet.

Then he offered his hand, and said softly, "Admiral Morgan? I'm David Gavron . . . Shalom." The solemn greeting of peace, from the land where Abraham forged his covenant with God.

"Good evening, General," replied Admiral Morgan. "It was good of you to come. Just a very simple inquiry."

Both men laughed and shook hands. The admiral poured coffee for them both—knowing the Israeli would never dream of touching alcohol. But he wasted not one second of time. "My question may not be simple, but I think it's at least an easy one," he said, grinning. "Can you tell me the whereabouts of one of your best submarine commanders, Mr. Benjamin Adnam?"

General Gavron was ready. "Well, we are conducting some exercises in the Med at present. I suppose he could be out there. I believe they are working with the new Upholder Class submarine we bought from the Royal Navy. As I recall, Commander Adnam was scheduled to take her out into the Atlantic."

"I have no doubt about that," replied Morgan. "But I do not really need to know what he was scheduled to do. I need to know absolutely, is he, or is he not, on that submarine, right now, as we sit here? No bullshit."

The Israeli was slightly taken aback by the directness of the admiral's assault. "Well . . . I expect you know that for security reasons, we never tell anyone anything about our unit commanders, or their seniors, in any of the branches of our services. We have many enemies, some obvious, and some unseen. It would be more than my career is worth to inform anyone of such detail."

"David," replied Admiral Morgan, in a more conciliatory tone, "I am asking for your help. And I appreciate the constraints upon you, although I doubt that your government would be keen to lose the services of such a distinguished officer as yourself.

"But if you feel unable to tell me where he is working right now, could you tell me this—is Commander Benjamin Adnam still a serving officer in the Israeli Navy, as we know he was ten months ago?"

"Well, I assume he is. I am not in the Navy myself, but I know his reputation. I would have to make a few inquiries, which would take a while. It's 0230 there now, tomorrow."

"General Gavron, you came to meet me tonight, fully aware of what my question is. There are several people at the Navy base in Haifa who know what my question is; there are several others in the Shin Bet Intelligence office in Tel Aviv who also know what my question is. That means the Mossad knows what my question is. I must now assume that you have been sent here to stall me. And if that is so, it may be necessary for my government to make one or two things clear to your government."

"Your government, Admiral, is very good at that," replied the general, smiling.

"Yours ain't so bad at it either," replied the admiral.

And so they sat, two ex-military men, both unused to compromise, both brought up to treat the problems of their respective countries as if they were their own. Deadlocked in this Virginia bar, they sipped their coffee, the American uncertain how tough to get, the Israeli uncertain how much to give away, not sure when to pose the question he knew he must ask.

"General," the admiral persisted, "I have to find out about Commander Adnam, and it may be in both of our interests for you to tell me."

"Admiral, I cannot tell you. No one has told me. Deliberately, I suppose. But I too have a question which I would like to ask you. Why do you want to know about Commander Adnam?"

Admiral Morgan had hoped it would not be necessary to deal with this. But he was ready. He sat in silence for thirty seconds, and then he said: "General Gavron, we are considering the possibility—and it is only a possibility—that the accident in the *Thomas Jefferson* may not have been an accident."

"Hmmm. You mean someone may have taken her out?"

"Yes, Someone may have. With a torpedo fired from a small, silent submarine."

"Nuclear-tipped?"

"Probably."

"And why should you think it was driven by Commander Adnam?"

"What should concern you a great deal more, General, is that we may think the submarine was Israeli."

"*Israeli! Us?* Blow up a United States aircraft carrier. No. No. No. Not us. We are friends."

Admiral Morgan was amused to see this cool Army officer from the Holy Land in temporary disarray. But he recognized genuine incredulity when he saw it. "General, we know there are people in your government who have never forgiven us for letting Saddam Hussein bombard Israel with Scud missiles, then leave him still in power.

"We have our enemies in Tel Aviv, as we have them in most places in the Middle East. And the Israeli Government would know, that if they did commit such an atrocity as obliterating a U.S. carrier, we would instantly blame Iran or Iraq. And so you see, General, your nation is very much under suspicion by us."

"And where, Admiral, does Adnam fit in?"

"Well, would anyone be foolish enough to open fire on the U.S.A. with a submarine that was in their known inventory? So we think they may have acquired one from Russia, and driven it out through the Bosporus. We keep a list of all high-flying submarine commanders in the world—real experts, the best of their profession. Every one of them is accounted for. Except Adnam. And you guys are being very, very cagey. It is just possible we may decide, in the next twenty-four hours, that you are deliberately lying to us, and then we might get very, very ugly.

"I hope you have enjoyed having a Navy for the past few years."

Morgan knew he had shaken the Israeli. David Gavron betrayed no fear. But neither did he reply. He took a sip of coffee, and ruminated upon the fact that unless his government cooperated with Admiral Arnold Morgan there was likely to be big trouble, on a scale no one could cope with.

"Admiral," he said. "I must confer with my superiors. I am sorry our meeting has been so brief. Can you let me have a number, or numbers, where I can speak to you later tonight."

The admiral handed him a card with his office phone and fax, and his home number scrawled on the back.

"I'll be waiting," he said.

General Gavron headed back to his embassy. Admiral Morgan drove directly to Fort Meade. He ordered a roast beef sandwich, more coffee—the latter loudly . . . "*Black with buckshot!*" his own word for the tiny white sweeteners he used. He called Admiral Dunsmore in the Pentagon, and advised him to put any meeting at the White House on hold until the morning. Then he retired to his computer, conducting yet another search, for any submarine in all of the world which could, conceivably, have crept up on the *Thomas Jefferson*. Two hours later, he arrived at the same conclusion he had arrived at earlier. The only submarine not accounted for was the Russian Kilo reported sunk in the Black Sea.

He ran the CIA program of leading submarine commanders from all over the world for the sixth time in two days. There was no one on that list who was anywhere near the Black Sea at the appropriate time. The arrival of Bill Baldridge had presented him with the only real suspect—the Israeli, Adnam.

Admiral Morgan knew they had no real record of the man's obvious brilliance. Everything about Adnam was shaded. To Morgan's deeply skeptical mind, Adnam did not add up. And there had been an instant conspiracy by the Israelis to shield their man from investigation. Morgan believed General Gavron might not know Adnam's whereabouts, but he believed there were some people in Tel Aviv who did.

The digital clock on his wall approached midnight. He sat in his armchair and turned on the television, picked up a West Coast baseball game, checked CNN occasionally. By 0100 he was asleep.

At 0210 the phone rang, and he reached for it like a striking cobra, wide awake in an instant.

"Admiral, this is David Gavron."

"Shalom, David," said Arnold Morgan.

"It took my superiors a while to gather the information you need. I am sorry to call you so late. It is just after 0900 in Israel."

"To tell the truth, David, I don't have anything much more pressing to do," replied the admiral.

"No. I suppose not. Anyway I am instructed to inform you that the man you seek left the service of the Israeli Navy in November of 2001, eight months ago. We have no record of his present whereabouts."

"What do you mean, 'left'? Did he resign, desert, or was he fired?"

"I think it would be better if we spoke face to face. Can you come here right away. I'm at the Israeli embassy. I will meet you at the gate."

"I'm leaving now."

Morgan pulled on his uniform jacket and charged for the door, down the corridor and into his car. This was it. The Israelis were about to come clean. Adnam had plainly skipped town. The question now was, who was he working for? And where the fuck was he?

Two minutes later the admiral was racing south down the Baltimore-Washington Parkway at over 90 mph. He had never put it to the test, but he considered that in a straight fight between the Maryland State Police and the Director of the Office of National Security on an emergency mission, there would be only one winner—not the troopers.

Five minutes later, the tires of the staff car squealed as he hit the Capital Beltway at Exit 22, heading west across the northern end of the sleeping city. It took him under ten minutes to cover the twelve miles to Exit 33, the Connecticut Avenue intersection. He swung south toward Washington, turned off after a couple of miles, and came to a halt at the tall iron gates that guard the entrance to the embassy of Israel, some three miles out of town. Gazing through the dark at the striking stone building, with its great archways and Middle Eastern architecture, Admiral Morgan felt he could have been sitting right in the middle of Jerusalem.

Silently, General Gavron appeared at the car window and, as the gates swung open, instructed him to drive straight through. The admiral parked the car and stepped out onto Israeli territory. Silent guards observed him from the shadows. As he walked with the general across the great courtyard he could feel the atmosphere of this tough, brave little country, no bigger than the state of New Jersey, so often under attack, and even here in Washington surrounded completely by a protective fence, the iron wrought in the decorative style of the homeland. Everywhere you could feel it, a kind of gallant bracing against the unseen threat.

They slipped unobtrusively through a door and stepped into a large, airy building, of the type favored by modern Arab sheiks, where thousands of years of desert tradition collide, finally, with modern Western technology. They walked down a corridor, past a portrait of David Ben-Gurion, another of General Moshe Dayan, and into a small anteroom, comfortably furnished, with two sofas and three big, burgundy-colored armchairs. The antique Persian rug, spread on the marble floor, was probably priceless. A white-uniformed Israeli serviceman stood by to bring them tea or coffee. And David Gavron asked the admiral to be seated. He then answered the three questions that Morgan had fired at him on the phone.

"We do not know what happened to Commander Adnam. He just . . . er . . . well . . . vanished. Into thin air. He was on station one day, and gone the next."

"David, are you telling me the absolute truth? Because if you are not, the consequences might well be monumental."

"We are a long way past telling lies, Admiral. I swear to you— and this is the solemn word of an Israeli officer, and friend to your country, Commander Adnam vanished. Plainly, I could not have told you this without the highest possible authority. In fact, I did know something of this when we met earlier. But I was under orders to reveal nothing."

Admiral Arnold Morgan silently cursed himself for having even considered he was being told the entire truth by a member of the Mossad on the previous evening. But he understood the Israeli's predicament. And forgave him now that the upper hand was clearly American. "Did anyone conduct an investigation when Adnam was first discovered missing?"

"Of course. He was our top submarine commander. The Navy was very shocked. There was a time when we thought he might have been murdered. But Adnam had just taken off. We simply never heard anything, ever again.

"The Intelligence Service had a fairly thorough look. But I spoke to them again, a couple of hours ago. The whole matter remains a mystery. Commander Adnam's parents were both killed in a small village which was bombed during the October War of 1973. As you know, our Achilles heel is poor records of immigrants. And they found no details of Adnam's parents beyond about 1965. But there's nothing suspicious. Except that it is a little unusual that no solid background information would be available on a man so prominent, and in such a sensitive area of our national defense. But that's how it is for now."

"Will your Intelligence services look again?"

"In the light of what you said to me, we consider the matter to be critical. We are reasonably sure Adnam is no longer in Israel. If he was, we'd have found him."

"Will you keep me informed?"

"Of course. You have our deepest sympathy for the men who died on the carrier. As you know, we do not approve of surprise attacks for no apparent reason."

Morgan smiled. He stood up and explained that he must go at once.

General Gavron said he understood, of course, and he escorted the American back, past the guards, to his car. It was 0320 when Morgan pulled through the gates, with the window down. And he heard General Gavron say very firmly, "Admiral, we did *not* hit your carrier. Do not waste your time thinking we did. And you can count on our support for *anything* you may need."

Admiral Morgan saluted him as he left. And he could see the Israeli still standing alone, beyond the embassy fence. A nice man, he thought, in a big and dangerous job. "And now," I believe, "a truthful man, which I suspect he likes better."

He drove at a more leisurely pace back to the parkway, swinging off to his home in Montpelier, a few miles before the turning to Fort Meade. He lived now in an official government residence close to his office complex, but he still owned and often visited the small, secluded, single-story frame house he had lived in while married. These days he had a housekeeper five mornings a week, and the place was spotless, but it looked and felt like a Navy officer's wardroom. Admiral Morgan had never been long on chintz and deep sofas.

He poured himself a deep glass of bourbon on the rocks, called the Pentagon, and asked a duty officer to relay a message to the CNO after 0600 that he would be awaiting him in his office at 0700, with information of a highly sensitive nature. He then put in a call to the headquarters of the Black Sea Fleet to check the arrival of Vice Admiral Rankov, and was agreeably surprised to hear he would be in Novorossisk later today.

He hardly touched the bourbon, and at 0420 Arnold Morgan hit the sheets and set his alarm for 0530. It had been a long night, but his adrenaline was still high, and most of the seventy minutes of rest he had allocated himself were wasted. His mind kept racing over the same questions. How long would it take the Mossad, and the U.S.A., to find Commander Adnam? And where was he now and, worse yet, where was his fucking submarine? Had young Baldridge been right when he had suggested the unnamed enemy might strike again? Admiral Morgan was out of bed before the alarm even considered awakening him. He was showered, shaved, and dressed, and on the phone to Baldridge before 0540. Told his new field officer to be at the Pentagon by 0640 for a briefing.

Inside the Pentagon, he and Bill Baldridge pondered the revelations of General Gavron. "It's changed the rules, hasn't it, sir?" said the younger officer. "Either Adnam helped the Iranians get one of their Kilos into action very quietly—Bandar Abbas being so damned close to where the CVBG was working. Or he helped them get a new Kilo out of the Black Sea. And, if we accept he could have helped the Ayatollahs, I guess he could have helped anyone else do the same thing. It brings Iraq right back into the picture . . . and Libya . . . Syria . . . Egypt . . . Pakistan . . . any of 'em. Because if any one of those nations had Adnam, the only other thing they needed was money."

"Yeah. To rent or buy a Russian boat and crew. But we still have to look at motive. And the nations with the most powerful motives are Iran, and, I guess, Iraq. The others are lightweight for something this big, and also would be much more afraid of the consequences. I don't think we should take our eyes too far off the most obvious ball."

"No. Guess not. And do you write the Israelis out of the list of suspects now?

"Almost. I'll make another couple of calls this morning. See if I can get Lessard on the line. Then we'll have to see whether they find their lost commander. Or at least find out who he really is. Meantime I think we should brace ourselves for the fact that this President wants action. Right now. And I'm not sure what to advise. When you are as big and strong as we are, it's damn difficult to punish someone on a large scale without starting World War III."

At 0710, the Chief of Naval Operations walked through the door. Admiral Dunsmore beckoned both men to follow him into his office and ordered coffee, which was rapidly becoming a staple of Arnold Morgan's diet. He then ordered the Intelligence Admiral to tell him everything.

The conversation lasted about five minutes. Admiral Dunsmore said little, absorbing every detail. Then he called General Josh Paul and said he thought they should meet with the President at the earliest possible time. He replaced the phone, and it rang within five minutes. The CNO just said, "I'm leaving now. I'll be by your office in three."

Admiral Morgan then called the Navy Intelligence office and left a message with an assistant to Admiral Schnider that

Lieutenant Commander Baldridge would be working out of Fort Meade for the remainder of the week. Bill shrugged, and the two men headed for the garage. By the time they made it, General Paul and Admiral Dunsmore were already bound for the White House.

Seated in the back of the staff car, Scott Dunsmore ran over the situation with the Chairman of the Joint Chiefs, told him of the rising suspicion that Benjamin Adnam was the commander of the submarine which they now believed had destroyed the *Jefferson*. He informed him of the defection of the Israeli Navy officer, how they had been promised the support and help of a very worried Mossad, and how Iran remained the prime suspect.

General Paul asked one question. "Do you guys think that this Adnam could have got one of the Iranian Kilos out through the Strait of Hormuz, hit the *Jefferson*, and then got back into Bandar Abbas without us knowing?"

"No. We don't really. But since we thought the carrier was just about impregnable, and we were wrong about that, I suppose we have to accept the possibility that the guy who successfully got into the Battle Group, might also have successfully chugged in and out of the harbor without being spotted by the overheads. Specially during the monsoon."

"Yeah. Guess so. We're still not seeing three boats in Bandar Abbas. Just the two, right?"

"Uh-huh. But the third one still might be in that big covered floating dock. We just can't get a look in there."

The car pulled up to the West Wing entrance. The Secret Service men were there to meet them, hand over their passes, and escort them immediately to the same conference room they had used for the breakfast meeting with the President eight days previously. When they arrived, the Defense Secretary, Robert MacPherson, and the Secretary of State, Harcourt Travis, were already seated. The National Security Adviser, Sam Haynes, arrived within moments. Five minutes later the President himself walked in accompanied by his press chief, Dick Stafford. The doors were shut firmly behind them by the Marine guards, who remained on duty immediately beyond the door.

A military quorum of five was now seated around the table;

five men who, if they acted in harmony, had the power to do almost anything they wished on the international front. They were five men whose unanimous decision could unleash the terrifying power of the U.S. Navy on an enemy. The sixth man, Travis Harcourt, was there to supply wisdom on a wide international base; the seventh, Dick Stafford, to ensure, professionally, that their actions would always be perceived by the American nation as justified.

The President sat at the head of the table, flanked by Mr. MacPherson and Mr. Travis. General Paul and Admiral Dunsmore sat next to them, opposite each other, with Sam Haynes and Dick Stafford at the end of the table. The President greeted everyone by their first names, and thanked them for coming. He then requested that Admiral Dunsmore brief the meeting formally with the latest update on the list of suspects.

It took about ten minutes, since the President and his cabinet officers had not yet been appraised fully of the situation regarding the drowned Russian sailor, nor of the importance of Commander Adnam, nor of the grave consequences of the Israeli admission of his disappearance.

"Scott," the President said at the conclusion of the CNO's briefing, "we have a submarine, sealed up tight, going along under the water, trying to stay quiet and remain undetected. Since they are all locked up inside, how can someone fall overboard and drown?"

"I'm sorry, sir," the CNO explained. "We should have made that clear. If someone should drop a hammer on a metal deck inside the submarine, that clang could be heard for possibly fifty miles under the water. The enemy of the stealthy submarine is noise . . . any noise . . . it is regarded with immense concern by every member of the ship's company.

"Remember, every bit of machinery in a submarine, bar the propeller, is set upon heavy rubber mounts, all designed to deaden noise and vibration . . . to ensure that the hundreds of rotating parts throughout the ship make no more racket collectively than the hum of your computer. At least, not beyond the hull.

"Now suppose something, a bracket, a wire, even an old oil can, gets loose somewhere up in the casing and it starts to rattle. The moment that noise is heard, something has to be done about it. Invariably, the submarine must come to the surface as soon as it is safe to do so. And fix it.

"A party must go up on deck and stop that rattle no matter what. In a big sea at night, that is really dangerous. Whenever there is a man overboard on a submarine, we assume it's probably something like that. If they had not bothered to fix it, that rattle would have served as a beacon to anyone listening within fifty miles.

"No competent submarine commander would ever make that kind of mistake—even if it cost the life of one of his crew."

"Cost more than that," replied the President. "But I'm grateful to have it cleared up."

He then asked the same question General Paul had asked. "Could Commander Adnam have piloted one of those Kilos out of Bandar Abbas, and then back in again, without being seen by the U.S. satellite reconnaissance systems?"

Scott Dunsmore gave him the same answer he had given the General. Highly unlikely, but not absolutely impossible. After all, the guy had somehow achieved the impossible anyway, by getting into the heart of the invincible CVBG.

There were no other questions at this time, because it was clear the President himself was thinking very carefully. It was almost one minute before he spoke, And when he did, a tense silence gripped the table.

"I am proposing, gentlemen," he said, "to take those three Iranian Kilos out of our lives for good. I want them destroyed. And I want it done fast. By the time it is done, we may know we have hit the exact culprit. If not, we may still have hit the right nation, because the chances are they merely used another submarine we do not know about. Let's start by getting rid of those Kilos. I expect you all remember, my predecessor tried to stop them being delivered in the first place. But the Russians somewhat outwitted everyone.

"Those submarines have been a pain in the ass ever since.

They have caused us to start moving squadrons of fighter aircraft into Bahrain for the second time in five years. And now we know they may have attacked a U.S. warship. I'm sick to death of this crap.

"Those three Kilos are a continuing threat, an endless problem to everyone. Get rid of 'em. All three of them—if all three of them are there. If not, hit two, and we'll get the third one when the sonofabitch returns home."

Robert MacPherson spoke first. "Mr. President, I want to clarify just one thing. Are you proposing we just fire up a fleet of fighter-bombers and go in an destroy the entire Naval base, straight in the front door and take the place off the map? Not that it would be any problem."

"I simply want all three of those submarines removed. Permanently."

Dick Stafford was next: "Sir, can we assume you would like to avoid starting World War III?"

"Yes, you may. But I don't want the military attack compromised because of it."

"Sir," said General Paul, "I think it would be better to take them out in what would appear to be mysterious circumstances, so that no one, least of all the Iranians, would ever be exactly sure who had done it."

"I'm with you on that," said Stafford.

"Any chance it would just seem like an accident?" asked Harcourt Travis.

"Yes," said the general. "They would find themselves in very much the same position we are in. They would have to announce an accident, otherwise they would be spreading alarm and panic among their own populace. And they would not want to lose face with their Arab neighbors. But they would know the destruction of their Russian-built submarines had been achieved by a very powerful military force."

"Would you like to be any more certain that Iran is the nation which hit our carrier?" asked Stafford.

"No. I think we're certain about that. But I'm happy to get rid of their submarines anyway. And I'm perfectly happy to hit them, and anyone else as well, if that's what it takes to ensure we teach the right nation a very severe lesson. I have given it much thought, and as far as I am concerned, those three Kilos are history. I'm looking forward to hearing how it's going to be done."

"That's easy," said General Paul. "It's a Special Forces job."

"It's an easy answer, and a correct answer," said Admiral Dunsmore. "But it is not an easy mission. The water in the three harbors at Bandar Abbas is very shallow. We'd need a nuclear submarine to bring in a SEAL team, and then an SDV to complete the last part of the journey. I'm guessing, but I would say they'd have to travel fifteen miles in, and fifteen miles back on a battery-powered underwater vehicle. That's a nine-hour job, it's quite dangerous, and it can't be set up overnight."

"Maybe we should just go in by air and obliterate 'em," suggested MacPherson. "Less dangerous, far less chance of getting anyone killed, and very efficient."

"Nonetheless, we'll be branded a bunch of reckless maniacs by the international community," said Stafford. "And then they'd all start asking questions. Why should the U.S.A. hit the Navy of Iran? What's Iran done to deserve that?

"And then they'll be asking if the *Jefferson* was really an accident? Was this outrageous airstrike against Iran because the Pentagon believes the fate of the carrier was no accident? Because the Pentagon believes the *Jefferson* was hit by an Ay-rab in one of those Kilos?"

"Yes," murmured the Secretary of State, "I suppose that would be very bad news indeed."

"Yes. That would be hopeless," said the President. "Gentlemen, I think it would be in my best interest to leave the meeting now. You may of course stay here as long as you wish, and perhaps Dick can inform me of anything particularly pertinent. However, the less I know about the technicalities the better.

"I just hope to see in the newspapers a couple of weeks from now that there has been a most unfortunate accident to three submarines at the Iranian Navy base in Bandar Abbas."

"How long was that, sir?" asked Scott Dunsmore.

"Couple of weeks, Scott. Is that all right?"

"Sir, I think I would be inclined to allow a month. Just because it may take us that long to get a specialist submarine into the area, especially one we can equip with the new SDV, which also has to be transported. It's over twelve thousand miles from our San Diego base. Also we have to allow the SEALS time to rehearse the mission."

"Yes. I understand. But try to get it done in two weeks. Especially as I would like to have it done tomorrow."

At which point Admiral Dunsmore said formally, "Well, gentlemen, since I am plainly the person to be charged with carrying out the Chief's wishes, I would be happy to tell you any more details you may want. But I think it best that I get back to the factory and put this all in motion; then maybe we can meet tomorrow somewhere and I'll brief you all further. By the way, the Navy likes the plan. We can't wait to get rid of the Ayatollah's submarines. I think this is a great call by the President."

"Sure was. All my guys will be relieved," said General Paul. "Matter of fact I think Scott and I should go back together right now, and get this thing moving."

The meeting broke up. And the two Service Chiefs left the White House immediately. In less than one hour Admiral Dunsmore had contacted the most elite combatant force in the Armed Services, the SEALS. It is the U.S. Navy's Special Forces Unit, where each man must possess a nearly unique combination of physical, intellectual, and emotional strength. Aside from speed and strength, and a natural agility in the water, he also requires a first-class memory and a thorough knowledge of dozens of weapons, systems, and demolition techniques.

The United States runs eight teams of SEALS. Three of them are based at Little Creek, Virginia, numbered Two, Four and Eight. Numbers One, Three, and Five work out of Coronado, California, home of the U.S. Navy Special War Command—in the trade, SPECWARCOM—which oversees all SEAL missions anywhere in the world.

The admiral in command of SPECWARCOM, John Bergstrom, answered his telephone on the island of Coronado at 0835 on that Thursday morning. He was greeted by the Commander of the Fifth Fleet, Vice Admiral Archie Carter, who was visiting San Diego, and requested his presence at the main Navy base forthwith.

When he arrived, Admiral Carter was standing at a big desk using a pair of Navy dividers and a metal ruler. Before him was a Navy chart of the area north of Jazireh-Ye Qeshm, a long, parched island in the Strait of Hormuz. He was measuring the waterway between the eastern end of the island and the harbor directly opposite; this was the right-hand harbor of three, in a twenty-mile stretch along the southeast coast of Iran.

Admiral Bergstrom peered over his shoulder, gazing at the name at the head of the chart, "The Port of Bandar Abbas." He noted the big radar domes marked clearly behind the harbor. He noted the narrow channel, only twenty-seven-feet deep, running between the pincer-shaped claws of the outer harbor walls. He noted the length of the long breakwater.

There could be but one reason why he had been summoned to this room, where the Commander of the Fifth Fleet was examining a chart of a potentially hostile foreign navy base: to organize its destruction. The SEALS specialty.

In his mind he imagined the base as his men would see it from the dark waters as they swam in . . . the flashing green light on the right, perhaps just illuminating an armed sentry on the harbor entrance. He noted the sheltered interior reaches of the harbor, tucked behind the sandy headland on the right. A death trap if they were seen. He wondered how carefully it was all guarded, what chance his men had of survival, and how many they might have to kill to get out.

"Morning, Admiral," he said breezily. "What do you want us to do, blow the entire thing to pieces, or just destroy the warships?"

Admiral Carter smiled at the insight of the top man from SPECWARCOM. "Not all of them, John. Just three, all submarines. Orders direct from CNO. We've got fourteen days to get there and take them out. I understand the decision was made less than two hours ago in the Oval Office."

"How close can we get to an SSN?" asked Bergstrom instantly.

"John, I'm very much afraid no nearer than thirteen miles."

"Jesus. That means they'll have to go in with the new Mark IX SDV. It's untried. And it only makes five knots. But it'll hold ten people, and it has a big battery, should run for twelve hours."

And he stared down at the chart, looking again at the narrow confines of the harbor entrance. "Are the submarines all in the water?" he asked.

"No. Unfortunately, we think one of them may be in a covered floating dock, shored up on her keel, and probably guarded."

"You want us to go in and take out the guards before we start?"

"No. I'd prefer you not to take out anyone, if possible. This is a completely clandestine operation, and ideally I would like the Iranian Navy to be wondering what the hell's going on for as long as possible. Maximum damage, minimum noise, no traces left behind. Except three rather large, very wrecked, Russian-built submarines, which will never go to sea again."

"Yessir. I understand. Will someone send the biggest, latest charts and overhead pictures over to us? And if we are pursued by armed Iranian patrol boats carrying depth charges, do I have permission to sink our enemy?"

"John, with this President we always enjoy that freedom. Shoot to kill in self-defense, if your lives are in danger. But in general terms I believe the White House would very much prefer you did not start World War III."

"I'll certainly try to avoid that, sir," replied Admiral Bergstrom.

0930 Thursday, July 18.

I T TOOK ADMIRAL BERGSTROM NINETY MINUTES TO establish his initial plan of action, in the SEAL compound, surrounded by barbed wire, behind the Coronado beach.

The admiral had ordered all of the commanders involved to enter "brainstorm mode"—and he had already presided over the short-list selection of the hit squad which would strike against the Ayatollah's underwater Navy.

There are 225 men on each SEAL team, of whom only 160 are active members of the attack platoons. There are 25 people in support and logistics, technicians and electronic experts, with 40 more involved in training, command, and control. Each SEAL strike squadron requires enormous backup.

The senior commanders had recommended this job for the Number Three Team. They had then selected one of the ten platoons of sixteen SEALS, which made up the team. They would then choose the final squad, of probably eight, which would make the "takeout" deep inside the port of Bandar Abbas. Their leader would be Lieutenant Commander Russell Bennett, a thirty-four-year-old veteran of the Gulf War, graduate of the U.S. Naval Academy, Annapolis, leading classman in the SEALS murderous indoctrination course, BUD/S, known colloquially as "The Grinder," and son of a Maine lobsterman.

Bennett was medium height, with thick, wide shoulders, dark blue eyes, and a generous but well-trimmed mustache. He had forearms and wrists which might have been made of blue-twisted steel. He was an expert on explosives, a superb marksman, and lethal with a knife, especially in the water. He could scale the smoothest steel plates of any ship. He could swim anywhere in the coldest seas, and he could climb anything. Any enemy who ran into him was probably looking at the last five seconds of his life.

His subordinates worshiped him and called him "Rusty" because of his short-clipped red hair. Like most SEALS he ignored all forms of correct uniform, and went into action with a head bandage instead of a hat, calling it his "drive-on rag." His colleagues swore he pinned his coveted SEAL golden Trident badge on his pajamas each night at Coronado. He had never gone into combat without that badge, carefully blacking it up before leaving, even more carefully burnishing it bright on his safe return. Lieutenant Bennett was typical of the kind of Navy SEAL SPECWARCOM considered adequate for platoon command.

He had twice done a stint as a BUD/S instructor, pounding tirelessly along the burning Pacific beaches at the head of his class, driving them up the sand dunes, and then down into the freezing sea, driving them until they thought they would die of exhaustion. Then driving them some more. Using the time-honored SEAL punishments, he sent shattered but still defiant men just one more time through the underwater "tunnel," then made them roll on the beach and complete a course of grueling exercises under the agonizing grazing of the clinging wet sand.

Twelve years previously, other instructors had done it to him, driven him until he thought he had nothing more to give. But he did. And they made him find it. They forced him ever onward, through the assault courses, through the brutal training of "Hell Week," which breaks 50 percent of all entrants, until at the end, he believed in his soul that no one on this planet could ever *hurt* him. At least not worse than he had already been hurt.

When he was selected as leading classman, and, in his full-dress uniform, chimed the great silver bell at the end of the course, Rusty Bennett was the proudest man in the United States Navy. And still, in the high summer of 2002, he was as hard-trained and impervious to pain as any human being could ever be.

Rusty's father, who still set his lobster traps in the deep, ice-cold waters of the rocky Maine coast, south of Mount Desert, had long assumed that his unmarried eldest was crazy.

And now Rusty was in "brainstorm mode," in the operations room, staring at the chart. This was the initial session involving SEALS high command and the team leader. They were dealing with absolute basics. Which submarine? Where is it? How long to get to Diego Garcia? Admiral Carter of the Fifth Fleet would have theater command, once they move into the area.

Rusty too was asking elementary questions: Strength of the current? Tide and depth? Conditions on the bottom? Guards? Patrol boats? Searchlights? Possible alarms? Likely weather conditions? Phase of the moon? Underwater visibility? How many SEALS do we need to go in? Not until these basic matters were clarified would he call in his second-in-command, who would drive in the SDV.

He made a drawing of the two Iranian Kilos in their precise positions, as provided by the satellite photographs. He sketched in the big floating dock, in the position it was last seen. He marked the place where they would leave the SSN. Marked another spot where the SDV would wait, in the outer reaches beyond the harbor, once they were all in the water.

He conferred with the weapons officers and the explosives experts, formulating the precise charge necessary for the "sticky" mine they would carry in and then clamp to the under-side of each Kilo's hull. The explosion would drive upward, through the casing, through the hull, right under the gigantic battery.

The charge had to be powerful enough to blow a big hole in the pressure hull, and ignite a major internal fire. The overall game plan was that the blast, the intense heat and searing flames, would immediately overcome the crew, while the onrushing flood of seawater would sink the submarine.

Another "sticky" mine, blasting upward, under the stern, and bending the propeller shaft, would make double-sure the Kilo never left the harbor again.

It was understood that it would take two SEALS to destroy each of the two floating Iranian submarines. The third one, the one which could be inside the floating dock, would undoubtedly prove a bit more difficult. But it had to go. After all, it might be the very one which had hit the *Jefferson*.

Everyone realized the floating dock might be empty, which would at least confirm they had definitely hit the right nation. But now they had to make their plans and behave as if it was *going* to be there—even though this submarine would be four times more tricky to take out than the others. The commanding officers knew they faced the age-old problem of big business— they were about to spend 80 percent of their effort on 33 percent of the problem—and all of that 80 percent might be wasted if the third Kilo was not there.

The action required on the first two was relatively straightforward by SEAL standards. The one in the dock involved a lot of educated guesswork, but the principle of standing up a 2,356-ton submarine in a dry dock was universal. The huge ballast tanks under the dock were flooded, on the same principle as the submarine itself, and the dock routinely sank sufficiently for the boat to be floated in.

She entered right down the middle of the dock, above a series of huge wooden blocks arranged precisely to accommodate the shape of the submarine's keel, and spread the load of her colossal weight. The ballast tanks under the dock were then pumped out until the dock rose a few feet, and the submarine nearly settled.

Mooring wires, controlled by powerful dockside winches, were then used to position the boat in exactly the right spot over the keel blocks, accurate to the nearest inch. Eight giant wooden "shores"—around eighteen inches square, twice the thickness of a telegraph pole, and probably thirty feet long— were set against the hull, a fraction over halfway up, four on either side.

These great beams, easily strong enough to bear the weight of several men, were wedged into place with sledgehammers, to prevent the submarine from toppling over sideways.

At this point operators would start to pump out the ballast tanks, and the massive edifice would begin to float upward, very slowly, not much faster than the outgoing tide. With the dock on the surface, the submarine stood high and dry, ready for the engineers and shipwrights to begin work. It was one of the more time-consuming, difficult procedures in any dockyard. If a submarine went into dry dock it had a major problem, involving repairs below the waterline.

The floating dock in Bandar Abbas had a roof built right across the top, turning it into something the size of an aircraft hangar, anchored to the harbor bottom by monstrous steel and concrete moorings. It was not going to wreck anyone's life in the Pentagon if the SEALS wiped that out too. But that would depend on how much "kit" the SEAL swimmers could carry.

Admiral Bergstrom, himself a SEAL veteran, made a key recommendation here. "I don't think we need 'blow' the third Kilo at all," he said. "If we could somehow smash all four shores on her starboard side, she'd crash down on her own, probably take out the entire wing wall of the dock, and possibly drive her way straight through the floor. Two and a half thousand tons is a pretty good weight to drop—it would certainly smash the dock to pieces, and put the whole lot on the bottom of the harbor with very little explosive effort on our part."

"Yes," replied Commander Ray Banford, "but those things are damn finely balanced. She may not fall immediately, and the noise we make blowing the shores might just alert them, maybe give 'em time to bang in another shore if they happen to have a few spares around. Just one could stop her falling."

"She'd go if I blew a damn great hole in her starboard holding tank at precisely the same time we took out the shores," said Lieutenant Bennett. "I guess the slightest tilt of that dock would do it. And that big float tank, full of seawater, would tilt her over half a degree in about one minute flat. She'd go then."

"Yes, I guess she would," said Commander Banford. "Actually

I think our real problem here is the amount of guys we might need to get those shores out."

"One man on each," said Rusty. "That's four. I'll go in first, under the dock, and attach some kind of a mine to the tank. Then I'll stand guard while the guys wire up the shores. We'll use det-cord. We'll hook up the explosives to the same detonator, give ourselves time to get clear, and the whole lot will blow together. She'll go. No doubt, she'll go."

"Right here, we're talking a lot of guys," said Banford, the ex-submarine commander, who would oversee the mission. "We need four men for the floating Kilos. Four for the shores. Couldn't two guys do two each?"

"Too dangerous, sir. Don't forget we'll be working close to the guard on the deck of the submarine, but just out of his sight-range. If he hears one sound he'll start looking, then I'll have to take him out, then someone else might hear, then we'll end up taking a dozen of 'em out, with all hell breaking loose.

"No, sir. I think we should move at twice the speed, with four men, one on each shore working simultaneously."

"Yes, Rusty. I do see that, it's just the number I'm worried about. Four men on the two floating Kilos, four men on the shores, you blowing the float tank and standing guard—that's nine, plus the driver of the SDV. That's ten, and the SDV only holds eight."

Admiral Bergstrom spoke next. "Well, Ray, we do have a new Swimmer Delivery Vehicle, delivered in the past few weeks. It does hold ten. They call this one an ASDS, an Advanced Swimmer Delivery System, electric-powered, made by Westinghouse. It has a longer range than the old Mark VIII, probably twelve hours, and it does hold ten guys.

"If you assume three hours to get in and three hours back, plus four hours waiting, that's ten hours, if nothing goes wrong. She only makes five knots, but she's nearly perfect for us. Trouble is, I don't know whether she's operational yet. And I believe we only have two SSN's fitted to carry her . . . "Tommy!" He beckoned over to Lieutenant Tommy Schwab, asked him to check out the submarine situation with SUBPAC, Vice Admiral

Johnny Barry, Commander, Submarine Force, Pacific Fleet.

Meanwhile they agreed in principle to a ten-man team. And Lieutenant Rusty Bennett then threw another curve ball. "I think we should blow the boat in the dry dock at the earliest possible time," he said. "It is likely they will have a sentry patrolling the walkway around the top of the floating dock. If we leave that det-cord in place for one and a half hours while we get away, he's got a good chance of spotting it if he's sharp. He only has to notice it on *one* of the shores and they'll find the whole detonation network and cut it.

"I think we should set the det-cord to blow ten minutes after we hit the water. We'll be a few hundred yards away by then, and we're not talking huge underwater explosion, just the minor blast on the float tank. That won't affect our eardrums. The rest of the explosives are high up in the dock, and the damage is going to be slow motion, zero-blast underwater, all in the same place.

"If we just let the submarine crash through the dock, they won't even suspect they were hit by anything military. And there will still be chaos in the base when the other two Kilos blow. We can set them to go two hours after we leave, by which time we'll be back in the SDV and well on our way across the bay. I'm figuring they'll want an hour to get their act together and come after us with a patrol boat. We'll be in the SSN before they get a sniff."

"Good thinking," said the admiral. "It sure would be god-damned irritating if we set the whole thing up and then they found the det-cord before we blew out the shores.

"One question . . . have you guys thought yet how you're going to work up high, on the side of the submarine? I mean A, how are you going to get up there? B, how will you avoid being seen? And C, what protection do you have?"

One of the senior instructors, a Chief Petty Officer, stepped forward. "According to these drawings we have here, the shores will be positioned about thirty feet from the floor of the dock," he told the group.

"Well, we can't climb the curved sides of the submarine, nor can we risk going up onto the walkway around the top of the dock. So we have to go straight up a rope to each shore. We'll use fairly thick black nylon, with a big foothold knot every two feet, and a small, padded black steel grappler on the end. The guys will twirl and throw the grapplers from the floor, up and over the beams. When the hook grabs and digs into the wood, they go, straight up, and straddle the beams.

"They'll work close in, maybe five or six feet from the hull of the submarine. That way the sentry *cannot* see them without crawling right down over the edge, in which case he'll fall off. Most likely he will be in a chair, possibly asleep, right in the middle of the deck, under the bridge, looking aft.

"Most of these big floating docks have steel ladders at the ends and one about halfway along the wall which goes from the floor up to the walkway. Rusty will position himself as far up there as he needs to be, just enough to train his sights on the sentry's head. Rusty's gun will of course be silenced.

"The guys will wind the det-cord around the beams probably about six times, that means they will each want about forty feet of the stuff up there, with another forty feet hanging down and another eighty feet to connect to the next beam. Our stuff is dark green in color, and det-cord's not too heavy. It's thin, and we can wrap it tight. It'll be awkward swimming in, but we've done much worse.

"I estimate the guys will be up on the wooden beams for no more than four minutes. Rusty can make the joins, and fix the detonator and timing mechanism as soon as he gets down the ladder. He says ten minutes, maximum."

"Thank you, Chief," said the admiral. "You starting practice today?"

"Nossir, I'm fixing up for us to use AFDM–14, the big floating dock right here in San Diego. They have a submarine in it right now, on shores. I thought we'd spend two days over there, by which time this team will be world experts with a thirty-foot throw with rope and grappler.

"Most of them have done it before, sir, but we must eliminate every possibility of a mistake. What we don't want is for one of those ropes to fail to fetch the beam, because then the damned grappler will fall and thump on the steel floor of the dock, and then Rusty may have to kill the goddamned sentry."

"Guess so, Chief . . . "

Just then the door flew open and Lieutenant Tommy Schwab rushed in. "Sir," he said, "we just got lucky. Real lucky. The SSN we want is one of those old Sturgeon Class boats, *L. Mendel Rivers*. She's recently been converted to take the new ASDS. She was one of the two SSN's with the *Thomas Jefferson*, and she's *in* Diego Garcia right now."

"Perfect," said the admiral. "What about the ASDS?"

"Yessir. She's about ready for ops, but she's still right here in San Diego. So we'll have to fly her out in a C5A with the SEAL team. But the *Mendel Rivers* is ready and waiting, being serviced right now. We're all set."

"Now that's great," replied Admiral Bergstrom. And turning to the Chief Petty Officer in charge of training, he said, "We can get the SEALS familiarized with the new vehicle right away. When do you reckon they'll be ready to go?"

"Well, we have swimming and weight tests, plus the rope training. Weapons testing. A couple days' instruction on operating ASDS. Plus a day coordinating everything. They'll be ready to fly out next Thursday night on the regular Navy flight out to DG, you know, the old C5A Galaxy right out of San Diego."

"Well done, Chief. Couldn't be better . . . oh, Tommy, call CNO's office and make sure he's told about all this, will you? Top secret. He's waiting."

"Aye, sir. Thursday night flight, right?"

At this point the broad plan for the mission was formally approved by Commander Banford. Rusty Bennett routinely informed his men they were now, officially, in isolation. Phone calls were banned, even to wives and children. No letter could be written, not even postcards. No faxes, no fraternizing with *anyone* not involved with the planning and training. In that way, there was no chance of anyone, however unintentionally, compromising the mission.

The men were permitted to update or write their wills, and

these would be held in the SEAL archives until their safe return. Or failing that, they would be pronounced legal by the Navy.

Rusty Bennett spent the first evening in conference with his whole team, thinking it through, measuring accurately on the charts all of the distances. In particular the navigational plan for the ASDS—from the *Mendel Rivers* to its waiting position outside the port of Bandar Abbas. His second-in-command, referred to as 2IC, a lieutenant junior grade, David Mills from Massachusetts, sat in on these meetings, since he would drive the miniature submarine in while Rusty navigated. The other eight men would sit behind them, in the dry but cold air, breathing through tubes connected to a central air system in the ASDS, as it crawled slowly and silently through the ocean, fifteen feet below the surface.

The sea miles were plotted with immense care. Rusty Bennett himself called out the information . . . "Total distance SSN to ASDS waiting position at 56.12E, 27.07N . . . is 12.93 miles . . . course three-three-eight . . . two hours and thirty-five minutes at five knots . . . add thirty minutes for the launch . . . at ten and a half miles there's a red flashing light every seven seconds marking a long shoal to port . . . water's only about twenty feet deep in there . . . if we see the light we're plenty close . . . it should be about 750 yards off our port beam as we pass . . . we don't want to be way off course on the right either, because there's a wreck marked there—in about thirty feet of water very near the inward channel."

Rusty Bennett was in fact *never* off course, having been brought up in his father's lobster boat, creeping his way through the fog that often blankets those enchanted pine-tree islands off the Maine coast. Rusty Bennett was reading ocean charts when most kids were still busy with Mr. Rogers. His father was a native of the outward island of Monhegan, and his mother's maiden name was Lunt, the famous Down East family that ran the boatyard and lobster fleet out of Lunt Harbor, Frenchborough.

The sea was in this particular SEAL's blood for generations. And he came from a cold, dangerous northern sea, in which the big marker buoys, with their chiming navigation bells and flash-ing lights, were often the *only* means of avoiding a catastrophic loss of bearing and direction. Miss one of them in bad weather, and death might be staring you in the face. Unsurprisingly, Rusty Bennett was one of the best navigators the SEALS had ever had.

Every time he spoke, someone took down his words. By the time he turned his attention to the Iranian submarine base, there were two note-takers, one Senior Petty Officer double-checking every figure, and another following Rusty's progress on a second chart . . . checking, checking, checking. Another man on the computer keyboard was entering the navigation plan in a file now marked "Operation Vengeance."

Rusty Bennett kept talking. "Probable distance from ASDS anchorage to right-side harbor wall . . . five hundred yards . . . bearing two-eight-four . . . there's a green navigation light on that wall . . . we may even see it. Right there we turn right . . . bearing zero-zero . . . heading for the inner harbor . . . thirteen hundred yards . . . this wants counting carefully . . . because we make a right there . . . that's two hundred yards beyond a second green light . . . this one flashing quickly . . . water's only about nine feet deep in here close to the wall . . . after that second right turn we swim for a thousand yards on a nine-zero bearing . . . right there we should be outside the floating dock . . . five of us bail out there and get up on it . . . possible four- or five-foot climb . . .

"The other four keep going on bearing . . . the Kilos berthed either side of the jetty will come up inside 50 yards . . . total swim distance in is thus 2,800 yards . . . it's gonna take us one hour to swim that, then we've got 160 yards further to go . . . allowing for nav stops . . . say ten minutes . . . that's sev-enty minutes from exit ASDS to the dock."

They finally wrapped it up just before 2300, and headed thankfully to bed. The chief who ran the training program wanted all five of the dock team ready to leave for the San Diego base by 0630 the following morning. Rusty mentioned that since he wasn't throwing the grapplers over the shores, maybe

he was unnecessary. The chief's reply was curt. "What if someone gets hurt, and you're not sure about getting the grappler
over, first time, sir?"

"Yes, guess so. But who would cover the guys then?"

"That's SOP, sir. Either your wounded man can get up the ladder to do it, or you shoot the fucking Iranian guard, nice and
quiet, before you start."

"Oh yeah, right, Chief."

Shortly before 0700 the next morning, the Navy jeep drove
onto the jetty alongside the huge floating dry dock, *Steadfast*,
positioned deep inside the San Diego base. Six men jumped out
of the vehicle, and immediately the chief began to speak. "Now,
you can all see the size of it, right? The wing walls are 83 feet
high, and close to 260 feet long. I should think the one in Bandar
Abbas is nearly identical, because a Russian Kilo is 242 feet
long.

"See those two cranes high up, on top of the wall? Well, they
can lift thirty tons and you find them on top of all floating docks.
Also up there you are going to see a control tower, and in there
you may see a guard and an operator, or just an operator who
doubles as a guard. In front of him are the hydrovalves and
flooding systems, and he has a set of illuminated dials which
show him the angles of the dock in the water.

"They are really just like spirit levels. Theoretically, when
Rusty blows a hole in the starboard-side ballast tank, the dock
will begin to tilt. What we don't want is for the guy in the tower
to notice something very early and then compensate for the list
on the dock by flooding the opposite tank as well. But I don't
think he will have time. A little later, we'll give that a bit more
thought, and then we'll go up and act out the scenario a few
times ourselves, just to see what might happen and to get accurate times.

"Meantime, let's get into the dock, and see how good we are
at hurling the grappler ropes up and over the shores."

All five men took their rope coils out of the jeep and headed
for the engineer's platform which was moored on the stern of
Steadfast. They crossed from the jetty, and walked into the

floating dock, all of them for the first time. From water level it looked massive, and so did the submarine propped up inside. They stood alongside the boat, and above their heads they could see the big wooden shores, four of them in a line, about thirty feet above the steel deck.

The trainer told them the secret of standing at least twenty feet in front of the unseen perpendicular line from the beam down to the floor. "That way, you pick your angle, and throw the rope up, underarm, in a dead straight line making sure it goes above the beam. That way when it drops, it *must* come down on the far side, and then you just pull, and the grappler will come up and dig into the wood. You want to give it a good jolt, but nothing too loud.

"The trick is to learn to twirl the hook in a large circle, clockwise as you look at your right hand. You need to know exactly when to let go. That's just practice. Okay, Lieutenant Commander, show 'em how it's done . . . "

Rusty got into position, and began to whirl the hook around until the noise made a hum in the air. He gazed upward and let go. Too low. The grappler flew twenty feet above the ground like a rocket at least ten feet below the beam and crashed down onto the deck with an unnerving, echoing thump and clatter.

"Well, sir, I'd say you just came up with a pretty good way of getting all five of you killed right there," said the chief. "I said you needed practice and that's what you're gonna get."

One by one the SEALS aimed their hooks up and over the beam; only one made it the first time, but he missed the next time. Seven hours later they were still there, and the standard was now almost flawless.

"In the end, it's like riding a bike," said the chief. "Once you know how, you never forget. I'm getting pleased with you, but I shall want each of you gentlemen to throw six perfect passes over the beam, one after the other. Anyone misses, you all start again, until we get thirty passes all sailing over. No mistakes."

"You ever consider becoming a basketball coach?" asked one of the SEALS.

"Sure I did, but only for the money. I wouldn't have saved so many lives . . . missed . . . the way you've been missing since this morning . . . too low . . . because you're letting go a fraction of a second too soon . . . now come on, get yourself centered . . . three twirls . . . rock steady rhythm . . . then let go . . . one! . . . two! . . . three! . . . *Release!* . . . You got it . . . straight over . . . stay centered . . . five more times . . . "

In Fort Meade, Admiral Morgan was still pursuing the Black Sea theory and had received a report from Admiral Sadowski in Pearl Harbor. It had been filed originally in Diego Garcia by a Navy pilot, Lieutenant Joe Farrell. The lieutenant wished to bring to the attention of any inquiry that he had spotted what he thought was the "feather" of a submarine at 1130 on June 28, one thousand miles due south of the Battle Group.

The white trail in the water had been clear to him, as had the total absence of any ship. Lieutenant Farrell had landed on the carrier and reported his sighting immediately to Captain Baldridge. At the specific request of the Group Operations Officer he had then made an official report to the ops room stating the time and position of the suspected submarine.

Unfortunately, there was nothing of this left, but Lieutenant Farrell had entered all the details in his flight log, including the fact that he hadn't seen anything on the way back to DG. It was a copy of this report which was exercising the suspicious mind of Arnold Morgan right now in his command center.

He was bent over a large map pinned to a high, slanting desk with a light positioned right above. In his hand was a pair of dividers, and they were measuring out the distance from the Strait of Gibraltar to a point one thousand miles south of the Battle Group's position at 1130 on June 28. He put that point at 9N, 67E.

He measured the distance, fifty-four inches on his map. He checked the scale—the distance from the Strait of Gibraltar to the point where Lieutenant Farrell thought he saw a submarine was 10,800 miles exactly. Everyone agreed it had probably been making eight knots through the water at periscope depth most of the way, sometimes in lonely waters a little faster, twice stopping to refuel. That meant it was traveling on average 200 miles per day.

Admiral Morgan divided 200 into 10,800 and came up with fifty-four days. He then checked his records for the precise time his operator had picked up the mysterious five-blader in the Gibraltar Strait—May 5 at 0438. From May 5 to May 31 was twenty-six days. The remaining twenty-eight days of June brought him to the precise time and date of Lieutenant Farrell's sighting—June 28, 1130. 9N, 67E. "As blind coincidence goes, that one ain't bad," growled the admiral. And now he didn't even bother with a telephone, just bellowed through the door at his Flag Lieutenant: "*Try Rankov again . . . and don't listen to any bullshit.*"

Unknown to the lieutenant, this was going to become even more difficult, and embarrassing, as the day wore on. Because while Admiral Morgan was raging at the world in general, Admiral Vitaly Rankov, the six-foot-six-inch head of Russian Naval Intelligence, was spending much of it in an ancient converted military aircraft, rattling and shuddering its way due south from Moscow on a laborious eight-hundred-mile journey.

Admiral Rankov hated aircraft, almost as much as he hated Naval mysteries. Right now he also hated the persistent, ill-tempered, and irritatingly powerful American Intelligence chief, Arnold Morgan. Which, generally speaking, made the Russian three times more edgy than he normally was on an interior Russian flight.

Admiral Morgan was the *only* foreign executive who had ever snarled at him, and then threatened him. "Rankov . . . there are always two ways to do things," Morgan had said. "The easy way and the hard way. If you do not do as I say in the next hour, I shall call my President, and have him call your President, and see how you come out of that little confrontation."

Admiral Rankov had slammed down the phone, and called the American's bluff. Two hours later he had indeed been in the Kremlin in front of the Russian President, and damned nearly got fired.

And now Morgan was being, for the second time in two

years, a royal pain in the rear. He must have called Admiral
Rankov's office eight times in the last twenty-four hours. He had
yelled at four different aides, and the Russian admiral knew precisely what he was asking: the same question he had been asking on and off for the last ten days—have you found that goddamned Kilo you told me you lost in the Black Sea ten weeks
ago. Except that now he also wanted to know whether a
drowned sailor washed up on some Greek island had been a
member of that submarine's crew.

Admiral Morgan's last message had requested the name on
the next-of-kin-list. This is the record every modern Navy keeps
in case of a disaster at sea. The trouble was they did not seem to
have a firm next-of-kin-list for the missing Kilo, which was at
best tiresome, and at worst embarrassing in the extreme.

In fact the High Command of the Black Sea Fleet was useless. They had been unable to salvage, or even find, the missing
Kilo. They had not even been able to trace the name of the
drowned man. And there was the problem of the next-of-kin
list.

They had the book at the base, and it contained a full crew
list, but apparently they had not received the standard signal
from the submarine, updating it before they left—recording perhaps a couple of men who had not made the trip, plus two or
three others who were sailing but were not entered in the NOK
list. Thus the whole system was out, every name was now ques-
tionable. Without the final signal from the Kilo, no name was
definite, and the NOK list in their possession was too suspect to
be quoted. As far as Admiral Rankov was concerned the
drowned man could have deserted.

And now this American bastard was on the phone, and
Admiral Vitaly Rankov considered it only a matter of time
before he was back in the Kremlin to explain himself to the
Russian President, and God knows who else.

Which was why he was now in this rattletrap of an aircraft
flying to the Aeroflot terminal in the southern Russian city of
Krasnodar, home, on the northern Caucasian plains, of the
Kuban Cossacks.

It was also the nearest commercial airport to the port of Novorossisk, in which the Navy was conducting its endless meetings, discussing the possibility of re-siting there a new Russian headquarters for the Black Sea Fleet. The long, laborious process of moving from historic Sevastopol, 250 miles west across the water in the Ukraine, had been driving everyone mad for eight years now, and nothing had been done, nor, in the opinion of Admiral Rankov, would ever be done.

The trouble was, no one knew what they were doing, nor indeed what they were expected to be doing. Thus you could *never* find anyone. Every time you wanted to see a high-ranking officer from the Black Sea Fleet, he was either in Sevastopol, or up in some shipyard gazing at an aircraft carrier which would *never* be completed, or wandering around Novorossisk talking rubbish about building projects no one could afford.

And now the admiral faced a seventy-mile car ride from Krasnodar airport.

He *must* find out about the missing Kilo before Morgan caused an uproar. He regarded Morgan's increasingly angry persistence as sinister. Something was going on, he knew that, but he did not want to get caught on the phone to Washington, probably being taped, with his pants down. A four-hour ride in that god-awful airplane had been preferable to that.

Admiral Rankov settled back in the deep and comfortable rear seat of the limousine which had arrived to collect him, right on time. He enjoyed the drive across the plains, and on down to the big commercial shipyard on the eastern shore of the great inland sea. He had been born just a few miles to the south in the lovely Russian resort city of Sochi, with its temperate southern climate and perfect beaches. The mountains, snow-capped and spectacular, lay to the northeast.

Right now, driving in some luxury into Novorossisk, with the warm southwestern breezes drifting across the sea from Turkey, and up the southern Russian coastline, Admiral Rankov wished no man ill. Except for Arnold Morgan, from whom there were already two urgent messages awaiting him at the temporary Navy yard reception desk.

"Jesus Christ!" groaned Vitaly. "Can I never get away from this fucking maniac?"

The SEALS sat together in the rear of the gigantic long-range Galaxy as it inched its way forward, twenty-five thousand feet above the Pacific Ocean. The forty-foot-long ASDS, winched on rails into this military freighter, was crated in a container in the hold. The SEALS sat in the close, silent camaraderie of fighting men who have nothing much to say to anyone except to each other. They wore their regular Navy uniforms, for a change. Also packed in the hold, with the miniature submarine, were crates containing the combat equipment they would use on their mission to disembowel the Iranian submarine service.

Each man owned a highly flexible, custom-made, neoprene wet suit, which provided excellent thermal protection; even eighty-four-degree water will sap the heat out of a man's body if he stays in it long enough. The big SEAL flippers, for extra speed, were also custom-made. On the instep they bore the student number each man was awarded when he finally passed the BUD/S course. That lifetime identification number is worn with pride. At least 50 percent of every class fails.

All of Rusty Bennett's men had with them a couple of modern commercial scuba diver's masks, the bright Day-Glo orange and red colors carefully obscured with black water-resistant tape. Not one of the nine swimmers would wear a watch on the mission, because of the slight danger of the luminous dial being spotted by a sentry.

Underwater, SEALS travel with a specially designed "attack board," a small two-handled platform which displays a compass, a depth gauge, and a more unobtrusive watch. The lead swimmer kicks through the water with both hands gripping his attack board, never needing to slide off course to check time or direction. These details are laid out right in front of his eyes on the board.

The second man usually swims with one hand lightly on the leader's shoulder, both of them kicking and counting. SEALS have a special technique for judging distance. If one of them has

IRAN

Bandar Abbas

Súrú

SEE INSET MAP

2

6

2

4

6

6

9

6

10

16

wreck
10

9

9

10

10

9

10

10

10

16

15

22

20

Khúrán Clarence Strait

16

9

6

Jazíreh-ye qeshm

N

0   1   2   3
Sea miles

Qeshm

'Mendel Rivers'
waiting area

51

DETAIL OF HARBOR

Radars

Floating
Dock

West
Breakwater

East
Breakwater

1

3   3

7

1

12

0   0.5
Sea Miles

ASDV
waiting area

to swim three hundred yards, and he knows he moves, say, ten feet forward with each kick, he knows he must count ninety kicks to be on top of his target. According to SEAL instructors, a trained underwater operative develops a near-mystical judgment of these relatively short journeys.

The SEALS would swim into Bandar Abbas behind four attack boards: three standard pairs, with the overall leader, Lieutenant Rusty Bennett, bringing in two men behind him. Each of them would carry the big fighting knife of their preference. The selected firearm weapon for this mission was a small submachine gun, the MP–5, made by the upmarket German gun company of Heckler and Koch, deadly reliable at close quarters, spot-on at twenty-five yards. Only three would be issued, one for Rusty and two extras for the rope-climbers. Their principal protection would be the dark waters of the harbor. Only in a case of dire necessity would the Americans open fire inside the floating dock.

Stowed separately in the hold was all of the SEALS' destruction kit—five limpet mines, plus one spare, specially shaped for an upward blast, and reels of det-cord, cut into eighty-foot lengths. The specially prepared black nylon climbing ropes, with their steel grappling hooks, were stored in a separate wooden crate. Rusty Bennett had also packed two small Motorola MX300 radios, plus two compact digital global-positioning systems which display your exact spot on the surface of the earth accurate to fifteen feet. These satellite-linked electronic gadgets were regarded as a godsend by marauding SEALS teams, but unhappily did not work well underwater.

Lieutenant Bennett knew that the principal weapons of this particular hit team were stealth, surprise, cunning, and skill. He hoped not to need any extraordinary aids, except strength, brains, and silence.

The SEALS from Coronado landed at the American base on Diego Garcia at 2100, Saturday night, July 27. The thirteen-thousand-mile flight had taken thirty-four hours with a short delivery and refueling stop at Pearl Harbor.

After a light supper, they were ordered instantly to bed, in readiness for an 0600 departure the following morning, on board the USS *L. Mendel Rivers*. The 2,600-mile journey in the hunter-killer submarine would take them almost due north, up to the Gulf of Hormuz; five and a half days, running at twenty knots.

They knew it would be cramped because the 4,500-ton nuclear boat needed all of its 107 crew and 12 officers for a mission like this, which required the ship to be on high-alert on a permanent basis. But at least the *Mendel Rivers* had been especially refitted to transport a platoon of SEALS. Each man would have a bunk, and Commander Banford was already in residence.

After six hours of sleep they awakened to a warm bright Sunday morning, the last daylight they would see for more than a week. Their equipment was already loaded and stowed, as the sun rose out of the eastern horizon of the Indian Ocean. The ten men stood on the dock and stared at the giant bulge on the deck right behind the sail. Inside, the miniature submarine which would take them in was already in place. While they had slept, a team had worked through the night unloading, uncrating, and lifting it aboard, ready for its final engineering check. Dave Mills would have five days to familiarize himself with the controls, but he was already trained to drive this new underwater delivery system.

They all knew the procedure. At the appointed time they would climb the ladder from the main submarine up into the DDS (dry deck shelter). There they would get aboard the tiny craft, and the hatch would be clamped into place. Oxygen supply would be checked, and the shelter flooded. Four divers would somehow wrestle her out into the ocean around thirty feet below the surface. Lieutenant Mills would fire up the engine and they would brace themselves for the uncomfortable thirteen-mile ride across the strait which divides Qeshm from Bandar Abbas.

It always felt freezing cold to the SEALS in an SDV, because the air they breathed came direct from a high-pressure storage bottle, and the temperature dropped noticeably in the manufactured, but normal, atmospheric conditions of the little submarine. The inner chill was always the same going in, and the SEALS knew this one would be no different.

The first three days of the journey to the Arabian Sea passed uneventfully. The submariners knew they were transporting the elite fighting men of the U.S. Navy, and the SEALS knew they were traveling with one of the most highly trained battle-ready crews in the world—officers who were also nuclear scientists, others whose knowledge of guided missiles was unrivaled, others who could diagnose the sounds of the ocean, sniffing out danger in all of its forms, often miles and miles away.

As Thursday night began to head toward Friday morning, nerves tightened. Commander Banford went over the plan again and again, until it was written on the heart of each SEAL. They were advised to sleep after an early lunch on Friday, and begin their final preparations at 1730. Each man should be ready by 1845, with his Draeger air system strapped on, the limpet mines, det-cord, ropes, grapplers, knives, and machine guns and clips buckled down, and waterproofed as far as possible for the swim. The official start time for the mission was 1900, at which time the ten men would enter the ASDS, just before dark.

During the final ninety minutes, the instructors and the Chief Petty Officer who had trained them, never left their sides. The talk was sparse, encouraging, as if defeat was out of the question. The SEALS' little corner of the SSN was like the dressing room of a world heavyweight champion, as each man prepared mentally in his own way. The atmosphere was taut, focused, as if deliberately ignoring the underlying fear of discovery, and probable death.

The rest of the submarine seemed quiet, but sharp, as the navigation officer guided her toward their waiting-station in the last deep water available to them . . . one hundred and fifty feet on the sounder. Position: 26.57N, 56.19E. Speed five knots.

The captain ordered them to periscope depth, grabbed both handles as the periscope came up from floor level. A three-second electronically coded message was fired up to the satellite for collection by the operators at DG, and a note was made of the flashing light guarding a sandbank off Qeshm harbor, five hundred yards off their port beam. The periscope of the *Mendel Rivers* was down again within twelve seconds.

And now, with the ship silent with anticipation, the SEALS, faces blackened with water-resistant oil, began their climb into the dry deck shelter, an exercise they had been practicing three times a day since leaving DG. They slipped up through the hatch with slick expertise, and then climbed through the second hatch into the ASDS. Rusty and Lieutenant Mills occupied the two separate compartments in the bow, which housed the driving and navigation seats. The dry shelter flooded quickly, but the actual departure took longer than expected. Finally the divers pushed and shoved the little submarine clear, released the tether, and swam back to the shelter before the SEALS started the electric motor.

At 1937 they moved forward, course three-three-eight, which would take them on a dead straight line to the drop-off point outside the port of Bandar Abbas. Rusty put Lieutenant Mills on a course which would narrowly pass the shoals off the eastern end of the island of Qeshm, and they kept the boat running at fifteen feet below the surface.

Neither could see anything through the dark water, and the entire journey was conducted on instruments. Behind the two leaders, the eight SEALS could speak, and they could hear each other, but conversation was kept to a bare minimum. Noise, any noise, was magnified underwater.

The first two hours passed quickly, but everyone was feeling very cramped as Lieutenant Mills slid up to the surface for a "fix," and then aimed the little boat across the final two miles to the harbor. They skirted the big sandbar which stretched in front of the entrance, and waited as the minutes passed until Rusty Bennett said softly, "This is it, guys. Right here." Their position was 56.12E, 27.07N. "We're going to the bottom," said Dave Mills. "It's about forty feet. Stand by to flood rear compartments. Connect air lines, activate your Draegers, flippers on and fasten."

All the men felt the little ship settle on the bottom. In the back they adjusted valves, shoved their feet into the flippers, clipped and fastened. Then they signaled everyone was ready. Lieutenant Mills opened the electronic valve and the seawater began to flood into the bigger "wet-and-dry-compartment," and into the tiny one occupied by Rusty Bennett.

Neither space would be pumped out until the men were safely aboard after the mission. But Lieutenant Mills, in his little cockpit, would stay dry during his long wait for his charges to return.

As the pressure equalized inside and outside of the ASDS, the SEALS were now sitting like so many goldfish in a completely flooded area. Then the three hatches were opened, and one by one the SEALS popped out. Rusty was first, holding his "attack board" rigidly in front of him, getting the feel of the water, stabilizing his breathing, coming to an operational depth about twelve feet below the surface. If the oxygen in his Draeger was to last four hours, every action had to be steady and relaxed. Sudden panicky movements could drain it in sixty minutes.

Rusty felt his two colleagues touch him on either shoulder. The other six men he could see swimming into position right behind. And with long steady kicks the red-haired lieutenant commander from the coast of Maine began to drive his way toward the Ayatollah's submarines.

He steadied the compass on bearing 284. There was five hundred yards to swim before the first turn. He hoped that he would be able to accurately judge the distance by counting his ten-foot kicks, and spotting the reflection of the green light on the harbor wall. Failing that, he would risk shoving his head above the surface to use a global-positioning device. He knew by a certain brightness in the water that the moon had risen, and he hoped to see the channel into the harbor.

They covered the five hundred yards in under fifteen minutes. Rusty spotted the green light through the surprisingly clear sea. Though the light seemed directly above, he knew it was fifty feet away because of the refraction effect of the water. He made his seventy-six-degree turn due north, fixed the compass bearing on zero-zero-zero degrees, and headed up into the harbor. With eleven hundred yards to swim, he had to concentrate.

It was almost 2230, and would be a little after 2300 when they passed the next light. They would stay out in the channel away from the very shallow water for the following two hundred yards.

They swam, kicking steadily, breathing as they had been trained to. At this point, everyone knew for certain that their brutal training—the years of running, swimming, lifting, and the killer assault courses which had broken so many of their colleagues—was paying off as the nine SEALS made their way through the alien waters.

These men had not broken. If the pain of the long swim became too great, each would dig deeper, searching for and finding more willpower. Each was too proud, too brave, to fail.

They passed the light, kicking forward to the point where they would make a ninety-degree turn toward the inner harbor. Rusty was beginning to feel the pace now, but knew he must kick three hundred more times, and keep his breathing steady. He kept his eyes down and his mind clear, and he kicked and counted . . . kicked and counted . . . a nagging pain beginning to settle high up in both thighs.

He passed two hundred and fifty, and sensed his team was still together in a tight group. The last minute seemed to take an hour, and up ahead he could sense a long blurred line in the water. He made right for it . . . and came to a halt. It was a huge dockyard chain. Rusty swam to the surface, and looked around him. He was in the shadow of a gigantic floating dock and there seemed to be no light. The chain ran up to its stern on the basin side. The far side was even darker, closer to the jetty, and in deep shadow. He could see an engineer's platform there, which almost certainly had a ladder into the water.

High above his head Rusty could see the ten-foot-long, scimitar-shaped blades of a propeller. . . five of them, engineered in bronze. It was the propeller of a Russian-built Kilo submarine.

Rusty dived again, swam across the stern of the dock, and climbed onto the deserted, unlit platform. He waited for his four black-suited colleagues. No sound passed between them. They unclipped their flippers and carried them into the great cavern of the dock. Each noted one single arclight positioned directly above the submarine, possibly fifty-five feet above the dock floor. The ship itself cast a giant oval shadow over the deck beneath. It towered above them, finely balanced, and it looked as big as a New York apartment block.

Four SEALS unclipped their Draegers, which weighed thirty-four pounds out of the water, and placed them with the flippers deep in the shadows of a dark corner. If any passing sentry as much as looked into that corner, they would blow a hole in his head with a silenced MP–5. With no Draegers, and no flippers, the SEALS would be marooned in this hostile, untenable land.

They whispered briefly. The four men would conduct a quick recce, prepare their climbing ropes, and place their det-cord in a handier place. Silently Rusty ran back to the starboard side, put his flippers back on, and slipped into the water without making a sound. He was carrying a limpet mine instead of his attack board. His target area was easy to locate, and he clamped the mine effortlessly onto the hull. He screwed a length of det-cord into the priming mechanism, and headed for the surface unraveling the cord as he went.

Rusty bobbed up right at the corner, tied his cord onto another piece being held five feet above him by one of the other SEALS, and headed for the port-side platform. Back inside the dock, he removed his flippers and Draeger, and checked the clip on his MP–5.

The SEALS exchanged information in whispers. "There's a guard with a machine gun up on the submarine . . . a chair right behind the sail facing aft . . . and there's someone in that tower high up on the portside corner . . . He's not moving . . . but he may when the det-cord blows and splits those shores in half . . . "

All five had seen the four wooden targets, thirty feet above their heads, holding the great submarine in place, stark against the glare of the arclight. "It's too bright . . . we'll have to work real close to the hull . . . either that or shoot these two pricks before we start . . . there's a ladder up the side of the dock right where we thought . . . in the middle . . . you'll get a good view, Lieutenant . . . watch that fucker with the machine gun, willya?

If that guy wakes up and as much as scratches his balls, he's history . . . "

Rusty Bennett headed up the ladder. They were right. It was bright, but the shadow of the Kilo was protective. He could remain in that shadow and still see the head of the sentry. He hooked one leg and one arm through the ladder so that he could stand safely without using his hands, checked his gun, and aimed it carefully at the forehead of the dozing guard, sixty feet away.

He took his left hand off the weapon and placed his forefinger and middle finger in a V over his nose, signifying that he had the enemy in his sights. Then he raised his left arm and jammed his index finger in the air. "Go." Immediately he heard the soft whirl of the roped grappling hooks as they circled clockwise. Each one flew up and over one of the four shores. They dropped quietly like spent fireworks, and for a moment he watched the four SEALS pull on the ropes. His heart beat faster as the black steel hooks bumped and then bit, hard, into the wood. No sound yet. No danger. Yet.

Rusty concentrated on his job, watching the sentry, but out of the corner of his eye he could see the confusion of pipes and equipment on the casing. There were huge gaps in the hull, several steel plates missing altogether, where a massive part had been removed from the interior. This was a submarine well into a six-month overhaul. To him, it was inconceivable that she had been fully operational, making her way back from the Arabian Gulf just twenty-four days ago.

Down below in the gloom he could just see his fellow warriors setting off, up the knotted ropes, each man moving carefully but relentlessly upward. They reached the shores at the same time, and Rusty saw them swing their right legs up and over the beams in a grotesque airborne ballet.

They each leaned forward, deeper into the shadow of the Kilo, clinging on with their knees like flat-race jockeys, pulling the det-cord up from the dock bottom. This was the tricky part, winding this explosive detonator line six times around the shores, while holding on to the rest, trailing below.

The SEAL on shore number two made the mistake. For a split second he lost his balance. With practiced skill he shoved the cord in his mouth and held it between his teeth, grabbing the beam with both hands to save himself from crashing thirty feet to the ground. The sure knowledge that no SEAL is ever left dead on the battlefield was no substitute for two-handed safety.

But the long end of the cord got away, and the whole sixty-odd feet dropped toward the dock bottom, landing noisily on the metal. The sudden sound of the cord hitting the deck, splitting the silence, terrified all five men.

Rusty Bennett lifted his left arm, fist clenched, fingers outward, the SEALS' signal to "freeze." But the armed guard on the submarine deck began to stand up, turning to his left, raising his machine gun in the approximate direction of the frozen SEALS. "*Heh! Who's there?*" he suddenly called out. It was the last sound he ever made. Lieutenant Rusty Bennett shot him clean between the eyes, sending him backward over his chair with a leaden thump against the tower.

The silencer on the German weapon had done its job. The airborne SEALS had heard just the tiny, familiar "phuttt," followed by the thud. There was no further noise as the four men completed their tasks of wrapping the cord around and around the shores. Six turns of that stuff would cleave the trunk of a big oak in two.

Rusty watched his men climb back down the nylon rope. Then he too descended the ladder and handed his machine gun to one of them while he went to work. He connected the four strands of det-cord in series. He took the end of the line of cord which went down to the limpet under the dock and tied that to the end of the line from the four beams. He took a further length of cord from his pocket and jammed it in between the rest and taped it firmly together.

That final piece of cord was then fixed into the timing mechanism, which Rusty carefully primed set for twenty minutes. No mistakes. No risks. Det-cord burned at five miles a second—when a bundle of it was wrapped together, as it was on the shore, it blew with serious impact. The SEALS all heard the almost soundless clock begin to tick.

"Now we've got ten minutes to get the fuck out of here," whispered the SEAL leader. "Let's go."

They walked single file to the dark corner on the starboard side and put on their flippers. They replaced their Draegers, turned on the valves, breathed slowly, strapped the three guns on their backs, pulled down their masks, and lowered themselves over the edge. It was a five-foot drop. Rusty, holding the attack board in one hand, went first, taking his weight with his right hand still on the dock until the last second. He made hardly a ripple. The others followed him immediately, and they submerged together.

Rusty Bennett took a bearing of two-seven-zero and began the first of his three hundred kicks to the turning point out of the inner harbor. He guessed correctly that the other four SEALS, who had mined the two floating submarines, were somewhere out in front. They had clamped on their four limpets, primed and set them, and left the way they had come in. Probably went past the floating dock while Rusty had been connecting the det-cord.

He kicked, trying to gain as much distance as possible between his team and the dock when the det-cord blew. He guessed a quarter of a mile was the best he could hope for.

Meantime, high up in the tower on the seaward, port side corner of the floating dock, Leading Seaman Karim Aila, aged twenty-four, was reading a book. Every half hour or so he walked out onto his little balcony and gave a wave or a yell down to his colleague Ali, who was seated below the sail of the submarine. He could not see him, at least not while Ali sat in the shadow, but they usually shared some coffee every couple of hours on this long night watch, which lasted from 2000 to 0600.

No one else was on duty on the dock, though outside there was a fully staffed guardroom for the sentry patrols. Occasionally there would be a visit from a duty officer, but not that often. Iran's Navy, eighteen thousand strong, and extremely well organized, tended to be a bit slack during the hours of darkness.

It was ten minutes after midnight when Karim heard the noise through his closed door. It sounded like a short, sharp but intense *crack*! Like someone slamming a flat steel ruler down hard on a polished table. He thought he heard a couple of dull vibrations far below, thuds in the night. He looked up, puzzled, put down his book, walked to the door, and yelled, *"Ali!!"* Silence. He gazed at the great Russian submarine. Everything seemed fine. Nonetheless, he decided to take one of his rare walks around the upper gantry of the dock.

He popped back inside to collect his machine gun, and set off down the long 256-foot port side, passing under the big lifting crane. He did not see the crumpled figure of his dead friend lying against the tower of the sail. At the end of the walkway he made his turn and walked slowly across the narrow end of the dock, staring down at the motionless bow of the submarine. He had traveled about fifty feet along the starboard side when he noticed the first shore was missing. He peered over the edge and could see at least one piece of the wooden beam lying in the glow of the arclight far below on the steel deck.

That was it. That was the *crack* he had heard. The shore had fallen out. Karim did not wait around. He raced back along the walkway, up the circular steps into his control room, and grabbed the phone. Then he saw it . . . a red light flashing, indicating one of the starboard tanks was either malfunctioning or filling with seawater. He slammed the phone down, and crossed to the screen which showed the horizontal level of the dock.

"My God!!" She was listing one quarter of a degree to starboard and still moving. Karim knew what to do. He must flood the port-side tanks instantly to stabilize the dock, level her out. He grabbed for the valve controls . . . but he was too late.

There was something terribly wrong. Outside there was more noise, a kind of heaving and wrenching.

He dived through the door, and before his eyes the huge submarine began to move. Karim stood transfixed, horrified, as the Kilo gathered speed, toppling sideways to starboard. All two and a half thousand tons of her was twisting downward as if in slow motion. The sail smashed into the steel side of the dock, buckling it outward, and ripping the tower clean off the casing. Then, almost in slow motion, the hull of the submarine crashed down to the floor of the dock in a mushroom cloud of choking dust and a thunderous roar of fractured, tearing metal. Her entire starboard side disappeared as the dock floor completely caved in.

Karim Aila felt the whole dock shudder from the impact, and then lurch as the sea rushed in through the gaping breach below the wrecked submarine. He was afraid to run, afraid to stay where he was, because it seemed the dock would capsize. The submarine, her hull irreparable, her back broken, her tower hanging up the side of the starboard wing wall, was already half under water. Karim debated whether to jump the eighty feet into the harbor, or try to walk back along the grotesquely tilted gangway. He gazed down, turned away, and went for the gangway, inching his way along. He made it fifty feet before the huge lifting crane directly in front of him suddenly ripped away from its ten-inch-wide holding bolts and plummeted downward like a dying missile.

The massive steel point of the crane, built to withstand the full lifting-weight, came down from a height of eighty feet and speared straight through the thick pressure hull on the port side of the stricken Kilo—an already dead whale receiving its last harpoon.

Karim still clung to the high rail, now only thirty feet above the water, as the dock settled on the floor of the harbor. The control tower was angled out like a bowsprit, and since there was now no way of reaching the jetty, the young Iranian climbed back to it. He sat on top, precarious, but safe; surveying the scene of absolute catastrophe over which he had presided.

Rusty Bennett kept swimming and kept counting. The five SEALS reached the first turning point and set off, due south, out of the harbor. They had been back in the water for one hour, when Rusty made the left turn toward the ASDS. Five hundred yards to go. And now he was listening—listening for the regular light-frequency "peep-da-peep-peep" of the homing signal which would guide them in. When he heard it once, he would hear it every thirty seconds. Rusty picked it up while they were still in the shadow of the harbor wall.

The rest was routine. Lieutenant Mills saw them from his cockpit as they moved around the hull and climbed into the open, flooded compartment. The other four SEALS were already in place, and offered a cheerful "thumbs-up." Rusty clambered into his solo navigation compartment, and each man seized the air lines to the central system.

Dave Mills now closed all canopies, and they heard the hum of the pumps as the water was drained out and replaced by air. The compartment was quickly dry again, and as the little ASDS crawled away at her five-knot maximum speed, Rusty Bennett said simply, "Well done, guys. How long before the other two blow?"

One SEAL in the back answered succinctly. "0145. Thirty minutes from now."

Rusty made a few calculations in his head. He guessed that the Iranians were not at this point even considering they had lost their Kilo by any kind of military action. The submarine had somehow fallen and that was that. But when the next two exploded, burned, and sank, the Iranian Navy would arrive at the inescapable conclusion. The issue was, how soon?

Commander Banford and Rusty had gone over the main strength of the Iranian Navy several times. In addition to the three Kilos, they also ran two guided missile destroyers, three Royal Navy–designed frigates, two Corvettes, and nine midget submarines. They had a ton of coastal patrol boats, and a lot of backup auxiliaries.

Rusty knew the frigates were the problem. Built in the late 1960s, by Britain's vastly experienced Vickers Corporation in Newcastle and Barrow, these streamlined three-hundred-foot Vosper Mk 5's could make almost thirty-five knots through the water. Worse, they carried an anti-submarine mortar, a big Limbo Mark 10, which contained two hundred pounds of TNT. Fired from the stern, these things had a range of more than a thousand yards and exploded at a preset depth. With a bit of luck on their side, they could blow a submarine apart. But they could kill a diver at five hundred yards. Rusty Bennett dreaded those fast frigates, and he ordered Dave Mills to drive the last half hour as deep as possible.

The Iranian frigates could cross the strait from Bandar Abbas to the eastern end of Qeshm in twenty minutes flat. He estimated it would take them one hour to get the crew organized and get under way—one hour from the explosions under the last two Kilos . . . one hour from 0145. In Rusty's opinion that could, theoretically, put a high-powered Iranian mortar bomb right in the water close to the waiting-station of the *Mendel Rivers* by 0310.

Right now it was 0130 and they had a two-and-a-half-hour run in front of them. The ASDS was due to dock at 0400. Rusty tried to juggle the figures, tried to imagine the uproar in the Naval base, tried to imagine how quickly the admiral in command could get his act together. "I suppose it might just take 'em sixty minutes at this time of night to get a damage check from the experts. Then I guess it could be another hour to get one of those frigates moving," he thought.

"But, Jesus. Any damn fool who's lost his entire submarine fleet could work out that the attacker must have arrived in a submarine himself. And where is that submarine? He's right out there in the first deep water you come to, right off the coast of Qeshm. That's where he is. And he's waiting for his demolition guys to get back, riding in some kind of a midget submarine. I know what I'd do. I charge out there and bombard the area with mortars. If I had three of those frigates available, I'd send 'em all. I'd definitely catch the divers, and I might get the big submarine too.

"If the Iranian is sharp he will pass us overhead an hour before we reach the *Mendel Rivers*. If he's unsharp, he might not get there until 0410, in which case he's gonna be a bit late, but still dangerous. Either way we're in dead trouble . . . step on it, Dave, willya?"

The limpet mines beneath the Kilos blew, precisely on time. Both submarines were almost split in two. Both batteries were blown apart. The interior fires were still raging as they each sank beneath the dark waters of the harbor. The Iranian admiral, called from his bed to inspect the wrecked dry dock and the written-off Kilo, very nearly had a heart attack when the other two joined them on the bottom.

Every light in the harbor was on. The admiral wanted to know whether the radar sweeps had found any contact whatsoever throughout the night. No one had seen anything, heard anything, done anything, or knew anything. He called a meeting of the High Command. He placed a call to the Iraqi Naval Base at Bazra, where the operator inquired irritably, was there a lunatic on the line.

Slowly his commanders began to appear on base. But it was not until 0315 that anyone asked the three pertinent questions. It was a young Iranian captain who wondered, "Who did this? How did they get here? And where are they now?"

And it was not until 0405 that one of the frigates was under way, speeding toward the deep water where the admiral now assessed any marauding submarine would be.

The Americans had just docked the ASDS as the Iranian warship left. Too late. Commander Banford and the captain were already moving south, running deep, at twenty knots in the nuclear-powered *Mendel Rivers*. They had a twelve-mile start, and the strait grew wider and deeper with every turn of the propeller. And the Iranians did not know what they were seeking, nor indeed what to do if they found anyone.

Twenty minutes after they set off, the crew of the *Mendel Rivers* heard the first wild mortar shot explode, far back and deep. But the Iranians were much too late.

The SEALS were safe, the mission was completed. "Nice job, Lieutenant," said Commander Banford.

0520 Saturday, August 3.

THE *L. MENDEL RIVERS* WENT AS DEEP AS SHE DARED through the dark waters above the undulating, sandy seabed of the Strait of Hormuz. She ran at around eighty feet below the surface, making twenty knots toward the vast depths of the Gulf of Arabia. Nine exhausted Navy SEALS slept, as the big U.S. submarine headed south, away from the chaos they had caused in the Iranian Naval base.

Lieutenant Bennett sat in a small office with Commander Banford, working on the preliminary report of the operation in the port of Bandar Abbas. The commander sent his first half-page coded signal on the satellite direct to COMSUBPAC just before dawn.

"030530AUG02. 56.9E, 26.5N. Course one-three-five. Vengeance Bravo. Objectives achieved. No Blue casualties or damage. SEAL Leader reports Kilo in dry dock well into major overhaul, unlikely to have been operational during month of July."

The signal traveled quickly to Pearl Harbor, then via CINC-PAC to SPECWARCOM in Coronado, finally to the office of the CNO in the Pentagon where it was 1945 the previous evening, Friday, August 2. Lieutenant Commander Jay Bamberg was at his desk awaiting the message, wishing he were starting the weekend at home with his young family.

When a duty officer brought the communication in, Jay punched the air with a grim feeling of joy. The departing junior lieutenant grinned, "Way to go! Right, sir?"

"Way to go, Lieutenant."

Jay Bamberg called the CNO at home, and then Arnold Morgan in his office in Fort Meade. His first call had brought something approaching glee to Admiral Dunsmore, but Admiral Morgan had just snapped, "Yeah, thanks, Jay. I already gottit."

Lieutenant Commander Bamberg found this sufficiently puzzling to ask, "How so fast, sir?"

"Heard from the Mossad in Tel Aviv thirty minutes ago something had exploded in Bandar Abbas Navy Base, and what did I know about it? Told 'em I hadn't left my desk since lunchtime, heh, heh, heh!"

"Did they know much, sir?"

"Nah, very little. 'Cept the Iranians probably had a weaker Navy now than they had before midnight. I guessed the rest. But thanks for calling, Jay, I'm glad they're all safe."

"Yessir. Good night, sir." But the admiral was long gone, as usual.

By the time Lieutenant Commander Bamberg had replaced the receiver on the secure line to Fort Meade, Admiral Morgan was on his way to his car. He had a supper date at the Israeli embassy with General Gavron, a meeting to which he looked forward with great anticipation. When the Israeli officer had called asking if the American admiral would care to join him, he had insinuated he had an interesting conversation in store.

Morgan had resolved to hang around until 2000 awaiting official confirmation of the SEALS' activities, then he would split for the embassy. The call thirty minutes previously had told him two things. One, he need not hang around beyond 2000, and two, the goddamned Mossad was about four times quicker off the mark than anyone else, on almost any incident, anywhere in the world. Jesus, it was 0230 in the morning for them.

He hit the highway at his usual high speed, and his mind was racing over that signal Bamberg had read out . . . the last sentence . . . the bit about the Kilo in the floating dock being in the middle of a major overhaul: ". . . unlikely to have been operational during month of July."

The words kept turning over in his mind. That meant he and Baldridge had been right all along. The Iranians had *not* used an inventory submarine from Bandar Abbas to hit the *Jefferson*. They must have used a fourth submarine. Worse yet, that fourth submarine must be still out there. Waiting. Watching. Perhaps to strike again.

The more Arnold Morgan pondered the issue, the more certain he became that the underwater boat he sought was the lost Kilo from the Black Sea. The one from which the drowned Russian sailor had fallen, the one his own guys had heard in the Gibraltar Strait in the early morning of May 5, the one Lieutenant Joe Farrell had seen heading north up the Arabian Sea on June 28.

The one where *all of the dates fit.*

The one which that nitwit Rankov would not discuss.

Arnold Morgan, his adrenaline rising, glanced at the speedometer, which was hovering at around 104 mph. "Fuckit," he said, slowing down to 85. "If David Gavron has found this Benjamin Adnam, a lot of questions are going to get answered real fast. If he hasn't found him, we're going to have to twist the arm of the President of Russia. Hard."

Guards waved him through the gates of the Israeli embassy and directed him to a parking place. They then escorted him into the embassy, and up to a small dining room on the second floor where General Gavron was waiting. The two men exchanged greetings and the host offered the American admiral a glass of Israeli wine from the southern town of Richon-le-Zion, where Baron Edmond de Rothschild established the great vineyards at the end of the nineteenth century.

Since he was there for at least a couple of hours, Admiral Morgan did not rush into an interrogation with quite the anxiety he felt. Instead he chatted amiably about Israel and her ambitions and the question of where the Palestinians were ultimately going to live. They dined like true Sabras, beginning with Israeli eggplant salad made with *tahini* and then progressing to *shashlik* of spiced lamb with crispy, fried *mallawah* bread.

Arnold Morgan found himself feeling increasingly cheerful at this sudden break in his traditional working diet of coffee and roast beef sandwiches. He was enjoying a plate of *baklava* when he broached the subject he was here to discuss . . . Benjamin Adnam. He took a deep sip of wine—poured by the general from their second bottle, a sweet white wine the Israelis use principally for ceremonial occasions. Then the admiral said, very softly, for him, "Well, David, did you find him?"

The Israeli general smiled and tilted his head to one side. "Not quite yet, Admiral, but we are a lot wiser than we were last time we met. Would you like me to tell you what my Intelligence officers have been doing?"

Morgan grinned. "David," he said, "I'm going to sit right here, with this great glass of wine, and let you entertain me."

"Very well. On the day I contacted them to relay your message about your government's anxiety, our agents confirmed they had gone through Commander Adnam's apartment and personal property. To their surprise, he had taken nothing. All of his documents, passport, Navy papers, educational records, etc., were still in his desk. Which made them think again, he had either been murdered or run off.

"The following day, after my call, they launched a huge search throughout the country. Found nothing. We then sent half a dozen agents to the village where his parents had lived. Found nothing there either. But nearby, we did discover a friend of the family, who had no recollection of the family having a son born in around 1960.

"They had known the Adnams quite well, and were apparently very upset when the family disappeared after the village was bombed during the 1973 war. But they knew *nothing* of any Ben Adnam being away at school in England between 1976 and 1978, when he was apparently between sixteen and eighteen.

"After that, of course, we already know he returned from Sutton Valence school in Kent, and immediately joined the Navy.

Never went home, because there was neither home nor parents to go to. And that's where he stayed. In the Navy."

"You mean no one really knows where he came from, nor, now, where the hell he's gone?"

"You have just stated the case perfectly, Arnold."

"Hmmm. I guess he just filled in his details on the forms, probably while he was in England, and the Israeli Navy was happy to accept this well-educated Sabra from well-to-do farming parents, recommended personally by an eminent English headmaster . . . "

"*And* by a very senior military attaché from the Israeli embassy in London . . . who we now discover also had a boy at Sutton Valence school at the time."

"Christ! You can see how these things happen, eh?"

"All too well, Admiral. To make matters worse there are no death certificates whatsoever regarding the Adnam family. The village was bombed. They may have been killed. Or they may have just left, returning, as you say, to wherever they came from.

"Anyway both they and their 'son' have vanished, without trace . . . and we are keenly aware that all three may have been spies, the parents 'in place' on behalf of another nation. The young Adnam, perhaps an eighteen-year-old Fundamentalist fanatic, being seconded to their care on a deep, long-term basis. The kind of thing to which my own organization is somewhat partial. Which brings me to part two."

"What happened to Commander Adnam? I hope," said Arnold Morgan.

"Well, Admiral, once we found his documents it was pretty obvious he had left Israel in possession of a completely different identity. We practically ransacked our own airport records for two days. Nothing. So how did he leave? Well, our agents felt he had made his way by bus or taxi from East Jerusalem, as far as the Allenby Bridge. That's the only one which crosses the river into Jordan. Then it becomes the King Hussein Bridge. Right there, at the bridge, he had to get out of his taxi, or bus, in order to pick up Jordanian transportation, we think one of those JETT mini-buses.

"Now, I expect you know, there are all kinds of restrictions at the bridge. So he must have had a Jordanian passport. But he also had a visa *and* a permit to cross the bridge. Remember, you cannot get Arab documents in Israel, nor indeed at the bridge. So someone was looking after him extremely well.

"However, we do conduct a very stringent search at the bridge of anyone leaving Israel and traveling into Jordan. For instance, it's illegal to carry a camera with any film in it whatsoever, and once you have left, you may not return. No one can obtain an Israeli visa in any Arab country, except Egypt.

"And here, right at the Allenby Bridge, our luck turned. Certain people are pulled aside by our customs agents and searched very carefully. And in that area we do have a surveillance camera. So we commandeered all of that film for the three days following Commander Adnam's disappearing trick. We took it to Haifa and called in every Navy officer we could find who knew him in any way. We actually flew men in from the fleet exercise in the Med—where he should have been.

"We got him on the first reel of film from the first morning, November 25, the time frame up in the corner said 0924. He was in Arab dress, and our camera caught him answering questions in the customs office. Four different men picked him out. Separately. Three of them were submarine officers. No doubt. Commander Adnam left Israel as an Arab. I brought you a picture of him, not very good quality. But here he is . . . "

General Gavron leaned forward and passed a sheet of fax paper over to the American. They had blown up the photograph and then faxed it. Details were smudgy. But, wearing the Arab headdress, Commander Adnam looked more like a trader in some local Casbah than an Israeli submarine commander. Nonetheless, Benjamin Adnam it was. And the picture showed a dark, rather elegant and refined face with hard, deep-set eyes. Admiral Morgan thought he could have been Iranian, Iraqi, Jordanian, Syrian, even Egyptian. The question now changed slightly . . . who the hell was this guy?

Morgan's mind whirred. He better get that photograph copied and faxed to Admiral MacLean for a 100 percent identification.

He tried not to sound anxious. And he said with exaggerated calm, "What happened then, David? Did the trail go cold?"

"Certainly not. We have several very good agents in Jordan and four days ago they traced him. That first morning, very, very quickly he found his way to the Queen Alia Airport, and almost immediately boarded a Royal Jordanian Airlines flight to Cairo. Paid for his ticket in Jordanian dinars. God knows where he got cash.

"He was traveling on a Jordanian passport when he left, and he used it to clear customs in Cairo. Our agents did pull that record up. Then, because we do not think he is Egyptian, we checked out every major hotel in the area. But found nothing. He was not registered anywhere."

"Did you try the Mena House, out by the Pyramids?"

"Of course. And they actually *knew* him. But said they had not seen him for two years. One of our agents talked to the manager, who was uncertain where he came from. He had certainly been there under his own name.

"Our agents then searched through every record the Egyptian authorities would provide. In the end they decided he never left Cairo International Airport, stayed there and flew on. That night, we came up with only one 'Adnam' who had left Egypt on an international flight. He paid in cash, Egyptian currency, and bought a ticket to Istanbul. I regret to say he was a Russian. Old Soviet passport. Visa for frequent entry into Turkey. Not much help, eh?"

Arnold Morgan could not believe his ears. "Do the Egyptians have a surveillance camera which may have photographed the passengers for that flight?"

"They say they do, but it wasn't working. Anyway our agents considered the trail cold. They do not think the Russian was Commander Adnam."

"Well, if he didn't leave the airport, where the hell did he go? Your guys think he got a job as a customs officer?"

General Gavron laughed. "No, we think he just picked up a new passport and documents from his masters, and took off. Could be under any name, and now in any country."

"Well, why not the Russian?"

"Our guys just don't think it feasible. We do not think Ben was Russian. Nor do we think he was Turkish. We think he was an Arab, and we've done a lot of research. Why do you think he might have been Russian?"

"David, I don't think he was Russian either. But I do think he might have been going there. And since he seems able to conjure up documents and currency anyplace he travels, why not this guy on the Soviet passport?"

David Gavron ignored the question. And came back with one of his own. "Why do you think he may have been going to Russia?"

"Because, David, we think the submarine that hit the *Jefferson* was a Soviet-built Kilo, a diesel electric-powered patrol boat, which Adnam and his masters either bought, rented, or stole, right out of the moribund Black Sea Fleet. I say the Black Sea Fleet because there's no place else they could have gotten one. Also I've checked where every working diesel submarine in the world was on that night. They're all accounted for—even yours! Except for one, and that's Russian."

"I see. We will continue to do everything we can to assist you. As a nation we do not like sneak attacks, and my people are extremely upset about the aircraft carrier. Even more upset that you even considered blaming us."

"David, in our position you have to suspect everyone."

General Gavron looked thoughtful as Morgan sipped his silky-sweet wine. The silence between the two men grew, until, finally, General Gavron broke it. "We have an accurate date," he said. "If that Russian in Cairo airport was Commander Adnam, then he arrived in Istanbul late at night on November 25. If he was using his real name when he left Cairo, I would think he was still using it when he left Istanbul. We should run some checks on the passenger lists—airlines, maybe even ships, out of the city, the following morning.

"We have three or four good men in place in Istanbul. I suggest my organization gets a search started . . . then if we get nowhere in, say, three days . . . maybe your government could persuade the Turks to cooperate."

"Good call, David. Right now we don't want to be seen stirring up anything more than we must."

"Very restrained, Admiral . . . for a man who has, in the last few hours, destroyed the underwater Navy of the Ayatollah of Iran."

"Now, hang on, General. I told your colleagues I never left my desk. Anyway, how do you guys know what we did or didn't do?"

"I know that only three or four nations *could* have done it so smoothly. Not us, we'd have caused an international uproar and bombed the place to bits. The British could have. Possibly the Russians. But you have the capacity to achieve that kind of excellence any time you want. The issue is motive. Who wanted to damage Iran? Not us, particularly. Not the British. Not the Russians. Nice job, Admiral. As a nation, we are delighted."

Arnold Morgan just smiled at the suave Israeli officer. And he guessed, privately, as he had done a couple of times before, that he was indeed looking at the next head of the Mossad.

The following morning, August 3, twenty-six days after the disaster, the Saturday papers were still blazing with the story of the lost aircraft carrier but neither the *Washington Post* nor the *New York Times* carried even a paragraph about an accident in the Iranian Naval base at Bandar Abbas.

Admiral Morgan, Admiral Schnider, Lieutenant Commander Bill Baldridge, and Admiral Dunsmore were gathered in the office of General Josh Paul in readiness for a meeting with the President in the White house at 1100. Admiral Morgan briefed them fully on his dealings with General Gavron. But the subject was now more finely focused.

Scott Dunsmore believed the President would broadcast to the nation this evening at 2100, announcing unprecedented compensation for the families of the men who died in the carrier. Saturday night was most unusual for this kind of activity, but the CNO believed the White House press office had approved it for maximum impact.

The two Service Chiefs were afraid the President would

assume that with the bombing of the Iranian Navy base American revenge was complete and that no further action should be taken, pending the arrival of hard evidence. However, Admiral Morgan's now rigid belief that the rogue submarine was still out there was uppermost in all of their minds.

General Paul detailed his CNO to deal with it, to persuade the President that the United States hunt for the nation which had sunk the *Jefferson* must continue at all costs. "If necessary," he said, "get Arnold to read him a modest riot act about the implications of the same thing happening to another of our warships."

They left the Pentagon in two staff cars and met the President, the Secretary of State, and the Secretary of Defense, the President's security adviser, and his press officer in the Situation Room, one floor below the Oval Office.

The President greeted them warmly. "I'll say one thing," he said. "You guys sure know how to take an instruction literally. Dare I ask what happened in Bandar Abbas, beyond this Navy signal which Bob here gave me this morning?"

"Sir," said Admiral Dunsmore, "you did say you did not really want to know the details of the plan. I guess we took that literally as well."

"How large a force went in, Scott?"

"Nine swimmers, sir, plus the driver in the ASDS."

"Is that all? Many casualties?"

"None for us, sir. We have no idea how many Iranian crew were aboard the floating submarines. But one armed guard was marginalized in the floating dock."

"Marginalized?"

"Yessir. Removed from our area of operation."

"Shot? Killed?"

"Precisely so, sir."

"Delicately stated, Admiral," said the President. "Considering you run the world's roughest hit squad."

"Thank you, sir."

The President shook his head in wonder at the professionalism with which he was surrounded. He then slipped quickly into his own agenda, and, as expected, said he would make a rare

Saturday night broadcast to the nation, announcing his plans for special pension funds for the widows and children of the men who died in the carrier.

"I already know there will be objections from some branches of the Armed Services," he said. "But no congressman will object, not if he wants to continue working in the Capitol. The newspapers will be forced to applaud us, the public will approve. Also I'm counting on the fact that I'm too good a friend to the military for any of you to upset me!"

General Paul ventured to say that there would be objections to special pensions from people who had lost fathers and husbands in other conflicts but were not being given special treatment. That was why the military routinely opposed such schemes, and had done so throughout the twentieth century.

"The worst thing," the President interrupted, "the *very* worst thing that could happen to you guys would be for me to be driven from this office in the aftermath of this disaster. You would get a Democratic President, a Democratic Congress, and possibly a Democratic Senate. And they would have a great time dismantling the Navy, banning nuclear weapons, cutting out our shipbuilding programs, and above all ending the building of aircraft carriers for the foreseeable future. They would then take all of that money and do what they always do—give it away to the poor, the weak, the sick, the incompetent, the stupid, and the idle, and worse, the dishonest.

"The four billion dollars we spend on building an aircraft carrier each year keeps top engineers, ship builders, scientists, and steel corporations in real-time profitable work, honing skills, keeping this country out there in front . . . with an end product, which, all on its own, helps to keep every American safe.

"When you build an aircraft carrier you are making this country *happen.* And you get at least half of it back in taxes.

"Hey, I'm sorry, guys, you all know my views, and I hope you share them. But you have to help keep me in office. And I know that a special consideration from this government to those *Jefferson* widows is going to touch a real chord with the public. Besides, I want to do something for them.

"Now let's run over the situation regarding the unknown culprit who hit our ship. Do we still think it's Iran, and have we punished them sufficiently? Josh? Scott?"

The Chairman of the Joint Chiefs nodded, and Admiral Dunsmore stepped up to the plate. "Sir," he said, "we do think Iran was the culprit, but we do not believe they carried out the hit on the *Jefferson* with one of their inventory submarines in Bandar Abbas. We think they got their hands on a fourth Kilo from Russia."

"Okay," said the President. "Just remind me why we do not think it was one of the submarines from Bandar Abbas."

"Because the two floating Kilos have not moved for several weeks. And the leader of our special forces saw the third Kilo in what he firmly believes to be a major overhaul. He says there was a large section of the hull missing and a major piece of machinery removed from inside. He thinks it impossible that the submarine could have been operational during the month of July."

"Yes, I did read that. Do we believe him?"

"Very definitely, sir. Lieutenant Bennett has been in the Navy since he first went to Annapolis. His father is a fisherman on the coast of Maine. He's been with boats all of his life, and the disruption he saw to that Kilo left no doubt in his mind. Personally I think the engineers were repairing that submarine for a few weeks in June, before she went into the floating dock on July 2, for completion of the work below the waterline."

"Admiral Morgan," said the President, formally, "do you have a view on this?"

The Texas Intelligence chief was thoughtful. "Well, sir, in my experience, when a seasoned officer in the United States Navy makes a judgment of a technical matter, he's normally correct. I accept what the SEALS lieutenant observed.

"What concerns me more is that I am now very sure the submarine that hit the carrier is still out there. We have not found it, neither has anyone else. None of our overheads nor our surveillance people have seen it.

"And I am extremely worried that it may strike again. That

Kilo probably had two nuclear-tipped torpedoes on board, and no one's told me he fired any more than one of 'em."

"Are you telling me it was definitely a Russian-built submarine?"

"There is no longer any doubt about that, sir. The *only* submarine in all of this world which was missing on the night of July 8 was the Kilo they *thought* had sunk in the Black Sea. Well, they were wrong, which they now admit. That Kilo got out of the Black Sea. I believe it torpedoed the *Jefferson* . . . and I believe it's still out there, possibly just hiding, but possibly awaiting another opportunity.

"Mr. President, we have to find and destroy that submarine."

"Yes, Admiral. I see that. But *how* did it get out? Every expert I talk to says it is impossible to transit the Bosporus underwater. No one has ever done it. And you tell me the Turks say no Russian diesel boat has exited the Black Sea on the surface for five months."

"All true, sir. But it did get out. We have to assume that. Someone got it out. Some submarine genius drove it out under the surface, through the Bosporus. We are on the trail of the man we think did it. But we must assume he first achieved the impossible and took a submarine where no submariner ever took one before."

"That's a tall order for me, Admiral. And before I commit additional resources to another military reprisal, I am going to propose something to you. I want you to prove to me that it could have happened. I want you to select a couple of the best submariners we have, and arrange for them to make an underwater transit through the Bosporus from the Black Sea in a diesel-electric boat. If they make it, I will agree to put into operation a worldwide hunt for the missing Kilo, until we find and sink it, whatever the expense may be.

"If, however, they fail to make that transit for any reason, or get caught by the Turks, I will deem that the destruction of the *Jefferson* was a pure accident, and there the matter will rest."

Arnold Morgan gulped. "Sir, we don't actually own a small diesel-electric any more. We'd have to borrow one from the Royal Navy."

"Excellent. Go do it."

"Sir, may we use your authority to put this operation into action?"

"Of course."

"Sir, if they are forced to surface, and end up in a Turkish jail, may I assume you will use your best efforts to get the submarine back, and get the men out . . . both British and American?"

"Admiral, you may assume I *will* get them out. And I'll get the submarine back. But I don't want the Turks to know this is happening, and then to turn a blind eye. Otherwise it won't count, will it? I want our submarine to face the precise hazards your Commander Adnam faced. No bullshit."

"Very well, sir," said Admiral Dunsmore. "We will proceed on those precise lines. If our best men cannot do it, assisted by the best in the Royal Navy, then we will deem the entire thing to have been impossible all along. The sinking of the *Thomas Jefferson* will become an official United States Navy accident."

"Correct, Admiral . . . and unless anyone has anything else to mention, I would like to get back to my office and work on my speech for tonight. Thank you all . . . and by the way, I think that goddamned submarine *is* still out there, and I want our Bosporus mission to succeed, so let's get it done."

By mid-afternoon, Admiral Morgan and Bill Baldridge were back in Fort Meade, plotting and planning for the ride through the Bosporus. Baldridge would go as the official observer on behalf of the Pentagon. And he would reopen his talks with Admiral Elliott, and probably Admiral MacLean. Arnold Morgan had him booked out of Washington on a Sunday night flight to Heathrow. He put in a call to the duty officer at Northwood Navy headquarters to ensure the British Submarine Flag Officer was ready to receive him. They confirmed the arrangements in twelve minutes.

"Okay, Bill, you happy with all this?"

"Yessir. But I'll tell you one thing, I'd be happier running through the Bosporus with Admiral MacLean somewhere below the periscope."

"Well, have a chat with Admiral Elliott on Monday morning. I know the CNO is going to talk to the First Sea Lord in London tomorrow, and the Royal Navy will do everything they can. I just hope they've got one of those Upholder Class boats of theirs in some sort of shape so we can borrow it."

Bill Baldridge left the Fort Meade office in the early part of the evening, but Admiral Morgan settled in for what he described as "a long night." He would listen to the President speak at 2100, but his real business would take place in his office at 0200 in the morning.

In separate rooms, in separate places, the Navy's investigative spearhead, Admiral Scott Dunsmore, Admiral Arnold Morgan, and Lieutenant Commander Bill Baldridge, sat and listened to the President of the United States speak on television. They watched him walk to the podium in the White House briefing room, and they saw him take a sip of water, before beginning:

"My fellow Americans, tonight I stand before you to share with you my thoughts and prayers for the families of the men who died on the *Thomas Jefferson* last month.

"I expect that many of you are already aware that it has been the policy of generations of American governments not to single out certain special cases for those of our naval and military men who die in the service of their country.

"The official viewpoint has always been that even in the military, a life is a life, and none is more precious than another in the eyes of God. Therefore no President and no United States Congress has ever awarded financial benefits to those families left behind in what are always the cruelest of circumstances.

"Tonight I intend to break with that tradition. I intend to break with it after days and days of soul-searching with my Chiefs of Staff, and knowing that veterans' organizations all over the country will support me.

"The plain truth is, I don't happen to believe in a lot of the policies we have sometimes used to shortchange the families of those who died in the service of this great nation.

"I happen to believe that those who die bravely and honorably wearing the uniform of the United States Marines or Navy or Army or Air Force represent the very best of our men, and their sacrifice is the highest one of all. But I do not have the power to turn back the clock.

"I intend to be guided by my own conscience. And I will not tolerate hardship for those who held together the very fabric of our society, while husbands and fathers set sail in their great warship to police this world on behalf of the United States of America.

"It takes a while to fully understand what we owe to those men . . . for their devotion to duty . . . for their skill . . . for their courage . . . for their downright patriotism. And right here I'm talking about men who come screaming out of the sky in big seventy-thousand-pound fighter attack bombers, slamming them down at high speed into the heaving decks of aircraft carriers, risking their lives day after day.

"I'm talking about the skilled technicians who talk 'em down, about the navigators, the engineers, the flight deck crews out there in the wind and rain, working in constant danger, to make sure the rest of us live our lives in peace.

"My fellow Americans, I am talking about humanity, kindness, and decency. Most things are not fair. Over six thousand men died in that Carrier Battle Group, through no fault of their own, through no weakness of their own, through no circumstance which any one of them could have foreseen or prevented.

"And behind them, they have left devoted spouses, and children who need the finest education we can provide for them, because most of them will grow up to be Americans as fine and as honorable and as accomplished as their fathers.

"My fellow Americans, there are many times when I too am heartbroken . . . heartbroken at the injustices I see around me. And often, like most Presidents, I can do too little about it. But in this instance, *I can. And yes, I will.*

"I am placing before Congress a special bill that will provide each *Jefferson* serviceman with children a twenty-thousand-dollar-a-year additional pension, until the children have completed college. It applies to four thousand families and will result in payments of approximately $800 million ... substantially less than the cost of just one aircraft carrier ... about $3.25 cents for every American, spread over one decade. Is there any one person sitting out there who would dare to suggest this was too high a price for us to pay?

"In addition there will be increased military pensions for everyone involved. I am afraid I do not have the power to make that forthcoming law retroactive to benefit other families, bereaved through other wars. But I *can* do it for those who suffered innocently from the terrible accident which occurred in the *Thomas Jefferson*.

"Once more I would like to state again that my prayers, and those of my family, remain with you, and will do so for all of my days in this place ... Good night to you, and God bless you."

Admiral Morgan found himself standing up, his clenched fist held high. He watched Dick Stafford step forward onto the podium to announce that the President would take no questions. And he saw the great man walk away, alone.

Admiral Morgan shook his head. "That President of ours," he muttered. "Ain't he something? He just slaughtered 'em. Made a pure ball-buster of a speech, blew $800 million, rode roughshod over 150 years of military tradition, told Congress to get into line or else, and there's not a journalist or a politician in this country who would dare to utter one word of criticism about what he just said. Jesus. Sure glad he's on our side."

He picked up the phone and requested someone bring him his regular late supper. He then retired to his computer and pulled up a chart of the Bosporus, which he studied carefully for a half hour. "Shit," he said. "I'd rather Baldridge made that journey than I. That little stretch of water is really dangerous, and I hope to hell someone can persuade Iain MacLean to make the voyage." And he added, to the empty room, "If he can't make it, no one can."

He did not realize he was echoing the words of MacLean himself, speaking about Ben Adnam.

Meantime he tried to find a baseball game on television, and settled down to wait until 0200 on the Sunday morning. He called the operator, told him to wake him at that time, and send in coffee, then to connect him to a number in Russia, out on the Crimean Peninsula, a Naval base to which he intended, like the British in 1854, to lay siege.

The Black Sea Fleet's headquarters in Sevastopol was the admiral's target, and he barked the number to the operator . . . "011–7–692–366204 . . . don't speak to anyone. Get me on that line before they answer."

"Yessir. 0200 it is."

Admiral Morgan was tired. He ate his roast beef sandwich supper and fell asleep, leaning back in his big leather swivel chair. It seemed to him like moments before the phone on his desk rang. He picked it up instantly, heard a number ringing seven thousand miles away on the main Russian Navy Black Sea switchboard. He knew it would be a very quiet, almost deserted building this Sunday morning at 0900 local time. He knew also that Vice Admiral Vitaly Rankov was in residence this weekend, and he knew too that the Russian Intelligence officer made a habit of working Sunday mornings.

He heard the phone pickup announce the Sevastopol Fleet Headquarters. Admiral Morgan barked crisply in English, hoping to intimidate the operator: "Connect me to Admiral Rankov *right now* . . . he is expecting my call . . . and I'm calling from the United States of America. Hurry *up!*"

There was a single click, and the deep, calm voice of the ex-Soviet battle cruiser commander rumbled down the line in Russian: "Rankov speaking, and this better be important. I'm very busy."

"Vitaly, you bastard, you've been avoiding me," said Admiral Morgan, chuckling as he heard Rankov groan. "Jesus to God, Arnold, is there no peace left in all of the world?"

But he laughed. The two Naval Intelligence men shared many secrets. "You know I thought this was the one time I would be safe from you—what is it? Two o'clock in the morning in Washington?" Rankov asked. "Where the hell are you, and why can't you sleep like normal people?"

"Duty, Vitaly, a devotion to duty. These are busy days for me."

"I guess so. Did you just blow up half the Iranian Navy, by the way?"

"Who me?" said Morgan, practiced now in responding to this accusation. "Certainly not. I've hardly left my desk."

"What I meant," the Russian continued patiently, "was this: Did your special forces just take out the Ayatollah's submarines in Bandar Abbas?"

"No one has mentioned it to me," lied Admiral Morgan effortlessly. "Why, has something happened?"

The innocence in his voice was a betrayal to a fellow member of his profession. "You tell me a huge whopper, Arnold, when you know as soon as I do when something big breaks. You are an American bastard. Iranian Holy Man take out *fatwah* on you if you're not very fucking careful. Then you won't bother me no more. Those tribesmen slice your balls off."

"They better be a lot more careful I don't slice theirs off," growled Morgan.

"You're a terrible man, Arnold Morgan. What do you want, as if I don't know. The Kilo, hah?"

"Will you tell me about it, Vitaly?" said Morgan, his voice softening. "As a friend. I have to know."

"Will you tell me why?"

"I will. This is on the record, and I expect you to convey it to your superiors." He continued in a flat monotone. "Vitaly, we think someone got ahold of your Kilo, ran it out of the Black Sea, and sank the *Thomas Jefferson* with a nuclear-headed torpedo."

Admiral Morgan heard the Russian's sharp intake of breath on the other end of the line. Admiral Rankov's shock was unmistakable. "*Jesus Christ!*" said the voice from Sevastopol. "Are you kidding me?"

"No, old buddy, I'm not. And you've got about five minutes to convince me that a United States carrier with six thousand men on board was not vaporized for no reason at all by your fucking Navy. And if we happen to believe that is what took place, you won't need to think of reducing your Black Sea Fleet any more. We'll carry that little job out for you, real quick. You guys wanna buy some cheap crash helmets?"

"Arnold, *please*. Don't be ridiculous. Of course we did no such thing. You must believe that. Why would we? We're friends, aren't we? You have to believe what I say. Look at our history . . . we've never been *that* stupid. We are not under the control of fanatics."

"Matter of fact, Vitaly, I do not believe you guys had anything to do with it. Mainly because I never thought you had anyone that clever! I want you to help me, and I want you to tell me the whole truth about that Kilo, right now.

"After that, I probably want you to do a few other things. You say you are our friends, as we are yours. Right now I need you to prove it. My country will not forget your response, either way."

"Very well, Arnold. I will tell you what I know and you may judge for yourself. Our search for the Kilo revealed nothing. We worked below the surface for three weeks, used every electronic device we have to sweep the bottom of the sea. Nothing. We now believe it is not there, and never was. The drowned crewman on the Greek island was a member of the ship's company of Kilo 630.

"His name was very clearly on the Next-of-Kin List. But there we have a problem. When the Kilo left, it did not relay its next-of-kin signal. Therefore the whole list is now suspect. As you know, there are always three or four changes, men going out as replacements for two or three other men who are not going. So I could not swear the man was in the crew, though the odds are he was.

"We believe the submarine escaped, and absconded with a crew of about fifty. We have heard *nothing* since she left port. There's been much financial hardship in the Black Sea Fleet, and we guessed these guys decided to make a break, probably took their wives and made it to some island in the South Pacific or South America. The fact is, Kilo 630 has vanished without trace. And I'm sure you can understand why I was too embarrassed to call you back."

"Yes, I can. Not many navies as big as yours lose submarines. That kind of thing only happens in Third World countries, eh?"

"Yes, Arnold, like Iran."

The American ignored that one. And then he said, "You don't think another country could have bought the submarine, do you? From some Naval agency in the Ukraine?"

"Hell no. We might be short of cash. But not that short. We'll fulfill genuine export orders for submarines for almost anyone, the Arabs, China, the Warsaw Pact nations. But we would not just flog off a diesel-electric submarine with a fully operational crew to some guy dressed in a sheet and carrying a sackful of cash. Give us some credit. We have to live in the international community, like everyone else."

"Well, Vitaly, if you guys are innocent, and Kilo 630 just went missing, there are but two alternatives. Somebody rented it. Or somebody hijacked it."

"I know you think we are very inefficient compared to the mighty U.S.A., Arnold. But our investigations here in Sevastopol indicate nothing unusual occurred in the three days preceding her departure. Preparations were normal. The captain filed the correct documents for an exercise in the Black Sea, following a refit. Members of the crew made the usual phone calls to wives, three substitute crew members did not leave their homes until the morning of departure. Our security around the submarine jetties is always very high, and no one saw anything to suggest the captain was coerced, or that he left with a gang of armed terrorists on board.

"The first thing to arouse suspicion was the absence of the next-of-kin signal. And of course no one reported that for three days. We just assumed the submarine comms had forgotten. It was another twelve hours before we became concerned there had been no communication whatsoever from Kilo 630. Then we found the bits of wreckage, which we now believe were planted."

"So where does that leave us, old buddy? I agree with you, theft is out of the question. Your submarine was not hijacked. There would be some clues if Kilo 630 had left Sevastopol at gunpoint. And they would surely have got a SATCOM signal away. No, I think your submarine may have been rented."

"From whom? The President?"

"No, Vitaly. From the captain."

"Admiral, he only drives it. He doesn't own it."

"But what might he say if someone approached him, and asked him to undertake a mission? To bring his submarine, and fool his crew into taking part? In return for which he would be given ten million American dollars?"

"But he would know he could never come home, not if he stole a Russian submarine."

"Home? To what? A run-down apartment in a dockyard town on the Black Sea where everyone's broke? Bullshit, Vitaly, I could buy a Russian submarine captain. So could anyone with a vast amount of money. And that money would also buy you the crew and the boat."

"But, Arnold, these men have wives and children. We have checked them all. No one knows anything. They just believe their men are dead. We have not made public our suspicions that this may not be so."

"Let me ask you one thing, what kind of torpedoes was this Kilo equipped for?"

"Her basic inventory was for the SAET–60's—you know, 533 millimeters, 7.8 meters long. They run at around forty knots, with a fifteen-kilometer range. Regular stuff, antisurface vessel. She was fairly new, a Granay Class, Type 877M. She was fully loaded with about twenty of them, with a couple of tubes specially for wire-guidance."

"How big's the regular warhead?"

"Four hundred kilograms."

"Can they take a nuclear variant?"

"Yes."

"Did this one have any on board with that variant?"

"Yes."

"How many?"

"Two."

"How do you know?"

"Because everyone involved in our internal inquiry knows every fucking thing there is to know about Kilo 630."

"May I now assume you will do what you can to help us?"

"Arnold, you can count on us to help find her, and to share information. Any information. I assume you also will share with us if you find her before we do?"

"We will find her first."

"How do you know that?"

"There's an old saying in the States—because we want it more."

"You're a terrible man, Admiral Morgan."

"I'll tell you what I do want. I want you to keep a clear eye on the families of the crew of Kilo 630. See if anything might be going on . . . you know, anyone spending a lot of money, or anything."

"You mean you think someone paid every member of the crew to go and blow up the carrier?"

"No. I don't think you would need to. You just have to present the captain with a cash fortune. Let him con the crew into believing they are on some secret mission on behalf of the Russian Navy. What would the crew do? Take a huge payoff, possibly a half million dollars apiece, and run, if they have any sense. Make a new life somewhere. Just watch the widows and orphans for me, willya?"

"Sure I will. What else?"

"Not much. Except I would like to send one of my men over to Sevastopol when you are in town, maybe a coupla weeks. You could show him around, give him the updates, and he will tell you personally what's happening in our own investigation."

"Okay. Let's try to find Kilo 630, shall we?"

Admiral Morgan tossed his old coffee cups and paper sandwich plate into the wastepaper basket, pulled on his coat, and checked the time, 0256. He was about to switch off the lights and his computer, when the phone unexpectedly rang.

"Morgan, speak."

The voice on the end of the line was foreign and struggled for English words. "Admiral Morgan. I am Israeli Intelligence. Ask to speak you by General Gavron. I am in Istanbul, and I find your man. He leave here on Black Sea ship, November 26. Bought ticket for cash, Turkish lira to Odessa. His name, Adnam, on passenger list. Ship docked November 27, 1300. He no jump overboard, he get there too. General Gavron hand over to colleague in Odessa now. Don't think your man come back here. Bye, Admiral, I go now."

The line from Turkey clicked dead. For a change Admiral Morgan was still holding the phone. "No he didn't go back there. He went straight past—right through the harbor, at periscope depth," he said to the empty room.

He walked to his sprawling maps and charts on the big sloping desk. He switched on the light, pulled out the one of the Black Sea coastlines, and went to work with his dividers, muttering as he considered the maps. "Istanbul to Odessa . . . 375 miles . . . at fifteen to twenty knots he's in the next day."

The admiral then measured the distance from Odessa, across the water to Sevastopol, "Two hundred miles to the southern headland of the Crimean Peninsula. Did Benjamin Adnam make that journey . . . to meet the captain of Kilo 630?" he asked aloud.

He returned to his desk, thinking deeply. "Let me stand in his shoes. I'm in Sevastopol, the headquarters of the Russian Black Sea Fleet. I intend either to keep an appointment, or find the captain of a Russian diesel-electric submarine. What do I need? I need cash, a ton of it, that's what I need. And I can't get it in Odessa or any other Russian city, not without attracting a great amount of attention to myself. Same with Cairo. But I *could* have gotten it in Istanbul."

Admiral Morgan picked up the phone and told the operator to connect him to the CIA immediately. The admiral asked to be put through to the senior duty officer, and told him to get Major Ted Lynch on a secure line to the Director of the National Security Agency.

He slammed down the phone before anyone was tempted to remind him what time it was. He sat back in his chair and waited. The CIA major was on the line inside five minutes. "Admiral, hi, Ted Lynch."

"Hey, sorry to wake you, but I have a lead you might be able to help with. I think our man may have picked up a very large bundle of cash, probably American dollars, more than 5 million, maybe up to 10 million, in Istanbul on November 26 last year. Any way of getting close to that?"

"Istanbul is a very cosmopolitan place, but they value United States business. They'll probably cooperate. We're almost certainly looking for someone in Buyukdere Street, the place is full of international banks—Bankapital, Iktisat Bankasi, Garanti Bank. They are fairly secretive, but we have connections there. And they mostly have branches in New York.

"I doubt if they'll give us names or anything—but if we ask for an unusual amount of U.S. dollars being picked up that day in cash, like a suitcase full, they'll probably give us a straight yes or no. We'll decide where to go from there. I'll get moving 0200 tomorrow, that's Monday, right?"

"Hey, thanks, Ted. Good luck, I'll wait to hear from you, early tomorrow morning. I'm in 0600. G'night, pal."

"Hey, Arnold, one thing," the voice of the CIA man rose, trying to stop the admiral from putting down the phone. "I gotta question . . . you still there?"

"I'm here."

"Admiral, if I am going to pay a Russian submarine captain a huge bundle of cash to take his submarine out of the Black Sea in early to mid-April, I sure as hell am not going to give it to him in late November."

"Beautiful call, Ted. You sure as hell are not. You're probably going to give him twenty grand, earnest money, in November. And then arrange to give him the big payment . . . maybe five million for himself, which would travel on the submarine with him, and another five million to take care of the crew, which would also be carried on board."

"Sounds much more like it, Admiral. But there's no way I

could get a trace on a small sum like twenty grand on November 26. What we're really after is maybe 10 million U.S. dollars, say between April 7 and 13. There's got to be a record of that somewhere."

"That's it, Ted. Second week in April is much more likely. Do what you can. I'm grateful."

The admiral replaced the receiver, picked it up again, and dialed the Maryland number of Bill Baldridge. The clock on the wall now said 0338. But the Kansas scientist answered swiftly in a reflex action honed by years of coming on watch in the smallest hours of the morning. If he was not alone, he sounded alone. "Yessir, that's me. Hi, what's hot?"

"Bill, we are making progress. The Russians recognize their Kilo was probably hired by an operative from an Arab state. They are on our side and you are going to visit a buddy of mine who heads up the office of Naval Intelligence, Vice Admiral Vitaly Rankov. Not till after your stuff in London and Scotland. Then I'm sending you down to the Black Sea, so pack plenty of things. You may be gone for several weeks.

"Meantime the Mossad are seriously on the trail of Adnam. They have traced him to Odessa. He went by sea from Istanbul on a Russian passport. He also had a stamped Turkish visa. I'll say one thing, that guy has no trouble with documents. Right now it looks like he went on to Sevastopol with a moderate bundle of cash and paid a Russian captain to prepare a mission with his submarine and crew."

"Steady, Admiral. You can't just turn up and start bribing Russian Naval officers to pinch a submarine and bamboozle their crew into doing something diabolical that is going to make them the most hunted men in the world."

"Yes you can, Bill. Find me a Russian captain with little money, and I could offer him enough cash to do anything. Just get in the boat, tell his crew they were going on a secret Navy exercise, and then depart. My terms would be simple . . . carry out the job, here's half the money. The rest is in a bank in South America, from where you cannot be extradited. Nor, with a bit of luck, even found."

"How much are you paying?"

"How about half a million dollars?"

"No chance. He's gotta live on it for the rest of his life, and his family's."

"Okay, three million."

"Not enough to wreck a big Navy career and leave your homeland forever."

"Five?"

"Possible."

"Ten million dollars."

"Sounds pretty good to me."

"I'll make it twenty million, if you like. But I'll get him. Because my government's oil money is nothing to me, but it's everything to him. And to his family. I think we've got the answer, Bill. This is how they did it. And I'll tell you something else. Those new Kilos in the Black Sea have a full complement of torpedoes on board already. Probably twenty. And two of them are nuclear-tipped."

"Jesus Christ! How do you know?"

"Rankov told me."

"You mean when that Kilo set sail, Ben Adnam was on board and the killer missiles were already in place."

"No. I think they picked Ben up somewhere in Turkish waters. He would not have risked security checks inside the Russian Navy base. But the captain knew that Ben had access to a colossal amount of cash. And he knew that the cash was his for the asking. With another half to come when the mission was completed. Payable in some foreign country. The torpedoes were ready though. The Russian captain saw to that. Part of the deal, right?"

"Are the Russians sure the Kilo went through the Bosporus underwater?"

"No. They just know it's missing, and they know something very fishy is going on. But they realize it may well have gone through the Bosporus because of the drowned sailor on the Greek island. He *was* a member of the ship's company of Kilo 630."

"Rankov confirmed that?"

"He did."

"Will I see you tomorrow before I leave for London?"

"Yes. Come to the office. Early afternoon. We'll get a final briefing from CNO. Then you can leave straightaway for the airport. Also I would like you to pick up a portable phone scrambler. Do you know how to work it?"

"Yessir, but we'd better run over the operating procedures. Can I hook it up to you from abroad?"

"It'll work from anywhere. And it's damned important. We cannot risk *anyone* listening in."

"Okay, sir."

But Admiral Morgan was already off the line. He was hunched over a chart at his sloping desk with the big light. This time he was poring over a larger-scale map detailing the northern coastline of Turkey, which stretched from the Bulgarian border one hundred miles west of the Bosporus along the seven-hundred-mile coastline which runs east of the Bosporus, out to the old Soviet border at the Georgian city of Batumi.

He was asking himself the question he always asked himself. "What would I do?"

The clock ticked on past 0400. Washington slept. Arnold Morgan did not sleep. He lit up a cigar, opened his door, and demanded a cup of coffee.

Time had no meaning for the admiral, who like many ex-submariners was accustomed to the cocoon of the great underwater ships, which did not distinguish between day and night. Only the watch changes marked the passing of the hours.

Morgan brandished his cigar theatrically. "Let me start that again," he said to the deserted room. "I have just arrived in Sevastopol. I am carrying two big suitcases stuffed with U.S. dollars. I have already given one of them to the captain. The other one will be given to him when I step on board. Now when do I do that?"

Admiral Arnold Morgan begged the empty walls to bear with him while he gathered his thoughts. Then he said loudly, "Right. Now hold it. What would I *not* do? What would I not *dream* of doing, if I was about to illegally board a Russian submarine and steal it. Answer, I'd pick up my second suitcase full of cash, and I'd get the hell out of Russia, and board the sub someplace else."

The admiral looked pleased with his inescapable logic. He studied the map, mentally ruling out the seaports down the western coast—those near the mouth of the Danube in Rumania, and others down on the Bulgarian coast which sprawled to the Turkish border. "And I'd stay the hell out of there too," he added. "Countries too long under the Soviet fist. Too much suspicion, too many spooks."

He looked at the ocean off the northeast coast of Turkey, on the European side. "No good there, either. The real deep water's too far out. You'd have to run out to meet the submarine, maybe sixty miles offshore. Too far. Too much risk of being stopped by a patrol boat. That's Turkish water. They might find you, with all that cash, and probably a gun. They might even spot the Russian submarine, way off course, and on the surface. Very bad news."

He switched his survey to the other side of the Bosporus, to the east. And he trawled his magnifying glass along the shoreline, stopping suddenly at a seaport on a peninsula. Sinop. The admiral skimmed through his big suite of chart drawers. Pulling one out, he stabbed it with his dividers, took a reading on his steel ruler, and saw with some satisfaction that the peninsula jutted out into very deep water. It was, by miles, the closest point on the entire coast to a possible submarine waiting area. A gentle twenty-five-minute journey to deep water.

He checked again, then he pulled out a guidebook which told him that Sinop was a shipbuilding and fishing port with fine beaches, a secluded harbor, and many inexpensive hotels. Sinop was accessible by bus, three-hundred-odd miles from Istanbul. It was the birthplace of Diogenes, the cynic philosopher. That settled it. Admiral Morgan was at home among cynics.

"That's what I'd do," he announced solemnly. "I'd make my deal with the Russian captain, drive south down the coast to Georgia, and go by sea to Trabzon. From there I'd take the bus to Sinop. I'd park myself in one of those little hotels with a radio pack, and I'd wait for a signal from my Russian captain.

"Then I'd slip down to the harbor, and get aboard the deserted thirty-foot yacht I had scoped out, and sail quietly beyond the harbor wall on a little journey about fourteen miles out, using my little GPS to put me at 35.3E, 42.1N. As an experienced submariner I'd get alongside the waiting sub, bang a hole in the yacht's bilge, grab my suitcase, and board the Kilo real quick. Then I'd take effective command of the Russian submarine through her C.O. as agreed previously with him."

Admiral Morgan realized he might not be right, but he liked having a starting point. To his keen eye the little seaport of Sinop had stuck out "like the balls on a Texas longhorn." That was what he liked, a strong start-point. For the moment, he would assume Sinop was where Commander Ben Adnam had holed up.

Admiral Morgan would never know how close he was to the truth. And what concerned him, as he marched out of the building toward his car, was the destiny of the submarine *after* its secret pickup.

Did it creep back west, running deep in a thousand fathoms, to the yawning northern entrance of the Bosporus? And did Commander Adnam then calmly order his Russian captain to steer left rudder, course two-one-zero, into pitch-black, unknown depths, through the great gap in the underwater cliffs, where no submarine had ever ventured?

0700 Monday, August 5.

BILL BALDRIDGE WAS STILL REHEARSING THE UNPRECE-dented request he was about to make of the Royal Navy as the British Airways Boeing 747 banked over London and turned due west for Heathrow. "Oh, good morning, Admiral, I was wondering whether you'd lend me a brand-new Upholder Class diesel-electric submarine which we will probably wreck in the middle of Istanbul Harbor?"

No. Too harsh. Perhaps something a little more subtle. How about, "Good morning, Admiral, I wonder if you'd be decent enough to let us borrow one of your submarines for a few weeks. We'll look after it. By the way do you keep a salvage squad in Istanbul?"

His hope that Scott Dunsmore had prepared the way for him before he arrived at Northwood to make what was, by any standards, an outrageous request of the Royal Navy showed that Lieutenant Commander Baldridge had much to learn about the intricacies of inter-Navy politics. The American CNO and Britain's First Sea Lord could almost operate by telepathy, each perfectly prepared to be edged into something he did not really want to do. Just so long as the favor was returned. Preferably in spades.

Baldridge arrived at Northwood just before 0900 in FOSM's

personal staff car, which had been sent to meet him. The territory was familiar to him now, and he greeted young Andrew Waites with cheerful informality.

"Morning, sir," said the Flag Lieutenant. "Found that Perisher yet?"

"Not yet, but we're moving on him."

Bill was led immediately into the office of the Flag Officer Submarines (FOSM), and Vice Admiral Sir Peter Elliott stood immediately to greet him. "Lieutenant Commander, glad to see you again. Good flight?"

"Pretty painless," he replied. "Everything been moving smoothly since I left?"

The British admiral chuckled at the junior officer's jaunty manner and put it down to American spontaneity. "Well, no one in my flotilla has collided, run aground, burned, got lost, or mutinied lately, so I suppose we're just about winning," he replied.

Just then the door opened and Captain Dick Greenwood walked in, late but unflustered. "Morning, sir. Morning, Lieutenant Commander. I have those notes you wanted."

"Barrow?"

"Yessir."

"Very well. Now, if Andrew will bring us some coffee, we may as well get down to business. The subject is very complicated, and very important to the United States."

He looked over at Bill and added, "I spoke to the First Sea Lord last night, who has had a long conversation with your CNO. In the broadest terms I understand you want to borrow one of our diesel-electric submarines, and transit the Bosporus underwater, which as we all know is illegal. Do I have the general gist of the exercise?"

Bill Baldridge was relieved not to be obliged to make the speech he had been rehearsing on the aircraft. He said simply, "Yessir, you do."

"Then, since I am keenly aware of my own point of view, and that of the Royal Navy, why don't you outline for me the point of view of the United States, with which I am not quite so familiar?"

"Certainly, sir. As you know we have now spent almost a month trying to find out what happened to the *Thomas Jefferson*. And every path we take is leading us to the same conclusion—that the carrier was hit by a torpedo fired from a nonnuclear submarine which belonged to one of the hostile Gulf nations.

"We do not think they used a submarine from their own inventory, but nonetheless the boat was a Russian Kilo. If our deductions are right, the sub *must* therefore have come out of the Black Sea, through the Bosporus. And the Turks say they saw nothing. We believe it came through under the surface."

"Yes, that all adds up to me. But why do you now want to do the same thing? One of your television shows organized a contest?"

Bill laughed. "Not yet, sir. That's probably next. No, the truth is our President is perfectly prepared to order a global hunt for the boat only if someone proves conclusively that it is possible to transit the Bosporus, north to south, underwater. The main trouble being that several dozen people have already told him it *cannot* be done. By anyone."

"Yes, global hunts are apt to become obsessional," said Admiral Elliott. "And once started they run away with money, and people, on a rather alarming scale. Your President is wise to be cautious."

"Yessir. Almost all of his political advisers are urging him not to stray publicly from the 'accident' theory. And if we make the Bosporus journey, and there is any kind of a problem, he is going to stick to the only theory he has, and the only one he will ever admit."

"Of course," said the admiral. "Although that might turn out to be rather shortsighted if your Muslim enemy should strike again. The one good thing about losing an aircraft carrier was that it wasn't two aircraft carriers."

"Well, that's the view of most of our senior Intelligence men, and the submariners, sir. But I guess you see the President's point of view. In a way, we think he's being reasonable given the circumstances. He's just saying that if we want to conduct a massive search operation, costing probably a couple of billion dollars, he wants to know we are working on a premise which is at least *possible*."

"Very Presidential," replied the admiral. "Unless they hit again. Then he will be blamed, and slaughtered by his opponents for failing to take the grimmer advice of his senior military commanders."

"Yessir," replied the Kansan. "Guess that's just about what will happen. And some of us think they might easily be preparing to strike again."

"In these matters, Bill, as with legal contracts, you are *never* actually discussing what *will* happen. You must always be considering what *could* happen. However unlikely. In military matters, when you are dealing with a potential catastrophic loss of life, you *must* operate assuming the worst-case scenario. There is no other course. And in my experience, politicians have the utmost difficulty grasping that."

At this point Captain Greenwood entered the conversation. "Can you tell me, Lieutenant Commander, why you are so sure it was a Russian Kilo?"

"I can, sir. We have checked the whereabouts of every other submarine in everyone's Navy, including those from the Third World, which were either in refit, out of commission, or even sunk in the harbor in the cases of both Syria and Libya . . . "

"Sorry to interrupt," said the admiral, looking up at Bill, with a half-smile, and one raised eyebrow, "but didn't the Iranians have a similar problem a couple of days ago . . . ?"

"I don't really know about that," replied the American.

"Of course not," said the admiral, still wearing his half-smile . . . "Do continue, won't you?"

"Yessir. Well, having run all the checks we could, we came up with only one possibility. There was a Russian Kilo, which cleared Sevastopol in April, and was reported sunk in the Black Sea two weeks later. The Russians admit that they cannot find it after a long search, and they have reason to believe it may have escaped. Right now they are admitting it just vanished."

"Well, I suppose it could have just sunk in an awkward place and they have not been able to find it. These things do happen," said Captain Greenwood.

"Yessir. But if you were us, what would you believe?"

"I'd believe it might have attacked my carrier."

"Yessir. It was the only submarine which could have. Which brings us right back to the President's insistence that we prove the Bosporus underwater passage is possible."

"Before you bring out the big guns, correct?" said Greenwood.

"I shouldn't be surprised if there were a few senior officers in the Iranian Navy who consider that's already happened," said Admiral Elliott.

Lieutenant Commander Baldridge said nothing, noticed that the admiral still wore his knowing half-smile.

"It seems to me," said Captain Greenwood, "that you are proposing something which is entirely unnecessary. Why risk a boat and her crew to establish such an outlandish possibility? Even if we were to do it, and were successful, it would merely tell us that a first-class boat, manned by the best possible crew, could exit the Black Sea underwater.

"You could decide that, quite reputably, in this room, and save a lot of trouble with an extremely dangerous mission. In any event I doubt the rewards. Not to mention the fact that it's against International Law, *and* we could lose the boat in about thirty different kinds of accident, possibly drowning several dozen sailors."

"I did forget to mention, Bill," said the admiral, "that Captain Greenwood is my personal devil's advocate. I need one of those, because there are a lot of people who think I am only happy when I'm tackling something which could not, or should not, be done. Not true of course, but nevertheless a part of my reputation with which I have to live."

"Absolutely, sir," said Bill Baldridge. "But the answers to Captain Greenwood's concerns are simple. The President of the United States has spoken. He wants this journey made, in order to justify to Congress and to the Senate why he is about to spend untold billions trying to find an enemy which may not exist.

"This is one of the best Presidents we've ever had. He's a friend of the military and tries to understand the subject. He's tough. He's brilliantly clever, and always on our side. What he is trying to avoid is some smart-ass congressman second-guessing him about the Bosporus under the water, and a decision to spend billions of taxpayer dollars."

"Yes," said the admiral, thoughtfully. "I see. He needs proof of it."

Captain Greenwood was beginning to look despondent as he saw the boss warming to the subject, and he spoke up again. "Why don't you use a boat of your own?" he asked.

"That's easy," replied Baldridge. "We haven't had one for twenty years."

He referred to the old diesel-electrics which had been abandoned in a succession of defense cuts. U.S. strategists have long believed that America needed only big, powerful, long-range nuclear submarines as her operations were always across oceans.

"Matter of fact I thought there was a lot of sense in what the Americans did," said Admiral Elliott. "They really do need their long-range SSN's, and they only require a stealthy inshore boat on the rarest of occasions.

"Politicians here in the U.K. think we can do the same but they are incorrect because we live in different geographical circumstances. We need to be able to operate right around the European coastline, with expert inshore submariners in command. Those little boats can be lethal to an enemy, which is why the Russians are still making and selling them. Dammit.

"Our own situation is not much short of absurd."

"How do you mean, sir?" asked Baldridge.

"Well, in recent years we spent about 1 billion pounds on four Upholder Class submarines which are roughly the equivalent of a Russian Kilo. That included all the development costs, and they were going to get progressively cheaper.

"Then, from out of the blue, the politicians decided we did not need them, not even to keep under wraps for the day when we might. So in order to avoid any running costs whatsoever, however minor, they decided to sell 'em off cheaply to anyone who would buy. The Israelis already have one in operational service. The Brazilians are just starting workup. Followed by God knows who else.

"They are being sold for peanuts, and in the view of the Submarine Service this is a criminal waste of the taxpayers' money, and it shows an almost criminal lack of military foresight by our government.

"Lieutenant Commander Baldridge, you come to me not as a bloody nuisance, which others might think. But as a particularly interesting opportunity."

"Yessir. I understand. Because we now have a reason to get one of those babies up and running, carrying out an important joint operation between our two countries."

"Precisely. And we all know this may be a major Naval emergency on a global scale. And the only way we can help our principal military ally is with our maligned little Upholder submarine, whose case we have been pleading for a very long unsuccessful time."

"Well, sir, for our part, there was only one nation we could possibly come to. Not just for help, but for discretion and loyalty."

"Matter of fact, I wouldn't mind going myself," added the admiral predictably.

"Absolutely out of the question, sir," said Captain Greenwood, interjecting swiftly. "You simply could not be out of touch for that long, and also there would be an uproar if there was an accident and anything happened to you. No one could ever reasonably explain what you were doing on such a dangerous mission."

"Well, of course I wouldn't much care then, would I?" replied the Flag Officer. "But I suppose you're right. Still, the submarine would have to sail under British command."

"We assumed a British commanding officer," said Baldridge. "But my President requires me to be on board."

"Right. That's not a problem. The problem is the short notice. My U Class qualified CO's are simply not up to it. And there's no time to get them up to it. Whoever we appoint as captain will need a topman right at his elbow—a very experienced, conventional submariner."

Captain Greenwood interjected. "What about Admiral MacLean, sir? If he can't do it, then it can't be done."

"What a bloody good idea!" said the Flag Officer. "We might have to persuade him, though. He goes grouse-shooting for the last part of August. But I think he'd do it. The old boy has a strong sense of history—it just might appeal to him."

"He's not that old, sir. What would he be . . . fifty-six?"

"He'd definitely consider himself young enough to have a shot at becoming the first man ever to make the underwater passage through the Bosporus," replied Admiral Elliott. "Or the second."

"May I now assume you are leaning toward proceeding with this entire operation, sir. I mean the preliminary stages?"

"Well, Dick, I am looking at some very interesting possibilities. From our own point of view it is obviously very good—one in the eye for the government, for trying to give away our extremely valuable hulls for petty cash. If we succeed in the mission it might even persuade them to allow us to keep at least two of the Upholders in the fleet, ready for the day when we may need them.

"From the Turks' point of view it will provide them with some very valuable new information, should we wish to share with them.

"And, in the long term, the Americans will be pleased to see the Turks increase security around the Bosporus. You never quite know when the Russian Navy might rise again.

"I'd say there was much to gain and little to lose—for everyone, especially us."

"Well, sir," said Captain Greenwood, "We could lose a brand-new submarine and maybe a lot of people."

"Oh, I don't know, Dick," replied the Flag Officer. "I think we'd survive a ramming from one of those shallow-draft ferries. Might knock off a mast, maybe a fin. Expensive, but not terminal. And a lot of the chaps would get out. The water's not that deep."

"Sir, they would not survive a bad underwater collision in the dark with a wreck or a rock, nor would they survive colliding with one of those really big freighters which run through those waters."

"True. But we're going to lose the submarines anyway, even if we sit here and do nothing."

"Actually, sir, it was the chaps I was more concerned about."

"Yes, quite so, Captain, I see that. But I do not want to turn my back on an opportunity to retain possibly three of the Upholders for the Royal Navy. And without this mission, they're history."

"Yes. But also, sir, there is the question of Johnny Turk," said Captain Greenwood. "Are we going to tell him?"

"I don't think the President wants to tell him," said Bill. "But since it's your boat, you'd better decide. We would prefer to say nothing."

"Let me remind you of one possible scenario," said Captain Greenwood. "It's the middle of the night. For whatever reason we are driven to the surface by either a collision, or by shallow water. Johnny Turk's radar spots us. We go back to periscope depth and he comes out in a patrol boat, panics, and drops in a half-dozen depth charges which blow the submarine in half, causing most of the crew to drown. Should we not attempt to avoid that?"

"Yes, I think we should," said Admiral Elliott. "We're not at war with anyone, and we shouldn't lay ourselves open to that kind of reprisal. Johnny Turk is not going to be too cheerful about this, mark my words. So we are going to have to find a way to retain the integrity of the mission, by telling him, but not telling him, if you see what I mean.

"And there I might be able to help."

Captain Greenwood averted his eyes. He knew when his boss was going to play a major card. And this was it.

"A few years ago," said his boss, "I had the happy privilege of being selected from a large group of nonapplicants to escort an important visiting officer from Turkey on a sightseeing tour down the River Thames. It had all the makings of a total bloody disaster. He could not speak a word of English, and I could not speak a word of Turkish. I was told to settle for French, which I also hardly speak. Anyway, I stayed up all night with a couple of guidebooks until I was an expert on the historic sights up and down the river.

"The Turk and I made it through the day. Had a very good time, and after dinner at the club, I fixed him up with a hostess from the Stork Room. As I remember, Al, the proprietor, let him have one on the house. That Turk owes me, and that particular officer is now CNS of the Turkish Navy. How's that?"

"Brilliant, sir," said Baldridge. "Maybe we should send him a rain check for the Stork Room?"

"No good, I'm afraid. It closed several years ago. Too many freebies, I suppose."

Captain Greenwood chuckled, and Bill Baldridge laughed out loud. But the Flag Officer was all business. "I propose the following. I'll have a very quick word with my old Turkish buddy, in French. Bill here will head to Scotland immediately and talk to his new friend Admiral MacLean. I'll speak to him first.

"Then Dick can get on to the dockyard in Barrow-in-Furness and find out the precise state of readiness of that boat which is being sold to the Brazilians, *Unseen*, isn't it?"

"*Andrew!* Get the First Sea Lord on the line, will you. I'll get this past the MoD. I believe the Prime Minister has been alerted. The politicos have no objection, and would wish to help our American friends if at all possible. Can't have some half-assed tribesman blowing up the U.S. Navy, what?"

The admiral stood up and suggested Bill go next door and check if it would be okay to stay with the MacLeans again, and perhaps take a run down to Barrow tomorrow with Sir Iain, have a look at *Unseen*.

"We'll send a Navy chopper in to meet your flight and get you over to Inveraray, if that's okay with the MacLeans," he said. "If not, you can camp overnight at the Faslane base, and meet Iain tomorrow. You'd better get on your way, and we'll have a talk on the phone tonight, check that all the ends are coming together, as they surely will. Generally speaking we do not like disappointing the Pentagon. Especially when they're paying, and we have something to gain."

Bill Baldridge ran down the stairs and boarded the admiral's staff car. The driver already knew the American was on his way to Scotland, and they left for Heathrow immediately. It was raining in Northwood at midday and the traffic was awful on the M25. But they sped under the tunnel into the airport with time to spare for the Glasgow flight at 1440.

051835AUG02. 19.55S, 64.31E.
Speed zero. Position Indian Ocean,
three hundred miles due east of Mauritius.

"Stores looking good. About another thousand gallons of fuel, Georgy. You'll be on your way in a half hour."

"You really not come, Ben?"

"I can't come. I have to get off here and get on the oiler. And I have to get to our meeting point, because you cannot just unload fifty renegade Russian sailors and leave them in some South American village with a half million dollars apiece. I need to get us a boat. And we need to ferry these men away from the submarine two or three at a time, over a three-week time span. That's what we agreed. Slowly, carefully, and safely, the way we've done everything."

"But, Ben, what if I get to our place and you not come? You never show up? What then for me?"

"Georgy, you know where the final fueling point is. Nothing has gone wrong so far. And you have a Samsonite suitcase under your bunk, in which you have four million American dollars in cash.

"You also have the full documents for the bank account in Chile. You even have their fax confirming your right to operate the account and a letter of credit for a further 5 million from that bank. Your money is safe. The biggest problem you have is getting off the submarine without being seen. That's what I'm now doing for you. I have to go."

"Ben, I can't let you go. The crew want you stay."

"Georgy, you cannot leave this boat without me there to meet you with a launch."

"I can beach it on one of those islands. Then I'll share out the other money in the other case for the crew, and I'll get away, in small life raft, through shallow water, with my case and documents."

"Georgy. There are too many of you. And they'll find the submarine within hours. We have to keep it hidden while we evacuate. I insist you stick to the plan."

"If you go, Ben, I might be a dead man. With you here I think I survive."

"If I stay. Georgy, we'll both be dead men. You must do as I say."

"Ben, if I have to, I'll have you held here at gunpoint. The crew won't let you get off. They told me that two days ago. As soon as I told them what we had really done. Some of them are pretty upset. Even if we didn't hurt Russia."

"Georgy, don't be ridiculous. Bring to me the four senior members of your crew and let me speak to them. Let me explain the importance of the plan. My objective is that no one gets caught. You beach this thing on some island, we'll all get caught. If the Americans are onto us, they'll have everyone extradited to the U.S.A., and put to death for the mass murder of the crew of the Thomas Jefferson.*"*

"Okay, Ben, I get them. But they not change their minds. They want you on the journey. So do I. You stay."

"Georgy, before you even consider brandishing a Kalashnikov at me, remember one thing. I was perfectly happy to die for my country on this mission. I still am."

Bill Baldridge gazed down from the helicopter onto the shining waters of Loch Fyne. To the northeast of the MacLean house he could see the little town of Inveraray. From the air it was dominated by some kind of a castle, or at the very least a fine manor house, with four round towers, surrounded by great lawns and gardens; Inveraray Castle, home to the Dukes of Argyll.

The chopper came clattering down onto Sir Iain's lawn, and Bill stepped out into a sunlit late afternoon in the west of Scotland. He carried his case to the door, and was greeted by

Lady MacLean, who shook his hand warmly and announced that her husband had been held up in Edinburgh and would be back in a couple of hours.

They walked into the hall, where the faithful Angus wished Bill good afternoon, and took his case upstairs. Lady MacLean led the way into the drawing room overlooking the loch and told him they would have tea in a few minutes. They sat on opposite sofas and exchanged formal pleasantries, during which the Scottish admiral's wife implored him to call her Annie. It took a while before she ventured, "I believe you are planning to take my retired husband on a little holiday to Turkey."

"No one has told me yet whether he has agreed to come," said Bill. "I was at the meeting when Admiral Elliott was informed that *he* could not go. Next thing I knew, they were planning to contact Admiral MacLean. They were supposed to have had a talk while I was on the plane."

"Well, I believe they did talk. And I also believe they have the matter under consideration, and I think we all know what the outcome will be. Iain will take his place on that journey as the senior officer on board, and end up taking all of the responsibility, just as he has done all of his life."

"Annie," said Bill quietly, using her name for the first time, "do you not want him to go?"

"Of course not. I have been a Navy wife for almost the whole of my adult life. I've waited for him for years. Sometimes I've waited for him to come home for months at a time, when he was out in the Atlantic or in the Barents Sea, risking his life every moment of every day, hundreds of feet below the surface. Right in the Russians' backyard. The weeks I was by myself, never hearing, always wondering.

"I think of the hours and hours I have spent in this house, in the night, wandering around, always alone, just praying for news of him. Any news. All through the Cold War, all through the Falklands War. Until last year, I finally got him back. And now this. Some kind of suicide mission in a submarine, in waters not much bigger than a wide ditch."

Bill looked thoughtful. "I suppose, if you talk to him, he

might decide not to do it. I have to be there myself, under orders."

"But, Bill, you are so much younger, and I don't believe you have a wife, do you?"

"No, ma'am, I do not. But I've got a stack of very close relatives back in Kansas, and we've just lost my brother Jack, who was really the head of the family. I guess my mother might feel the way you do."

"Navy wives and mothers have a very lonely and worrying time. And it lasts for years. I suppose I am just a little bit shocked. I had believed it was over."

"Well, at least no one's going to shoot at us. We're just going to make the trip. It's only about sixteen miles. Won't take more than about four hours, once we get set up. I don't think you should worry. We'll be fine. And if Sir Iain decides to come, we'll be really fine. Because he believes it can be done. And he's the best."

"Oh, he will definitely be on that submarine," said Lady MacLean. "Whatever I think or say. He'll actually enjoy it. Because it will take him back to his happiest, most exciting days in command. Doing the things he believed only he could do."

"A lot of people seem to think he was the best submarine commander the Navy ever had. Maybe this is part of his destiny. Do you believe in destiny, Annie?"

"Yes, Bill. After all of these years, I'm afraid that I do."

Angus brought in the tea, and when he had gone, Baldridge and Lady MacLean sat and sipped in silence for a while. Finally Bill said, "How long does it take to drive to Edinburgh from here?"

"About an hour and a half to Glasgow, then another hour to Edinburgh if the traffic's reasonable. It's less than fifty miles between the two cities, straight along the M8."

"Still, that's five hours behind the wheel," said Bill. "Guess you wouldn't want to make it every day."

"Oh no. It's hardly commuting distance. Really it's right across this narrow part of Scotland, west to east. Still, it's not too bad for him today. He's got Laura driving him."

Bill looked up sharply, smiling to disguise the heartbeat of excitement he felt. They had not spoken since they parted on the lawn of this house three weeks previously.

He tried to slow the conversation down, and very nearly succeeded. "Oh, I had no idea I'd be meeting one of my chief informants again," he said, grinning.

"And, I believe, one of your fellow opera enthusiasts," replied Lady MacLean. But she betrayed no sense of knowing, nor sly insight, when she added, "My daughter liked you very much."

"Does she have the little girls here—the ones I never met?"

"No, Bill. They've gone off with their father for a few days, up to his brother's grouse-moor. The season starts next week, and everyone gets frightfully busy in the days leading up to the first shoot. Laura hates the ritual of it."

"So she comes over here for a few days on this spectacular loch," said Bill.

"Yes. Actually we've seen quite a bit of her just lately. She's never really been content living in Edinburgh. And her husband's charming. Of course she's never got over that frightful Adnam boy. She told me you knew all about that."

"Yes. She was amazingly helpful about him. If we get him, she'll probably never know how important a part she played."

"Do you really think he blew up your aircraft carrier?"

"When I was last here I thought he might have. Right now, I know he did."

"Can I know how?"

"Not in any great detail, I'm afraid," said the lieutenant commander. "But he was not Israeli. We think he was Iranian. But he could have been Libyan, or Syrian, or an Iraqi. His identity has baffled even the Mossad."

"Iain thinks he could have been Iranian. Especially after Laura told him about that strange visit they made to the mosque in Cairo."

Just then the telephone rang. Lady MacLean hurried away to answer it across the room. "Yes . . . yes . . . he is here . . . I'll get him." She beckoned to Bill and told him to take the call in the admiral's study across the hall. "It's probably top-secret," she said, smiling. "It's my husband's old office."

Bill found Lieutenant Waites on the line. "Hello, sir. Hold on a moment. I have Captain Greenwood for you."

"Good afternoon, Bill." The deep, somber voice of FOSM's Chief of Staff was unmistakable. "Just a short progress report. First, we've been cleared politically. The mission is to proceed immediately. The boss ran Admiral MacLean to ground at some office in Edinburgh and Sir Iain's coming. That's all decided.

"The submarine we want, *Unseen*, is in Barrow, in a state of near-readiness for the sale to Brazil. We've canceled that for the moment, and the admiral has ordered a crew to be brought in. That will take a week. Then we will have a two-week workup period to familiarize everyone with the SSK. Barring accidents, *Unseen* will clear Barrow on August 25, and arrive in the area on about September 7. It's 3,700 miles, and we'll run at around twelve knots all the way."

"How about the landowners?" asked Bill, avoiding naming the Turks on the telephone. "Are we spilling the beans?"

"No, we're not. I believe the admiral is going to talk to their boss tonight in very guarded terms. He has already spoken to Admiral Dunsmore at the Pentagon, and, so far as I can tell, you are the only American on board. Admiral Elliott is naming the captain tomorrow. I expect it to be the former *Upholder* XO, Jeremy Shaw. He and his team have been training the Brazilians, so he's well up to the job."

"Sounds good to me."

"Oh yes, two other things. Tomorrow we are sending the chopper over to take you and Sir Iain down to Barrow to get a look at the boat. And will you expect a call in a half hour or so from Admiral Morgan?"

"Okay, sir. I'll be here, enjoying my little vacation in Scotland."

"Not for long, I hear. Admiral Morgan said he was sending you to Russia on Thursday. You have to pick up a special visa at the embassy in London before you go."

"Jesus," said Bill. "There's no peace, right?"

"Not if you want to catch your man. No, Bill, there's not."

★   ★   ★

A half hour later the lieutenant commander had just lowered himself into the steaming spare-room bathtub, along with the other half of the jar of blue crystals, when he heard a tap on the door.

"Sir, there's a call for you. I've put it through to the phone by your bed."

"Thanks, Angus, old buddy," he said. "Be right there."

Cursing the exquisite timing of Arnold Morgan, he wrapped himself in a towel, and picked up the telephone, warning immediately, "Admiral, this is not a secure line."

"Okay, Bill. Gottit. I hear we're all set. I spoke to Scott Dunsmore this morning and he says the President is definite. The minute he hears you're through the slot, he'll authorize a massive search for the Kilo. Meantime, I want you to get out to Sevastopol and spend a little time with Admiral Rankov.

"He's as anxious as we are to locate his employees. But he'll show you around, so you can get a feel for the area, and the families of the crew. Sorry to turn you into some kind of detective, but everyone is anxious not to expand the circle of people who actually know about this. So I guess you're doing nearly everything."

"What about my travel arrangements to Russia?"

"Admiral Elliott's office is taking care of it all. You need to pick up tickets, visa, and cash in London before you go. I thought Thursday or Friday, after you've taken a look at the submarine. Anyway call the admiral's Flag Lieutenant in Northwood. They got it covered."

"Okay, Admiral. Will I come back to the States after Sevastopol?"

"I guess so. You'll be through with Rankov by around August 13. You might just want to meet the guys working up the submarine after that. Then there may be something else over there for you.

"If not, you might as well come back, and we'll go on playing detectives together. Anyway, you'll be ready to go aboard on September 8, I understand with Admiral MacLean."

"Guess so, sir."

"Good. See you, Bill." The line went dead.

Back in the hot, scented water, Bill Baldridge reviewed the situation. The fact was, the "search-and-destroy" operation was on hold pending the successful transit of the Bosporus. Thereafter the President would be relentless in the pursuit of Adnam. It was curious how certain he was that the Israeli officer had made that journey. Even more curious that Ben's Teacher was now trying to follow him.

Downstairs he was just walking across the hall when he heard the tires of the Range Rover on the drive. He opened the front door and saw the admiral step out of the car, pursued by the omnipresent Fergus, Muffin, and Samson. God knows what those Labradors had been doing in Edinburgh.

He noticed the spring in the step of the admiral as he walked briskly toward him, smiling in greeting. He noticed too, the gentle wave of the driver through the windshield, as she gathered up her jacket and bag. "Hello, Bill. Delighted you're here. Understand we're going on a little jaunt together?"

Bill shook hands with the admiral, fought off the dogs as they leapt all over him. "Coupla days sailing off Istanbul, paid for by Uncle Sam, shouldn't be so bad, sir?"

"Certainly not. I'm rather looking forward to it, tell you the truth."

By now Laura was out of the car and walking over to join them. "My God, she's beautiful," thought Bill. And he grinned rakishly as she held out her hand. "Hello," she said. "I didn't expect to see my inquisitor so soon."

Lady MacLean emerged through the front door. "Hello, darling," she said. "Good journey?"

"Yes, fine, except when Daddy loosed off the dogs in the forest about an hour from here. That ridiculous Fergus wouldn't come back. Found a rabbit or something. Cost us twenty minutes. I don't know why we had to take them in the first place. They were sitting outside a lawyer's office for two hours, and in the car for five, with only two breaks."

"You know how your father is with those dogs. They go everywhere with him. Except London. And they behave like lunatics most of the time."

In the distance Bill could see them right now. A boisterous black trio of running, barking, rolling, pushing energy, two of them having already rushed into the loch. "Don't let those wet Labradors into the house," Lady MacLean called out to her husband.

Laura took Bill by the arm. "Come on, Inquisitor, let's have a drink. It's almost half past seven."

It was a good start to a long evening. Angus had cooked yet another Tay salmon, and the wines were identical. Admiral MacLean expounded more on the Bosporus and how he intended to guide *Unseen* safely through. Bill thought this was strictly for the benefit of his wife. It was eleven-thirty by the time dinner ended and the group retired to bed. The admiral and Bill were being collected at eight-thirty in the morning.

Strapped by the rigid propriety of their surroundings, the lieutenant commander and the admiral's daughter retired to their separate rooms, forty feet and a thousand miles apart on the second floor. Bill himself wondered if he would ever see her again. In two days he would be gone, and he might not return. He could never telephone her here, and he sure as hell was not anxious to call her husband's house in Edinburgh.

He knew he would have to wait, to find out if she would call him in the States. And where could such a course of action take her? Nowhere, except to Kansas. And he hardly knew her. Christ, he didn't even know if they had any *au pairs* in Kansas.

The Royal Navy chopper arrived precisely on time. The lieutenant commander and the admiral strapped themselves in for the one-hour ride to the sprawling home of Vickers Shipbuilding and Engineering Ltd., the British corporation which had constructed all of the Royal Navy's nuclear boats, from Polaris to Trident.

Most shipyards in northern Europe were situated in bleak, windswept areas, and this was no exception. The Vickers yard sat on the southernmost peninsula of Cumbria, on the northwest corner of Morecombe Bay, opposite the coast of Lancashire. Technically, it juts out into the Irish Sea, unprotected from the westerly rain and gales except by its own enormous buildings. Across the sound lay the flat, eight-mile-long sand spit of Walney Island, which contributed approximately nothing in the way of a weather lee.

A small welcoming party of Naval officers greeted the admiral and his guest, and almost immediately they were driven down to the Buccleuch Dock, home of the unwanted Upholders. The single-shafted *Unseen* was secured alongside. She was a jet-black 2,500-tonner, over 230 feet long, with an 8,000-mile range and a top underwater speed of 20 knots. A big Paxman diesel-engine/generator combination powered up the giant submarine battery, which in turn powered a 6,500 hp GEC motor. She was scheduled to carry a complement of McDonnell Douglas sub-harpoon guided missiles, and twenty-one torpedoes, Marconi Spearfish. *Unseen*, silent at under five knots, was lethal to any enemy. The crew knew that the British Government was in the process of almost giving her away. They also knew that the Royal Navy was appalled. Just as appalled as back in 1981 when politicians elected to sell the only two operational aircraft carriers the Navy owned, which actually caused the Falklands War, since the Argentineans then believed Great Britain could not defend the islands against a major attack. They were wrong, but only by six months. The carriers were still in RN service.

Bill Baldridge could feel the resentment in the Royal Navy toward the government as he walked alongside the unused submarine. No one wanted her to be sold and by now all the senior officers knew that her potential savior was this visiting American lieutenant commander. Bill was being treated like a hero.

They boarded *Unseen,* and while Lieutenant Commander Baldridge was given a tour of the weapons area, Admiral MacLean spent two hours in the sonar room reviewing the Thompson Sintra Type systems and the passive ranging Paramax 2041. After lunch they took a tour of the yard, crossing the Michaelson Bridge. The bridge separated the Buccleuch and Devonshire Docks, which could be raised to allow ships to pass between the two. Beyond Devonshire stood the gigantic Trident building sheds. It was a cloudy day now, gray and gloomy along the water. To Iain MacLean it had always been a complete mystery why these stark backwater docks of the defense industry should each have been named after one of Britain's greatest landowning dukes.

He showed Bill the narrow dredged channel which curved out of the inner basin and then swung right through the otherwise shallow waters of the bay past the twin headlands of Roa and Foulney islands and out into the buffeting chop of the Irish Sea, beyond Hilpsford Point. "Literally hundreds of new submarines have followed that route out to the Atlantic," he said. "And in World War II, a hell of a lot of them never came back. This shipyard, and the men who work in it, represent the soul of the Royal Navy's submarine service. Generations of skills, often taken too much for granted by various British governments."

"I sure liked *Unseen*," said Bill. "She had a great feel to her, sleek, quiet, and solid. I'm really looking forward to this."

"So'm I," replied the admiral. "She's as quiet as any boat in the world, and she handles extremely well. We'll be all right."

At 1600 hours sharp they took off for Inveraray, clattering over the gray, melancholy streets of Barrow, where life for the engineers and shipwrights was so uncertain in these days of canceled orders and abandoned Navy building programs.

Down below, out of the starboard window, Bill Baldridge could see the docks, and he craned to see the submarine that would take him through the Bosporus. But the cloud cover was too low.

On the flight back, the dreary landscape soon slipped away behind them, but there remained a feeling of despondency between the two men as they reflected on the hard lives of people in a shipbuilding town like Barrow. Only the welcoming sight of the former Miss Laura MacLean waving from the lawn as they flew up the lock and turned in to land cast a near-depression from Bill's shoulders.

"You been waiting long out there?" he asked her.

"No. Just a few minutes. That helicopter always leaves

Barrow at four o'clock when Dad's on board. That means you'll be home just after five, and that's what it is. Did you have a good day?"

"We had a great day, and the admiral's home for tea. Can't beat that."

Laura gazed at Bill. She had never seen him in uniform, and he did, she thought, cut a commanding figure. So why had no one landed him?

"Laura?" he asked, "why are you staring like that?"

"Oh, I'm sorry. I've never seen you in uniform before. I was just getting used to how official you look."

"Oh, I'm official all right," he chuckled. "Right here on the business of the U.S. Government. And dressed for the part—stiff collar and battle honors."

"You have those too?"

"Nothing won in the field of conflict," he said. "But I've had a few private moments."

"He's a rascal," thought Laura, "but he's nice."

They watched the chopper climb away over the loch for its short journey back to Faslane. Lady MacLean called out from the doorway that tea was ready in the drawing room, so would everyone come in. "And Iain . . . keep those bloody dogs outside, will you?"

The evening, it emerged, was already planned. They were going up to the village pub, the George, in Inveraray for supper. "Sweaters and no ties," said Lady MacLean. "They'll give you a good Aberdeen steak, Bill . . . good even by the standards of an American rancher."

"But you don't know what his standards are, Mum," said Laura.

"Neither," said Mum, "do you."

There was something knowing in that remark. Bill picked it up, and so did Laura. They did not look at each other. But their thoughts were intertwined. And they both knew that too, without looking anywhere.

The admiral sipped his tea, read his paper, grunted but once. "Damn U.S. stock market. Goes up fifty or sixty points one day, then falls back fifty or sixty points the next. Been doing it for two weeks. Needn't have opened at all. Save everyone a lot of trouble."

They left for the George at seven o'clock, Laura driving the Range Rover up to the village and past the church. Admiral MacLean ordered a minor detour, and pointed out the town jetty, showing Bill where his old submarine mooring had been. "We used to stop out there overnight, and then come into the pub for a few drinks when we were exercising in the loch," he said. "This is a very strange little village for a submariner, because the first thing you see is a rowing boat containing His Grace the Duke of Argyll and his ghillie. He calls on visiting submarines in his capacity as Admiral of the Western Isles.

"It used to be quite a ceremony. We'd pipe the duke aboard and give him a dram of whiskey, and he'd tell us what was happening locally. He once told me his wife was the constable of Scotland. I suppose that might apply to any wife of any duke of Argyll. It'd be rather amusing if one of 'em married a chorus girl, don't you think?"

The George itself had a beamed low ceiling and was almost empty. The steaks were excellent, and a couple of bottles of red wine were perfectly good. Bill insisted on paying, and said the President of the United States would be furious if he encroached upon the MacLean hospitality for one more evening. His last evening. Tomorrow he must begin his journey to Russia.

Back at Inveraray Court, Lady MacLean took charge. "I'm taking my husband to bed immediately," she said, laughing. "Barrow today, Edinburgh yesterday, eight here for dinner on Sunday night. Fishing all day on the Tay on Saturday. Golf at Turnberry last Friday. He'll be too tired for the Bosporus. Night, you two. I expect you'll find a way to amuse yourselves for another hour."

"And don't drink all of that expensive port," muttered the admiral as he clumped up the stairs. "See you tomorrow. Early, Bill. I'm driving you over to the base. They've got a man to take you on to the airport."

Bill and Laura retired to the study, where the American put a couple of logs on the remains of the fire, and Laura slipped *La Bohème* onto the CD player. "Nothing too advanced for you, Inquisitor," she teased. "Don't they call this the beginner's opera?"

"They do. And it is still probably my favorite, although I know I'm supposed to grow out of it."

Laura said, "Mine too," as she poured two glasses of Taylor's '47, and handed one to her guest. With Herbert von Karajan's Berlin Philharmonic in the background, they sat quietly in the big chairs on either side of the fireplace, and sipped the admiral's vintage port. Pavarotti's Rodolfo and Mirella Freni's Mimi completed the musical spell, woven almost a hundred years ago in northern Italy by Giacomo Puccini.

The time slipped by very quickly. They talked of music, and of Kansas, and of Ben Adnam. Laura shook her head despondently. The Israeli officer she had once loved was now the most wanted man on earth.

Absentmindedly, she remarked, "And now the two men in this house are planning to go off on some suicidal mission in Turkey . . . all because of bloody Ben. I don't want you two to die. And I don't really want you to go to Russia tomorrow either."

"But, Laura," Bill said, "you have to go back to Edinburgh. And I have to catch Ben's submarine."

Laura stared at him hard for the second time that day. Her green eyes were open wide, and she said again, very firmly, "I still don't want you to go to Russia tomorrow."

Bill Baldridge was silent for a few moments, as the implications slowly sank in. Then he asked her, "Would it make any difference if I told you I'd rather be going to Russia with you, than without you?"

"Yes," she said, "it would make a difference. It would turn a situation I already find difficult into one which I would find almost impossible."

"Laura, I recognize real danger when I see it. I have taken a few risks in my career, and sitting here discussing the immediate possibility of absconding with the married daughter of a senior British admiral, *while* I am on official U.S. Navy duty for the President of the United States, is not only beyond all my known limits . . . it's way beyond yours as well."

They sat and stared together, and while Rodolfo and Mimi made their respective confessions of love just beyond the horizon, Lieutenant Commander Baldridge heard himself saying the words he suspected would have a major bearing on his life. "Laura," he told her, "I'm leaving the Navy when this mission is completed. At which time I'll be back in Kansas, a free man answering to no one. Would you like to stay in touch with me until that time, as best we can?"

"Yes, I would."

Laura stood up and brought over the decanter of port, and poured a little into each of their glasses. As she did so, she bent to kiss him for the first time. It was a swift and electrifying moment. Laura stood up and looked down at him. She caught her breath, pushed her hair off her face, and said, "You are a very beautiful man, but for the moment, anyway, I'm staying up here on the moral high ground."

They finished their port almost in silence, smiling gently at each other. The iron link which bound them was made. Laura sent Bill to his room while she took the glasses to the kitchen. She retired fifteen minutes later, and all through a largely restless night, she refrained from considering the perilous journey through the minefield of the creaky passage outside her parents' room, to that of the American Naval officer.

The following morning the admiral drove Bill away, before Laura was awake. The two men supposed they would meet in Istanbul on September 6. Meanwhile Bill would stay in touch via the Northwood office, to which he was now headed.

Collection of visas, tickets, and cash took him a few hours to complete during the morning in London. Admiral Elliott had provided a car and driver at the airport, and during the afternoon had proved a fountain of information.

He had spoken to the Turkish admiral, and informed him that he would like to run an Upholder Class submarine through the Bosporus on the surface for a goodwill visit to a couple of Russian ports.

No problem there. But the Turk had nearly done a double take when FOSM ventured that the British submarine might like to make the return journey underwater. But he saw no real harm in it for the Turkish nation. Perhaps a collision, for which they would be amply compensated. But not much else to worry him. There would be no nuclear weapons on board, and he would be firming up friendships with both the U.S. and the Royal Navy. Also, he would be glad of whatever information there was, after the mission was completed.

On one aspect of the mission, FOSM had been adamant. "We do not want you to say anything to anyone. We want to make the transit under completely normal circumstances, to see if it can be done.

"We will be making the journey back sometime between September 12 and 20—and all I'm really asking is that you do not rush out and depth charge the British boat, *if* you find her in the normal course of your surveillance."

The Turkish admiral had laughed. "No, Peter, we won't do that! I think it is quite an interesting idea. I will know you are doing it, but no one else will. And if all goes according to your plans, I will certainly improve our Bosporus security. Meanwhile, I will make no extra effort to find you. But I will be very interested to hear from you."

Admiral Elliott did not quite believe him. The Turk would almost certainly sharpen up the surveillance, hoping at least to spot the British submarine. He would allow his men to attack and arrest, but he would not depth-charge them. And he would say nothing to anyone in advance. That way, if the British were not caught, the CNS alone would find out what had happened, and then he alone could strut around making "necessary national security improvements."

Meantime Admiral MacLean and Lieutenant Commander Jeremy Shaw would make the treacherous north-south transit under almost identical circumstances to those likely undertaken by Commander Adnam. The biggest danger would be, as it had been for him, that they might crash and drown in the dark, fast-flowing, narrow waters.

It was also decided that Lieutenant Commander Baldridge should enter Russia the same way the Mossad thought Adnam had. A regular British Airways flight to Istanbul, and then by ship up the Black Sea to Odessa and Sevastopol.

It was possible to fly direct from London to Kiev, the Ukrainian city which lies 450 miles to the north of the Crimean Peninsula. But travel from there to Sevastopol was difficult, because the great, secretive Russian Navy port had been virtually a closed city for so long. Old securities, endless delays, irregular transportation, few flights, except military, made it a traveler's nightmare. Better for Bill to arrive quietly by boat, with the correct papers, and be met by Admiral Rankov's staff.

Bill stayed overnight at a hotel on the edge of London airport and made the flight to Istanbul the following morning, arriving in the ancient capital of the old Ottoman empire at six in the evening. The traffic was heavy as his taxi made its way through the old Sultanahmet area of the city to his hotel, which was situated in an old mansion block between the Blue Mosque and the waters of the Sea of Marmara.

He debated calling Laura at Inveraray Court, which now seemed about a million miles away, but decided against it in case her mother answered.

The telephone in his room was ringing loudly as Baldridge entered his room. "Well, it's not Laura," he thought glumly. "She has no idea where I am." He was right. It was not Laura. It was Major Ted Lynch of the CIA, who was in Istanbul and wanted to come over right away. There were things to discuss, he said.

Bill liked the beefy ex-Ranger officer, and was delighted he was in the city, particularly since Major Lynch was the kind of guy who would know precisely what and where to eat and drink. He told the CIA man to come right over to the hotel on Amiral Tafdil Sokak.

Big Ted showed up within fifteen minutes, kept his cab waiting outside, and summoned Bill to the lobby. They shook hands and Bill was hustled into the taxi, which made a U-turn and swung back west, weaving through the crowded streets toward Kumkapi, the packed waterfront area of Istanbul, with literally dozens of excellent fish restaurants sprawled along the shore.

On hot August nights, the place gave the appearance of an immense street party, and the haunting beat of Middle Eastern music filled the air. The smell of a million spices mingled with the aromas of grilled fish, hot, frying peppers, and night-black Turkish coffee.

Bill noted the throngs of handsome couples: suave men and beautiful, expensively dressed women. Cabs hooted endlessly as they deposited their fares outside packed restaurants.

Ted Lynch had booked a table on an outside terrace, and ordered drinks as they were seated, two glasses of the ferociously strong aniseed *raki*, which he, like the Turks, would cut with water, half-and-half.

Bill still sucked in his breath as he took his first sip of the diluted Turkish firewater. "Christ!" he said. "You could start up the Concorde with this stuff."

The CIA man chuckled and said, "I thought we'd sit here and chat for an hour or so, and then eat at around nine o'clock. The waiter will be here in a minute and I'll order us some Turkish *meze*, and then some fish, which is wonderful here. I expect you know, Turkey is supposed to have the French cuisine of the East."

"Not the kind of regular intelligence they throw around in Kansas," said Bill, grinning. "Nor, since you mention it, in Maryland. But I'm with you—let's jump right into the old *meze*— what the hell is it, by the way?"

"Big selection of hors d'oeuvres—things like *borek, kabak dolmasi, patlican tava*, and *yaprak dolmasi*. You're gonna love it."

"You got me," said Bill. "Bring on the belly dancers. I'm going native for the night." And he took a true sportsman's swig of his *raki*, which almost pulverized his gullet.

Ted Lynch laughed. He was suddenly serious and said, "Bill, I don't actually give a rat's ass whether we knocked over the Ayatollah's submarines or not last Saturday. I haven't asked, but like everyone else I've guessed. Those Kilos were a goddamned nuisance at best, and a serious threat to the security of the Gulf at worst. So screw 'em.

"But I'm obliged to say, the more I conduct this investigation, the less I think Iran did it."

"You don't?"

"Uh-uh. There's not a whisper, *anywhere*. Zepeda's back in there again this week, heading for Tehran on a train, right now as we sit here. He left Istanbul last night, crossed into Iran at the border station, Razi. Then ran on down into Tabriz and then Tehran. He speaks Arabic, which gets him by, and he has so many contacts.

"But he says there is not a hint that the Ayatollahs had anything whatsoever to do with loss of the *Jefferson*. There is also not a hint of money being moved. If they're covering something up, they're doing a hell of a job. Jeff says he would be amazed if they were involved."

"Well, Ted, I guess we have to listen to that."

"We certainly do. And there's something else."

"Yeah?"

"From two quite separate sources, Jeff and I did hear a whisper."

"You did? Who?"

"Iraq."

"Jesus. Nothing firm, I guess?"

"No, but you don't get anything firm in the Middle East. You get a lot of shrugs, smiles, nudges, and head-shaking. It's a place of innuendo, and from those innuendoes you have to try to surmise correctly.

"Mine was from a member of the Syrian secret service operating out of Cairo. A man I have known for years. He had already said to me, 'Well, Ted, I did hear several months ago that Iraq was considering purchasing a submarine from the Russians. It would make a big difference to them to have a weapon like that.'

"Then, on a separate occasion, sitting in a café in a very seedy part of the city, the same very well-informed man told me, 'They are not as ignorant about the military structure of the Middle East as you think. Iraq's biggest enemy is Israel, and their knowledge of the Israeli Navy's habits and capabilities has always been uncanny. I've often wondered if they had a man deep in there.'

"In Arabia, that's a huge hint. And one week later Zepeda picked up a tip that a very large sum of money had been taken in cash, millions of dollars, from one of the Iraqi bank accounts in Geneva. Nothing more. But together those suggestions add up to about three hundred times more than we have picked up on Iran."

"Will we firm any of it up?"

"I've been working with the local guy from the Mossad on it. He's one of their top men. Works in combination with General Gavron. They are right on top of the Iraqi money situation. God knows how. Last time I heard from him he thought he would have something in about two weeks."

"What do you think will happen if we nail Iraq for the *Jefferson?*"

"I shudder to think. The President is perfectly capable of a preemptive military strike on Baghdad. He's like Reagan. He would not hesitate if he thought that damnable country had killed six thousand Americans."

"You're right. He'd do it."

"And, Bill, there was just one other thing I haven't mentioned to anyone. My Israeli buddy here says the Mossad tapped into a very mysterious international phone conversation in Geneva during March. It was between Switzerland and Cairo, and involved ten million dollars. They spoke in Arabic and the phone belonged to the guy who handles Iraqi money in Switzerland. The Mossad eavesdroppers' main observation was that both parties came from the same town."

"Is that significant?"

"It is when it's Tikrit, the birthplace of Saddam Hussein, and most of his government."

0730 Friday, August 9.

B ILL BALDRIDGE DEEPLY REGRETTED HAVING STAYED
out half the night in Istanbul with the CIA man from
Washington. He leaned over the rail of the northbound ship and
wished, fervently, that he had never laid eyes on a bottle of *raki*.
His head throbbed, he felt repulsively ill, and there was a mild
tremble deep within his body. He had been leaning on the rail
for almost two hours, and the gentle rhythm of the teal-blue
waters of the Black Sea was causing his condition to worsen.

There were two questions banging around in his aching
mind—what was he going to find in Sevastopol to prove
Benjamin Adnam had been there? And, was Benjamin Adnam
really an Iraqi who had been working for years, undercover, in
the Israeli Navy?

They were big questions. And he wished he felt better able to
cope with them. Ted Lynch was still waiting for a report from
the Mossad on the wire-tapped Geneva conversation. But by
now Bill felt certain there must be *some* evidence in the Russian
submarine port to suggest that someone, somehow, had been
paid a huge amount of money.

He hoped Admiral Rankov would be cooperative. And he
hoped he would get into Russia as easily as Admiral Morgan had
predicted. Twenty-four hours later, very early on the still-dark

Saturday morning of August 10, his faith in Arnold Morgan was confirmed. He was met by a young Russian Navy officer, Lieutenant Yuri Sapronov, who spoke excellent English and marched him through Odessa's dimly lit customs and immigration rooms without missing a beat. He carried the American's suitcase, but not the briefcase, which contained the phone scrambler, and he explained they were immediately boarding a Navy vessel which would run them across the water to Sevastopol in under six hours. They would arrive by 1300.

The ship turned out to be Russia's fastest attack patrol craft, a Babochka Type 1141, with an anti-submarine capability. Lieutenant Sapronov said the boat was capable of forty-five knots and was making the crossing from Odessa to its home port of Sevastopol. Admiral Rankov had personally instructed Sapronov to pick up Lieutenant Commander Baldridge.

Recovered from the excesses of Thursday night, Bill enjoyed the journey, chatting for much of the way with the young lieutenant, who turned out to be a native of the Crimean coast, from the easterly dockyard city of Feodosiya, where the Babochka was originally built.

"Everyone here worried about the missing Kilo," Lieutenant Sapronov had admitted. "Admiral Rankov has been yelling and bellowing about it for two weeks. And he's a very big guy to yell that loud. He's my boss. I'm his Flag Lieutenant. At the moment we are in just a temporary office, thin walls. The whole fucking place shakes whenever anyone even mentions that Kilo. He can't understand how a submarine can just disappear. Tell you the truth, neither can I.

"Each day I look after his signals and letters back to Moscow. He's very concerned that Americans think we are lying. Last week he sent a long communiqué to Moscow to Admiral Zubko—he's the C-in-C, and Deputy Minister of Defense. He said Americans suspicious the Kilo had something to do with that aircraft carrier which blew up in the Gulf. He said it was essential we help Americans all we can. Zubko faxed back right away he agreed with everything. I guess that's why you're here."

Bill reckoned that was all a bit too fluent not to have been rehearsed. But Admiral Morgan had said he could trust Rankov and he was certain the Russians were ready to help any way they could. "Sure is a mystery," he told the lieutenant. "Have you guys been following up on the families of the crew?"

"Oh, sure we have. We've had people visiting them, even watching some of their homes. Guys from the old KGB. But no one has found a sign of anything. No money around, no one looks as if they have been bribed. Everything seems desperately sad but essentially normal. Admiral Rankov gets crosser every day. I heard him yelling down the phone to someone yesterday."

At this point Lieutenant Sapronov did a deep imitation of a fairy-tale giant's voice, and continued: "*There's nothing fucking normal about this. Nothing!! Do you hear me?*' I guess the guy on the other end nearly had a heart attack. But we still didn't get anything new."

Bill laughed. He liked Russians, as almost everyone does who meets them. They are usually very frank and open, with a good sense of fun, and an unfailing irreverence about authority, once they get loosened up. He and the lieutenant enjoyed a good breakfast of kolbasa, the smoked sausage native to the Ukraine, with scrambled eggs, toasted *lavash* bread, and Russian coffee, which Bill thought was not a whole lot different from that at Chock Full o'Nuts.

Afterward they sat on deck in the morning sun, sipped *vody Lagidze*, the cold Russian mineral water mixed with various syrups, and watched the fast-approaching coastline of the Crimean Peninsula. Right after 1230, the Babochka cut its engines for the run into the short bay of Sevastopol, and Bill was on the jetty before 1300. Admiral Vitaly Rankov was there to greet him. The towering ex-Soviet international oarsman, whose eyes were as gray as the Baltic Sea, and whose handshake resembled that of a mechanical digger, was an imposing figure.

"Welcome, Lieutenant Commander," he rumbled in a deep bass voice, which Bill thought would probably have done justice to the role of Sparafucile in *Rigoletto*. "I know you are one of Admiral Morgan's staff. I know Arnold well, and I do not envy you. He is a terrible man!" Admiral Rankov joked as they walked along the dockside. They came to a group of newly built offices that resembled those on a New York construction site. Admiral Rankov and his staff occupied about six of the wooden structures during the weeks he was working with the High Command of the Black Sea Fleet. Every step he took in his office made the place shudder, every door he closed threatened to bring down the ceiling. Bill thought the floor might give way altogether when he banged his huge fist on the desk for emphasis. This was a man, he thought, who belonged in the vast, vaulted stone halls of the Kremlin, where Admiral Morgan felt he would most assuredly end up.

"Right, Lieutenant Commander," he said, once he had attended to his more urgent messages. "I instructed Yuri to give you a little background on our progress, but if there is anything you particularly want to know, please feel free to ask me. By the way, we still have no hard evidence about the fate of the Kilo."

"Well, sir," said Bill, "I think the main purpose of my visit is to try and discover whether any suspicious-looking character from the Middle East was seen around here at all. You see, we think someone bribed your captain with a huge sum of money. Someone must have seen him."

"Yes," replied Rankov. "Arnold Morgan told me what you have worked out, and I'm just beginning to think you may be right. What other explanation can there be? We can't find the wreck. The drowned sailor who was a member of that ship's company? Found off the coast of Greece? The Kilo must have got out. But it's still very difficult for us to find out how. This place is crawling with people from the Middle East. The Iranians have a fucking office here!"

"How about the Iraqis?"

"No office. But they're not strangers. They want to buy two or three Kilos, but right now they have no money to spare, and we're giving no credit to anyone, however good their credit might be. Right now it's—how you say it?—cash on the drum."

"Barrel," said Bill.

"Right. Cash on the barrel. The Iraqis have been arms customers of ours for a long time, as you know. But if they can't pay, we can't supply. Things here are very bad financially. And we just don't have the backup to go around giving away submarines for which we might get paid, sometime. Also you Americans have things wrapped up pretty tight now. We'd rather be your friends, and we don't much want to do anything which will endanger that friendship."

"No submarines for a mad dog like Iraq?"

"Lieutenant Commander, I have to be straight. If anyone comes in here waving a billion dollars for submarines, we *will* supply. We don't care if they're Chinese, Arabs, Persians, or even Eskimos."

"We have noticed that," said Bill, grimly.

"You don't know what it's like to have your backs to the wall over money," said Rankov. "For a big nation like ours, it's a dreadful thing. And it's been happening here for almost the whole of the twentieth century. And it's still happening now we're in the twenty-first."

"Yes, I suppose so. But would you have noticed a stranger who looked like he came from an Arab nation hanging around here at the time, early April?"

"Well, I certainly would not, because I was not here at the time. But I do not think anyone else would either. There are just too many people who would fit that description. Anyway, I do not think your man would just have been hanging around. He could not have got in through the gates, not without being brought in by a Russian official or at least a serving officer.

"Quite honestly, I'm inclined to agree with Arnold Morgan. I think his rendezvous was arranged. And he bought the captain with a massive amount of money, and then that captain fooled the crew into going on a secret exercise on behalf of the Russian Navy. Nothing else fits."

"Who was the captain?"

"A very well-respected Russian officer. A native Ukrainian, as so many of our submarine commanders are. Captain Georgy Kokoshin. He's very experienced without being brilliant. Man of about forty-two. Married to a much younger woman, Natalya. They have two young children, six and eight, both boys. The family lives on the edge of the city in one of those new high-rises. We've been checking there on and off for over three months now. Ever since the submarine was reported lost. But everything seems normal. Mrs. Kokoshin was very, very upset over the death of her husband."

"When did you last check?"

"I believe I had a report in on Tuesday morning. The children were at school as usual."

"No new cars, new clothes, nothing extravagant."

"Nothing."

"Did you search their apartment? Ransack it from top to bottom?"

"No. We did not. Captain Kokoshin was a senior Russian commanding officer, presumed dead. He was very popular, and no one wanted to treat his widow as a criminal. In some respects we are in a similar position to yourselves. You do not wish to admit your carrier was hit by an enemy. We do not wish to admit we have mislaid a submarine and its crew. If we start harassing the wives of the officers, word will get around that something is wrong."

"Yes. I guess so. Have you done any checks at all on any of the families of the other senior officers?"

"All of them. We found nothing."

"And the Kilo sent no signal whatsoever once she had cleared the port of Sevastopol?"

"Nothing."

"Well, would you mind if I have a look around? Could you just show me the area where the submarine was moored, let me see where the captain and some of his officers lived? I have to make a report about this visit to Admiral Morgan."

"Certainly. I will show you what you wish to see, as I promised Arnold Morgan."

It was a short walk to the submarine area. When they arrived Lieutenant Sapronov was awaiting them, standing in front of a Kilo, identical, Bill supposed, to the one he believed had hit the *Jefferson.*

"This is where she lived, Hull 630. This is where she was last seen. This is where she sailed from, at first light, on the morning of April 12." Admiral Rankov spoke as a man who has gone over the ground many times.

Before him Bill could see another slightly shabby, black-painted submarine, similar in size to *Unseen*, which he had visited four days previously. The Kilo looked a bit basic compared to some of the modern American designs, but he knew she ran deathly quiet beneath the surface, probably quieter than the U.S. boats, and he knew that her torpedoes were both accurate and lethal.

He stared up at three of her masts, jutting out from her long, slim sail. And he imagined in his mind, the dull, familiar clunk of the big SAET–60 exiting the tube, the whine of the engine as the underwater missile raced straight toward its target, its nuclear clock ticking, its warhead primed to explode and incinerate. The ice-cold eyes of Ben Adnam somewhere beneath the periscope.

Bill shuddered. He gazed around at the uniformed Russian Navy personnel walking by. There were a lot of people around the submarines. In just the few moments he had been here, four different crew members had left the Kilo, two of them officers. He assessed that it would have been impossible for an Arab hit-squad to have penetrated this dockyard and commandeered the submarine.

No. Someone *bought* Captain Kokoshin. And that someone was Benjamin Adnam. He had the brains, the backup, the know-how as a submarine commander himself, and the cash. He also had the arrogance. Jesus, Bill thought, the guy even traveled here the first time under his own name, despite being on the run from the Mossad as a deserter from the Israeli Navy. He was a cool customer, no doubt about that.

"You want to go aboard?" asked Admiral Rankov.

"Can I see the weapons area, the tubes and the warheads?"

"No. I'm afraid you can't inspect that area. No one can, except for the captain, the weapons officer, and his staff."

"I am a weapons officer," said Bill, smiling.

"Wrong Navy!" laughed Rankov.

Bill laughed with him, and then made his first formal request. "Can we go and have a talk with Mrs. Kokoshin?"

"We can, certainly. But I'd rather do it in the morning. I have some people to see this afternoon. And I had thought I would have someone take you to your hotel. You can get yourself unpacked and have some coffee. Then I will meet you at around 1900 for dinner. I stay at the same hotel when I'm here."

"Sounds pretty good to me," said Bill. "Okay, I'll take off. I'll call Admiral Morgan from the hotel, and meet you later."

The two officers shook hands. And Lieutenant Sapronov led Bill to a black Mercedes limousine parked right off the jetty. The engine was already running, and the lieutenant issued an instruction to the driver, who jumped out and opened the rear door for the American. They drove out slowly, pausing at the security building adjacent to the dockyard gates. Bill counted at least eight armed guards in proximity, and he again thought it impossible for an armed squad of men to penetrate this place. So much more efficient to "rent" your submarine.

The Mercedes rolled through the gray, run-down streets. There were few people to be seen, and cars were rare. The surface of the road was appalling by Western standards. The omens of decay were everywhere. The woeful streets, with their high apartment houses, all around the outer dockyard area of Sevastopol, made Barrow-in-Furness look like Fifth Avenue.

Beyond the inner city, Bill thought the place looked a bit more cheerful. But Sevastopol, steel-ringed by the Soviet Navy for generations, was not long on hotels. This was one of the last areas in all of the Ukraine to acquire a hotel built by a foreign corporation. As late as 1995 there was no such establishment in the entire state, not even in Kiev.

But, by the turn of the century, one of the enterprising Finnish hotel groups was on the move. They had constructed a new hotel on the outskirts of the city which had housed the Soviet Black Sea Fleet. It was called the Krasnaya, and it existed for the scores of visiting foreign executives who had journeyed to Sevastopol to buy ex-Soviet warships, and in some instances, new ones. Kilos.

The place was full of non-nationals, from the Middle East, East Asia, South America, and all kinds of Third World republics, who were either trying to buy warships to frighten their neighbors, or to protect shipments of drugs. Some of the better-heeled patrons, from the Gulf states, had matters more sinister on their minds. It was a perfect place for the huge, apparently genial Russian Naval Intelligence officer Rankov to stay. And Bill Baldridge summed that little scenario up in short order, before he even registered.

Up in his room he prepared to call Arnold Morgan. He took the portable phone scrambler from the depths of his suitcase, placed it on the bed, and opened the lid. He then put the hotel phone handset into a special cradle in the case, and set up the electronic crypto system, which would render their conversation unintelligible to an outsider. Then he made the call on the regular open line. When the admiral answered they would go over to encrypted mode simultaneously. The process was tricky, but very effective.

"Morgan . . . speak."

"Baldridge . . . preparing to speak. Stand by crypto August 10."

"Roger, standing by."

"Crypto three, two, one. Go. How's that, Admiral?"

"Terrible, Bill. But I can hear enough."

Arnold Morgan explained that he had been in touch with Major Lynch, and that the spotlight of suspicion, which had shone for so long on Iran, was now shifted to Iraq.

The Mossad had given orders to tap into the telephone system in the lakeside mansion of Barzan al-Tikriti, one of Saddam Hussein's half-brothers, and Iraq's Ambassador to the United Nations in Geneva.

The Mossad knew better than anyone how to follow money, particularly counterespionage money. Barzan was one of Iraq's leading financiers. He had helped to mastermind the plan which enabled the Iraqi dictator to siphon off between 3 and 5 percent of every barrel of exported oil, and turn it into a multibillion-dollar hoard of cash and gold in Geneva.

The money had traveled efficiently from the Iraqi Treasury into an account called Patriotic Revolutionary Guard Number 473 in the Central Bank of Iraq. From there it was wired to a private bank in Vienna, where numbered accounts were still used. And from there into the account of a Swiss corporation in Geneva, administered by Barzan al-Tikriti. At the last count there was more than 2 billion dollars in that one account, and it was from there that Saddam Hussein broke every international law with regard to purchasing arms.

A relatively small matter, like withdrawing 10 million in cash in order to strike a secretive and massive blow at the "Satan of the West" was kid stuff to an operator like Saddam. Just as long as he had the right man for the job.

The Mossad's agents had been very certain in their reports to General Gavron. The Iraqis would have trusted no bank, no broker, no wire transfer, in moving the money on its final step from Geneva to Istanbul. That was why Ted Lynch had drawn a complete blank in the Turkish banks.

The vast amount of cash required to "hire" a Russian submarine would have been crammed into a couple of hard, specially rimmed suitcases, and would have traveled on a direct flight, in the first-class luggage cupboard of a Swissair Boeing, under the watchful eye of Barzan's highly paid personal assistant, a statuesque Austrian blonde named Ingrid Jaschke. She, in turn, was always accompanied by an Iraqi bodyguard, bagman, and professional assassin, who traveled behind her in a business-class seat, probably on a highly respectable Egyptian passport. Kamel Rasheed was the name he went by.

Ingrid never went anywhere without a small custom-made German pistol, which fired snub-nosed bullets designed to spread on impact, thus leaving a tiny entry hole, but a massive exit wound. She was fully licensed to carry the pistol, and she always checked it with the airline, and then collected it on landing. There are many really lousy ideas associated with international arms dealing. One of them would be to try and rob Ingrid Jaschke, anywhere beyond the airline arrival gate.

Right now four men from the Mossad were combing the main hotels in the mysterious city of Istanbul, utilizing charm, cash, and persuasion, to try and establish whether Miss Jaschke, and/or Mr. Rasheed, were in residence in the city between April 7 and

April 13, 2002—these were the nights most likely to have seen the second arrival in the city of Commander Benjamin Adnam.

The admiral explained to Bill that this was not such a daunting task, since Miss Jaschke was not the kind of woman to shack up in a youth hostel. If she was in Istanbul that night, she would have been in one of the best hotels in the city. It is, after all, against no law to walk around with a couple of big cases full of cash. So long as you own both the cases and their contents.

The Mossad was also trying to check the airline, but Swissair was apt to be more secretive than even the Swiss banks. However, one Israeli agent thought he could get his hands on the passenger lists out of Istanbul to Switzerland in the first half of April. Safe behind the encrypted technology, Admiral Morgan explained all of this to his Kansas-born field officer.

"It beats me how those Israeli guys are so efficient," Admiral Morgan finally growled down the telephone to Bill Baldridge. "I don't know where they get their information half the time. But every time I talk to the embassy they have advanced the search further. Every time I talk to the CIA we have nothing more than the Mossad is telling us. And there's twenty-five thousand people on the staff in Langley. Christ knows what they're all doing."

"I guess it's because the Mossad is so damned small and tightly controlled," said Bill. "What have they got, twelve hundred people—only thirty-five case officers? What are they called? *Katsas?*"

"Yeah. But there's something more to it, Bill. Israel has a ton of people, all over the place, who are deeply sympathetic to its plight, and its fears. They are a kind of unseen army, numbered in their thousands in almost every country. They are always there to help any Mossad agent. The Israelis call them 'the *sayanim*'—and they have vast computerized lists of 'em. That's how they tap into real information.

"I guess that's how they got into Barzan al-Tikriti's phone line. A Swiss Jew involved in the telephone system in Geneva. A favor from a proud member of the *sayanim*, for his spiritual home in the Middle East. That's how it works."

"So right now they're looking for a helpful Turkish Jew in the hotel business in Istanbul," replied Baldridge. "A guy to see them on the right track, to call a couple of friends, check out those guest registers?"

"You got it, Billy. That's how it's done. Stay close to Rankov. He wants to find that Kilo too. And stay in touch. Call me if you get anything."

The phone went dead. Bill was still holding the receiver, as always. "Oh, thank you very much," he said sarcastically. "It was so nice to talk to you, Admiral Morgan. Have a nice day, rude asshole."

Bill showered and changed, gazed out of the window at the soulless spread of Sevastopol. In the near distance he could see the giant cranes of the shipyards. He decided to wander downstairs, have some coffee, and then go to the bar to meet Admiral Rankov. The coffee was pretty nondescript, and he skimmed through a copy of an English-written Arab newspaper he found on the next seat.

There was a picture of the wrecked floating dock, jutting out of the water in the harbor of Bandar Abbas, but the caption carried no suggestion of anything more than an accident in the dockyard area.

Bill signed the check, and decided to play a mild hunch. He knew now that the Kilo had sailed on April 12, which he had not known before he talked to Rankov. And he felt instinctively that if Adnam had been in Sevastopol in the days leading up to that sailing, he had stayed in this hotel. Everyone in the shipping and arms business did. But, unlike the Mossad, he could not spend days trying to get into a Russian hotel guest list for the first part of April. They would never reveal anything. Not here.

But there was one thing he could do immediately, and he strolled outside to talk to the waiting limousine drivers who inhabit the forecourts of hotels such as this.

The first man he spoke to wore a gray uniform. No, he had never had a long distance run to the southern border of Georgia and Turkey. But he thought Tomas did, back in the spring, and Tomas had just arrived back in the forecourt. Bill then sought out Tomas, a thick-set, blond young Russian. Aged around twenty-five. Yes, he did once have such a customer. Back in April. They drove all through the night, stopping only for gasoline. He remembered it well, because it nearly caused him to be divorced. "My wife was not at home so I could not tell her, and the man wanted to leave immediately. So I just went. Made it in fourteen hours—six hundred miles, right down the coast road, through Sochi. He was an Arab gentleman, paid me two and a half thousand American dollars, cash. Best job I ever had."

"How come you nearly got divorced?"

"I forgot it was her birthday. We were going out to celebrate with friends. It was awful, I phone her from Batumi. She says she never speak to me again. Slammed down the phone. I drive all the way back not knowing if I'm still married. If I had not agreed to share the money with her, I would *not* be still married."

"Do you recall the name of the man?"

"No, he never told me that. He hardly spoke."

"Do you recall what he looked like?"

"Not really. He was an Arab. Dark-skinned, tight black hair. Not very tall, about my height. But well built, muscular."

Bill reached into his pocket for his wallet, took out the grainy, fax machine photograph of Benjamin Adnam in Arab dress—the one they had taken in the Israeli search room at the Allenby Bridge. It was absolutely useless except to the eyes of someone who knew Adnam well. But Bill held out hope for the Russian driver.

"Could this have been him?" he said, handing the photograph to Tomas.

"Well, it *could* have been," he replied. "But the man I took to the border was not wearing a headdress. I cannot really tell from this. It was night, and I hardly saw his face. He rode in the backseat. This photograph could be any one of fifty Arabs I have driven for. I could not say this was the man I drove to Georgia. But then, I probably wouldn't recognize him if he was standing here right now."

"Where did you leave him when you arrived in Georgia?" asked Bill.

"In the town. There was another car there to pick him up,

and take him on. I think he was going to Turkey but I could not tell whether by road, or on the hydrofoil to Trabzon. I have never seen him since."

"Thanks, Tomas," said Bill, pressing a ten-dollar note into the driver's hand. "By the way, when's your wife's birthday?"

"I never forget that again. April 11."

The time was now 1858 and Bill Baldridge wished the driver good evening and walked back into the hotel to find the bar. He was mildly surprised to find the admiral already there. His Russian uniform cap was on the seat beside him, and the admiral was sipping a glass of *gorilka z pertsem*, vodka with a small red pepper floating in it. The vodka was a special Ukrainian variant, and Bill, wary of his last run-in with foreign liquor, settled for a scotch and club soda, which was not so elegant in flavor as that at Inveraray Court.

Admiral Rankov was enjoying his drink, taking steady gulps as they talked. Bill half-expected him to hurl the glass over his shoulder in some kind of crazed Cossack ceremony. But before he could, a bell captain came over to announce a phone call for the admiral.

When he returned, Vitaly Rankov's big, handsome face was grave. "This is trouble," he said. "I can sense it. That was young Sapronov. The KGB observers' daily report says Mrs. Kokoshin's children did not attend school today. And they were not there yesterday either. They want to know what to do. The school knows nothing, except they are absent."

"I know what I'd do," said Bill. "I'd get round to her apartment real quick. And I would not alert the entire secret police force of the Ukraine either."

"You mean now?"

"Hell, yes. You got the address?"

"Sure I have."

"Then let's go. I might be able to help."

"This is a bit irregular, conducting a search of a Russian officer's premises in the company of an American Naval officer."

"Do you want to be in partnership with the U.S.A. in the search for the boat?"

"I not only want to be, I am instructed by the Kremlin to work with you all the way."

"Then let's get the hell out of here and see what shakes with Mrs. Kokoshin."

The admiral signed the check, and they headed out to the car. Rankov gave the new driver the address, and told him also to step on it.

The Kokoshin family lived only ten minutes away. Their apartment building stood about ten stories high. There were glass swing-doors, but no doorman on duty. The captain's family lived on the eighth floor, number 824, and Bill stood aside while the admiral rang the bell twice. They could see there were lights on in the apartment, and they could hear a radio or a television in the background.

No one answered. Rankov hit the bell again, this time three rings. They waited but no one came. "Maybe she just went to see a neighbor," said the admiral.

"Why don't we check?" said Bill. They walked along to number 826 on the same side of the central corridor. The admiral rang the bell, and again there was no reply.

"Let's have a shot at 822," said Bill. And there they were more fortunate. The woman who answered the door did know Mrs. Kokoshin. She had not been home all day, nor was she home yesterday when her own children had come from school and tried to find the Kokoshin boys.

She suggested the admiral try the lady on the opposite side of the corridor, number 827, who was a good friend of Natalya Kokoshin and might even know where she was. "Sometimes she goes to see her mother, who lives about forty-five minutes from here—little place called Bachcisaraj."

The bell didn't work and they knocked on the door. Another Ukrainian housewife answered, and was unable to offer much help. "I have not seen her for two days, which is unusual," she said. "She was late home the day before yesterday, because her boys called here for the key. She arrived at about five o'clock and returned the key. I haven't seen her since."

"Do you still have the key?" asked the admiral.

"Yes, I do, but I don't think it would be right for you to borrow it."

"I assure you it would," boomed Rankov. "I was her husband's boss, and my business is *very urgent indeed*."

The neighbor fled from the wrath of the gigantic uniformed Intelligence officer, and returned with the key a moment later.

The admiral thanked her profusely, bowed low, and waited until she had closed her door. Then he walked quietly over to the home of Natalya Kokoshin and her children. The key turned easily. Rankov pushed open the door. The lights were on, and he could see the television turned on in the living room. The occupants were long gone.

The place was tidy. But hollow. There was nothing in any bedroom cupboard, the drawers were empty. It was obvious the clothes had been taken, along with shoes and coats. But all the furniture was in place and the kitchen was untouched. The windows were closed and locked. The Kokoshins, observed Bill, were history.

"Do we go back and grill the neighbor opposite?" asked Rankov.

"Hell, no," replied Bill Baldridge. "That would be like taking out a half-page ad in the *Ukraine Times*, or whatever it is. Since we now know what has happened, I think we should turn off the television, close the drawers, put out the lights, return the key, and leave. Quietly.

"Then, if I were you, I'd get your KGB guys to check airports, border crossings, the shipping lines, and all the routine stuff we do when we are searching for missing persons."

"You're right. Let's get back to the hotel. I'll call Sapronov and put plan in action."

"Not that it will do the slightest bit of good," said the American.

"Why not?"

"Because I think that lady is carrying a suitcase full of dollars. And you can cover a lot of trails, a lot of rules, and a lot of miles, with that kind of cash to speed your way. She's been gone for two days. She could be on the other side of the world by now. She'll be hard to track down."

"I wonder how she got out of Russia," said Rankov.

"With that much cash she had a thousand options," said Bill. "She could have hired a car and driver and headed for the border. She could have hired a boat and headed down the coast, but that's probably too slow. She could have hired a small private plane, or even a helicopter, to get down to Georgia, and then cross into eastern Turkey. The cash makes almost anything possible, and if she has the same backup we think she has, documents are going to be no problem whatsoever."

"How would you do it, Bill Baldridge?" asked Admiral Rankov, slipping into the Russian habit of using both names.

"I'd make for Georgia, as fast as I could get there, and enter Turkey at the border-crossing post at Sarp, or cross over on the hydrofoil which takes non-Georgian nationals from Batumi to Trabzon. It would depend on what documents I had for myself and the two boys.

"I'd guess Natalya has been stockpiling clothes and possessions at her mother's house for several weeks, and paid a private driver, say, five thousand dollars, to take her through the night to Batumi. They probably walked out of their apartment empty-handed at around six the previous evening. Nothing remotely suspicious about that. Then they hit the road. First stop, Mum's house, second stop gas station, and on to the southern border.

"I think it's about six hundred miles down the east coast, but if they averaged 40 mph and made one night gas stop on the way at around 2300, they'd do it in fifteen hours. That would have put them in Trabzon yesterday morning around 0900."

"And then where, from Trabzon?"

"Oh, that's easy. No hurry. There are direct flights from Trabzon to Istanbul, and she's had four months to make sure she arrived at exactly the right time to catch one of 'em. Then she took the British Airways evening flight to London, and on to wherever the hell she's headed. Probably South America. If I had to guess I'd say she was out of Turkey and on her way to London, or even Paris or Madrid, last night. And, remember, she's broken no law. She's just taken her children to live somewhere else. So what? The South Americans will never extradite her, even if you find her."

"You Americans are so very accepting of human behavior," said the admiral with a smile.

"That's right. That's why we're rich, and you're broke. Go with the flow, old buddy. Saves you a lot of time and trouble."

"Well, I guess we'd better give back the key, and head back to the hotel. I do have to report all of this, of course."

"Sure you do. And what's more you *must find her*. Because where she is, is where Captain Georgy Kokoshin is headed, right now, with his crew."

On Sunday morning, August 11, the U.S. lieutenant commander traveled with Admiral Rankov in a military aircraft as far as Kiev, for an overnight stop en route to London. He checked in to the Ukraine Hotel on Taras Schevchenko, and prepared to call Admiral Morgan at his home in Maryland. It was 0900 in Washington. Once more he unpacked his telephonic scrambler case and placed the hotel phone in the electronic cradle.

"Morgan . . . speak."

"Baldridge . . . preparing to speak. Stand by crypto August 11."

"Roger. Standing by."

With the crypto locked on, and their conversation now protected from prying ears, Bill explained that the Kokoshin family had fled. He passed on Admiral Rankov's kindest regards. "If you want him this week, he's in his office in Moscow."

Admiral Morgan confirmed it was looking more and more like Iraq, but he had not yet heard whether they had run Ingrid Jaschke to ground. He had spoken to Scott Dunsmore the previous night, and the CNO reported that the President was unflinching in his attitude to a global submarine hunt. "Get through the Bosporus underwater," he had said. "Then I'll authorize anything you want. But I'm not doing anything if you guys fail on the mission."

Bill's news was critical. And it fired up the American admiral. "Does Rankov want us to help find her?" he said. "He's welcome to all of our resources."

"He didn't say so, sir. But I think he's very worried about his own position. They just lost a submarine, which is about to embarrass the entire nation, and his guys have allowed their prime witness to slip through their fingers. Old Vitaly's a bit depressed, to tell the truth."

"Guess he would be. Hey, where are you? You on your way home? Or you going back to see MacLean?"

"Right now I'm in Kiev. Then I'm headed back to London, and I guess home. Unless you want me to stay in Europe."

"I don't think so, Bill. You need to be in Istanbul on September 6. But there's no need to make the outward journey to Turkey in the boat. Come on back, help me start preparing this report. See you Tuesday."

The line went dead. And this time Bill just laughed.

The following three weeks, which he spent in the United States, went by very fast. The detailed intelligence report Baldridge compiled with Arnold Morgan on the destruction of the USS *Thomas Jefferson* would become a case document for Naval investigations for years to come.

In the middle of Bill's third week at home, the Mossad made another major breakthrough. General Gavron called Admiral Morgan to report that they had traced Ingrid. On April 7, she and her bagman, Kamel Rasheed, had checked into the Pera Palas Oteli, off the great pedestrian walkway of Istiklal Caddesi.

They had stayed two nights, checked out on the morning of April 9. The rooms had been reserved with an American Express card which the hotel had not checked. Then Ingrid had deposited $1,500 in cash on arrival.

Ingrid had dined alone in the hotel restaurant on both nights. No charges were forwarded to American Express, and there was no trace of either billing or payment. By the time the Mossad got hold of the number, the card was obsolete. And American Express would disclose nothing.

Nonetheless, Ingrid Jaschke, the Iraqi courier, was suddenly in Istanbul five days before Kilo 630 set sail.

Arnold Morgan liked what he now knew. He liked Ingrid's sudden presence in Istanbul. He liked the man fitting Adnam's description who made an overnight run to the Turkish border just hours before the Kilo sailed. "A thousand coincidences," he grunted at Bill Baldridge. "They gotta add up to something. And right now they're telling me our man Adnam is an Iraqi. No wonder Gavron's upset. Those Israeli military guys *hate* their organizations being penetrated. Especially by a country like Iraq. I shouldn't be surprised if they do our dirty work for us in the end."

He walked over to his chart desk and stared again at the map of the northeast coast of Turkey. Once more he stuck the prong of his dividers into the now worn pinhole at the Turkish port of Trabzon. The other end he placed on the resort harbor of Sinop. "Two hundred and thirty-five miles," he muttered. "With a coastal road joining the two towns."

He glared now at the coastal navigation chart, noting the jutting point of Sinop, the most northerly headland on this stretch of coast, so close, so conveniently close, to a deep-water submarine waiting area. "That's where they picked Adnam up."

"Sir?" said Bill.

"Oh, nothing. Just imagining Adnam's point of departure. If your man Tomas drove him that night, I'll bet there was a moored yacht missing from Sinop harbor a coupla days later. I gotta feeling about that place."

The British Airways flight from London touched down at Istanbul's International Airport late afternoon, September 7. Admiral Sir Iain MacLean stepped out of the first-class cabin, accompanied by a steward carrying his old dark leather suitcase. They made their way briskly to the immigration desks, where Lieutenant Commander Bill Baldridge waited.

The admiral's passport was stamped quickly, and they were escorted though customs and into the car Bill had hired from the hotel.

Baldridge had also arranged for a corner table in the hotel restaurant, where the two could speak privately. They were due to board the Turkish pilot boat around lunchtime the following day, when they would join HMS *Unseen* as she sailed up from the Sea of Marmara to the Bosporus. The admiral said *Unseen* was scheduled to clear the Dardanelles at 2100, and would make ten knots toward Istanbul throughout the night and morning, a distance of 150 miles.

Before they went down to the dining room, the admiral presented Bill with a double-CD pack of Georges Bizet's opera *Carmen*. The recording was sung by Agnes Baltsa and José Carreras, with maestro von Karajan conducting the Berlin Philharmonic. "Bill, Laura gave me this for you. It's the one you wanted and apparently asked for on your first visit. She said to say sorry it took so long, but she had to order it specially."

Bill, who had not the slightest idea what Sir Iain was talking about, made a sharp recovery, and asked him to thank her very much. "I couldn't get this recording in the U.S.A.," he said. "It was good of her to go to so much trouble."

He placed the CD's on his bedside table, and left, joining the admiral outside the elevator. On the way he asked the question which had been concerning him for several weeks. "Sir, if the Turks sweep the Bosporus with radar, from one end to the other, as they claim, does this mean we can't come up to periscope depth without running a risk of being detected? I mean, that mast on the Upholder will leave a damn great wake—surely they'll spot us easily, maybe without even using radar, if they are alert."

"Yes. They do sweep the surface of the Bosporus pretty thoroughly. And since I want to stay at PD for much of the way, we'll have to box a bit clever."

"Sure will. But what do we do? What did Adnam do?"

"He almost certainly did what I intend to do. He got into position in a southwesterly holding area in the Black Sea, and he waited for a good-sized freighter to show up with the kind of cargo to suggest it was going right through. Then he took a range on its stern light to get on the correct angle, and distance, and he tucked right into its wake, about a hundred yards behind. He set engine revolutions to match speed, and followed it through."

"Gottit. His periscope wake obscured by the much bigger wake of the freighter?"

"That's it."

"We gonna do that?"

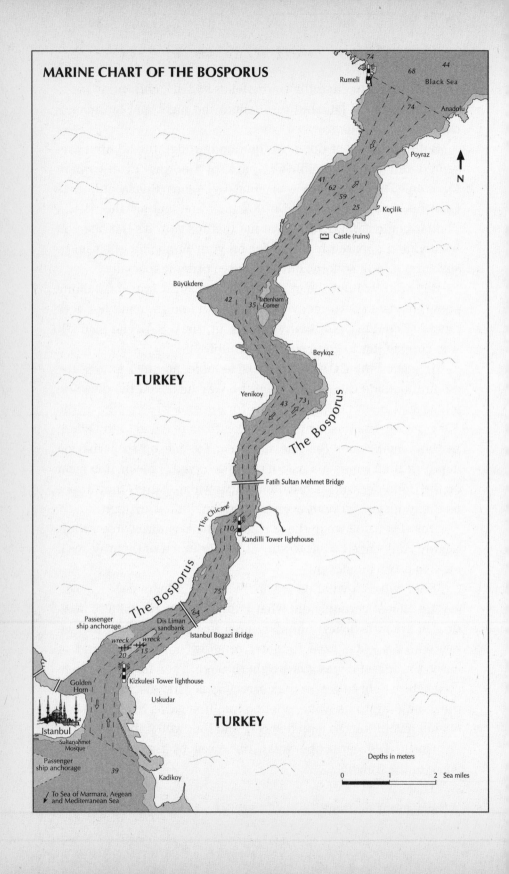

MARINE CHART OF THE BOSPORUS

Rumeli

Black Sea

74

68

44

Anadolu

74

Poyraz

41

62

59

25

Keçilik

🏰 Castle (ruins)

Büyükdere

42

35

Tattenham Corner

Beykoz

TURKEY

Yeniköy

43

73

The Bosporus

Fatih Sultan Mehmet Bridge

"The Chicane"

110

Kandilli Tower lighthouse

The Bosporus

75

Passenger
ship anchorage

Dis Liman
sandbank

64

Istanbul Bogazi Bridge

wreck

wreck

20

15

Kizkulesi Tower lighthouse

Golden
Horn

Uskudar

Istanbul

Sultanahmet
Mosque

TURKEY

Passenger
ship anchorage

39

Kadikoy

To Sea of Marmara, Aegean
and Mediterranean Sea

Depths in meters

0   1   2   Sea miles

N

"We are."

"Jesus. What if he stops suddenly, or goes off cours[e] water deep enough for him, but too shallow for us? W[e] run straight up his backside, or hit the bottom."

"We will if we are not careful. But we are going to be careful. That's what Ben Adnam must have done. That's what we're going to do."

"Is Jeremy Shaw up to this?"

"Oh yes, he's extremely good. And he's used to doing precisely what he's told. I know his Teacher. Actually I *taught* his Teacher. And he was young Shaw's boss for a good many years. Those old Navy habits die hard, thank God."

"When do you want us in position?"

"Well, I think we should vanish from sight an hour north of the Bosporus. Just so no one has the slightest idea where we are. The Turks will see us come through on the surface, but as the light starts to fade, we will disappear.

"Then, I'd like to be at our Black Sea station, set up and ready, periscope depth, just before dark, around 1930, about thirty-five miles north of the Bosporus entrance. Just so we have enough light to identify a freighter making ten knots in the correct direction, hopefully going right through to the Med.

"We'll get in behind him. Then we can snort down to the entrance, at PD, get a good charge into the battery, and hope the merchantman doesn't see us. He probably won't, because the light will have gone completely within a half hour of our picking him up. With a bit of luck."

Bill shook his head, and smiled. "Guess I'm talking to the von Karajan of the deep."

"Who's he?" grunted the admiral. "U-boats?"

"No, sir. He's the conductor on the CD Laura sent me. One of the best ever. Maestro Herbert von Karajan."

"Oh yes, I see. Of course. I'm not much good at opera, really. But it's good of you to say so, even though it's not true. I'm just a retired officer volunteering for a job no one else wants."

"As the personal choice of the Flag Officer of the entire Royal Navy Submarine Service, sir."

"Yes. Of course, I used to be his boss too. He's probably trying to get his own back."

Dinner was subdued. The topic of conversation was anchored in their own anxieties about the perilous task they faced tomorrow. Bill had never been involved in a crash-stop in a submarine, and he finally summoned the courage to ask the admiral how it worked. He did not mention the real question he wanted to ask—what do we have to do to avoid slamming right into the freighter's massive propellers?

"It's only dramatic if you're not ready," replied the admiral. "Which makes your sonar team even more critical than usual. They have one vital task—to issue instant warning of any speed change, the slightest indication that the freighter is reducing its engine revolutions.

"Which means they have to keep a close check on the freighter's props. If she slows, we're talking split seconds, otherwise we *will* charge right into her rear end, which is apt to be rather bad news.

"If the water's deep enough, we will slow down, dive, and try to duck right under him. If it's not, and there's a bit of room out to the side, we'll go for the gap. If there's not enough water, no room to the side, and we're late slowing down, I think you'll probably end up at Jeremy Shaw's court-martial. If any of us survive it, that is."

"Christ," said Bill. "Are there any procedures I ought to know about if we have to stop in a hurry?"

"There are a couple of things. All the time we are close to the freighter, we will want to be at diving stations. But we must be on top-line to shut down to a specially modified collision station.

"None of us knows much about the water density changes, and we have no idea if we'll be in vertical swirls. So we may need old-style trimming parties. That means our watertight doors have to be open for them at all times, so the men can go for'ard or aft at high speed to help keep the boat level.

"I have had several talks with Jeremy Shaw, and I have recommended he posts bulkhead sentries throughout. Everyone will be on permanent stand-by. However, when we broadcast 'crash-stop,' the bulkhead doors will not be shut and clipped. They'll be open for the trimming parties."

Bill chewed his kebab thoughtfully, and then took a long swallow of red Turkish wine. He had never operated in a diesel-electric submarine, but he knew the basic collision procedures. In any tricky situation, the bulkhead doors should be kept shut and clipped in order to contain fire, or onrushing water if the submarine crashes or is holed. He knew too the terrifying dangers, especially if they were running deep.

The admiral remained sanguine, chatting away cheerfully about hair-raising scenarios below the surface of the Bosporus. "Actually, Bill, I'm hoping we'll get a bit of practice quite early on if the freighter stops to pick up a pilot at the northern end. We'll be right up his backside at that point, with the current sweeping us down the channel. Then we'll find out how quick we are, and how easy it is to hold the trim, when two and a half thousand tons of steel traveling at ten knots suddenly slows down."

Bill took another swig of wine, and they remained in the dining room for only another few minutes before returning to their rooms and turning in for the night. "Possibly my last night," Bill said as he shut and clipped the bulkhead door of room 1045.

He opened the CD pack, and took out the two slim, sealed plastic holders and the glossy libretto booklet. No obvious message there. No note from Laura. He tipped up the outer box. Nothing there either. Then he began to leaf through the booklet.

He found it stapled to page 105. It read very simply:

I am back in Edinburgh now, and feeling a bit desolate not
being able to talk to you. Please, Bill, look after my father, and
for God's sake look after yourself. I don't think I could bear it if
anything should happen to you both.

She signed it, "*Laura*" and placed a small line of three crosses beneath her signature.

But beneath the note were greater depths. Outlined in a pink highlighter were three lines sung by Carmen in the divine duet with Carreras during the ninth scene of Act One—translated from the French: "*It's not forbidden to think! I'm thinking of a certain officer who loves me, and whom in my turn, I might very well love!*"

"That Bizet," said Bill. "A guy with real perception."

After a night disturbed by nerve-racked dreams, he felt unaccountably full of energy when finally he packed his bag and headed downstairs to meet the admiral. He paid both accounts with a credit card, and they headed down to the docks in a cab.

The ride out through the harbor, south along the Sea of Marmara, afforded them a spectacular view of Istanbul, the great pointed minarets of the Blue Mosque, Hagia Sophia, and the Topkapi Palace. The specter of the giant Bogazi Road Bridge, which spans the Bosporus three miles upstream from the Golden Horn, shimmered in a light heat-mist this morning as cars streamed across, two hundred feet above the water.

The captain of HMS *Unseen* held her stationary in the current just north of the Turkish Naval anchorage on the Asian bank. In flat, calm water Bill Baldridge, the admiral, and the pilot made their ship-to-ship transfer, bags being hauled by sailors with hooked ropes.

Both officers and the Turkish pilot expertly climbed the rope ladder, and were helped up onto the casing by two brawny young lieutenants. The newcomers joined Lieutenant Commander Jeremy Shaw on the bridge for the surface ride north through the Bosporus.

The CO greeted Admiral MacLean with the due deference Bill Baldridge had witnessed in all of his travels. He was more welcoming to Bill, and briefly outlined the high points of the long journey out from Barrow-in-Furness to Turkey. He was pleased with the submarine, and the crew had easily mastered the systems in the two-week workup period before they left England. It usually takes five weeks, but of course on this occasion they had not had to bother with weapons.

The ride north was highly instructive. Admiral MacLean assessed the width of the channel, the lights on the two big bridges, particularly those on the much narrower one, three miles north of the Bogazi, the Fatih Sultan Mehmet, already nicknamed by *Unseen*'s crew as the "Fatty Sultan."

He noted the water depths in the narrow right-left "chicane" immediately south of the bridge, marked by the navigation control station at Kandilli, on the Asian side. The first big corner they would meet, a hard left and then a hard right, was equally as dangerous because the channels narrowed dramatically. The admiral took notes in small neat handwriting: "*two bloody great shoals to port, five meters only.*"

The sunlit waters of the Bosporus seemed wide on the surface, and not at all menacing. Only the charts revealed the hazardous nature of the seabed below. All the way north, Admiral MacLean was trying to establish the treacherous shape of the underwater contours.

Two hours after they set sail, *Unseen* cleared the Bosporus, and the men on the bridge said good-bye to the disembarking pilot. Then Captain Shaw ordered a northerly course, zero-three-zero, across a calm sea to their waiting point.

At 1730, Captain Shaw decided they should vanish: "Officer of the Watch, dive the submarine."

"Aye, aye, sir."

"Clear the bridge."

"Upper lid shut, one clip . . . both clips on."

"Open main vents . . . Group up . . . half ahead main motor."

"Main vents open, sir . . . Telegraph to half ahead . . . Group up, sir."

"Five down. Seventeen and a half meters."

"Twelve meters, sir."

"Ease the bubble, Cox'n."

"Eighteen meters. Bubble forward, sir."

"Very good. Shut main vents. Group down."

"Up ESM . . . particularly looking for commercial X-band radars coming in from the north, say three-one-five to zero-four-five."

"Looks a pretty good trim," said Captain Shaw. "I want you to stay in this position while we find a merchantman heading for the Bosporus. He'll want to be under ten knots. An eight-knotter will do us fine. Stay reasonably furtive. Though he won't be looking for the likes of us. Tell me if you get one, please."

"Aye, sir. Blue watch . . . watch diving . . . patrol quiet state."

"I'll be in the wardroom with the admiral and our American guest. You have the ship, Number One."

"I have the ship, sir."

The Commanding Officer, the admiral, and Lieutenant Commander Baldridge immediately retired to the wardroom for a conference.

"The bottom's mostly marked as shingle, Admiral," the C.O. said. "We don't want to be stern-down if we hit it. The trimming parties are going to be very important to us. But I can't help feeling that in the narrows a lot of that shingle will turn out to be rock, which could be very nasty. Thus, I intend to stay at periscope depth, at almost any cost, well outside normal rules."

"I think you need my written approval for that, Jeremy," said Admiral MacLean. "I'll enter it in the log. But I do agree with you—it'd be much better to write off a periscope on the bottom of a freighter, than leave yourself with a bloody great rock shoved straight through the hull."

The three men stared at the chart. Jeremy Shaw was frowning, and said suddenly, "The tricky bits are here . . . here . . . and here." He pointed to the big sharp bends with his index finger. We are going to call them Tattenham Corner—after the left-hander on the English Derby racecourse—and the Chicane. Usual reasons. Men under a lot of pressure often react faster to familiar words. These places are all unpronounceable Turkish, and represent mass confusion to everyone."

"Good idea," said the admiral.

"On the left-handers here I expect our leading freighter to keep right and not cut the corners. But he may be tempted to do so if there's nothing coming up the other way. If he stops or does something bloody silly, and I can't stop, or get under him, I'll evade to port. And that's when we may have to correct trim in a big hurry."

"Yes, Jeremy. But if we have to evade, and there is a queue

coming up the other way, I think we'd be better to surface astern of him, for a bit more control. You never know, he might not even notice. Amazing what you can get away with if you have enough brass nerve."

"Yes," Bill chimed in. "I once heard of a really insolent British warship getting right up to one of our carriers disguised as a curry-house."

Jeremy Shaw burst out laughing. The admiral feigned innocence. "What about depths, Jeremy?" he said.

"Well, sir, we need seventeen and a half meters to run at periscope depth, plus five meters below . . . about twenty-two and a half meters minimum. The worst bit, easily, is right below the Bogazi Bridge, where the chart shows twenty-seven meters, but there's a couple of wrecks marked right in the middle of the channel, one of 'em only fifteen meters below the surface.

"Right there, I can't go to the right, because of the mooring buoys, and the merchant-ship anchorage. I can't go down the middle because of the wrecks, and I can't go left, because you can't see round the big bend. This makes the other lane very, very dangerous. Not least because it's only thirty meters deep anyway, which would prevent us ducking under a big oncoming freighter.

"If our leader looks as if he's going to drive straight over the wrecks, I think we'll *have* to surface, for a half-mile, only three minutes. Trouble is, it'll be damned bright up there from the shore lights. That's where the Turks might spot us."

"I suppose we'll just have to keep our fingers crossed, then," said Sir Iain. "And hope for the bloody best. By the way, have you got a personal list of 'call off' factors, Jeremy? Like visibility, etc."

"Just the usual things, sir. Defects on the nav system, losing our leader early on, before the last narrows, the Turks making it damned obvious they've seen us, or if trimming the ship is just too damned difficult in the currents. Aside from those, anything sudden, unexpected, which takes us beyond the last limit of our already-stretched margins for error.

"Basically, if the unforeseens pile up on us, until we have no way out. I'm hoping to rely on you and Bill to bear all those things in mind, while I get on with the minute-to-minute detail."

"Good. We'll just stand at the back with our teeth gritted until we can't stand it another minute. You do have final responsibility for your ship, Jeremy, but I can't help feeling I've put you here.

"Remember, you can always say, 'Stop, I want to get off,' and no one will think worse of you. We're only here to see if this is possible; not to give a concrete demonstration that it's not."

"Okay, sir. I'm going to the control room for a look. Supper at eight. No wardroom film tonight, I'm afraid. Not even for the first-class passengers." But they had a long wait . . .

092025SEPT02. HMS *Unseen*. 41.55N, 29.37E.
Course 180. Speed 5.

"Captain, sir. I have a possible . . . zero-two-zero . . . fifteen thousand yards . . . I'm about twenty on his starboard bow radar . . . gives him 8.5 knots on 180 . . . we've got a strong commercial nav radar right on the bearing . . . no other traffic within five miles . . . turning toward for a proper look before the light goes altogether."

"Right. I have the ship."

"You have the ship, sir. His higher masthead light comes out at twenty-eight meters by comparison with radar, sir."

"Okay. Up periscope. All round look."

"Target setup. Up. Bearing that . . . zero-two-two. Range that . . . on twenty-eight meters. Fourteen and a half thousand yards, sir . . . put me twenty-five on his starboard bow . . . target course one eighty-five . . . distance off track six thousand yards . . .

"Group up . . . half ahead main motor. Revolutions six zero . . . five down . . . forty meters . . . turn starboard zero-nine-five.

"Team . . . I'm going to run in deep to close the track for fifteen minutes. We want a good look as he passes on his way south. Then we'll turn in behind and follow him . . . Make a broadcast, Number One . . . we're going to be at diving stations from about 2030. And it's going to be a long stretch. Eight or nine hours. Fix cocoa and sandwiches for 2300 and 0300."

092040SEPT02.

"Take a look, Admiral. I think she'll do. I'd say about six thousand tons. Small container ship . . . nationality Russian, from what I could make out on her funnel.

"She might not be going right through. But she fits nicely for time and speed. I think I'll just swerve back in under her, check her draft while there's plenty of water. Then I'll slot in behind at PD."

"Very good, Jeremy. She'll do."

HMS *Unseen* proceeded to match the freighter's speed at forty-two revolutions, 8.2 knots, and began to track the Russians back toward the entrance to the Bosporus. They ran for almost four hours, and shortly after midnight at 0030 Captain Jeremy Shaw got his visual fix.

"GPS and soundings all tie in, Admiral. Rumineleferi Fort bears two-four-zero . . . two miles. Leader still on one-eight-two . . . eighty revolutions, making 8.7 over the ground, 8.2 through the water. Current's behind us, should go to one knot in the next two miles. Expecting our leader to come right, to about two-one-seven, any second . . .

"There he goes, sir. Starboard three. Call out ship's head every two degrees please."

"One-eight-four . . . one-eight-six."

"We're up close, Admiral. Bow right behind his stern. Range locked on his stern light."

"We have about twelve minutes on this course before he picks up his pilot."

Locked together, traveling at precisely the same speed, the Russian freighter and the Royal Navy submarine headed on down to the Bosporus, separated by only one hundred yards of white foaming water, the bright phosphorescence gleaming in the pale moonlight.

No one in the merchant ship noticed the periscope sliding

through the wake, as they were tracked along their course, unwittingly leading the aptly named *Unseen* into a kind of Naval history.

The degree of precision being practiced by the officers of the underwater boat would have been beyond the comprehension of even the most experienced merchant seaman. They kept station to the nearest few yards, observing the angle of the beam on the freighter's stern light, knowing that if it increased they were going too fast and dangerously close-in. If it decreased, they were slipping behind and out of the wake.

They cleared the northern limit to the Bosporus, crossing the unseen line which stretches from the fort to the headland of Anadolu, with its light flashing every twenty seconds. They ran on down the channel for another two and a half miles before the freighter began to slow down for the pilot pickup.

Jeremy Shaw was ready. They had already picked up the revs of the fast diesel pilot boat, and when the submarine captain ordered the "crash-stop" it was accomplished with maximum efficiency with nearly two hundred feet of water below the keel. As it happened, *Unseen* came to a halt more quickly than the freighter. So far so good.

They ran on south in the pitch-black depths of the water, rounding the big left and right turns, still at periscope depth, right behind the freighter. They slipped under the "Fatty Sultan" at 0130, and prepared to meet the sudden right-and-left turn of the "chicane" off Kandilli, where the channel was narrow but deep, and the current fast and awkward.

But the freighter skipper steered steady and true, straight down the middle of the lane. He kept his speed constant, and the unseen watchers a hundred yards astern detected no alter-ation in the revs of his engines. No one was yet aware of the covert Anglo-American submarine operation. Above *Unseen* the military radar of Turkey swept silently over the water, but noth-ing locked onto the lone periscope slipping along in the turbu-lent white water which marked the trail of the freighter.

Jeremy Shaw eased the helm, steering course two-three-two, as they came into another straight area, where the channel grew more shallow, with the great span of the Bogazi Bridge almost overhead. They had been unbelievably lucky.

Through the periscope, *Unseen*'s CO could now see the yellow quick-flash of the bridge light to starboard, and the quick-white to port. The span passed overhead at 0141. A ferry crossed west to east up ahead, but well clear of the oncoming freighter and her shadow.

They were two minutes short of the shallow sandbank in the middle of the south lane—the one with two wrecks already on it—when the first danger signal flickered into life. Up ahead, running hard toward them, almost on the middle line of the shipping lanes, was an oncoming contact. They could see she was very wide on her course, going fast, rounding the right-hand corner marked by the Kizkulesi tower. What they did not know, at this stage, was that she was a twenty-thousand-ton Rumanian tanker.

The submarine would meet her just as they too had to swerve to the center to avoid the second wreck. There was not sufficient water here to go deep and get under her. There was only thirty meters at best charted on the edge of the shoal. The tanker drew about ten meters. *Unseen* would need at least twenty more.

Admiral MacLean and Jeremy Shaw had about five minutes to come up with something. Their options were running out.

"Christ! This thing is a fucking size," the CO reported as he peered again through the periscope.

Then, just to compound matters, he spotted what looked like another ferry up ahead, crossing east to west right in their path. Then the totally unthinkable happened. The sonar officer called suddenly, "Control Sonar . . . our leader's revolutions are decreasing, sir."

Jeremy Shaw showed signs of real strain for the first time. "*Jesus!*" he exclaimed. "We really do not need this. No wonder it's fucking illegal."

Unseen was now on an underwater collision course with the Russian freighter's screws, a life-threatening maneuver for everyone who sailed in the submarine.

Captain Shaw recovered his composure . . . "Revolutions twenty . . . turn fast starboard two-four-zero."

Now the Russian freighter too began a long starboard swing toward the docks on the European side, but at least he kept going. The navigator called out that the fifteen-meter wreck was passed. But the Rumanian tanker kept coming, five hundred yards now, still too wide.

Jeremy Shaw and Admiral MacLean knew the shallow-drafted ferry could go straight over the casing provided it missed the fin and periscopes. But if the submarine pressed on down the left side of the down lane, they would be unable to avoid being mowed down by the Rumanians, who were not only blind to the submarine, they were running too wide and too fast.

Unseen was unable to move right because of the shoal and the twenty-meter wreck, unable to veer left because that would take her onto the Kizkulesi bend, and, while the tanker might miss them, they had no way of knowing that another big merchant ship was not driving round on the inside of the bend.

All the admiral could do was to suggest they make like a "dead pig"—that is, show as little periscope as possible, drifting just below the surface with the south-running current, easing over the sandbank, making no speed until they could go deep around the next corner. "That should keep us marginally out of the line of collision with the tanker, and the Turkish radar operators will take us for a hunk of flotsam," said the admiral.

"If their helmsman makes even one minor mistake, he's going to break this submarine into two very large pieces," muttered the captain.

It was a passive maneuver, and the more courageous for that. But it was their only option. Within seconds they heard the propeller of the big tanker come thrashing down their port side, missing them not by the two hundred yards Admiral MacLean had estimated—cutting his normal safety margin by 60 percent—but by about forty yards.

The swirling turbulence in the wake of this massive hull, twenty thousand tons of steel barging through the narrow waterway, threw the submarine well off-course. She swiveled fifteen degrees to port before she steadied. "Ah yes, we're head-ing straight toward Asia now—that was rather a novel way of doing it," the admiral muttered.

"Not so bad, sir," said the navigator. "We're a bit late for our turn to the south round this bend anyway. I'm happy on the western side of the channel. The water's deeper."

Just then, a new call rang out in the Royal Navy submarine, which was still making like a "dead pig," with only her periscope showing intermittently. "Control Sonar . . . *new contact!* Designated track four-three. Bearing one-eight-five."

"*Christ!*" snapped the C.O. "This is a big bastard and we're right ahead of him, bang in his path. Put him at seven hundred yards. Give him twelve knots. Bloody hell, he's in the wrong lane."

"We'll *have* to go deep," snapped Admiral MacLean. "*Jeremy* . . . half ahead . . . four zero revolutions . . . five down . . . thirty meters . . . call out the speed."

"*Sir . . .*"

"Two knots."

"Christ. He's turning. Midships. Starboard thirty."

The C.O. barked, "*Down all masts. Ease to ten . . . steer one-eight-three . . . thirty-one meters.*"

"Twenty-five, sir."

Then the sounder called the depth below the keel, "Sounding ten meters, sir."

"*Slow ahead.*"

"Still one-eight-five. He's louder. All other contacts blanked."

"Thirty-one meters, sir."

"Sounding five meters, sir."

The admiral: "Yes, here he comes, Jeremy. That's his bow pressure pushing us down. *Foreplanes full rise.*"

"Sounding two meters, sir."

"Nice and level, Jeremy. Don't want to put the propeller in the mud."

"Right, sir. Depth holding . . . that's the suction along his hull."

The admiral gave out his last commands: "*Half-ahead. Four*

zero revolutions. Seventeen and a half meters . . . But keep her level at first, Jeremy."

The words of the sounding operator—"Two meters, sir"— were almost drowned out in the roar of the big freighter's props as she thundered overhead, charging through the water at twelve knots.

"Track four-three right astern. Bearing zero-zero-four, sir. Very loud. Doppler low. Same revolutions, one-two-four."

Admiral MacLean stepped aside as the submarine headed back up toward the surface of the mile-wide and now deeper waters of the harbor of Istanbul. Slowly *Unseen* climbed to periscope depth as she silently entered safer waters.

Fifteen minutes after the near-miss, life was just about back to normal in the control room and plainly the worst was over. Captain Shaw handed over to his first lieutenant, joined the admiral and Baldridge for a cup of tea in the wardroom.

"I'm sorry I was a bit pushy there, Jeremy," said Admiral MacLean. "But I reckoned I'd seen a lot more of those shallow-water, close-quarters situations than you had."

"Absolutely, sir. I was getting a bit mesmerized looking through the periscope. Anyway I think I had missed the navigator's clue that we were in deeper water, and could go under him. Thank you, sir."

Unseen headed out of the wide southerly channel which flowed past the eastern shoreline of the old city of Istanbul. There was more than fifty meters of water here, and less than three miles to the open reaches of the Sea of Marmara.

Jeremy Shaw wondered when they should send in a satellite message to the duty officer in Northwood. "And one to Washington?"

"I'd say we ought to do it right away," said the admiral. "We've done it. And that's that."

"Do you have a code word for a successful mission, Bill?" asked the captain.

"Sure do—*home run*—that's what they're waiting for. Straight to Admiral Morgan, Fort Meade, Maryland. It's nine o'clock at night there, but he'll be around in his office, waiting to hear."

The CO sent for a messenger to take a drafted signal for transmission. Then he left the wardroom, leaving the admiral and Bill alone.

"Let me ask you something, sir. Would you have done it, if you had known in advance what it was going to be like?"

"No, Bill. I would not. I understood the risks, but I did not think we would run out of luck quite so often! We were nearly killed twice in ten minutes. That first freighter that nearly hit us was closer than I have ever been to death. I actually thought the second one was going right through us."

"If it hadn't been for you, sir, she might have."

"Oh, I expect Jeremy would have thought of something in time."

"Well, I was pretty glad we did not have to hang around and find that out, sir. You saved us. So did Jeremy. And all you have to show for it is a bit of history. Senior officer in the first submarine ever to transit the Bosporus underwater."

"Not even that, Bill. We were the second."

Admiral Arnold Morgan received the signal with delight. *"Home run."* They're through. He called Scott Dunsmore to break the news. In turn the CNO called General Josh Paul, who informed him the President awaited his call, and that the admiral should make it personally. One minute later, the President stepped out of a formal dinner to speak on the telephone to his Chief of Naval Operations.

"They did it? . . . Good . . . Yes, you have my full authorization to commit resources to find and destroy the Russian Kilo, using whatever means you must . . . I'll leave that entirely to you . . . "

Admiral Dunsmore replied, "Thank you, Mr. President."

"Go get 'em, Scott," said the Chief Executive.

2200 Monday, September 9.

THE EVENING OF SEPTEMBER 9 WAS ONE OF TOE-
curling anxiety for Arnold Morgan. Trapped in his office,
still awaiting the satellite signal from the south end of Istanbul
Harbor, he had rampaged through his beef sandwich, spilled coffee on his diary, and growled at everyone still working in the
building. Happily there were not many, but his general mood of
tightly wound exasperation was sufficient to encourage the late-
night staffers to stay the hell out of his way, if possible.

The *"home-run"* signal had restored the rueful grin to his
face. And in the following four minutes he had passed on the
information to Admiral Dunsmore, and then burned rubber on
the driveway en route to a rendezvous with General David
Gavron, in the cool privacy of the Israeli embassy.

The general had made the telephone call to Fort Meade personally, and the admiral found himself worried about the edgy
demeanor of the urbane and gracious Israeli officer. He always
enjoyed their talks, but tonight General Gavron had not been
relaxed, and the admiral sensed tension and worry in the
Israeli's words. And whatever that worry was, it was plainly
something to do with Benjamin Adnam. Otherwise David would
not have requested this meeting.

Inside the gates of the embassy, he was joined by an Israeli

guard who escorted him to the upstairs room with the big burgundy-colored chairs, where he and the general had first come
to terms. General Gavron was sitting back, holding a glass of
white wine, and smoking a rare cigarette.

"Hi, David," the admiral said. "Sorry to be so late. it seems to
get harder rather than easier to get out of my factory these days."

"Welcome, Arnold," replied the general. "Let me pour you a
glass of that dessert wine you liked so much. I have things to tell
you."

"What's on your mind?" said the admiral.

"As I expect you have guessed, it's about Commander
Benjamin Adnam. I am afraid, Arnold, that circumstances may
have overtaken us. Let me backtrack for a moment. You remember you told me a couple of weeks ago that your man Jeff Zepeda
was working on the outskirts of a major Iraqi Intelligence cell in
Cairo?"

"Sure I do."

"Well, we have been onto that for several years. In fact we have
had a man working deep inside it, in place since 1998. He's an
Iraqi, with Jewish grandparents. We established this cell right
after the Gulf War, with some of our top guys operating on the outside. It has been an invaluable source of intelligence on the inner
workings of the Iraqi Government. I do not need to elaborate
upon the extreme danger our case officer is permanently in."

"You do not."

"Arnold, he has disappeared. We have heard nothing from
him for nine days. He has always operated on a one-week contact cycle. He's never missed his Saturday check-in. Even when
he has nothing to say."

"What can I do?"

"Nothing really. It's just that two weeks ago I gave an instruction to him, that if he came up with anything about Commander
Adnam, or indeed the missing Kilo, I wanted to know ASAP.

"He never uses electronic equipment for obvious reasons.
And I'm wondering whether you have received anything, anonymous of course, from Cairo. Because if you have, it might just
be a last-ditch effort from our man."

"No. I have not received anything. And I'll let you know if I do. Do you think his disappearance has something to do with the *Jefferson* incident?"

"Yes. Mainly because I imagine that everything is heightened in Iraqi Intelligence right now. I am sure they have guessed that you hit the Iranian submarines in retaliation. They must know they might be next. I think anyone asking questions about the *Jefferson* operation would be in a high degree of danger. The Iraqis may seem irrational. But they are quite ruthless."

"Yes. I agree with all that."

"If our agent did find something, and somehow managed to tip the Americans off, he might already have been fingered. Anyway, he did not even have time to call for help from us. But he knows how urgently we want Adnam back. The man is a deserter and a senior officer of the Israeli Navy with access to highly sensitive information. We'd like him alive, to find out how badly we have been betrayed. Then we'll know what to change."

"He may be a deserter to you, General. But he's an international terrorist to me. And I want him first. Dead or alive."

"We do not care who finally kills him, but we'd most certainly like to pick him apart first."

It was long after midnight when Arnold Morgan left the Israeli embassy. He drove home slowly, slept for three and a half hours, then showered, dressed, and drove to his office, where his daily special delivery mail package was waiting for him.

At 0515, he found it.

Admiral Scott Dunsmore thought he was ready for anything. He had four Los Angeles Class nuclear attack submarines on warning for special ops in Norfolk, Virginia. And he had one at Diego Garcia and two more at Pearl. In tenuous anticipation of the Kilo making a break across the South Atlantic en route to South America, satellite observation points had been adjusted, on the off-chance that one might betray the sudden surface appearance of a Russian Kilo in strange waters.

What the admiral was not ready for was a phone call at 0520. Not even from Arnold Morgan, whose careless disregard for time was fabled, even among submariners. The CNO reached out of his bed for the phone, and was unsure whether to be furious at the sharp, daytime tones of the Director of National Security, or merely appreciative of the sheer devotion to duty of the senior U.S. Navy Intelligence officer.

Admiral Morgan, as ever, wasted no time. "Sir," he said, "we may have found the Kilo. Tip-off. I'm leaving now for your office. See you there." The line went dead.

Admiral Dunsmore's feet had hit the carpet even before the line cut off. He opened the bedroom door and yelled downstairs for someone to have his car outside and ready to exit the Navy Yard in eight minutes.

Morgan beat him into the Pentagon by minutes, having knocked twenty-three seconds off his own all-time record from Fort Meade to the military headquarters of the United States. It was a little after 0600.

He had already organized coffee—black with buckshot—for both of them. And in his hand he held a sheet of expensive, cream-colored writing paper, which he handed to the boss. "Came this morning. Air mail letter postmarked from Cairo, Egypt. Addressed to the Director, Office of National Security, Fort Meade, Maryland. U.S.A. No zip."

In the center of the almost empty sheet there were just four very short lines, composed on a word processor:

120630APR024436N3332E.
050438MAY023557N0548W.
082103JUL021992N6395E.
251200SEP025440S6000W.

Nothing else. No date. No signature. No address. "I get the mail before everyone else," said Admiral Morgan, irrelevantly.

"Yes, I had realized that," replied the CNO. "What is it? Dates and times, written in Navy style. Plus chart positions."

"That's correct, sir. It was the second line which got me. That "050438MAY02." That's the exact date and time we heard the submarine in the Gibraltar Strait. Those numbers are written on

my heart, 050438. I almost did not have to check the map reference . . . 35.57 North, and 05.48 West. It's in the probability zone
given for its detection.

"Then I checked the first line. And that's the exact date and
time of the Kilo's departure from its home port, according to
Baldridge's report, which he based on information from Admiral
Rankov. April 12, first light. The position, 44.36 North, 33.32
East, is that of Sevastopol.

"The third line is the precise date and time of the sinking of
the *Jefferson* . . . July 8, three minutes after 2100, The map reference is slightly more refined than ours, but identical."

"So, Arnold, is the fourth line, which begins with a date fifteen days from now, where we might expect the Kilo to show up
next? Or, where the writer would like us to think the Kilo will
show up next?"

"Precisely, sir. I do have some idea of where the note came
from, but nonetheless, it *is* anonymous. The interesting part is
its information, because most of it has been available to only
very few of us. Line one, the departure time and date, was
known to several people, although not to us, until Baldridge
found out three weeks ago.

"Line two, date, time, and position of the Kilo in the strait.
The time is exact to the minute. Well, a few of our people might
have known what was heard, but there you'd be talking about a
hoax. And I don't see any U.S. serviceman joking about this. No,
sir. The *only* people who knew the time and date *and* position of
the ship when that noise was made were the guys who made it."

Admiral Dunsmore nodded slowly. "Yes," he said. "And they
also knew the time, date, and departure from Sevastopol."

"Correct. None of us knew that before Baldridge told us. And
since then, only you and I, and maybe two or three staff members, were acquainted with his report. It's never left Fort Meade,
except with me."

"Right. That narrows things down a bit."

"Which brings us to line three, the *Jefferson*, date, time, and
position at the moment of destruction. The accuracy in this note
is precise, it's possibly better than our own.

"Now, our accident analysis guys have worked on this, and they know the position of the carrier. But not one of the analysis people is connected in any way with the information path involving the sonar contact in the Gibraltar Strait. That leaves us with very few suspects among ourselves—six altogether, you, me, Baldridge, your Lieutenant Commander Jay Bamberg and his assistant. And my lieutenant. I exclude them all, categorically."

"So do I. That means we're looking for people outside who could have known all of these things."

"Sir, there's no place else to look. The author must have been aware of the doubts expressed about the lost Kilo; he must have known it made a detectable noise off Gibraltar; and he must have known the *precise* time, and *precise* place, where the *Jefferson* was hit. My conclusion is that the author of this note was either in that submarine, or was in possession of a full report from that submarine."

"That's just about where I was getting to, Arnie."

"Kinda obvious, really. Which means they *intended* it to be obvious. The author established impeccable credentials in the first three lines, in order to establish his fourth line as that of an unimpeachable source."

"Has he done it?"

"I think he has. His intention is plainly to make us believe that the Kilo will be found on September 25, at the time and position he gives in statement four."

"I see it's in the South Atlantic. Where exactly?"

"It's about a hundred miles due south of the Falkland Islands. Four hundred from Cape Horn, east-nor'east. Now, I haven't the slightest idea where the Kilo's headed, but it must be going to South America somewhere. Which makes sense, I guess, if you happen to be the most wanted ship's company in history."

"Yes. It does. And since all of our evidence suggests they have been operating on behalf of Iraq, we might wonder whether that old alliance between Iraq and Chile could be at the heart of their escape route."

"Well, sir, I'd rule out any Argentinean Navy base. They're too far south for that. The obvious port that Kilo's heading for would be Punta Arenas, which is in Chile, right opposite the northwest end of Tierra del Fuego.

"That way, its route would be around Cape Horn into the Pacific, then north up the South American coast, turning east after about 250 miles, into the Cockburn Channel. Then on into the Magellan Strait. Punta Arenas is right in there, sheltered, with a lot of deep water. It's also full of deserted little islands. If ever you wanted a great place to hide out in a submarine, staying underwater, coming up to the surface just to let guys off, every coupla days, that's the spot."

"Yes, Arnie. Especially if you have a ton of money for each one of them, and a boat to run 'em ashore."

"Are you getting the feeling, sir, that this escape has been very well planned?"

"You could say that, Arnold."

"That's my feeling too. The question is, are we being led into a trap? Or does the writer of this note just want us to go down there and blow the Kilo out of the water?"

"Arnold, if this Adnam character is a Muslim Fundamentalist he may have expected to die with the *Jefferson*. But right now he is on the loose, apparently in the South Atlantic, driving a Russian submarine which is *still* armed to the teeth with torpedoes, one of them nuclear. This could be a trap. He could just be down there, waiting for our SSN's to show up . . . just as he waited for the carrier. In a submarine battle, fought sub-surface, the advantage lies, as you know, with him who gets there first, with him who is lying in wait."

"Yes. And, maybe, sir, he who does not give a shit if he dies."

"Right. But let's just go over our options . . . first of all, we write off hoax. That's out of the question. Secondly, we assume the author of this note is either in the submarine and sent it out to colleagues via satellite. Or, it was sent by someone not in the submarine, who was in a controlling position. Are we agreed, so far?"

"Yessir."

"Therefore this is either a trap designed to wipe out another couple of big expensive U.S. warships or it is a straightforward ploy to get us to blow up the Kilo."

"That would seem rock solid, sir. But it wouldn't be a trap. There are so many easier ways to blow up our ships, without making a date."

"So, what do we do?"

"We get down there with a lotta muscle and blow the son-ofabitch to smithereens. That's what we do."

"Do we investigate the possibility of a new, unknown friend?"

"Sir. I was just coming to that. I think we do have a new friend. And I think I know who he is. Was. But I just wanted to run this entire sequence right through, to acquaint you with the full picture and all of its ramifications."

At this point, Admiral Morgan explained in full his conversation with General Gavron. "It is possible, sir, the letter was dispatched, directly or indirectly, from a doomed Mossad man in Cairo. And I think we should act on it right away."

"I agree. I'll order four SSN's into the South Atlantic immediately."

Admiral Morgan paced the office restlessly while the CNO alerted his senior Atlantic Flag Officers. He spoke to the Commander of the Second Fleet, Vice Admiral Ray Mapleton. And he spoke with even more urgency to the Commander of the Atlantic Submarine Force, Vice Admiral Joseph Mulligan.

Arnold Morgan heard him order all four of the submarines he had placed in readiness for a possible mission to clear Norfolk as soon as possible. It was going to take them two weeks to get down to the Falkland Islands, almost eight and a half thousand miles away. The big nuclear boats would run underwater at twenty-five-plus knots, night and day, covering six hundred miles every twenty-four hours. That would put three of them off the southern coast of Argentina early on September 24. The Kilo was due to show the following day, probably at the earliest.

It was, Admiral Morgan knew, critical they arrive on station well *before* Commander Adnam's Kilo. That way they would have time to settle into the area, and become used to the normal sounds of the underwater jungle.

The Intelligence officer was enjoying the experience of listening to the CNO in action. He was crisp, economical, and decisive,

recommending Admiral Mulligan consider a three-boat submarine trap, north to south, barring the way to the eastern entrance
to the Magellan Strait, and the southern route to Cape Horn.

It was made clear to Joe Mulligan that the boss thought only
one U.S. nuclear boat, the fourth, should be deployed in the
Falkland Islands area.

Admiral Morgan also heard Admiral Dunsmore end the conversation with the diplomacy and tact for which he was renowned.
"Very well, Joe. Just a few thoughts. Take them for what they are
worth, and I'll leave the rest to you. Keep in touch, g'bye."

The CNO turned back. "Oh yes, Arnold, I forgot to mention.
We're taking Bill Baldridge and Admiral MacLean off *Unseen* by
helicopter in the next couple of hours. We've got a Spruance
Class destroyer, *Fletcher*, in the area. She'll run them into
Athens. They'll both fly direct to London from there."

"Any thoughts about getting Baldridge down to the South
Atlantic as our official observer?"

"I hadn't quite got to that yet, Arnold, but plainly he ought to
be there. What do you think?"

"Oh, very definitely. First because of the official report.
Second, he may be pretty damned useful. He knows more about
Adnam than anyone else. And he's just spent a lot of time with
his Teacher."

"Agreed. Let's get him down to Roosevelt Roads. He can pick
up *Columbia* right there. It's hardly out of the submarine's way.
Bill needs the London-Miami flight, then American Airlines to
Puerto Rico. I'll have Jay fix it."

"Perfect. Before I leave, sir, there are just two other things I
wanted to mention. Admiral MacLean was the sonar officer in
the Royal Navy submarine which sank the *Belgrano* in the
Falklands War. It took place right down there somewhere south
of the islands, exactly where we're going. I think someone
should get his input. The man's a submarine scholar."

"Agreed. Lieutenant Commander Baldridge can do that
immediately. We'll get a detailed report of our action plan to the
Fletcher, and Bill can debrief Sir Iain on the way to Athens. We'll
detail *Columbia* to make the Falkland Islands patrol, and Bill

can give the captain the benefit of the admiral's knowledge on the way down."

"The last thing, sir. Should we put the CIA onto the Iraqi money situation in Chile? If that Kilo is really on the course the note is telling us, there's gotta be a big bank somewhere near Punta Arenas with a lot of Iraqi cash in it. Unless the entire submarine is stuffed with hundred-dollar bills."

"For the moment I'm going to say not. Let's just concentrate, very quietly, on slamming the boat which destroyed our aircraft carrier. Meanwhile I had better give the President the news."

At 1400 on Tuesday afternoon, September 10, three American nuclear submarines, each of them 362 feet long, weighing seven thousand tons dived, with a crew of 133 men, 13 of them officers, began to head out of the Norfolk Navy shipyard into the Hampton Roads. In the space of two hours they had all made the familiar warship exit, out through the wide ocean gap, beneath which the road bridge becomes a tunnel, then on through a near identical gap in the Chesapeake Bay Bridge Tunnel.

Before them were the broad reaches of the Atlantic, and one by one they turned southeast . . . USS *Asheville*, USS *Springfield*, USS *Charlotte*. They were all Los Angeles Class, all armed with torpedoes, Tomahawk and Harpoon guided missiles. All were capable of speeds over thirty knots. They were approximately twice as fast and twice the size of the Russian-built Kilo they sought.

USS *Columbia* was the newest of the four SSN's allocated to the task and was scheduled to leave five hours later at 1900, bound for Puerto Rico, then to the Falklands. Built by General Dynamics in Groton, Connecticut, she was launched in 1994. The big single-shafter operated on two nuclear-powered turbines which generated thirty-five thousand hp. The submarine was capable of operating a thousand feet below the surface.

The U.S. Navy owns sixty of these ultramodern attack nuclear boats. They are the workhorses of America's underwater strike force, range unlimited. Nine of them were on active duty in the Gulf War.

Columbia's commanding officer was Commander Cale

"Boomer" Dunning, a forty-year-old career officer from Cape Cod, Massachusetts. As his nickname suggested, "Boomer" had spent a working lifetime devoted to nuclear submarines. He had completed a two-year spell in Holy Loch, Scotland, in the Poseidon program back in the late eighties, and had been promoted to commander in 1997.

Commander Dunning was a fair-skinned, burly-looking man who might have appeared more at home grinding in the mainsheet on an America's Cup yacht. He had big shoulders and forearms, and tree-trunk legs. He was an excellent, lifelong racing sailor, when he had the chance, and still kept a beautiful wooden skiff at his parents' home on the Cape, to which he and his wife would most certainly retire one day.

Boomer was married to a perfectly lovely, failed television actress, named Jo, whose father ran a boatyard in New Hampshire. They were, in the most generous sense of the phrase, a family of sea dogs. Boomer was a wizard at the helm of any boat, from a little skiff to a big racing yacht. His reputation in a nuclear submarine was, if anything, higher.

Serving under Boomer Dunning, tactical expert, sonar expert, weapons expert, navigation and nuclear engineering expert, was to serve under the command of the best of the breed. The 132 men who worked for him in *Columbia* had grown in confidence with every passing month. Generally speaking, they reckoned they were the best nuclear boat in the Navy. When they learned they had been selected for a secret mission in the South Atlantic, on direct orders of the Navy High Command, they assumed that High Command knew precisely what it was doing.

As ever, Commander Dunning had his ship in top order. All of the electronic combat systems had been checked and rechecked. She carried fourteen Gould Mk 48 wire-guided torpedoes of the old, but reliable, ADCAP type (Advanced Capability), tube-launched. Internally she carried eight Tomahawk missiles, with a 1,400-mile range, plus four Harpoon missiles with active radar-homing warheads.

If the Kilo should get off an underwater shot at them, *Columbia* had an arsenal of decoys, Emerson Electric Mk 2's, plus a MOSS-based Mk 48 with a noisemaker, designed to seduce any incoming weapon away from the submarine. Her IBM sonars were the BQQ 5D/E type, passive/active search and attack. On station, *Columbia* would use a low-frequency, passive, towed-array, designed to pick up the heartbeat of any prowler, which Commander Boomer Dunning, and his sonar team, would then designate either harmless or hostile.

Columbia's Combat Systems Officer was Lieutenant Commander Jerry Curran, a tall, bespectacled, slightly stooped figure from Connecticut, who had a master's degree in electronics and computer systems from Fordham University. According to Commander Dunning, "Jerry's the best bridge player in the Navy."

With only four hours to go before *Columbia* sailed, Lieutenant Commander Curran was below talking to the sonar chief. The navigator, twenty-nine-year-old Lieutenant David Wingate, was poring over his deep-water charts of the South Atlantic near the Falkland Islands.

It was back in the nuclear area where the activity was still intense. The Marine Engineering Officer, Lieutenant Commander Lee O'Brien, and his team had taken the nuclear reactor critical some hours previously, or "pulled the rods" in the vernacular. This a slow and methodical process, getting the power plant up to temperature and pressure, ready to provide *all* of the power requirements of the submarine—roughly the amount required for a small town in winter.

Lieutenant Commander O'Brien, an Annapolis graduate with a degree in nuclear sciences from MIT, was the busiest man in the ship. Commander Dunning had been down to see him a couple of times since lunch, but generally speaking he left the thoughtful Boston Irishman to his work. "He doesn't need me looking over his shoulder," he said to Lieutenant Wingate, "he needs peace. The guy's got six children at home, five of 'em boys. He's good under pressure."

By 1830 the telegraph systems from the bridge to the control room had been tested for the final time. At 1850, Commander Dunning signaled to the engineers.

Out on the casing, the deck crew prepared to cast her off.

The Officer of the Deck ordered, "*Let go all the lines . . . pull off!*" Commander Dunning, standing next to his navigator high on his bridge, said crisply, "The ship is underway . . . *shift the colors*." Back astern, the Stars and Stripes was hauled down. Up for'ard, the Jack, the flag with just the field of blue and fifty stars, was also lowered.

As the tugs began to haul *Columbia* off the dock, the flag of the United States of America was raised high above the bridge. Forty feet out into the harbor, Commander Dunning ordered the tugs to let go, and put his telegraph to "Engines backing . . . one-third . . . Okay . . . Ahead two-thirds."

The great jet-black hull began to move slowly through the harbor waters, now under her own power, a deeply sinister, menacing sight, no matter how bright the day.

This evening, the light was beginning to fade as *Columbia* cleared the Hampton Roads and headed out into the Atlantic. Commander Dunning remained on the bridge with Lieutenant Wingate. They made twelve knots through the outer reaches of the Norfolk approach, and down in the communications room they relayed back to shore the final adjustments to the Next-of-Kin list.

They set a course of one-three-zero, heading southeasterly out toward the Bermuda Rise, five hundred miles out. But Boomer Dunning would dive the submarine, and swing onto a more southerly course long before that, as soon as the water was deep enough, due east of Cape Hatteras. Right now, running fair down the channel, Boomer ordered, "All ahead standard [fifteen knots]."

102200SEP02. On board USS *Fletcher*, Aegean Sea, northeast of Athens.

Orders for Bill Baldridge had been received in the ship's radio room—Athens-London-Miami-Puerto Rico, to meet *Columbia* en route to the South Atlantic.

He explained the situation to Admiral MacLean, who was wryly amused by the U.S. Navy's total disregard for distance—planes, ships, no problem. They could get anyone anywhere, anytime.

When Bill informed him of the possible position of the Kilo on September 25, the retired submariner looked pensive. "Yes, she's heading to South America, isn't she?" he said. "I expect you chaps will try and get her south of the Falklands, hmm? May as well stick to the one piece of hard information you have. But it's not that easy right there."

"Can you give me the main problems?"

"Yes. Have you ever heard of a place called the Burdwood Bank?"

"No."

"The Burdwood Bank is a pretty large area of fairly shallow water on the edge of the South American continental shelf. It runs two hundred miles from east to west, passing a hundred miles south of East Falkland. Right there it's about sixty miles across, north to south.

"Now, further south, the Atlantic is two miles deep. But on the bank, the bottom rises to only a hundred and fifty feet below the surface. The shoals are quite well charted. But it's a lethal place for a big nuclear submarine, which wants to be at two hundred feet to avoid leaving a wake on the surface.

"But that's not really your problem with it. Because you do not have a surface ship enemy. Your problem is noise. And that bloody bank is one of the noisiest spots in the entire ocean. It's full of fish, shrimp, whales, and God knows what else. It's impossible to listen for an oncoming boat because of the general racket. Never mind one as quiet as that Kilo is going to be."

"From what you say, sir, the Kilo is probably not going to cross the bank. He's obviously coming from the coast of South Africa, with a course set nearly due west, to get around Cape Horn."

"I agree, Bill. It's worth remembering that the southernmost point of Africa is around seventeen degrees further north than Cape Horn. So he's running west-southwest. I think he will deliberately avoid the Burdwood Bank, not only because it's so shallow, but because it's quite widely patrolled by British military aircraft. My guess is that your enemy will come at you from out of the east. And, Bill, you must get into position before he gets there.

"My advice is to get in fairly close to the bank, so your sonars are pointed in an arc, east and south out toward the much deeper water. That's where he's coming from. And out there it's quiet. Actually, you'll find it relatively silent in those waters—until Ben Adnam shows up. You'll probably want to stay on passive sonar until the very last moment. So it is important to be aiming the beams across a wide zone which is as quiet as possible."

"Right, sir. Do you think it's dangerous?"

"Anytime you are dealing with an enemy as cunning and brilliant as Ben Adnam, it is going to be extremely dangerous. But you will be in a very superior submarine, with top-class people, and you will be waiting for him. I hope. His main strength is his stealth. He's silent under five as we know. However, he will not be expecting you, which is a big advantage.

"But he'll fight, if you give him the least opportunity. Have no doubt, Benjamin Adnam will fight, as he's been trained to do . . . as, I am rather afraid, I taught him. The second you go active, he'll open fire with one of those Russian torpedoes. Have your decoy men on top line at all times. Be ready every minute. It happens fast down there. And I don't particularly want you to die. I suspect that may also apply to my daughter, but probably not so much to my wife, who thinks you were the cause of my little underwater holiday in Turkey."

"Just between us, sir, I'm also hoping to give death a miss."

130700SEP02. USS *Columbia*, 18.22N, 65.38W. Waiting off Roosevelt Roads, on the easternmost point of the Caribbean island of Puerto Rico.

Commander Boomer Dunning was in his shirtsleeves on the sunlit bridge, watching a U.S. Navy helicopter clatter across the bay from the north, bearing the lieutenant commander from Washington who would accompany them on their long journey south. The arriving officer had, he knew, been one of the prime instigators of this investigation since Day One. Commander Dunning had met his brother, Captain Jack Baldridge, who, he knew, had died on the *Thomas Jefferson*.

Bill Baldridge came out of the blue West Indies sky, and was lowered from the chopper onto the casing of the submarine. His bag came down on a separate line, and he disappeared down the hatch, where a young officer met him and showed him to his quarters.

The CO handed over control of the ship to his Executive Officer, Lieutenant Commander Mike Krause, another New Englander from Vermont, and went below to chat with the newly arrived official guest from the Pentagon.

As they talked, Lieutenant Commander Krause turned *Columbia* north, to make a wide easterly sweep around the Virgin Islands and Anguilla. By nightfall they would be out in deep Atlantic water, three and three-quarter miles below the keel, all through the Puerto Rican Trench, the submarine running swiftly four hundred feet under the surface.

Boomer Dunning and Bill Baldridge had much to discuss. They sat in the captain's tiny cabin, where the submarine commander expressed misgivings about taking out an enemy nobody knew, or had even seen, far less found guilty of anything.

Bill Baldridge set Boomer straight on that one in short order. "Have no doubts, sir," he said, agreeably recognizing the seniority of the commanding officer, despite the exalted circles he usually moved in these days. "We have spent weeks and weeks ensuring that there was only one submarine in all of this world which could have taken out the *Thomas Jefferson*. Every other underwater boat capable of moving forward, above, or below the surface was checked out, over and over.

"The carrier was sunk by Russian Kilo 630—even the head of Russian Naval Intelligence recognizes that. It was 'hired' by the Iraqis for a huge bundle of cash—we think probably 10 million dollars payable to the captain. Most of the money is probably on board now. We even found out which of the old Saddam Hussein accounts it came from in Geneva. We even know how it got to Sevastopol a couple of days before the Kilo sailed. We have pieced it all together bit by bit. The tip-off, informing us where the Kilo will show up, came from an impeccable source.

"Sir, we do not want to waste much energy worrying about

the Kilo's guilt. We know what it did, and we know the man who commanded it. He's our problem. He's an Iraqi, but he operated for years as a submarine officer in the Israeli Navy. He was trained by the Royal Navy in Scotland. He had the Brits' greatest-ever submariner for a Teacher, and he was the best potential submarine commander that Teacher ever instructed."

"Jesus," said Commander Boomer. "How the hell do you know all this?"

"By some fluke I've been involved right from the start. I was called in originally as a nuclear weapons expert—from there I just never got away from it. But I was proud to do the job. I expect you know my brother Jack was killed in the carrier."

"I did, Bill. And I was really sorry to hear that. I met Jack a few times. Just a super guy. And one hell of an officer by all accounts."

"Left a big gap in our lives," said Bill.

"Did you ever talk to the Teacher about this bastard?"

"Sure did. For hours at a time. I also got quite a bit of advice from him about the area where we're headed. He was the submarine sonar officer when the Royal Navy sunk the *General Belgrano*, south of the Falklands twenty years ago. I doubt you *need* any advice, but he did suggest a few things you might find helpful. I tried to write it all down on the plane from London to Miami, but I was so tired I just fell asleep. I'll get to it in the next couple of days."

"That'd be great. If we're fighting some kind of a submarine genius we'd better be well coached, I guess."

"He may be a genius," said Bill. "The first thing he did after leaving Sevastopol was to transit the Bosporus underwater."

"You're kidding me? No one's ever done that, have they?"

"They have now. Matter of fact it's getting to be a regular occurrence. Did it myself earlier this week!"

Bill explained the insistence of the President that someone complete that journey before he would order the U.S. Navy into action against the submarine. "That was before we got the tip-off from the Mossad, and at that time I guess we were looking at a huge expenditure for such a search, over possibly months and months. If, in the end, we found nothing, the President was not anxious to be accused of wasting billions on a scenario that was known to be impossible."

"So he sent you guys to make the transit from the Black Sea in a nuclear?"

"No. We used a Royal Navy diesel, with a British crew, which included the retired admiral who taught the Iraqi."

"Was it easy?"

"It was for a long way. Then it got really tricky. We were almost killed twice in ten minutes. Both times I thought it was all over. I noticed that when we finally got through the second trauma of being mowed down by a twenty-thousand-tonner, the XO's hands were shaking so badly he couldn't light a cigarette ten minutes later."

"But this Iraqi did it?"

"Yessir. He did. Then they lost a man overboard in the Greek islands, and he turned out to be a member of the ship's company of Kilo 630. We heard them accelerate in the Gibraltar Strait on exactly the right date for a submarine moving at eight knots through the Med. Then one of our mail aircraft spotted a 'feather' in the Indian Ocean, again on exactly consistent time and date for a submarine making a couple of hundred miles a day.

"We picked them up very briefly on sonar near the Battle Group. Sent up choppers, laid down a sonar buoy. But he never crossed it. The next day the *Jefferson* was hit."

"Jesus. This guy is really something, right? He actually got through the Bosporus submerged, *and* got through all of the billion-dollar defenses of a U.S. Battle Group, *and* vaporized an aircraft carrier?"

"Correct, sir. He really is something."

"Well, Bill, I guess it's critical we get down there before that Kilo. We want to be waiting right on that position. There's no doubt in your mind that if we find a Russian-built Kilo down there, it's gotta be the one?"

"Commander, I know there is not one Russian-built Kilo on either SUBLANT's or SUBPAC's boards within three thousand miles of the Falkland Islands in any direction. Except the one we seek. The Russians are helping us. They have confirmed all other Kilos are at home. The only Kilo that's going to come rolling past us is Number 630, driven by an Iraqi."

"That at least puts my mind at rest. I don't much want to face my maker one day having dispatched sixty innocent men to their deaths. Meanwhile our rules are pretty simple. We have been cleared to shoot only at a positive ident Kilo. Once we have a good trace on his engines, and we're dead sure he's a single-shaft, five-blader, we just have to check the surface to make sure he's not a Japanese trawler or something. At that point he's a positive ident. And right after that, he's a dead positive ident."

"That's it, sir. Sounds easy, right? And I think it would be—but for this homicidal Iraqi maniac at the helm."

Commander Boomer laughed. "I'll tell you something else. No one would ever believe that we were once parked in the middle of nowhere, waiting to shoot live weapons at a passing submarine which exists only as a result of a weird letter from Cairo."

"Yeah. That one would be hard to imagine. But we're correct here. And when you think about it, it is the natural place to go, South America. *If* you're on the run. Nazis, train robbers, and God knows who else have headed there after the crime. And, if you were heading across the South Atlantic from the Indian Ocean, you would pass right by the Falkland Islands."

"You think we're going to find that Kilo, Bill?"

"Yessir. Yes, I do. I think the information we received is golden. I'm told it may have cost the Israeli agent his life. I didn't ask questions. Some things you just don't much want to know."

For the next five days *Columbia* rushed along the northern coastline of Brazil, running deep, southeast, all the way down the Guiana Basin, putting six hundred miles behind her every time the sun rose out of the east. It was a sun the crew never once saw rise or set; and, the further south they ran, the fiercer the rays became on the glaring tropical waters above them. But where the Americans traveled there was only darkness, pitch-black water being split apart by the onrushing black hull of the nuclear attack submarine from Norfolk.

At 1900 on Tuesday evening, September 17, *Columbia* crossed the equator. Three hundred miles later she was somewhere off Cape São Roque, on Brazil's huge jutting eastern headland. Right there Commander Dunning and Lieutenant David Wingate altered course to due south, for the sixteen-hundred-mile run down to the bright waters off Rio and São Paulo, great South American cities which *Columbia* would leave eight hundred miles off her starboard beam.

The only man who ever saw the daylight, albeit for just fleeting seconds, was the CO himself. Every twelve hours he slowed the submarine down and slid up to periscope depth for the routine fast-passage procedure—checking the satellite for messages. Boomer Dunning would order the radio mast raised. The comms room would "suck it right off the satellite" in the merest seconds, and the CO would order *Columbia* deep again, back into the endless darkness, barreling on south, to meet the rogue Kilo, which had caused such universal agony in the U.S.A.

All through the headlong rush of the voyage to the Falklands, officers quietly caught up with their paperwork, sailors who had completed their watch played cards and watched videos. Bill Baldridge sat writing his long, detailed report of the Bosporus transit. Sometimes he and Commander Dunning dined together, while Lieutenant Commander Krause took the ship. It did not much matter how hard they tried to vary the conversation, it always came back to the Kilo, the difficulty of sonar-listening near the Burdwood Bank, and the nerve-racking possibility that the Iraqi commander, Benjamin Adnam, would hear them first.

At 2300 on the night of September 20 they altered course off São Paulo to two-one-five, for the final southwesterly journey down the coast, which would take them past Uruguay and along the vast Atlantic expanse of Argentina. Commander Dunning headed *Columbia* another hundred miles further east in order to pass the Rio Grande Ridge in deeper water. And from there it was a straight four-day run down to the Falkland Islands.

They arrived off the eastern coast of the islands in the small hours of the morning of September 24, one day early. Commander Dunning stayed east and deep as he passed the

British territory, for whose few people Margaret Thatcher had been prepared to fight a war to the death in 1982.

"There's a lot of people I don't really care much about upsetting," said Commander Boomer. "But I'd sure hate the Brits to get really pissed off at me, if I was creeping around their island in a submarine without telling 'em. Those guys are fucking dangerous. I'm staying well clear."

Bill Baldridge, who was sharing a pot of coffee with him at the time, chuckled. "They know precisely where you are, sir. They've been working with us on this almost since the start. They identified Adnam for us."

"Just don't want any misunderstandings," said Boomer, laughing.

And now for the first time, he ordered a decrease in speed. They headed south, running at only fifteen knots standard across the sixty-mile expanse of the western end of the Burdwood Bank. For the sonar team, the noise of the shallow water was heightened to a point where everyone understood the impossibility of finding *anything* over those fish-laden shoals.

It took them four hours to make the crossing. Commander Dunning came to periscope depth twice, once to take a look at the weather, which was awful, foggy and windy at the same time, with big South Atlantic swells heaving in from the turbulent southwest, where the Atlantic and the Pacific first meet, right off the stark, tormented rock-face of Cape Horn. The second time was to access the comms satellite.

The crew now deployed the towed-array, the great electronic tail the submarine towed behind—weightless in the water—while on patrol, enabling her sonars to "see" everything in all directions, except the thin triangular cone of water right astern.

This "blind" spot was dealt with in a strictly routine way. Every few hours, but with careful irregularity, the submarine made a turn to port, or to starboard, to check the stern-arc's clear. If anything should be stalking her, the sonars picked it up very quickly. They called it "clearing the baffles."

With the passive-sonar array strung out behind her, *Columbia* swung east, running quietly at seven knots, with the giant underwater cliffs of the Burdwood Bank ranged along her port side. Commander Dunning, who now had a copy of Admiral MacLean's recommendations on his desk, planned to run the whole length of the bank, then set up patrol in the dark shadow of those cliffs. Awaiting the arrival of the Russian Kilo.

In the midafternoon of September 24, he once more accessed the satellite to report his own position and receive any new orders or information. There was one signal. It told them *Springfield* was on patrol at the eastern entrance to the Magellan Strait. She was 120 miles due east of Cape Virgenes, the jagged headland which separates the coastline of Argentina, allowing free international passage through the strait.

Charlotte was right on the fifty-fourth parallel north of Cape San Juan, guarding any northeastern approach to the waters off Tierra del Fuego. *Asheville* was in deep water twenty miles southeast of Cape Horn. All three U.S. submarines were on station in case *Columbia* should fail. There was no way Kilo 630 was going to round the tip of South America in one piece.

But the real tension at this stage of the operation was in *Columbia*, whose CO anticipated the Kilo was probably one day east of the bank now, running at around seven knots, coming up only to snorkel occasionally, to recharge her huge, vitally important battery.

Commander Dunning and his team reached the eastern end of the bank shortly after 0030 on September 25. They were reasonably sure they had not passed the Kilo, and they knew that if they were too late, it would almost certainly be picked up and caught by one of their three colleagues. Dunning turned his boat back to the west.

Bill Baldridge had an implicit belief in the validity of the tip-off from Cairo, and did not expect the Kilo to be there before the date and time stated, 1200, September 25, on latitude 54.40S, longtitude 60.00W. Right where they now ran, slowly through the dark water.

The bells of the watch came and went. All through that night and morning, the great electronic ear of the passive sonar swept, unseen, through the icy depths, aimed always into the silence of the deep, away from the racket of the bank itself. The daily "weapons check" report came and went again.

Every six hours they reported the self-noise check on the array. And *Columbia* lay in wait, with the noise of the bank behind her, holding what was once called in days of sail, the "weather gauge."

When, they all wondered, would the rogue Kilo come sliding eerily out of the deep Southern Ocean? Whenever that was, the Americans had their cover. The submarine running west would be forced to aim his sonars at the noisiest part of the ocean, which obscures, eclipses, and ultimately camouflages the noise of another submarine.

Boomer Dunning and Bill Baldridge, now together as underwater comrades-in-arms, knew that every advantage was with them in this grim and deadly game of hide-and-seek.

Noon came and went on Wednesday, September 25. It came and went too, on September 26. Still nothing. The afternoon wore on, and no sound of a softly turning single-shafted five-blader was detected by the sonar room. All through the evening they remained on full alert. The watch changed at midnight. At 0400, Captain Dunning came once more to periscope depth to access the satellite. No messages. All four of the U.S. submarines, in their separate waters, waited alone for the missing Kilo. But it was *Columbia* which stood bang in the middle of the offensive line.

Men came on duty for the second watch of the night as Boomer Dunning ordered his submarine deep again, into ice-cold seas in which nothing stirred.

At 0600 there was a glimmer of activity in the sonar room. Chief Petty Officer Skip Gowans was muttering that he might have heard a very slight rise in the background noise, "just an increase in the level, coulda been a rain shower, just swishing on the surface. But I thought it was something . . . give me a few minutes."

Lieutenant Commander Jerry Curran was standing right next to him, and at 0604, the chief spoke again. "I have a rise in the level," he said. "It's hard to explain unless it's the weather."

At 0614 an electric charge shot through the submarine . . .

"*Captain—sonar* . . . I have faint engine lines coming up on the array. Relative 92. Alter to 135 to resolve ambiguity, please. They fit the sample, sir."

"Sonar—Captain . . . I'll be right there."

Lieutenant Commander Curran crossed the room to the "waterfall" screen on which it was now clear that there were definite engine lines. The computer had already compared them with the Kilo engine sample built into the system. "They fit, sir, no doubt."

Boomer Dunning stepped into the room. "Nothing else on this watch?" he said.

"Nossir, nothing except that zoo up on the bank."

"What's the range?"

"Not close, sir. Could even be first convergence. The bearing hasn't moved. I assume she's coming dead toward."

Commander Dunning stepped back outside and talked to Baldridge. "What would your admiral do right here, Bill?"

"He said to keep moving back off-track to the north, trying to get the bank in behind us, for more noise cover, just in case the Kilo goes completely quiet on us."

"Right now he's snorkeling, on course west, making a lot of noise, for that boat. But we'll head north as you suggest."

Forty minutes passed with agonizing slowness. Bill heard the next call from the sonar room.

"Solution looks good, sir. He's still way out to the east, still coming our way. Still snorkeling, not cavitating. So he's less than nine knots."

"One and two tubes ready, sir . . . we're about three thousand yards to one side of the Kilo's predicted track."

"Okay," said Boomer Dunning quietly, as if even the sound of his voice would betray their presence. "I'm going to hold it right here, dead slow . . . then let him go by, and fire from his stern arcs, so he has zero chance of picking up the firing transient."

"Yessir."

"Meantime I want to get the best picture I can of his masts at CPA. 'Posident,' they said. 'Posident' they shall have."

Fifteen minutes went by, and now the Kilo was seven miles

closer than he was at first contact, two miles to the south of *Columbia*.

"Up periscope . . . Here, Bill, you're the official observer. You've got to tell the CNO it was a real live Kilo. Take a look."

Bill Baldridge peered through the lenses, across the gray waters, at the tiny masts coming and going with the long swell . . . "Yup. Tallies close enough with the book. It's hard to be sure, but that's no trawler."

"Down periscope. Firing in five minutes. Sonar, make sure you get full recordings."

"Sonar, aye."

Three minutes later . . . "Captain—sonar . . . target dynamic stop, sir. He's stopped snorkeling. I'm getting transients on the bearing in broad band, but the lines have all gone. He'll be all quiet in one minute."

"*Shit.*"

The sounds and signs from the Kilo died away. One minute passed, and Boomer Dunning made his decision, to fire at range three thousand yards on predictions from the last-known bearing, sending the Mk 48 torpedo off quietly at thirty knots, staying passive until sixty seconds from impact. Then *Columbia*'s Torpedo Guidance Officer would go to active sonar for dead accurate direction, and simultaneously accelerate the missile on its way, leaving its hapless target without hope, or even time for retribution.

"Stand by one . . . "

"Last bearing check . . . "

"*Shoot!*"

In the sonar room they heard the dull metallic thud of the big wire-guided torpedo launch out of the tube. *Columbia* shuddered faintly.

"Weapon under guidance, sir . . . "

"Arm the weapon."

"Weapon armed, sir."

One minute passed . . . "Weapon two thousand yards from target."

"Sonar—*Switch to active. Single ping.*"

"Aye, sir," called the sonar officer as he hit the button which would send the powerful telltale beam straight down the predicted bearing of the Kilo, and then echo back to give them a last-minute check on the fire control solution.

260713SEP02. 54.40S, 60.00W.
Course 255. Speed 5. East of Burdwood Bank.
Depth 16 meters.

"*Captain—sonar . . . one active transmission . . . loud . . . bearing Green 135 . . . United States SSN for sure. Real close.*"

"*Stand by Tube Number Two. Set targets bearing Green 135. Range three thousand meters. Depth one hundred meters. Shoot as soon as you're ready.*"

"*Hard right. Steer zero-three-five. Shut off for counterattack. Full ahead . . . ten down . . . two hundred meters.*"

"*Two Tube fired, Captain.*"

"*Captain—sonar . . . torpedo active transmission . . . possibly in contact. Right ahead . . . Interval nine hundred meters . . .*"

Turned straight toward his enemy, charging forward at maximum speed, in the reckless, but classic, Russian torpedo evasion maneuver, Captain Georgy Kokoshin snapped out his last command . . . "Decoys . . . Thirty down . . ."

The American torpedo slammed into the top of his bow, detonated with savage force, blasting a huge hole in the pressure hull. The water thundered in for'ard, flattening the bulkheads.

Captain Kokoshin looked up at the five-foot high, three-inch-thick steel door which protected him, just in time to see it catapulted toward him, exploding inward before eighty-six tons of solid water pressure. He died in his Navy uniform on active duty. But not on behalf of Mother Russia, the nation he had served for all but the last five months of his working life.

Back in *Columbia*, they had already picked up the incoming Russian torpedo, which, in a lightning, last-ditch reaction, the Kilo's weapons team had got away.

"Captain—sonar . . . *Possible discharge transient on bearing.*"

Boomer Dunning was calm. "Captain, aye . . . Ahead flank.

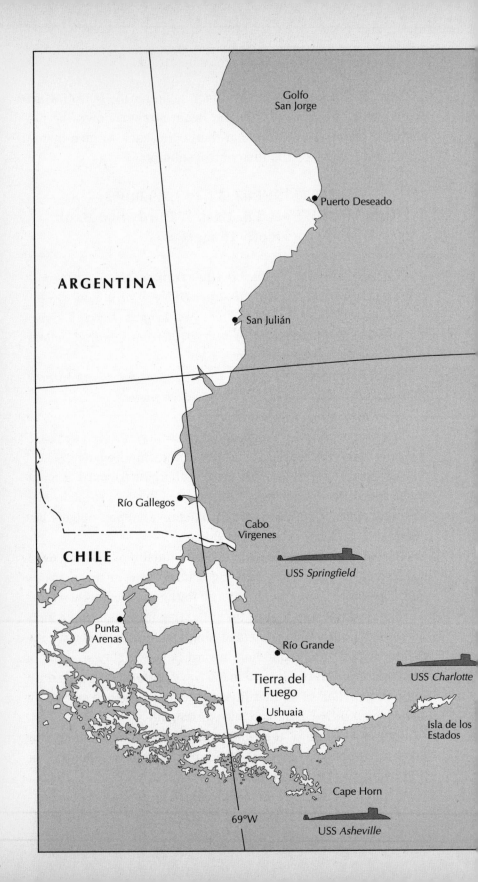

Golfo
San Jorge

● Puerto Deseado

ARGENTINA

● San Julián

Río Gallegos ●

Cabo
Virgenes

CHILE

USS *Springfield*

Punta
Arenas

Río Grande ●

USS *Charlotte*

Tierra del
Fuego

Isla de los
Estados

● Ushuaia

Cape Horn

69°W

USS *Asheville*

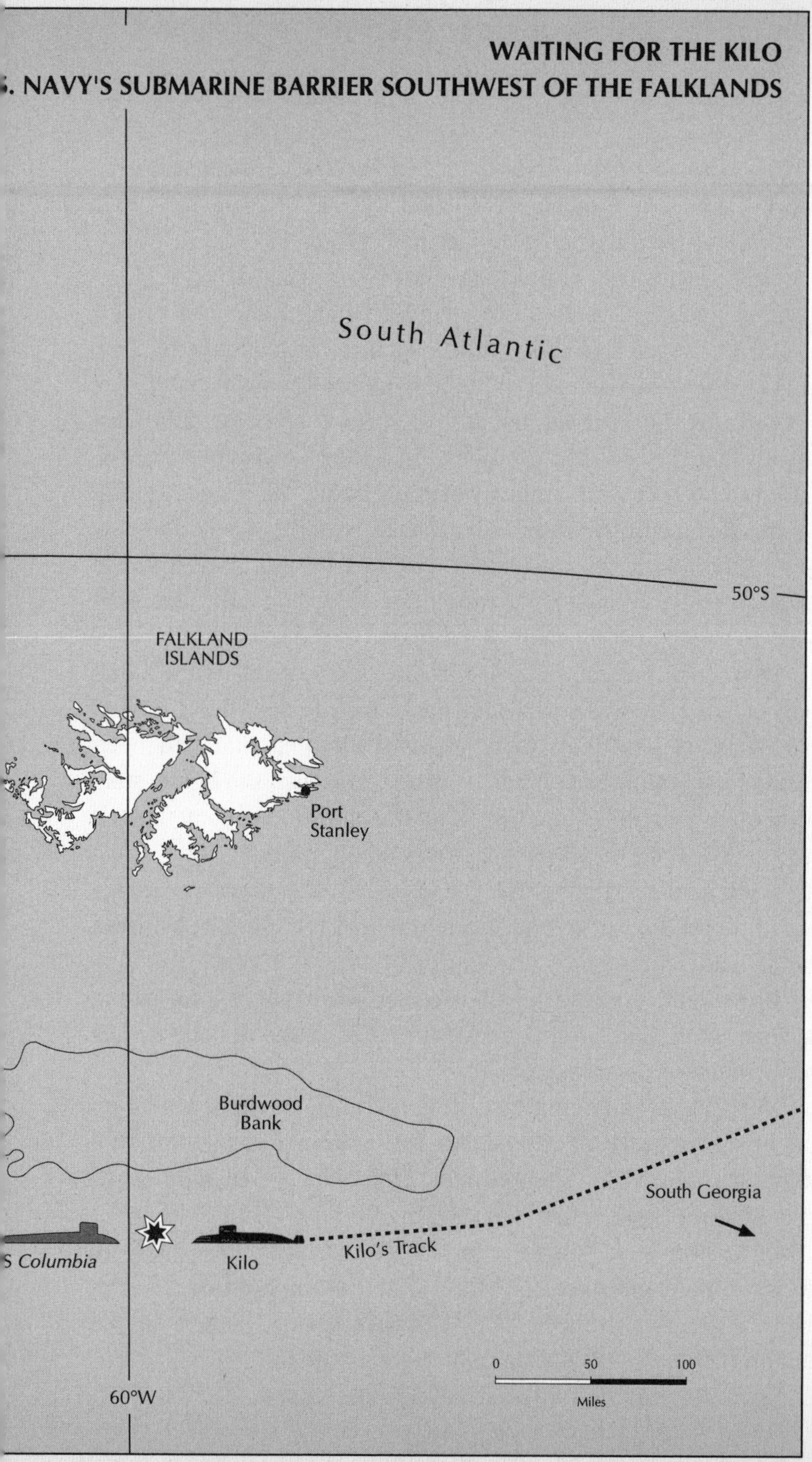

WAITING FOR THE KILO
. NAVY'S SUBMARINE BARRIER SOUTHWEST OF THE FALKLANDS
South Atlantic
50°S
FALKLAND ISLANDS
Port Stanley
Burdwood Bank
South Georgia
S Columbia
Kilo
Kilo's Track
0
50
100
Miles
60°W

Right full rudder . . . thirty down . . . nine hundred feet . . . *Decoys one and two.*"

"*Torpedo—torpedo—torpedo* . . . bearing 260 . . . sweep mode . . . moving left. *Fast* . . . still in sweep mode."

"*Rudder amidships*," snapped the captain.

"Still moving left . . . but fainter, sir. *She's missed.*"

"Yes, she has," replied Commander Dunning. And he turned to Bill Baldridge and added, in the rich, salty, language of their calling, "Beats the shit out of me how he got one away at all."

And now he ordered his ship to surface and was quite surprised that the swell in the ocean had died down very quickly. Off to the west about a mile away, they could see a smooth area on the surface of the water. All alone now in this bleak and desolate South Atlantic seascape, *Columbia* turned toward it and drove along the surface, through the calm and now flat gray waters, to identify, formally, the remains of their "kill."

There was not much to see, really. A lot of oil, a few small bits of wooden wreckage, and unsecured items which looked like Navy jackets and other items of clothing that had been blasted out upon the torpedo's impact. The rest, the heavy steel structure, weapons, engines, and the ship's company, rested now on the floor of the ocean, two and half miles below.

Commander Dunning, Bill Baldridge, and Lieutenant Wingate stood up on the bridge and stared down at the minute remnants of the Kilo.

Down on the casing, a half-dozen crew members were taking a closer look, just a final check for bodies. Russian bodies, they supposed. But there were none.

No one said anything for a few minutes, possibly out of an unconscious mark of respect for the unknown dead. But suddenly a young sailor shouted out: "*Hey*, what's that right down there? *Right there*, where I'm pointing."

But no one else could see anything. And the sailor looked up to the bridge, embarrassed at his outburst, in front of the captain. "Sorry, sir," he said. "But I coulda sworn I saw a coupla hundred dollar bills floating right there, in the oil."

Only Lieutenant Commander Baldridge smiled.

EPILOGUE

THE PENTAGON—1100,
Thursday, October 10.
Office of the Secretary of Defense.
Third Floor, E Ring.

ROBERT MACPHERSON PRESIDED OVER THIS PARTICULAR
debriefing meeting personally. Seated around him in the conference room were the Secretary of State, Harcourt Travis, the
CJCS, General Josh Paul, the CNO, Admiral Scott Dunsmore, the
Intelligence Director, Vice Admiral Arnold Morgan, and the man
who had tracked the Russian Kilo from day one until it was finally
destroyed, Lieutenant Commander Bill Baldridge. Major Ted Lynch
of the CIA was invited to sit in, having compiled a dossier on the
Iraqi's financial involvement in the *Jefferson* disaster. At 1115, the
President of the United States was expected to join them, but not
to preside.

They were assembled to discuss the formal report of the
secret demise of the Russian Kilo. Here in this room behind
closed, guarded doors, the men who occupied America's three
great Offices of State would finally confer with the most senior
officers in the Pentagon, to make a decision not to admit any-

395

thing. The Iranians had said nothing whatsoever about their written-off submarines, the Russians had already agreed to say nothing about the Kilo, and the Israelis intended to say nothing about Commander Benjamin Adnam. Nor indeed about their probably murdered field officer in Cairo.

Governments like to put things to bed. The United States of America was about to turn out the light on the death of the *Thomas Jefferson*. Assuming the President was not hell-bent on flattening Baghdad for all the world to see.

Robert MacPherson suggested that the President was in no such frame of mind; not with the Kilo, and its crew, *and* Benjamin Adnam all resting at the bottom of the South Atlantic.

Everyone at the table had read the accounts of the hunt and "kill," most of which had been written by Lieutenant Commander Baldridge, and refined by Admiral Arnold Morgan. The financial document from Major Lynch had provided critical pieces of the jigsaw, and a private addition to the report, furnished to Admiral Morgan from General David Gavron, had more or less confirmed that Commander Adnam was an Iraqi agent who had been in place in Israel since he was eighteen.

The Mossad had run a set of computerized voice-matching tests on the conversation they had taped from the lakeside home of Barzan al-Tikriti. At first they had learned only that the two parties both came from the same hometown, which was plainly Tikrit, a small town located further north up the Tigris from Baghdad.

But the Mossad technicians now identified the other party. It was, without question, Benjamin Adnam, also of Tikrit, like Saddam Hussein and most of the Iraqi Government. The Mossad nailed Adnam five days after his death, comparing the Geneva conversation with an instructional tape Ben had helped to make for trainee Israeli submarine officers.

The loose ends were tying together smoothly when the President arrived. He greeted everyone warmly, using first names as he always did, and confirming that he had, of course, read all of the reports very thoroughly, and that there seemed little further they could advance, save to declare war on Iraq, which on reflection was not a great idea.

The President wanted to talk for a while about operational improvements which might be made for the future patrols of Carrier Battle Group, and he was particularly interested in the blow-by-blow account from Commander Boomer Dunning of the sinking of the Kilo. But he appeared preoccupied today, as if he wanted, finally, to lay the *Jefferson* to rest. For the moment he seemed content just to have the knowledge that the Iraqis had been behind the atrocity. Almost as if he was biding his time over any future retribution.

"Well, gentlemen," he said, "I would like to thank all of the investigative team for the great job you all did. I wish someone would express our gratitude also to the Scottish admiral. We owe him a great deal. I would very much like to meet him, if that could be arranged.

"Meanwhile, we are naturally agreed on a policy of silence. And now, unless anyone has anything of paramount importance to impart, I guess that wraps it. For the moment." He looked around the table, smiled at his team, and added, one final time, "Anything else?"

"Sir," Lieutenant Commander Baldridge said firmly, "we did not get Commander Adnam. He was not on the submarine. And he's still alive. And I just hope he does not have it in his mind to try anything else."

All heads turned in unison. The President looked amazed, but recovered his composure very swiftly. "Bill!" he said in mock outrage. "Haven't we been through a similar routine to this, once before?"

"Yessir."

"Well, you were right then. I guess I'd better sit right here, and hear you out."

Admiral Dunsmore interrupted. "Commander, the President is very busy. Could you not have mentioned your new theory to me a few days ago?"

"Not hardly, sir. I only just got it. Just dawned on me. I didn't even tune in when I stood by and watched them wipe out the Kilo."

"What's on your mind?" said the President. "I may be busy. But I'm not too busy for this."

"Okay, gentlemen," said Bill. "If you turn to page fourteen of Captain Dunning's report, you will see that we fired the wire-guided torpedo, and let it run at thirty knots for two thousand yards. Then, with about one thousand yards to go, we took a single ping and switched the weapon's sonar to active, to give it a good look at its target, and then we increased its speed. The report from *Columbia*'s sonar room says it *hit* only thirty seconds later.

"That means the Kilo's defense was classic 'Crazy Ivan.'"

"Crazy what?" asked the President.

"Crazy Ivan. Submariner's jargon for the regular Soviet method of getting out of the way of a torpedo. Sonsabitches just turn around and run straight back down the bearing *toward* the incoming missile, going deeper at top speed all the time. They think this tactic throws the torpedo's sonar into confusion, and will force it to miss. And so it does. Sometimes. But no Western-trained submarine commander would ever dream of doing anything like that.

"Our own method is normally to accelerate forward in the same direction as the incoming missile. That means that if the torpedo is making forty knots, and we're doing twenty, he's only catching us at around twenty knots, and we have a head start. That gives us vital extra seconds to think of something, you know, decoys, evasion tactics. But we would not run straight *at* the damn thing, that's for certain."

The table was silent. And Bill Baldridge took it upon himself to add, "Kilo 630 accomplished its place in the Navy's Black Museum because it was handled by a master. It died because that master was no longer on board. Whoever was left in command was a Russian, Captain Georgy Kokoshin. Not Ben Adnam."

"You think Ben jumped overboard?" asked the President, wryly.

"Nossir. He got off when they were fueled. I calculated it somewhere in the Indian Ocean, before they made the crossing of the South Atlantic. Matter of fact I'd say they were topped up again with gas in the Atlantic, off West Africa. Ben left 'em at one of those two stops. That's why they were blown apart by the first torpedo fired at 'em."

The President stood up. "Thank you, Bill. Very interesting. Arnold, you'll listen out for Adnam's footsteps, I'm sure. Don't let's drop our guard. But for the moment, I think I'll just take some time to think about this."

Burdett, Kansas. October 30.

Lieutenant Commander Bill Baldridge resigned from the United States Navy and returned to the family cattle ranch. Two days later there was a memorial service for his brother, Captain Jack Baldridge. It was conducted by a Navy chaplain down by the river, next to the new bronze and granite memorial. The CNO, Admiral Scott Dunsmore, and his wife Grace were among the three hundred people who attended.

Camp David, 1130, November 12

Admiral Sir Iain MacLean and the President of the United States walked slowly in the glorious autumn foliage of the Blue Ridge Mountains. The path they trod, set deep in the 125 acres of the Presidential retreat, ran through a copse of maple, hickory, and locust, the red and butter-gold leaves lit by the morning sun. The route was so winding you could hardly see the Secret Servicemen and the Navy guards following on behind.

"Mr. President," said the admiral, "you have invited me to a very beautiful place."

"If I could, I'd give it to you, Admiral," replied the President, "after what you did for us. I'm just delighted you were able to come and spend a couple of days. I've invited Scott Dunsmore and his wife for dinner this evening so we can indulge in my favorite pastime, talking about Naval warfare."

"Yes. I'm really looking forward to that. We have a lot of mutual acquaintances. I did a stint at the British embassy in Washington, as Naval attaché. I knew the previous CNO."

"Ah, yes. Just before my time. I think you'll like Scott. He's a very fine officer, and much more fun than you first think. Damned clever too . . . like all you senior guys."

"You flatter us, sir. We're all very single-minded."

"So are defensive linemen," replied the President. "But that's not quite the same as being the commanding officer of a nuclear submarine or an aircraft carrier."

"Possibly not, sir, but I must say there was a really terrific chap played for the Redskins when I was here . . . "

The President laughed. "Before we get back for lunch, Admiral, let me ask you a question which you will not have the slightest trouble answering."

"Of course."

"You are in a nuclear submarine. Your enemy, positioned in your stern arcs, fires a wire-guided torpedo at you on passive sonar, from a range of three thousand yards. With one thousand yards to run, it switches to active, pings you, and accelerates hard, straight at you. What do you do?"

"I go full ahead and present my quarter to the torpedo, trying to hang on to my half-mile start. This means he is going to take something like another minute to catch me. At the same time I fire three or even four decoys to coax the torpedo away. I put the bow up and head for the surface at top speed. The torpedo gets very confused up there. The echoes off the waves interfere with its sonar once it gets within thirty feet of daylight. Also it can be confused by the turbulence in the water right behind my propeller. I'd almost certainly get away."

"Is that what you taught Benjamin Adnam, Admiral?"

"Yessir. That's exactly what I taught him."

"Thank you, Admiral, very much."

Dinner was arranged for the President's house, Aspen Lodge, the grandest of the many residences scattered discreetly among the wooded acres of the estate. A succession of American Presidents had loved this place, from Roosevelt, who founded it, Eisenhower, who named it after his grandson, to Jimmy Carter, who negotiated the Middle East peace treaty here.

Sir Iain MacLean was ensconced in Dogwood Lodge, where Anwar Sadat stayed in 1978. He spent most of the afternoon reading the reports of the *Jefferson* incident, then he strolled over to Aspen shortly after seven-thirty in the evening. He walked straight into the kind of discussion he might almost have predicted. The President and Admiral Dunsmore were wrestling with the question of whether Adnam was on the Kilo.

The introductions were made, but the conversation remained rooted in speculation, on the man who wiped out the American aircraft carrier. They explained the speed with which the torpedo had hit the Kilo, and they both heard Sir Iain murmur, "Mmmmm. Crazy Ivan."

Then Scott Dunsmore asked the Scottish admiral directly: "Would *you* say Adnam was on board when we hit the Kilo?"

"Absolutely not. And 'Crazy Ivan' merely clinches it for me. In my view there is only one man in all of the world who could have sent that four-line tip-off. And in my opinion that was Adnam.

"Gentlemen, I know the man. He is ice-cold, self-protective, and damned smart. There is no possibility he remained on that submarine. He would have considered that tantamount to suicide. He either talked his way off, threatened his way off, or fought his way off. But he would not have stayed.

"Besides, he had to get off. In order to complete his task."

"He did?" said the President.

"Oh, certainly. The Iraqis were never going to allow the Kilo to dock. I always assumed they would, in the end, scuttle it, and we'd just find a bit of wreckage. Adnam, however, went a step further. He didn't scuttle it. He didn't have to. He got you to do it for him, with one, short, simple, air-mail letter from Cairo to Fort Meade."

"Jesus," said the President. "That little sonofabitch. He's been one jump ahead of us all the way."

"Not just one jump ahead of you. He's been one jump ahead of everyone involved. One jump ahead of us, who misguidedly taught him. One jump ahead of the Mossad, one jump ahead of the Russians . . . three jumps ahead, I suspect, of the Iranians, the sworn enemies of his country. And a jump ahead of the United States. Tricky little bastard, wouldn't you say?"

"Clever, tricky little bastard."

"And the really worrying thing is, sir, there is not *that* much a great power can do about these bloody terrorist people. You could of course declare war, or even make a preemptive nuclear strike against Iraq. But it's awfully messy. Half of the international community would go off its rocker with indignation. The damned media would be full of pictures of destroyed Iraqi hospitals and schools. You know what it would be like."

"I'm afraid I do, Admiral. All too well. In the end I suppose we just have to accept that if we are to police the world, with a dozen Carrier Battle Groups, we are going to end up, sometime, somewhere, losing one. It's a terrible price, but the alternative is world chaos. And I am afraid the curse of the twenty-first century might very well be weapons of mass destruction in the hands of fanatics. Maniacs."

"Yessir. However, we are not powerless. We can persuade the Russians to cooperate by not selling those damned Kilos to nations of unstable government. But I hardly think you, Mr. President, could make a general policy to wipe out *any* small foreign submarine fleet you may consider may be a menace to the free world."

"No. We cannot go on doing that. But as you may have guessed, we did partly attend to that problem."

"I did guess that, sir. More or less the moment I heard about it."

"Meanwhile, there is not much more we can do, militarily, without admitting what happened to the carrier, which we will not do."

"There is of course the option of the dams," said Sir Iain.

"Which dams?" asked Scott Dunsmore.

"The ones on the Tigris. The ones the Iranians were trying to blow up during their war with Iraq."

"I remember that," said the President. "One of them was called the Samarra Barrage, correct?"

"That's it, sir," replied Admiral MacLean. "Back at home, I shoot a few grouse with a chap who works on the Iraqi desk in the Foreign Office. He was telling me about it quite recently."

The admiral outlined, as well as he remembered, the facts about the two great Iraqi dams—the Samarra Barrage, which stands 115 miles north of Baghdad and holds 85 billion cubic meters of water. The second one, five times as big, is called the Darband-I-Khan Reservoir, and holds three cubic kilometres of water. This one is situated on a tributary of the Tigris, 130 miles northeast of the city, near the mountain town of Halabjah, right on Iran's border, where three rivers converge.

"It was the huge Darband Reservoir the Iranians tried to blow," said the admiral. "But the Iraqis somehow found out and counterattacked . . . that was the battle of Halabjah. It later transpired the Iranians were also on their way to the Samarra Barrage, but they never got there either."

"Yes," said the President. "As I recall there was some talk of us taking one of those dams out during the Gulf War, but it was rejected because no one quite had the stomach to drown several million Iraqis. Matter of fact, I would not do that either."

"Quite so, Mr. President," replied Sir Iain. "But my chap at the Foreign Office says these things have been studied much more scientifically recently. They do not assess the loss of life would be anything like so great as the Iranians hoped if they blew the dams. Maybe even minimal. But it would certainly wreck the Iraqi economy for years."

"How difficult to do?" asked the President.

"Just a bit. But no more so than removing the Ayatollah's submarines. More important is the timing. To put Baghdad completely out of action my chap assesses both dams would have to go at the same time. It would have to be right when the winter snow melt in the mountains was happening, when there was maximum water. Then you could take Iraq right out of the world trouble equation for years and years. They'd be crippled financially, and probably emotionally."

"Then I guess we've got three months to consider whether the men of the *Thomas Jefferson* should be thoroughly avenged."

"Yessir. You do. But I won't be able to help much then. You won't need submarines . . . "

The President was thoughtful. And Admiral MacLean spoke again. "You know, sir, I'd be inclined to rethink the whole procedure of Carrier Battle Groups. Let's face it, we've just been shown, quite conclusively, that in these dangerous days, the big American policeman, on his world patrol, can be killed by a relatively unsophisticated knifeman. Because all defensive measures leak. No system is 100 percent certain.

"Perhaps we should put smaller, cheaper units up front, which will allow us to retain our military capacity less densely.

"If the guerrilla fanatic is going to strike at us, let's give him a lesser target . . . not a multibillion-dollar carrier with six thousand people on board. That perhaps should be kept further back, safe and ready, for when we decide to punish the aggressor.

"I expect you will have read, in the old days of Empire, we Brits always put a completely expendable gunboat up front, as a 'mark of our interest.' The battleship only showed up if the gunboat was attacked.

"Sir, if we have a troublesome area in a city, we send in police patrols. We do not send in the chief of police."

The President's face lit up as he cottoned on to the political advantages in such a new strategy. Admiral Dunsmore himself said, "Yes. It's an interesting and often-considered thought. A few years back I personally doubted the wisdom of placing a huge carrier right between Taiwan and China . . . "

But just then a uniformed security guard came through the door with a message for Admiral MacLean to call his daughter, Laura, at ten the following morning.

"It's a fairly local call, sir," he said, conditioned by years of parsimony in the Royal Navy. "She took a few days off to visit a friend in New York. They're going to a couple of operas or something. I think she's staying outside the city with friends, Connecticut or New Jersey, I suppose. It's a '3–1–6' area code.

"She sure is outside the city, Admiral," replied the President. "Three-one-six is just to the west of New York. About fifteen hundred miles, out near my country, in the southern half of the great American state of Kansas."

"Oh dear," said the admiral, wearily. "I was rather afraid of that. Her mother will be absolutely thrilled."

Fort Meade, Maryland. December 14.

Admiral Morgan carefully slit open the special-delivery package which had arrived on his desk. It contained a small newspaper cutting, mounted on a sheet of crested diplomatic paper from the Israeli embassy.

> CAIRO. Monday. The body of a man in his early forties, wearing Arab dress, was discovered by Cairo police in the precincts of the Citadel early this morning.
>
> According to Police Chief Hamdi, the man had been shot once through the back of the head. His officers were acting on information received by telephone shortly after midnight. No murder weapon has yet been found, but police are still searching the area around the Mohammed Ali Mosque where the body was found.
>
> Chief Hamdi said that the incident bore the marks of a professional killing, carried out by a person or persons unknown. The body, in his opinion, had been robbed. It contained no documents, identification, or credit cards. There was, however, "considerable cash." Police inquiries are continuing.

Admiral Morgan delved deeper into the outer package, and pulled out a slim leather cigarette case. Inside the case was a small military badge, an anchor entwined with a heraldic vine, set upon a silver submarine—the coveted insignia of the Israeli Submarine Service. Looking closely Arnold Morgan could make out faded initials in the leather, *"BA."*

The accompanying white card brought a smile to the face of Admiral Morgan. Scrawled upon it were the words, "Just to remind him he was still a commander! Arrogant little bugger, wasn't he? Best wishes, DG."

Admiral Morgan sat and thought. The leather cigarette case he would keep in his personal little military museum, which was comprised mostly of souvenirs from missions fought and won.

The little badge he resolved to give to the President, as a souvenir of the fight to bring to justice the killer of the *Thomas Jefferson*. In the end, Boomer Dunning's torpedo and the Mossad's bullet had provided an extreme form of rough justice. But nonetheless justice.

The White House. December 20. Midday.

The two Marine guards shut the door softly, leaving Bill Baldridge in the Oval Office, face to face with the President.

"Hey, Bill. Glad you could come," he said, striding around his desk to shake hands. "I've arranged a little lunch for us, with Admiral Dunsmore and Admiral Morgan. I wanted the opportunity to thank all three of you in private for a damned difficult job conducted with just super professionalism."

"Thank you, sir," replied Bill. "I appreciate that. Very much."

The President was silent for a moment, and then he said: "As you know, the operation was black, strictly nonattributable so there's nothing I can really do about a reward. I can't have you promoted, since you've retired from the Navy, and I cannot decorate *anyone* for their part in such a mission." He grinned and added, "So I guess you're just going to have to make do with my heartfelt personal thanks."

"That, sir, would be more than sufficient."

The President motioned for Bill to be seated and then he walked around to his desk once more. "Bill," he said. "I am not quite as stupid as some people think. I remember it was you who blew the whistle on the accident theory."

"Yessir. At the time it was a pretty lonely spot to be in."

"I know it was. I also know it was you who insisted that the Arab commander of that Kilo must have somehow left a trail. You went and found him, identified him for the Mossad. Had you *not* found him, we might still be scratching our heads."

"I was lucky in Northwood, sir."

"I also remember it was you who warned me that Adnam was not in the Kilo when we hit it."

"Crazy Ivan, right?"

"Crazy Ivan. The same words that wonderful Scottish admiral used. You got him for us too. And you were in *Columbia* at the final moment when we hit the Russian boat. Bill, I'd like to make you the youngest goddamned admiral in the Navy. But I can't."

"Don't worry, sir. There's not that many warships on the prairie."

The President smiled. And then he produced from his desk drawer a small package, which he gave to the rancher from Kansas. "Open this, will you? I'm just going to the next office for a few minutes, then I'll be back, and we'll go and meet Scott and Arnold."

The President left, and Bill Baldridge stood alone in the Oval Office. He removed the wrapping, and held a flat, black jewelry box in his hands. When he opened it, he saw only a sheet of official White House paper, on which was inscribed a careful hand-written note from the President, signed only with his first name.

The words were simple: *"For Bill. Because you were brave enough to warn me. And because you are my friend."*

Beneath the paper, pinned to the deep red velvet of the box, was a small military badge, an anchor, entwined with a heraldic vine, set upon a silver submarine.

AFTERWORD

BY ADMIRAL SIR JOHN WOODWARD

I SHOULD PERHAPS DECLARE MY PERSONAL INTEREST in this book, written by Patrick Robinson, who assisted me in the writing of my own autobiography back in 1991.

For *Nimitz Class*, he asked me for technical advice on submarine operations—a request for me to wear again the hat of Flag Officer Submarines, rather than that of the Falkland Islands Battle Group Commander.

He now informs me there is a senior retired admiral featured prominently within the pages of *Nimitz Class* who may be somewhat familiar both to me and to those who served under my command. However, I am happy to say that his fictional admiral does not coincide with my own personal view of myself. I'm not even sure I would have recognized him!

Nonetheless my purpose in writing these introductory words is to express my approval for this book, and the very real, you might say terrible, issues it raises.

Patrick Robinson used several consultants both in the U.K. and in the United States Navy during the two years it took to prepare—and I do know that every one was acutely aware of the enormity of the subject and the consequent dangers under which the U.S. Navy operates.

The author has turned this "worst-case" scenario into a page-turning thriller. He has not, however, strayed from the grim reality of terrorism on the grandest scale: the vulnerability of the modern military commander to the sly and cunning knifeman.

What happens in *Nimitz Class* could happen in the real world, with momentous consequences for us all. The United States Navy and the Royal Navy are all too aware of the threat. But even now, certain politicians on both sides of the Atlantic seem perfectly prepared to cut defense budgets regardless of stern warnings from the military.

I should perhaps remind them all that when countries such as Great Britain and the United States lower their guard in any way whatsoever, they end up paying for it, in blood, sorrow, and tears.

Margaret Thatcher, out of office now, but frequently still in our minds, remains a far-seeing politician of an entirely different class. In her historic lecture at Westminster College, Fulton, Missouri, on March 9, 1996, she told her American audience:

> The Soviet collapse has also aggravated the single most awesome threat of modern times: the proliferation of weapons of mass destruction. These weapons—and the ability to develop and deliver them—are today acquired by middle-income countries with modest populations, such as Iraq, Iran, Libya and Syria . . . acquired sometimes from other powers like China and North Korea, but most ominously from former Soviet arsenals.

She reminded her audience that by the end of the decade we could see twenty countries with ballistic missiles. Nine with nuclear weapons. Ten with biological weapons. Thirty with chemical weapons.

"On present trends," she said, "a direct threat to American shores is likely to mature early in the next century.

"Add weapons of mass destruction to rogue states," said Margaret Thatcher, "and you have a highly toxic compound."

She pointed out that many such states are led by "megalomaniacs and strongmen of proven inhumanity, or by weak, unstable or illegitimate governments." She added that the potential capabilities at the command of these unpredictable figures, "may be even more destructive than the Soviet threat to the West in the 1960's."

Patrick Robinson's book vividly illustrates precisely what the lady means. And in its pages it also raises the question of how, in a turbulent and dangerous world, we make our resolution plain, without excessive cost in both materiel and, more particularly, people.

Nimitz Class will, I hope, bring home to an even broader public the extreme pressures under which the Armed Services continue to operate. In particular I would suggest that serving Naval officers read it, perhaps especially Navy cadets, who may have ambitions to join the Submarine Services on either side of the Atlantic.

SANDY WOODWARD